Amanda Cinelli was born into a large Irish-Italian family and raised in the leafy green suburbs of County Dublin, Ireland. After dabbling in a few different careers, she finally found her calling as an author when she won an online writing competition with her first finished novel. With three small daughters at home, she usually spends her days doing school runs, changing nappies and writing romance. She still considers herself unbelievably lucky to be able to call it her day job.

Millie Adams has always loved books. She considers herself a mix of Anne Shirley—loquacious, but charming, and willing to break a slate over a boy's head if need be—and Charlotte Doyle—a lady at heart, but with the spirit to become a mutineer should the occasion arise. Millie lives in a small house on the edge of the woods, which she finds allows her to escape in the way she loves best: in the pages of a book. She loves intense alpha heroes and the women who dare to go toe-to-toe with them. Or break a slate over their heads...

Also by Amanda Cinelli

The Avelar Family Scandals miniseries

The Vows He Must Keep
Returning to Claim His Heir

The Greeks' Race to the Altar miniseries

Stolen in Her Wedding Gown
The Billionaire's Last-Minute Marriage
Pregnant in the Italian's Palazzo

Also by Millie Adams

A Vow to Set the Virgin Free

The Kings of California miniseries

The Scandal Behind the Italian's Wedding
Stealing the Promised Princess
Crowning His Innocent Assistant
The Only King to Claim Her

Discover more at millsandboon.co.uk.

A RING TO CLAIM HER CROWN

AMANDA CINELLI

THE BILLIONAIRE'S ACCIDENTAL LEGACY

MILLIE ADAMS

MILLS & BOON

First published in Great Britain 2023
by Mills & Boon, an imprint of HarperCollins*Publishers* Ltd,
1 London Bridge Street, London, SE1 9GF

www.harpercollins.co.uk

HarperCollins*Publishers*, Macken House, 39/40 Mayor Street Upper,
Dublin 1, D01 C9W8, Ireland

A Ring to Claim Her Crown © 2023 Amanda Cinelli

The Billionaire's Accidental Legacy © 2023 Millie Adams

ISBN: 978-0-263-30687-3

07/23

This book is produced from independently certified FSC™ paper to ensure responsible forest management.
For more information visit: www.harpercollins.co.uk/green.

Printed and Bound in the UK using 100% Renewable Electricity at CPI Group (UK) Ltd, Croydon, CR0 4YY

A RING TO CLAIM HER CROWN

AMANDA CINELLI

MILLS & BOON

For my grandmother Elda, who loves to read my books when they come out in Italian— even if they are a little spicy!
Ti voglio bene, Nonna

PROLOGUE

AT THE RIPE old age of nineteen-and-a-half, Crown Princess Minerva of Arqaleta was quite sure that she was completely immune to any kind of romantic attraction. She certainly wouldn't do something so foolish as fall in love with the surly, redheaded prince she was destined to marry.

The old-fashioned betrothal agreement between her mother and the King of Cisneros had begun when she'd been fourteen and, every year since, Minerva had obeyed and undertaken her scheduled four-week summer visit with Prince Oliveiro. There could be no two people more opposite in this world forced to spend weeks together in one another's company. Minerva despised reading and she despised silence and, by the time that first summer had come to an end, she'd been pretty sure she despised Prince Oliveiro too.

But…when she and the Prince had set eyes upon one another at this year's summer garden party…everything had changed.

A simple dance had turned into hours of talking and soon she'd found herself introducing him to her favourite place in all of Arqaleta, a teardrop-shaped lake on the edge of the palace grounds. She had found it when seeking out an errant arrow as a small child and had taken it upon herself to cut back most of the thorns and weeds, cleaning and polishing the old stone benches and statues and stringing up solar-powered fairy lights.

She told him all of this in a flurry of nerves as he took in every inch of her den, not knowing why it was so vital that he liked it, but that it was. She needed him to love this place just as much as she did. As usual, he hadn't spoken much, but, as he'd taken in the lake and the full moon reflecting upon the calm waters, she'd noticed his body visibly relax.

'It's so peaceful,' he'd whispered. 'Like we're the only two people in the world.'

Then he'd turned to her, their eyes meeting in the glow of twinkling lights, and everything else had ceased to exist. No duty, no differences, no watchful parents… it had just been them, boy and girl… Her hands had trembled in his as she'd closed the space between them and pressed her lips against his. Her first kiss…and his too, he'd later confessed.

They'd kissed for so long, her lips had felt swollen and her body had ached. He'd stopped every so often, staring down at her as though he were afraid she'd disappear at any moment. Then he'd taken her lips again, their bodies writhing against one another in the dark.

He'd asked her to call him 'Liro' that night—a name that only his mother had used for him, before her passing when he'd been a young boy. A name his father forbade him to use, as he did with everything that reminded him of the beloved wife he had lost.

He could barely look at the son who resembled her so closely. No one else knew of the name. For the first time, she'd seen a glimpse of something wild and furious beneath Liro's silent exterior. He was like an animal confined to a cage, pacing the length of the bars, consumed with the possibility of breaking free.

Their secret lakeside meetings became a nightly ritual over the following weeks. In the dark, she soon found herself offering up her own secrets too. Such as the long-drawn-out truth behind her parents' supposedly amicable divorce and her father's subsequent abandonment of her in favour of his new family. Liro always listened, her hand cradled in his.

They had never once spoken of the marriage arrangement that bound them, but she always felt it hang between them like a gauntlet of sorts. She knew that this summer eventually had to end and, when it did, Liro would leave. Only, this time, he would leave for obligatory military training in his home kingdom for two whole years and she would go to university in America. They'd be half a world away from one another.

On their last night together, she went ahead of him to the lake and waited, her mind swimming with all of the fears she'd tried to ignore. Would he think of her? Would he visit? Or would he abandon her without a thought, just like her father had?

That last thought stopped her in her tracks. Her own parents' marriage had been a royal arrangement, a public front for the good of the kingdom and their allies. As a child she'd been unaware of the tension but, as she'd grown older, their turbulent relationship had become impossible to ignore or escape. She had witnessed Papa's misery and resentment grow with each year he'd spent playing his role of King Consort.

Once they'd completed the terms of their betrothal… would Liro grow to feel the same way about her?

Her increasingly anxious thoughts were interrupted when Liro appeared at the lake's edge and made his way towards her in the moonlight. There were no lamps— nothing but the glow of the moon to illuminate the stern set of his mouth as he came to a stop a few feet away. She moved towards him, reaching up to claim his lips in a kiss, only to find his movement stilted and off.

'What's wrong?' she demanded, tightening her grip on his hand in a firm squeeze. His fingers were cold and he didn't squeeze her back.

'My father is here.'

Minerva inhaled sharply at the news, instantly understanding the change in him. King Guillermo didn't usually join his son in Arqaleta. Liro despised his father and they had spoken of him often, now that Liro actually spoke to her. She reached out to touch his shoulder, only for him to turn away and pace towards the lake.

'My father came to the archery arena yesterday to seek me out and instead he saw us…'

Minerva fought the wild urge to clap a hand across her mouth and scream like one of the characters in her mother's favourite soap operas. Liro had accompanied her to practice to watch her as usual, but then her best friend Bea had cancelled and unexpectedly they'd had the whole arena to themselves… She had barely taken a breath before both of them had been semi-undressed and writhing against one another on a pile of soft mats behind one of the equipment lockers.

Only, instead of stopping at the usual point of safety, for the first time they had gone all the way—another first for them both. It had felt special. A uniquely real and private moment in a life where so much had to be prearranged and approved by others.

Now, to learn that they'd been seen, and by King Guillermo of all people... She felt her stomach turn. For all that Arqaleta had become more modern and free, the kingdom of Cisneros was old and staunchly traditional in its culture. Would she be blamed for corrupting their son?

'What did he say?' She squared her shoulders, all trace of the previous excitement fully quashed by the reality of their situation. She noticed how Liro avoided her eyes, how his hands were clenched together so tightly the knuckles glowed white.

'He said he would speak to the Queen...' Liro's eyes searched hers. 'That we would need to be married straight away in case there was a child.'

'We were completely safe.' Minerva shook her head, furious. 'How dare he act as though we are a pair of errant children in need of punishment?'

A strange emotion shifted across Liro's face. 'Is that really how you would view marriage to me, Min? As a punishment?'

'That came out wrong.' Minerva inhaled a deep breath. 'What I mean is that it's too soon. I thought we would have years before we fulfilled the royal betrothal agreement.'

Liro's handsome features hardened at her words, his voice a low whisper in the semi-darkness. 'You knew about the agreement?'

'Of course,' she said, unnerved. 'Wait…you didn't?'

He shook his head once and Minerva felt her insides twist. He was utterly miserable at the revelation, that much was very clear.

'How long…?' He paused, clearing his throat. 'How long have you known that you were going to be forced to marry me some day?'

Minerva shivered in the cool breeze. This reminder of their reality was cold and wrong, his words slicking over her skin like ice water. 'I overheard them discuss the details on the day that you arrived, that very first summer.'

'Well…tonight is the first I heard of it.' He remained silent and still, his eyes scanning her with disbelief.

'I thought that you knew. I thought that was why you were so remome at first. You argued with your father that first day…you seemed so unhappy.'

'I *was* unhappy. I'm the youngest of three sons with a miserable father who only bothers to interact with his heir and his spare. Not to mention I'm the spitting image of the woman he can't bear to think about.' He closed his eyes and shook his head, a pained expression crossing his fair features. 'My father is unhinged. He's demanding that we get married as soon as possible, Minerva.'

She froze in his arms, a strange humming beginning in her ears. She'd been raised to believe that they were a progressive kingdom, that she would be free to rule as she saw fit whenever her time came. That she was trusted to know her own mind, to make her own choices, to experience some of the world for a while without the weight of her duty.

'We're only nineteen,' she said, taking a step back until she was fully out of his reach. She couldn't think if he was touching her, not when her body still hadn't caught up with the reality of their situation. 'I have plans to go to college, to compete with my archery. I don't want to give that freedom up yet.'

Silence fell between them, a fraught, empty sound filled with the suffocating weight of their situation.

'Who says we have to give up any freedom at all?' he said quietly. 'Why should we live by their plans and agreements? Why should we be treated as pawns?'

Minerva shook her head softly, 'Liro... I'm going to be queen one day.'

'You don't have to be.' He met her eyes, a strange wildness to his expression.

It scared her, that wildness. She took a step away, pulling out of his grasp and pacing towards the lake. 'Liro, I love my country, and I trust my mother's judgement. If this marriage is a necessary part of my duty, then I have to do it.'

He glowered down at her and for the first time she felt self-conscious under his gaze. She knew to others it might seem weak, always following the rules and expectations of her role. Of course, sometimes she got tired of being the dutiful daughter, the over-achiever. She was only human. These last few weeks, during their stolen moments of illicit pleasure, she had been Min. She had felt free with Liro… Maybe once they were married they could have the best of both worlds?

'You don't *have* to do anything,' Liro said quietly. He took a step closer, taking her hands in his. 'Min… haven't you ever dreamed of running away to start over somewhere new? Don't you ever yearn for a life of your own?'

'This *is* my life.' She frowned, pulling her hands from his grip.

Liro froze, his expression becoming strangely blank. The light summer breeze rustling the trees was a cacophony of sound against the unbearable silence that had fallen between them. Minerva didn't know what to say in the face of his hurtful words. She'd known that he wasn't fond of royal life back home, but did he truly believe her adherence to duty meant she didn't live a life of her own?

'I've never dreamed of running away from this, Liro.' She waited until he met her gaze before continuing. 'I've had five years to accustom myself to the idea of an arranged marriage. I didn't plan for these last few weeks, but… I see it as further evidence that we will make a compatible couple.'

'Compatible.' He stared at her for a long moment, his eyes hard. 'These past few weeks… Was this some kind of twisted exercise to test out our marital compatibility?'

'Of course not.'

Liro made a cruel, scoffing sound, his anger clearly the reigning emotion. For a moment she contemplated laying it all out for him—how she'd been fascinated by him every year and had yearned for his attention. How she'd never felt happier than she'd felt these past few weeks. But then that small voice from before returned, reminding her what happened when you allowed yourself to be vulnerable. If she wanted a sensible, arranged marriage that would last, she needed to keep her emotions at a safe distance.

'We can push for a long engagement.' She stood upright, forcing herself to look away from him as she tried to disguise the crushing disappointment from his reaction. Clearly, Liro was not okay with the prospect of marrying her. She took a deep breath and adopted her most practised calm, regal smile, ignoring the tremor quaking in her abdomen with every word she spoke. 'Who knows? It might not be so terrible. I believe it will be a good match.'

'Do you *want* to marry me, Minerva?' he asked, grey-green eyes pinning her in place.

'Of course I do. I've just said as much, haven't I?'

'Tell me why.'

She squirmed under his attention, hating every moment of this conversation. 'I l-like you, Liro. I think you would make a great consort. We've been friends long enough for our union to be…believable. We're both royals, we know what is expected of our roles. It makes sense.'

'You make it sound like a business arrangement.' Liro scowled. 'Marriage should do more than make sense, Minerva. What else?'

His demand, coupled with the harsh quality of his voice, made her feel small and uncertain. Like that younger version of herself who had called her father's number every night to leave embarrassingly long voicemails detailing every moment of her day. She hadn't been prepared for Papa to answer one day and coldly demand that she stop. The realisation that her own father hadn't missed her the way she missed him, that he didn't wish to be a part of her life any more than a couple of obligatory visits a year, had been the most crushing rejection she'd ever known.

Somewhere, in the last few weeks, she had let her guard down and now Liro had got under her skin. She had begun to rely on him, to long for him in a way that was far too much of a risk for their polite, royally arranged marriage. She needed to make things right. Needed to pull this betrothal back into safer territory, even if it hurt.

'We seem pretty good together in bed, is that what you want me to say?' She forced a smile, hating the flippant words as they left her lips. 'What else is there?'

Liro stiffened as though she'd struck him. His eyes drifted closed and Minerva instantly wished she could take it back. She felt a rush of foolish words threaten to climb up from her chest, needy phrases full of hope and longing that had no place in a safe, royal arrangement like theirs.

His hands gripped her shoulders, holding her away for a brief moment as he stared down at her. He seemed tortured, undone with a riot of unspoken emotions.

'You deserve more, Min,' he said softly.

'It won't be so bad,' she murmured against his throat. 'Not if this is how it can be.'

Giving in to her own weakness, she leaned in to

kiss him. No more than a few seconds passed before he groaned and kissed her back. He held her close, his grip intense and purposeful, as if he was afraid she'd disappear at any moment. He was usually careful with her, almost reverent. But this time as they tore off their clothes and began to make love it felt different, more urgent. She was still a little tender—it was only her second time, after all. But she didn't care, not if it meant they could stop arguing and just go back to *this* for a while. She loved how he made her feel. She loved being with him...so much.

Tears filled her eyes and she told herself to pause, to savour this moment before their relationship became public property, but his lips against her skin made her mind swim. Liro gripped her jaw, tilting her face up to claim her mouth in a hard kiss.

'I'll remember you like this, always,' he whispered. 'So wild and beautiful for me.'

Just for him. *Yes*.

She gloried in his words, in the way he held onto her so tightly. She *felt* wild as her body began to shake with the force of her orgasm. She felt it the moment he joined her, his entire body shattering in her arms. Afterwards, he held her close to his chest, not withdrawing or letting go until the chilled night air made her teeth chatter. They were silent as they walked back to the palace but she felt strangely light.

She'd never harboured fantasies of a grand wedding. But the idea of being Liro's bride...of having him as her husband...made her feel excited and vulnerable all at once.

He walked her as far as the palace gates, as was their habit to avoid being discovered, not that it was necessary any longer. His stiff hug and murmur about needing to take a walk to clear his head set off alarm bells in her mind but she shook it off, telling herself that she was just being sensitive. That tomorrow everything would be figured out. Liro's whispered goodbye against her lips felt cold and distant but she didn't question it.

She didn't question anything...until it was already too late.

CHAPTER ONE

Fourteen years later

MINERVA FOUGHT NOT to fidget with the heavy diamond tiara that had been secured artfully atop her head. Pins dug into her sensitive scalp, a scalp that had already endured three hours of glamorous torture with the royal stylist. Her waist-length curls had been washed, trimmed and tamed into the world's most intricate chignon.

A mirror was brought in front of her to survey the final look and she made sure to show her gratitude. These people were premium artists in their fields; it wasn't their fault that their princess would much rather be in jeans with her hair up in a messy bun. Doing away with the various dress codes she had been raised to adhere to for every event would be her first order of business once she became queen. Well, perhaps after she'd made a start on her kingdom's myriad other pressing issues, but still, it was pretty high on her to-do list.

Before she had a moment to compose herself, a small army of liveried staff entered the antechamber, announcing the arrival of her mother. Everyone rose, even Minerva, as Her Majesty Queen Uberta of Arqaleta appeared in the doorway, looking effortlessly regal as always.

Her mother crooned softly as she took in the antique Arqaletan gold-and-emerald tiara and matching jewels that adorned Minerva's ears and neck. 'I haven't seen these pieces in such a long time.'

'Master Nasir decided to bring out some of the pieces from your original coronation events, in honour of your celebration.' Minerva bowed her head towards their elderly curator, the man who single-handedly had preserved so much of her family's proud history over the years, and took huge honour in holding such a position. Minerva felt the same sense of privilege about her own role in their country's history, messy buns or not.

Queen Uberta was celebrating thirty years upon the throne on the same day as her sixtieth birthday. While Arqaleta was usually quite busy in the summer time, with tourists and their world-famous archery festival, this year they were holding a week-long celebration to honour their queen's momentous double milestone. There were to be seven days of events, culminating in a grand ball.

She met her mother's eyes and saw an echo of her own nervous excitement. Aside from a select few members of parliament and their royal administration, no one in the kingdom knew what was actually in store for them this week.

No one knew that the Queen had decided to change history by stepping down voluntarily. And not for any dramatic or sorrowful reason, simply because she wished to retire and pass on the crown. All of their late-night conversations, all of their detailed brainstorming sessions, were finally ready to be unveiled. Once the announcement was made on Sunday night, everything would change. A new era for their tiny island kingdom would begin.

'You look beautiful.' Her mother's hand gently squeezed hers. 'Nervous?'

'A little,' she said honestly, seeing no point in lying. Her mother could read her like a book anyway. She'd always been shocked to hear so many other royals describe deeply unhappy relationships with the people who had raised them.

But, then again, her mama had been a queen like the world had never known, changing traditions and forging progress even after the scandal of a messy public divorce and her refusal to remarry for the sake of propriety. The thought of having to fill such perfect shoes was a challenge Minerva knew she would not fully reach, but she would enjoy trying.

'You will have to get used to these public speeches, my love; they will only become more frequent.' Her mother sighed. 'You've hit an Olympic archery target live on television. Surely that was more nerve-racking than a week of playing host?'

'That's different.' Minerva smiled sadly, not entirely sad that her archery career had come to an end, but still not quite able to talk openly about the world she'd left behind. She'd had a good run, more than ten years of relative freedom to pursue her passion. When the time had come to return fully to her duty, she'd made the transition with ease.

'If you are not nervous about the speeches, then it must be about our other plans for this week.' Her mother stood by her side, brushing a non-existent fleck off the bead-encrusted shoulder of her gown. 'I still think it's a little unnecessary.'

Minerva shook out her shoulders and walked to the full-length windows that overlooked the crescent-shaped bay of Albo, their bustling capital city. Usually watching the steady movement of the ships coming in and out of port was one of her favourite calming techniques but not today. The harbour was in chaos, with hundreds of wealthy guests who had chosen to travel by yacht, and the harbour master was having quite a time trying to dock them all.

One particularly gigantic black super-yacht had drawn a small crowd of onlookers as it came to a stop a few miles out from the docks, bobbing in the bay like a gleaming obsidian mountain. There would be more just like that one and whoever owned it, more wealthy politicians, celebrities, millionaires, billionaires and whomever else her mother had decided might possibly be an appropriate match for the future Queen of Arqaleta.

For, while this week was about celebrating her mother's reign, it was also about securing Minerva's image as she prepared to become queen. There had never been an unmarried monarch at the time of their ascent to the throne of Arqaleta and, with public opinion inexplicably at an all-time low for their crown princess, Minerva had no other option but to find a husband…fast.

'Mother, you know that a brand-new unmarried queen upon the throne would cause uproar. Especially when your early retirement is already breaking tradition. It is what must be done.'

'But what if we just—?'

'I'm not arguing. I've already done all of the research, spoken to countless advisors, and every one of them said the exact same thing.' She imitated the rasping monotone of Robart, their royal parliament liaison. '"A life of service and dedication to this country is not enough; the Crown Princess must show allegiance in the form of matrimony and the intent to carry on the royal line".'

Queen Uberta frowned. 'I had hoped that you would have found someone eventually by yourself…after what happened.'

Minerva turned away, unable to stand the hint of regret in her mother's voice and the memories that came with it. The sting of Liro's abandonment, and the fact he had not trusted her with the truth, still hurt deeply. 'I much prefer a royal arrangement. It's easier.'

For a moment she thought her mother might have something to say on that matter, but she simply nodded once and let silence fall between them.

Her mother had been shocked and horrified after discovering the events with the former royal family of Cisneros. She had apologised for entering into the betrothal, revealing that it had been Parliament's idea originally to strengthen ties with their neighbouring kingdom. An alliance that had quickly revealed itself to be a dangerous one, as the Cisnerosi crown was revealed to be heavily in debt, and King Guillermo a master in corruption and deceit. Furious, the Queen had insisted that their entire royal family, including Prince Oliveiro, be formally

banished from her kingdom. Minerva had accepted her
mother's apology, but she would be the first to admit that
she had pushed the bounds of her own freedom further
than she'd ever intended before all of that had occurred.

She had played competitive archery in every country
in the world, spending more than a decade juggling her
passion and her duty. An unforeseen result of which was
that now she was met with resistance from Parliament,
which was now questioning the suitability of their unconventional royal.

She was not oblivious to the news headlines that had
dominated the press during her many absences from the
kingdom. She was portrayed as a flight risk, far more
curious about travelling the world and having fun than
doing her duty to her kingdom. Perhaps for the first
couple of years that might have been true but, once
she'd blown off a little steam, she had always strived to
achieve a balance. She had made it her personal mission
to show that she could nurture her own dreams and her
duty as crown princess. That she could love both roles
and be successful.

Her mother had wanted to give her an unconventional amount of freedom from the duties that would
have traditionally been expected, such as waving from
a parade carriage or shaking hands at gala dinners. But
Minerva had never missed the more important events.
Now, if she wanted to take her place as queen—which
she very much did—she would have to choose a royal
spouse to stand by her side.

But, as she gazed down at the thin rectangular speech-
cards that the team had prepared for her, she felt another

strange wave of unease pass along her spine—the same prickle of anticipation that had come over her earlier only now more intense. She shook it off, knowing that she should have slept later that morning and not gone down to the old archery arena to run circuits. She might no longer compete but there was no rule to say that she could not still practise.

'Are you ready?' her mother asked, extending her hand.

Minerva smiled, loving that this was one of the most famous images they had shown their people in the fifteen years since her father had left. They were a team—mother and daughter against the world. The Queen and Crown Princess of Arqaleta were an unstoppable force.

'Okay, let's go and find me a husband.' She laughed.

The garden party was in full swing when they arrived and Minerva was swept along a line of guests, greeting and bowing and accepting their well wishes. A brief moment of girlish excitement was allowed as she spied her best friend Bea, who had arrived to stay in Arqaleta for a number of weeks to work with the team at the palace's stables and horse sanctuary. They didn't get to see each other much nowadays, since Bea's work took her all over the world, and something within Minerva calmed a little at just having her friend home.

But, once they'd had a moment to reconnect, she was pulled away by duty once more. Her mother made a point of introducing her to a large number of handsome men, some of them recognisable celebrities or businessmen, some of them distant royals from neighbouring kingdoms.

She didn't consider herself classically beautiful, whatever that meant, but she knew that her appearance was pleasant enough on the eye—proved as each eligible bachelor gazed upon her with obvious interest. Her anxiety simmered in the back of her mind as she made the required small talk with a dizzying number of handsome counts, Formula One drivers and heirs. But, as the time for her speech grew nearer, she felt her nerves peak and at the first opportunity she could manage she wandered off in search of silence and refreshment.

Someone appeared suddenly on her peripheral vision and she turned, readying herself for another bout of polite chit-chat.

'Good afternoon,' she said, finding a red-haired man with dark sunglasses standing a small distance away. 'Apologies if we haven't been formally introduced yet. You are most welcome to Arqaleta.'

She prided herself on remembering names but she was pretty sure she would have remembered this guy. He was quite striking…handsome, with a sleek trimmed beard, impossibly tall and heavy with muscles in a way that seemed to contrast violently with the fitted black tuxedo he sported. Perhaps it was his thick red hair, a rare colour in these parts. It was a colour that reminded her of heartbreak, even after fourteen years.

She shook off that ridiculous thought, far more interested in another subtle undercurrent of emotion coursing through her—excitement. She rarely felt any kind of attraction to others, certainly never upon first glance, but it was undeniable that her attention had been piqued by this burly stranger.

Minerva shook off the thoroughly inappropriate sense of physical awareness coursing through her and busied herself refilling her glass of ice-water. She certainly needed cooling down. She subtly assessed the crowd behind her, noticing her mother's attention was firmly rapt upon them. Could it be potentially that this guy was one of the suitors Mama had hand-picked? The thought wasn't entirely uncomfortable. Or at least it wasn't at first, until he spoke again, this time in a low voice meant just for the two of them.

'*Gracias, princesa.*' His voice was a low rumble, startling her out of her thoughts.

That voice…

Minerva felt a shiver run up her arms as something within her reacted to his tone, like an odd sense of déjà vu. She frowned, taking him in fully. He seemed so very out of place in this calm, sedate garden party. As if he was merely adopting a formal façade as a disguise of sorts, a temporary mask to fit in. She rather wished he wouldn't. She found herself wondering where those hints of tattoos led…if they covered his whole body…

Shocked at the direction of her thoughts, she took a step backwards, almost knocking over a large ice sculpture of two kissing swans in the process. The man reached out, effortlessly catching the sculpture with one hand and tipping it back into place.

Without a word, he reached out with his other hand to steady her. His touch was warm and soft, despite the fact that his long fingers appeared callused and scarred. He had the hands of a man used to manual labour, his forearms corded with the kind of muscle that came from heavy lifting. The barest hint of dark tattoos was visible along the cuff of one white sleeve, quickly hidden as he straightened and stepped back.

Minerva let out a sigh of relief and ignored the small protest within her at the loss of his warmth. All in all, this man was possibly the furthest from polished royalty that a person could get. Almost as though he had heard her thoughts and wished to affirm their correctness, he growled and subtly pulled open the top button at his collar.

'Apologies, I take personal issue with the necessity of strangling oneself in the name of high fashion.'

Minerva let out a sound that was half-laugh, half-squeak as a small triangle of curling hair was revealed inch by inch. That was it; she needed to move away before she made an utter fool of herself. Saved by duty… An aide appeared to guide her to get ready her for her speech.

'My apologies, I hope you enjoy the rest of the festivities.' She smiled politely, noticing that he still hadn't bothered to remove his sunglasses. He hadn't introduced himself either, but there was no time now as he lowered himself to a polite bow and she was guided quickly away. But, even as she put distance between them, the strange, unsettling feeling of anticipation remained. She fought not to look back, to get one more good look at him…no matter how intrigued she was.

Liro scowled as Crown Princess Minerva walked away from him. He had fought not to imagine how their first meeting might go. He had been prepared for myriad potential scenarios...but not one in which she politely smiled at him like a complete stranger. But, of course, no one else here had recognised him, why would she after fourteen years?

He owned a mirror—he knew that he hardly resembled his younger self at all. Still, he felt the need to down the remnants of his fruity cocktail, unsettled as he watched Minerva's diamond-topped chignon disappear into the crowd.

When the invitation had arrived, signed by Her Majesty Queen Uberta of Arqaleta, Liro had believed it to be a practical joke. Why on earth would the woman who had formally banished him want him to come to her celebration event? Of course, once his own righteous indignation had passed, he had realised that there was a far more obvious and infinitely more hilarious reason...

Her Majesty, like most of the rest of the world, had absolutely no idea of the true identity of shipping magnate Liro San Nicolau. His alter ego had amassed a fortune and mystery like none other, allowing him a comfortable anonymity that he had never known in all twenty years of his former life. He felt no sense of nostalgia because it had been Prince Oliveiro of Cisneros who'd spent countless summers here. But, while Liro was quite used to crowds gathering around the hulking, sleek black yacht upon which he lived exclusively, he was not used to exiting said vessel and becoming the centre of attention himself. The afternoon sun was not the only thing that had made him sweat as he'd adjusted the sleeves of his sleek black tuxedo.

He had waited for a breath before he had entered

the palace grounds, every one of his senses piqued and ready to respond to the first sign of recognition amongst the crowd…but none had come. Murmurs of curiosity had been the predominant sentiment through the sea of faces, but none of them had shouted out his true name.

It had been fourteen years since he'd had last set foot on Arqaletan soil, fourteen years since he had come to this island kingdom for the last time before his lengthy exile, and it seemed that just enough time had passed to render him completely unrecognisable. Of course, he was not surprised, considering he had gone from a slender and pampered prince to a labourer aboard an international cargo ship—a job he still performed quite often, despite having worked his way up to owning that vessel and numerous others, amassing countless head-quarters around the globe.

He had built his wealth from nothing, fuelled only by pure anger and regret. Now, as he looked around the manicured gardens of the royal palace of Arqaleta, he waited to feel an ounce of sadness or emotion at the events that had set his new course in life.

Memories of countless balls that he had attended in these palace grounds came and went from his atten-tion. He felt no sadness or regret about the time he had spent here. He felt nothing any more. This was not an emotional plot for revenge, this was simply business.

Having been banished from Arqaleta under his royal name, he had been careful to avoid any trade with the small country for the entire duration of his rise amongst the shipping world, despite the kingdom's perfect place-ment in the Alboran Sea, midway between Spain and northern Africa. Its unique position had long made it an enviable trading partner and port and now, with recent plans announced, he could no longer ignore it.

Over the past year he had heard murmurs of plans for a large developmental tender in the works being pitched by new up-and-comers in the parliament. His own competitors had showed signs of readiness to jump at the first sign of availability.

So, when his secretary had informed him of an invitation to a week-long celebration of Her Majesty Queen Uberta, he had been able to see through the first flush of red anger that'd initially clouded his vision. After some careful research, he had discovered that Her Majesty had absolutely no idea that his alter ego had any connection to the young prince she'd once known. And as for her daughter the crown princess... He had no need to think of her at all.

He had chosen to come here to make connections, to hunt in the way he knew best. If there was a weakness in Arqaleta's parliament that he might exploit to his own advantage, he would find it. If there was an opportunity here for him to take, he would take it without question.

He stalked along the periphery of the crowd with ease, glad that he had decided against bringing any security. Guards and teams of assistants reminded him far too much of his father, and his business model was that he preferred to operate alone. Living on a ship, he had very little need for security escorts or personal assistants. He kept a skeleton crew on board to keep the vessel running, and he hired virtual assistants to deal with most of his correspondence. Most of his meetings were performed remotely, and any site visits were informal, quick things.

He was renowned for his unusual mode of operation: he did not throw fancy dinners or wine and dine potential clients or business partners. If he wanted something, he went in direct pursuit of it and he offered what it was worth. He did not play games and did not tolerate them.

He recognised numerous faces from past business dealings here among the elegant guests. That realisation should have filled him with pride at how far he'd come and yet, as the crowd pushed and the royal family procession moved out of his view, he felt more tense than ever.

Her Highness Crown Princess Minerva had been quite busy over the past decade, travelling the world as he had hoped she would. Her talent at archery had always astounded him every time he had watched her practice, which had been a lot, during the five summers he had spent here in his youth. He had enormous amounts of respect for her drive and the things she had achieved since...

The media had always had an unhealthy interest in the young princess, a fact that had not changed at all in present times, judging by the reporters camped out all along the boundaries of the royal palace compound.

He had watched from afar as Minerva grew from a beautiful, carefree young woman into a future queen. Still beautiful, but not the same girl whom he had followed around these palace grounds. With every interview that he had read from his tiny bunk, he had witnessed the irreverent sparkle in her eyes dim a little more. Even when she had won her first Olympic gold medal, the smile that she'd given the camera had never quite been real enough for him. It was a fact that had filled him with frustration and eventually led him to ban himself completely from keeping track.

He was self-aware enough to know that was what he had been doing. It had taken years to work away the remnants of his lovesick obsession. But work it away he had. He had taken on every extra shift available on board, working, lifting and hefting heavy ropes and crates until his hands had been raw and his body ached enough to fall asleep. His body had transformed and his mind had grown sharper and more able to manage the riot of thoughts and worries that always consumed him.

The work had helped. The solitude had helped. He was in control now, so the decision to return here to hunt down a deal had not been a difficult one. He was a businessman, after all. This wasn't personal.

He had the answer to his question when Princess Minerva once again came into view, her bright smile glistening in the sunlight as she waved and followed her mother out into the centre of the courtyard. He hadn't believed it possible for her to become more beautiful than she had been at nineteen. She had always turned heads with her tall, lithe build but, at some point in the last decade, she had stopped wearing her dark hair down in its loose, natural curls. She was always perfectly put together in tailored dresses and blazers, her brown skin glowing with just the barest hint of expertly applied make-up. It infuriated him. He had watched his own mother and brother undergo the same tightening down of their images, the same relentless attention.

'Every eligible bachelor in Europe must be here. We all know what that means,' someone nearby announced, speaking loud enough in a heavy Irish accent for Liro to overhear the conversation. He followed the voices, spying a trio of lavishly dressed men standing a few feet away.

'She's given up the archery now. I suppose it's time to start securing the line. Pop out some royal brats!' a tanned, blond man with an American accent answered, his smile much too wide for Liro's comfort.

'She'll need to find someone to marry first.' Another voice joined the conversation. The handsome black man leaned closer to the other two, his accent distinctly French and his demeanour one of supreme confidence. 'Why else do you think I accepted Queen Uberta's personal invitation?'

The other two men frowned, looking upon one another with shrewd interest. The Frenchman made a tutting sound as Minerva smiled brightly up at the stage. 'I wouldn't mind waking up to that face each morning, that's for sure. Game on, gentlemen.'

Liro felt a low growl in his throat and stopped himself from taking a step towards the men. Taking a deep breath, he tried to focus on the speech and ignore the urge within him to give the so-called eligible bachelors a piece of his mind. The sun had gone behind a cloud and Liro removed his sunglasses at the same time that the crowd in front of him moved forward.

The princess paused mid-sentence and her eyes became locked on him with a sudden intensity that made every fibre of his being stand to attention. She frowned, clearly trying to gather her words as the crowd waited with bated breath. He didn't move or turn away from her silent scrutiny. Instead he felt himself will her to look... to see the truth, as no one else seemed to.

For a man who had spent fourteen years cultivating his alter ego and burying his past, he felt no unease as he saw the confusion morph into shocked recognition on her delicate features. Almost in slow motion he watched as the ornate champagne flute she'd been clutching slid from her grip and fell to the floor, smashing into a thousand glittering pieces.

With recognition came a flash of fury in her eyes, so bright he thought she might send him into flames on the spot. Minerva had recognised him...and she was absolutely furious.

CHAPTER TWO

OF ALL THE ways Minerva had imagined softly spoken Prince Oliveiro reappearing in her life over the past fourteen years, one where he had morphed into a fiercely confident hunk with arms like tree trunks had not been one of them. She didn't know what had caught her eye from the opposite side of the garden—perhaps a reflection or a movement—but one moment she was looking out at the crowd and the next she was pinned by a familiar pair of green-grey eyes.

Shocked emotion blossomed in her chest as her mind tried to make sense of what she was seeing.

Liro.

No. How could it be him? Her mind struggled to process the slow smile that spread across his lips. A smile that was unmistakeably Liro's, despite the changes in the rest of him. She went onto full autopilot, somehow managing to get through the rest of her speech without crumbling into a babbling mess on the floor. Her heartbeat still hadn't slowed down, but her hands began to shake a little less once she'd practically run from the stage and downed an entire glass of champagne.

He clearly knew that she'd recognised him, and yet

he had not attempted to leave or approach her. Still, she felt his eyes upon her the entire time as she was forced to speak with various delegates and politicians. When the guests were called to the grand dining hall, she found that seats had been assigned well in advance by the event staff, her position flanked by some of the suitors her mother had selected. She took her seat near the top of the table, looked up and there he was, seated directly across from her.

Such was the width of the grand table that she could barely hear a snippet of his conversation with the elderly woman to his left, something about shipping lanes and the cost of transit. He smiled politely at the woman, but it was not his old prince's smile. This man was someone completely different. The young man she had fallen for had smiled with warmth and genuine affection, but this man seemed to exude nothing but cold indifference.

She hadn't realised she was staring until green-grey eyes met hers, and she saw the challenge in them, just as she had the moment she'd first recognised him from the stage. She had passed off her glass-smashing as simple nerves, but now she could feel her mother's attention upon her. *Stay calm,* she reminded herself. 'Crown princess' mode meant control and grace: *rein it in.* Was she imagining it or was he smirking at her ever so slightly?

As she listened to other guests comment upon his apparent success as a global shipping magnate of some sort, she felt her insides tighten. He was well known by his pseudonym, apparently, and had been leading a life of luxurious freedom upon a yacht. The same ridiculous, giant black super-yacht she'd stared down at from her bedroom window that morning. It felt as if fourteen years of repressed rage was building up through her skin with every bite of food she tried to force down.

How dared he? How dared he come here and use a false name, of all things? What was he up to? What was his motivation for blindsiding her this way? Revenge? She felt the mad urge to call the guards and have him thrown out of the kingdom all over again, just to see how it might feel.

Did her mother have any idea who she'd invited? Almost as soon as the idea entered her head she brushed it away: her mother had been the one to banish the prince, after all. Her mother had not played a role in his family's downfall, but she had heard rumours about those who believed Arqaleta had benefited from the fall of their neighbours. Perhaps Liro had decided to come for revenge.

Conversations blurred into one as dinner wound down and the guests began to move towards the lively band that had set up stage in the ballroom. The clammy air was stifling as she moved through the crowd, smiling at the handful of faces she recognised. The band was a mixture of traditional Arqaletan folk music and a more modern sound, and soon dancers filled the floor. She politely refused one suitor's quick request to join in and waited a beat before slipping quietly through an archway to the main hall.

She had made it no more than a few steps along the lamplit corridor before a large, looming shadow stepped out from an alcove, blocking her path.

The scent of cool sea air and cedarwood filled her

nostrils as she took in the utter absence of any sign of the boy she had once loved. It was not him, and yet it was. Really...how had she not seen it at very first glance?

His short red hair was bathed in the light from the candelabra above, burnished golden in places, but much darker than the strawberry-blond it had been when she had known him. Was that why she hadn't recognised him immediately? He had been wearing sunglasses too, a fact that offset the aquiline nose he had once so maligned.

Apart from that, his jaw was wider and covered with an expertly trimmed beard; he seemed broader everywhere, in fact, and more angular. The boy she had known had been tall but this man was huge. Large, taut muscles strained the shoulders of his jacket and the long cords of his neck. Prince Oliveiro could easily have been described as handsome, if a little awkward, but this man was brutally attractive. The fact that she had felt such an instant attraction to him without fully recognising his identity made her angry all over again.

'*How* are you *here*?' The words left her mouth in a furious rush, shocking her. She shook her head, holding up a hand to stop him from coming any closer. Or perhaps to stop herself...she didn't know. All she knew was that she'd woken up this morning, fully open to the idea of matrimony after fourteen years of bitterness and cynicism... And this was the day he decided to walk back into her life? Pain rioted within her chest, pushing against her carefully posed exterior. She was becoming unhinged.

'I received an invitation, princess. Just like everyone

else.' His voice was still as deep as she remembered. But had it always sounded so menacing?

'So that's how you're going to play this…feigning innocence? Did you think that no one would recognise you?'

'No one did, not even you at first.'

'So what? You planned to come here as your alter ego? To accept an invitation as one of my suitors…after what you did?' Her voice broke on the last word, the final shred of her control now dangerously thin.

He stepped close, his eyes strangely devoid of any emotion, eerily so. 'I accepted an invitation addressed to my business name, nothing more.'

'You're lying.'

'You think I would come here to parade myself in a line of men hoping to become your king?'

'No. You had your chance at that position once, I suppose. But you decided against it, didn't you?' She let a small, hard laugh escape her lips. 'It would have been nice to have been informed of your feelings before you disappeared without a trace—leaving me in a cloud of scandal, of course.'

'Minerva.'

She turned back to face him, fully intending to continue the speech she had practised over and over in her mind for months after he'd run from his duty. After he'd run from *her*. He deserved to know exactly how awful it had been. But he had stepped closer without her realising so that, instead of having a safe distance between them, she somehow wound up pressed flush against his chest.

Instinctively, her hands rose to push him away…or

at least, that had been her intention. And yet moments passed when she remained frozen in place with the heat of his skin scorching her hands through his dress shirt. His muscles felt hot and solid underneath her fingertips. He was so much larger and stronger than she remembered. What was she doing, feeling him up?

She looked up, saw the heat in his gaze and wondered if his memory was conjuring up the same illicit pictures that hers was. The same stolen moments of fervent, joyful discovery that she had tried and failed to forget.

'You can hit me, princess, if that's what you need.' He growled. 'Hell knows, I would deserve it.'

Was that what she needed? Would that make all of these ugly, tangled feelings go back to wherever she'd stored them all this time without him? That was what she'd wanted to do, moments ago. But now...she was staring up into eyes that she had never dreamed of seeing again. Soft lips that had once driven her out of her tightly wound royal shell and shown her what it meant to be just a girl—just Minerva. They hadn't needed anything else when it had been just the two of them, just each other.

She moved to pull away and felt his hands tighten upon her elbows for the briefest moment, holding her close. She held her breath, fighting to find just the right words that would cut him, hurt him, just as she had been hurt. But as their gazes met and held and that anger within her morphed into something infinitely more dangerous. Her breath seemed too much for her lungs as she waited, wanting everything and nothing all at once. A war waged within her as Liro's strong hands flexed upon the soft skin of her elbows, his nostrils flaring as he inched closer, only to pause at the last moment.

Something broke within her, splitting the final thread that had held in more than a decade of longing. It was so long since she'd allowed herself to let go. So long…and it was all his fault. She grabbed the lapel of his jacket, roughly pulling him down to her so that she could capture his full, traitorous lips with her own.

She kissed him with fury and a wild abandon that she had thought herself no longer capable of, filling the angry thrust of her tongue and lips against his with all the frustration she'd locked away. She was vaguely aware of his beard scraping her chin and hard, callused hands caressing her neck, trying to soften her…trying to calm the raging storm he had awoken.

But she had no patience for it. She growled against his mouth, pulling his hands down tight upon her waist, showing him what she needed and praying he followed suit. His answering groan was shockingly obscene and he finally gave in. He took control of the kiss, crushing her against him as one hand fisted in her hair to hold her in place.

Yes, the voice within her cried. *This.*

Liro's kiss was plundering, wild and infinitely more soul-shattering than any one of her illicit memories of their short-lived affair. He had always had the ability to get under her skin this way, awakening some fragile scared thing that he alone seemed able to coax out. He had always made her feel free. But, as his lips slowed down and her thoughts became louder, she did not feel free. Nor had she realised she was crying until she felt a tear trickle its way down her cheek. Liro's gaze was unreadable as he reached out to wipe away that single, mortifying drop of moisture from her cheek.

'I didn't come back here to hurt you again, Min.'

'*Don't.*' She breathed, taking a step back, the spell of whatever madness had just taken hold of her for those few ridiculous minutes fully broken.

'Don't hurt you…or don't call you Min?' he asked.

'Both.' She gritted her teeth.

He straightened, a shrewd look entering his eyes as he watched a couple exit the ballroom behind them and wave in their direction. Minerva exhaled sharply, realising how close she had come to ruining all of her plans again. How close she still might be if she didn't get rid of him before scandal had the chance to break.

'You need to leave.' She tried and failed to remove the slight wobble from her voice as she stood tall and met his gaze head-on. 'You should never have come back here.'

'Is this how you treat all of the eligible bachelors your mother has seemingly rounded up for you in there?' he asked with feigned nonchalance.

Minerva cursed inwardly. Of course he would have noticed all the suitors who had been invited; it would have taken a fool not to. That her mother had likely invited him as a potential candidate for marriage was a painful irony she couldn't quite process. Not when she had just kissed him in plain view of anyone that might have wandered out.

'I think I'm entitled to feel however I like, considering you are the one who walked away from our betrothal without a single word.'

He inhaled sharply, looking away. 'I thought it would make things easier...'

'Easier for whom?'

'For everyone.' He met her eyes. 'But mostly for you.'

Hysterical laughter bubbled in her throat for a split second as she took in the sincerity in his features. Did he truly believe that? Did he truly believe that walking away from the girl who had given him her first kiss... her first everything...had been what was best for her? Of all the patronising, self-sacrificing nonsense...

This night felt like some kind of strange fever dream...or perhaps it was a nightmare. Nothing good would come of his reappearance in their kingdom, that was for sure. No matter what riot of feelings he had re-awakened within her, she was going to become queen of this country. She had to protect them from scandal, and this man was a walking scandal directly tied to her.

'You need to leave,' she said again, harsher this time. 'You are banished from this kingdom; your very appearance here is in breach of the law.'

'I have business here other than festivities,' he said silkily. 'But, if you wish to have me publicly removed, my identity casting shadow over such an important week, that is entirely your prerogative, Your Highness.'

It was a direct challenge, there was no mistake in it. Her fists balled tightly at her sides but she restrained herself from delivering the strike he had asked for. She would not satisfy him by losing her temper. No... She would give him exactly what he had given her—nothing.

Pulling free from his gaze, she took one final look at his cold, stern expression, turned on her heel and walked away.

* * *

Liro watched Minerva run from him, knowing that he could not pursue her. Not after what he had just done. What on earth had he been thinking, following her out here? He should have given her some time and space... He should have walked away the moment she had recognised him. But something within him had refused not to at least speak to her. He had expected anger, maybe even disappointment. But, as far as long-lost-lover reunions went, that had been pretty explosive.

He stood alone in the silent corridor for far longer than was necessary, waiting for his body to relax, for his erection to subside. He had reacted to her like a horny teenager... But it really was not a surprise, considering their history. Being around Minerva had always been like standing next to a flame. He closed his eyes, calming himself and reminding himself that he was not here for her. He had spent far too long training his mind not to think of her, to dream of her. The urges to return here had taken months to pass, months of lying awake at night in the bowels of a crowded ship, his body tight with longing and regret.

He had been little more than a boy when he'd left this kingdom; maybe that was why he had not been able to resist confronting her with the man he had become. He'd wanted to see the look in her eyes when she realised he had made something of himself beyond the impoverished prince she had almost settled for. He had walked away from his title and built his own empire, leaving her here with her precious duty.

He had no idea what she would do, now that she had

discovered his return. He'd have no control over her if she desired to punish him by publicising his true identity. He had come to rely far too much on his new anonymity anyway; he had always known the day would come when somebody joined the dots. But he had not expected his reputation to lie in the hands of the Crown Princess of Arqaleta.

It was quite poetic, really; he laughed to himself as he took long strides across the palace grounds in the direction of the old town where he had a meeting. It was comedic, really, that the woman who had broken his heart and given him the purpose to reinvent himself and finally walk away from his toxic father and their corrupt family might be the one to try to break him.

She wouldn't, of course—he had worked for too long and too hard to build his empire to the point where very little could take it away. If anything, the public discovering that he was actually a former prince would only elevate Magnabest's global status. Not that it mattered. He had already ordered his yacht to be readied to set sail. He would be long gone from Arqaleta before night fell. Once he had completed the true purpose of his visit, of course.

He shook off the riot of feelings coursing through him as he walked through the old cobbled streets that he had spent so many summers traversing with Minerva by his side. The capital city, Albo, was busy tonight. The tourist season was in full swing and there was the added excitement of the Queen's celebration and all of the wealthy guests. He would bet there wasn't a free bed in the whole of the kingdom.

He did not begrudge them their success, nor did he blame them for the downfall of Cisneros. But still, seeing the obvious health and happiness of the people here felt a little raw. Once the marriage alliance had fallen through, and Liro had walked away from royal life, his father had continued to destroy their kingdom's economy to the point of revolt. His two older brothers had been instrumental in navigating a path for Cisneros to return to Spain, dismantling their historic monarchy piece by piece, but Liro had made the conscious choice not to return to help. He had invested in Cisnerosi companies and created jobs, but nothing more.

It had long been known that Queen Uberta was the main reason why Arqaleta did not make use of the shipping lanes that were so popular with most countries around the Mediterranean. Their enviable position in the Alboran Sea midway between Spain and Algeria made them an untapped resource that he was determined to get for himself.

If anyone was going to take advantage of this deal, it would be him. From the moment he had first heard whispers of plans to redevelop and rezone the land around the small harbour, he had been thinking of a way to try to claim it. So, when the invitation had arrived from Queen Uberta herself, he had laughed aloud at his own good fortune. Getting a meeting with one of the top politicians in charge of the rezoning project had been child's play after that.

The meeting was held in a private conference room at the top of Albo's iconic parliament building, a beautiful white marble-and-stone structure that had once housed

army battalions in times long past. Arqaleta was rich
in history like this: most of its streets were lined with
the plaques of UNESCO historically preserved build-
ings and the people worked hard with government in-
frastructure to keep their culture preserved. Arqaletan
people were proud and welcoming to the tourists who
provided most of their annual income. They might not
take well to the lengthy development and disruption
that would come from his redevelopment plans, but they
would come round to it once they realised the benefits.
He was sure of it.

As the government officials talked through the details of the harbour project, he wondered how much they
had even considered the balance between old and new,
but that was not something for him to consider. He was
here to invest, not preserve the kingdom which had done
nothing but reject him and remind him that he was not
worthy. He might no longer be the young, naive prince
who had been sent here to carry out his father's bidding,
but he'd still felt the sting of the reminder of his banish-
ment with every step he had taken through the palace.

One politician in particular, an elderly man named
Robart, seemed particularly eager to get him to name his
price and cement his offer. As a lifelong silent observer,
Liro considered himself to be a particularly good judge
of character, and something about this guy instantly put
him on guard.

'What does Queen Uberta think of this deal?' he
asked.

As expected, the men and women around the table

exchanged not so subtle glances, most of them directed towards Robart, who then took the lead in responding.

'Her Majesty has much to worry about, what with the unrest surrounding the Crown Princess's negative standing in public opinion at present. She is more concerned with ensuring that the royal line carries on. So we have taken the initiative in creating some new projects that ensure our kingdom is at the forefront of economic progress.'

'What is the nature of this negative public opinion?' Liro asked, using every ounce of his energy to keep his body relaxed and his expression slightly uninterested.

'There has been some unrest.' The old man smirked. 'She spent much time travelling as an Olympian—an admirable adventure, but not really one that instils confidence in the people.'

'A gold-medal-winning Olympian as queen makes them lack confidence?' Liro raised one brow.

'Her athletic prowess is impressive, but we are still a country of tradition. Her mother gave her life to this country from a young age. She married well and she carried on the royal line. Minerva's duty is to do the same, and yet she has not shown any interest in marriage or family. It's a bad look.'

'A bad look that the Queen is very occupied with trying to fix, it seems...' Liro mused, finally seeing the full picture. Minerva was being forced to marry to appease her people. The very thing that Liro had almost made her do a lifetime ago. He had walked away from her, from this kingdom, to ensure that she was not trapped into a loveless marriage of convenience.

'Congratulations to you, on being invited as a potential suitor. You have your work cut out for you with the others. I believe the Frenchman, Jean-Claude, is a firm favourite with the public.'

Liro thought of the suave aristocrat he'd spied monopolising Minerva's attention over dinner and felt his fingers grip his wine glass to the point of risking shattering it into a million pieces. Was this truly why the Queen had issued Liro San Nicolau, a man she had never met, a personal invitation? Did she believe a mysterious shipping magnate to be a potential future king of her kingdom?

'I'm here to do business,' he snapped, pushing away a sudden vision of any of the other men he'd met this evening taking Minerva as their bride. The very idea of her being pressured to choose from her mother's selection brought a sour taste to his mouth, but he brushed it off, bringing the conversation back to the final points he needed to know about the deal before leaving without another word.

It was only once he had returned to the solitude of his yacht in the harbour that he allowed himself to sit and think upon what he had just discovered.

Señor Robart was clearly pushing the agenda of Minerva being unsuitable to mask his own dealings behind the scenes. He would bet good money that Robart was also the reason why the royal family had been kept out of earshot of this deal until it was far enough along that they could not refuse the cash injection that it would provide.

It was none of his business and yet, when his captain came to ask if they should leave, he found himself pausing the order. It was not his duty to care for Minerva or shield her from the consequences of her own life. He was not her fiancé any longer and, judging by the events of today, she would have a new fiancé by the end of the week.

If Queen Uberta had not discovered the truth behind shipping magnate Liro San Nicolau, what on earth had she neglected to find out about the others? Thoughts crowded his peace, agitating him as he stared out across the sea towards the palace.

CHAPTER THREE

MINERVA TOOK A deep breath and stared bleakly at her reflection in the mirror. Even with twice the amount of make-up she would normally wear, the result of her sleepless night was still starkly visible. She had returned to her room the evening before in a haze of quiet shock, excusing her maid in favour of spending some time undoing the tiny buttons of her dress one by one. But, even after undressing and taking a long freezing-cold shower, she had still lain awake for the entire night staring at the canopy above her bed and trying not to think of the feeling of having Liro's lips consuming hers.

The thought of seeing anyone today while she was still so shaken up was unbearable. She'd half-toyed with the idea of faking an illness just so she could lie in bed. But that would only encourage her mother and Bea to come investigating, and she would already struggle not to tell them everything as it was. There was no need to tell them anything, not so long as their unwanted guest disappeared, as she'd told him to. Once he was gone again, she would relax. She was sure of it.

She'd hoped that her memories of their chemistry were exaggerated, that perhaps her nineteen-year-old self had simply been overwhelmed with her first experience of lust. But, of the small handful of other people she'd kissed in the past fourteen years, none had ever made her feel close to what Liro had. Closing her eyes, she tried to focus on the items in her wardrobe, but her mind kept going back to his words.

I didn't come back here to hurt you again, Min.

A harsh shock of laughter escaped her lips as she thought of just how ridiculous a statement that was. To think that he might actually believe that his sudden return to her life wouldn't hurt her just as badly as his disappearance had. Much as she had tried to put on a brave face as she'd headed off to college a free and single woman, she had lost a part of herself when Liro had left. It had reinforced some ugly thoughts about her own worth, having yet another man she trusted just up and leave her life without a second thought.

The Argimon-Talil women were unlucky in love, her mother often said. But Minerva refused to believe that what had existed between Liro and her had truly been love. Surely love was not something a person could just walk away from without a fight, without even a conversation? It was far more likely that she had simply been infatuated with him and with the excitement of their sexual exploration. He'd said it himself, that he'd thought leaving would make things easier. And it was even more likely that he had simply seen her as a summer fling, one he'd decided to run from like a coward once he'd discovered their betrothal.

She shook off her thoughts and slid her feet into her favourite ratty old sandals, the perfect accessory to the simple blue jeans and white T-shirt she opted for. Dressing casually at the palace while she was 'off duty' was a relatively new concept but, if she was expected to marry a complete stranger for appearances, she was pretty sure the people seeing their princess in a pair of jeans wasn't going to cause a scandal.

She wasn't against the 'gowns and tiaras' life; she was simply against the idea of needing to dress formally all the time. She didn't understand it, and she probably never would, considering she had been trained for this life from birth. But thankfully her mother had stopped forcing the issue and allowed her to get on with her own day-to-day styling, for the most part.

The palace was abuzz with movement, the remnants of the evening before being tidied away in favour of plans and preparations for the grand ball that would take place on Saturday night. There were no formal events planned until later today, when she would likely be required to do some social mingling and network-ing among the various house guests who had been in-vited personally by the Queen. She hummed to herself as she made her way towards the ground-floor dining room where they breakfasted each morning.

But, when she entered the sunny breakfast room, she found it completely empty. Frowning, she walked through towards the long patio at the rear of the build-ing where she could hear voices. The morning sun was warm on her skin as she stepped out onto the stone ter-race that overlooked the gardens at the rear of the palace. They never ate out here... She frowned, then noticed that a dining table had been set up and was filled with people.

'Darling, you're late.' Her mother frowned from her post at the head of the table.

'I wasn't aware that we had breakfast plans.' Minerva forced a smile, noticing Bea had even joined them, and was happily inhaling a plate of honeyed buns near the end of the table. Through a series of pointed looks, Bea alerted her to the tableful of eligible bachelors, and Minerva fought the urge to gulp.

'It was a last-minute decision,' Queen Uberta crooned. 'I thought a more informal setting would be nice for of our guests to sample some of our famous morning pastries.'

Nice indeed. Minerva took in the sight of the pretty blond Irishman, John, to whom she had been introduced the day before. By his side was the exceedingly handsome French actor Jean-Claude, and two spots down was Prince Lorenz, who quickly stood and pulled out a chair for Minerva to take directly beside him. She smiled obligingly and lowered herself into the seat slowly while still scanning the table.

Liro was not here. She had spent much of last night wondering what she might do if Liro did not leave as she had advised him to. Surely he had come to his senses and realised that his few moments here would only serve to endanger his new persona, and that she would not hesitate in revealing the truth of his origins? As she looked out to where the harbour was just visible in the distance, she felt a slight tightening in her chest, knowing that she would not see him again.

Breakfast passed with amicable conversation, with the trio of Mama's finest matchmaking selections still doing their very best to outdo one another with exciting tales of their achievements. Jean-Claude was quite funny and a born entertainer. John was charming, in a quiet kind of way, but the tall, dark and handsome Prince Lorenz seemed most intent upon captivating her.

He was well-educated and charming, without being overly confident, plus he had expressed a great interest in her charity work around the world with the Olympic foundation. He had been a former rower at university, and they shared a few moments talking about the psychological and physical endurance required for an athlete. He was the ideal candidate that she would've expected her mother to choose for her but, when she looked up towards where Her Majesty sat at the head of the table, she found her mother staring at her with a pensive frown.

'So sorry that I'm late—have I missed breakfast?' a familiar low voice asked from the stairs that led down to the gardens. Minerva turned to watch Liro stride towards them, looking fresh and unruffled as ever in a sage-green polo shirt and charcoal-grey slacks. Again, sunglasses shielded his gaze from hers and she did not even try to hide her annoyance as she narrowed her eyes upon him.

Was that a smirk gracing his lips as he passed her? He moved straight towards her mother, leaning down into a bow and accepting her hand to lay a reverent kiss upon it, as was Arqaletan custom.

'Señor San Nicolau, I was beginning to worry that you had abandoned your invitation.'

'I simply had a matter to attend to down in the harbour. It appears that a yacht the size of mine has garnered quite a lot of attention.'

'I was never one for the super-yachts myself,' the

brooding Irishman, John, mused loudly. 'What is it that they say about those who require extra-large vessels?'

'Over-compensating?' someone mused, earning a low murmur of uneasy laughter.

'Considering he owns most of the largest vessels in the world, I would shudder to think what he's over-compensating for,' Bea suggested loudly from the end of the table. Minerva coughed on the mouthful of croissant she'd just bitten into, eyes watering.

Liro smiled good-naturedly, laughing along easily as he sat down and removed his sunglasses. When his eyes met hers for a split second, Minerva felt her traitorous stomach flip.

'There is no need for you to stay on your ship—we have ample room here.' Her mother spoke over the din. 'In fact, it is considered the height of bad manners to refuse my invitation.'

'I understand, Your Majesty, truly I do,' he said 'But my yacht is my headquarters. I live there fifty-two weeks of the year and it is the best place for me to find a balance between work and…pleasure.'

Minerva ignored the hum of awareness that vibrated through her at the emphasis he placed upon that final word.

'An honourable decision.' Her mother nodded. 'I find a strong work ethic to be *such* a valuable quality.'

Minerva looked for any sign of recognition in her mother's serene features but it appeared she had no idea that the man she was praising was the same young prince she had banned from ever returning to their kingdom. Looking at how much he had changed physically, she supposed not many would see the similarities. He bowed his head once again in deference and Minerva fought the urge to roll her eyes. She could feel Liro's gaze boring into her, so she made extra efforts to renew the conversation with Prince Lorenz, laughing politely at his admittedly bland joke and offering to give him a lesson in target practice whenever he needed.

Once breakfast had finished, Minerva made to excuse herself, only to find the stable master striding across the lawns to inform her that their horses had been readied for the morning's excursion.

'Let me guess,' Minerva said to her mother. 'You forgot to tell me about that as well?'

Queen Uberta shrugged one delicate shoulder and sipped her tea.

Bea ran ahead to perform her morning checks on one of the newly rescued stallions with which she was working, who had become ill during the night. Minerva stood up, looking down at her mother, and tried to convey with her eyes as much as possible her absolute intention to have a very stern conversation once this day came to an end. She sighed with resignation as their group was guided down towards the stables.

Minerva rode her own horse, an impressively fast and agile white stallion named Grumpy that she'd raised herself from a foal with Bea's expert guidance. Most of their party opted for quieter horses, but she was unsurprised to see the selections of the three men who she'd begun referring to internally as 'The Suitors'. It was an old-fashioned term and one that felt entirely apt for this week's objective. She'd already whittled the larger crowd of eligible bachelors down to three. By the end of this week, she would be choosing one of them for marriage.

She tried not to stare as Liro opted for a politely tempered grey-speckled mare by the name of Strawberry who he proceeded to croon to in a low voice as he watched the stable hand ready her. They had all taken a moment to dress in clothes appropriate for riding apart from her, so Minerva slipped away to change in the changing rooms.

When she exited, all eyes were on her, and she fought not to squirm under the scrutiny. It was rather impossible to mount a horse without sticking out one's behind.

But, as she watched Liro slide one booted foot into a stirrup and effortlessly haul himself into position, she herself fought not to stare. His thighs were like tree trunks in the dark jodhpurs he wore like a second skin. His sage-green polo shirt had now been covered with a perfectly tailored black riding jacket, a matching helmet sat proudly atop his head. The overall effect made him look even more gigantic and intimidating, despite him having chosen a modest mount. The three other men flanked him upon their giant black and brown stallions, and Minerva could not miss the measuring looks upon their faces as they gazed upon their competition. If only they knew that Liro was no competition at all.

I did not come for you.

Once again that tight ball in her chest throbbed but she ignored it, kicking a heel back to guide her horse forward and leading their small group along a path that wound around the palace. They reached a crossroads, and for a moment Minerva contemplated taking them on the leisurely wandering path that best showcased the striking views down to the coastline. But then she remembered the smug look upon Liro's face when she'd seen him at breakfast and she instantly guided her horse to the right, down towards the rockier forest path.

'Hope you can all keep up, gentlemen.' She smiled innocently, taking off at a canter.

Liro was fast regretting his decision to return to the palace this morning. He should have stuck to his original plan and set sail the night before—in fact he wasn't quite sure why he had stayed. And he certainly had no idea what had possessed him to attend the breakfast this morning and join this ridiculous outing of socialites.

The Frenchman was getting on his nerves. Minerva laughed again at the charming actor, giving him her full attention. What on earth could he be saying that was so funny anyway?

He adjusted himself in his seat, trying to relax the death grip of his thighs around the wide barrel of the sturdy mare's back. He had never been a strong rider as a boy, and of course there was no real use for horse-riding skills when one lived at sea. But it appeared his new strength meant he was slightly more competent than he had once been. Still, the jostling and moving beneath him made him immeasurably nervous, a sensation that he'd rarely experienced in the past decade.

The other riders evidently noticed his discomfort, the Irishman passing a joke about him not having his sea legs. If it had been the Frenchman, perhaps he would have shown him exactly how balanced he felt; the charmer wouldn't last a moment on one of his ships. But the other two seemed like nice guys—decent, at the very least.

Still, he had ordered a private in-depth investigation into the three men to deduce exactly what had brought them here. He could have left it there, and sent on any information to Minerva anonymously in the event that she did actually choose one of these men as her...king consort. The word left a sour taste in his mouth. There had been no reason for him to remain, and yet here he was.

From the moment Minerva had emerged from the dressing room in her skin-tight leggings and perfectly fitted black polo-shirt, Liro had been on edge. She had the perfect form for every sport, it appeared: the way she'd mounted the horse with effortless grace had made his teeth grind together. And, even as he concentrated on questioning the other men under the guise of casual conversation, his eyes never strayed from her for long.

Minerva had the perfect balance of strength and curves, her long, lean frame sitting so proudly atop her mount. Her dark hair had been wound up into a tight bun beneath her riding hat, putting the full length of her neck on display. He remembered trailing a kiss down that neck the night before, right before she had pushed him away. The scent of her had lingered upon his dress shirt long after he had returned to the yacht, and he had only barely resisted burying his face into it to find some relief.

He was not a horny teenager any longer, he was a grown man, and he was here to ensure that nothing would affect his business deal, nothing more. He needed to know exactly what was going on here between the Crown Princess's supposed dilemma and the likely corrupt politicians in the capital. He needed to know if there was a connection between the two before he proceeded any further.

And, if you find out that there is no connection, what then? a small voice asked. What if he discovered that all was well here in this kingdom, and that the only thing threatening her happiness was his reappearance?

That thought bothered him more than it should have, leaving him scowling into the distance so much that he almost missed the sharp redirection of the party in front of him, down a rocky outcrop from the beaten path.

'Princess, are you sure that this is the best path for our party?' her usually eternally carefree and optimistic friend Beatriz called out, concern in her voice. 'You know how tricky this trail can be.'

'If anyone is not a confident rider, they are free to stay above on the easier path,' Minerva said sweetly, throwing an unmistakable glance back towards Liro.

Ah. He had wondered when his punishment would begin. Liro fought not to smile as he raised one brow in her direction, urging his mount forward so that his horse was nose-to-nose with hers. 'Is this little divergence from the trail all for my benefit, perchance?'

'Don't flatter yourself,' she muttered, her expression still deceptively serene. 'Still, you don't appear to be a very strong rider. We wouldn't want you to sustain an injury.'

'Wouldn't you?' he asked.

'Certainly not, Señor San Nicolau. This is your first trip to our beautiful kingdom, after all. There shall be no injuries or disappearances on my watch.'

It took most of his effort not to laugh at the saccharine sweetness of her voice, shocked that no one else could see the barely restrained malice in the golden-brown gaze directed upon him. If she wanted to challenge him, he would not back down. To his surprise, most of their small group of guests, including the formidable Prince Lorenz, soon decided to turn back to the smoother path, led by Beatriz. The Frenchman paused for a long moment, looking forlornly back and forth between the two parties, and then quickly came to the same decision.

'We will meet you down at the lake,' Minerva called to her friend, then swiftly turned and nudged her horse on at a remarkably faster pace than before.

They continued downhill, dodging tree branches and underbrush, Liro's heartbeat increasing at every possible misstep, but quite impressed at Strawberry's agility. He could not take credit himself, for the horse seemed to instinctively know where to step and where to slow down slightly, but his tolerance was tested significantly when the Irish man nudged himself forward, overtaking him. Seemingly gathering even more speed and bravery, the fool began to show off, overtaking Minerva and disappearing into the distance as he showed off his impressive horsemanship.

'Isn't he going a little fast?' Liro called out, just close enough that she could hear him. She didn't answer so he continued to ramble loudly, 'I suppose we will know soon enough if we find his body at the bottom of a cliff further down.'

Silence.

'I suppose you would rather it be me than him,' Liro

pondered loudly. 'Wouldn't want to sacrifice one of your eligible bachelors.'

Minerva paused her mount, looking back over her shoulder at him. 'You talk a lot more these days. It's quite annoying.'

Liro hid a smile behind his hand. 'Out of interest… which of the three charming fellows is in the lead so far?'

'Just three?' she answered easily. 'You removed yourself from the running so quickly?'

'Darling, we both know that I am in a whole other league.'

The ghost of a smile hinted at the corners of her lips now, but she turned away from him, holding herself at that maddening distance he knew he deserved. She was being sensible, behaving rationally. He was the one who seemed unable to toe the line. He was the one who had insisted upon staying here, appointing himself some kind of unofficial royal investigator of sorts, when it was clear he was unwelcome.

Was he trying to perform a penance for having left things so badly between them? Or did his motives run deeper than that, to a place he had long refused to look at or entertain?

'Why are you still here, Liro?' She exhaled on a long sigh as they began moving downhill through the forest once more.

'I'm a businessman. I'm here to hunt down a new deal.'

'We both know that Arqaleta plays no role in your area of business.'

Liro paused, processing the fact that his hunch was

right, and the royal family had not been consulted on this potentially large change to their kingdom's economy. 'Perhaps I'm just curious to know why a woman who remained comfortably single for the past fourteen years seems set to choose a husband based upon a week of courtship.'

'From the way you asked that question, I gather that you already know the answer.' Minerva shifted atop her saddle, pushing an errant strand of hair away from her face. 'I've had some bad press, but I always knew that the time would come for me to marry. And I have decided to solve that problem now rather than waiting until later.'

'So this is what *you* want?' he asked, needing to hear her say it with her own mouth.

'I'm the Crown Princess. It's what is required of me, in order to maintain the future of my kingdom, so of *course* it is what I want.'

'What a perfectly rehearsed response, Your Highness,' he said, feeling irritation rise in his throat. Of course, there had to be a more pressing reason why she had decided to marry so suddenly, but she was hardly going to divulge that to him of all people.

Silence fell between them as the trail became more demanding and he found himself entranced by her skill and followed her lead. When he performed a small jump over a creek without comment, he found her waiting for him, her gaze narrowed and watchful.

'You remembered some of my lessons, then.'

He smiled, remembering how she had forced him to practise his horsemanship once she'd figured out he was utterly terrified. His father had been a champion polo player in his youth, forcing the sport onto each of his sons. His older brothers had taken to the sport naturally, whereas Liro…had not. After a series of gruelling lessons and bad falls as a young boy, he'd instantly begun to have nightmares. His mother, a terrified rider herself, had taken to shielding him from the pressure, bringing him along with her to the library or the town fun fair when his brothers were at matches. His father hadn't resumed his pressure after her death, instead shifting to the outright mocking and derision of his sensitive youngest son.

'Your teaching methods were impatient but effective.' He moved his mare alongside hers, close enough that he could smell the delicious scent of coconut from the styling oil she had always loved so much. 'You were just as intent upon ignoring me then as you are now.'

'Says the guy who barely spoke to me for the first four years.'

'I barely spoke to anyone, not just you.' He shook off the discomfort at her reminder of his youth. As he had been a skinny, awkward teen in a family of much bigger and louder men, his father and brothers had often taken enjoyment in commenting on his uselessness. Perhaps that was why, when he'd been sent to Arqaleta with the oddly specific purpose of befriending the princess, he had taken it as an opportunity to show his worth.

She was right—that first summer, he'd hardly uttered a single word in her presence. He had always struggled socially and tended towards self-isolation, but around Minerva he'd been speechless for an entirely different reason. From the first moment he'd seen her, she'd made him feel uncomfortably seen. Her wide golden-brown eyes and open, friendly manner had made him feel as though he were staring at the sun for the first time after years spent in the dark. Add the fact she'd been the most beautiful girl he had ever laid his eyes on...

'I looked forward to coming here every summer. Being here, getting over my fear of riding, I was happy. Despite my silence.' He surprised himself with his honesty, knowing that she could simply wave him off and go right back to ignoring him all over again. But whatever part of him that had forced him to keep his yacht moored in the harbour last night was still very much in control, and it desperately needed her to know the important part she'd played in his life.

'Your silence was just you, Liro. Besides, I talked enough for both of us.' Her voice trailed off and he wondered if she was thinking about all the things she'd said when she'd thought he was ignoring her. Her sadness about her father, her worries about becoming queen one day. He had listened to every word, storing away each detail and wondering how he might help. He wondered who she talked to now—probably Bea or her mother. He wondered if they let her talk things out all by herself, as she needed to, or if they jumped in with suggestions, tangling her up. Maybe that was how she had wound up in this ridiculous week of marital matchmaking with strangers.

He let her stew over whatever thoughts were piling up in her mind, understanding that he was no longer one of her confidants. He had walked away from that position the moment he'd chosen to leave Arqaleta on a ship in the dead of night, like a coward.

There was no audience here as he kept pace perfectly behind her, no one to play nice in front of. He relaxed back and allowed his horse to navigate the rocky path down the mountain, enjoying the view, the rolling hills and the smell of the sea air in the distance.

But mostly he enjoyed looking at Minerva, the sweat just barely evident on her brow as she held her reins. She rode so effortlessly, with such smooth, subtle movements of her hips and thighs... It mesmerised him.

It had been far too long since he'd last indulged in any kind of sexual gratification with anything other than his own hand. He'd thought of her last night, after that kiss... He'd brought himself to the swiftest release of his life in a brief moment of weakness, accessing the memories of the brief few weeks he'd had her in his arms he'd stored away. He was so focused upon curbing his illicit thoughts that he was not prepared when the tree line broke and the ferocious midday sun blinded him momentarily.

'Be careful!' Her voice called out to him from a few feet to his left, where the path took a sudden, sharp turn. He pulled the reins hard, trying to get the horse to stop. By the time his eyes adjusted and he realised that he had veered close to the edge of a rocky cliff, there was little that he could do, only pull the reins harder, feeling the horse's hooves skid beneath him as the old girl tried to stop. He was aware of the sound of galloping and the sound of a shout before the sky tilted and he was thrown heavily backwards.

CHAPTER FOUR

THE WHOLE THING happened in slow motion. Minerva could do nothing but watch as Liro pulled too hard on his reins, startled by the sudden cliff drop-off that lay in front of them. The sun had blinded him momentarily but now his eyes were wide, darting towards her with realisation, right as his horse reared up and sent his body tumbling backwards towards the drop. He landed with a sickening thud upon the ground.

The horse skidded to a stop a few feet away, thankfully avoiding trampling him or more danger. But, as Minerva jumped down from her own horse, she felt real fear rise like bile in her throat. She had done this—she had brought him down this path, knowing that he was not a strong rider. She'd told him she wanted him gone, and in that moment it had felt painfully true, but that did not mean she actually wished him harm.

Liro looked past her, his face paling as he looked upon the edge of the cliff. In an impressive display of nonchalance, he slid himself a few inches away from the precipice before flopping back to the ground with a grunt.

'Are you okay?' Minerva breathed, falling down to her knees beside him. His small movements indicated a lack of serious injury, but one could never be sure.

She'd been there on the awful day when the stable master's daughter had been thrown from a temperamental horse. She would never forget the horror of it. Minerva had been by Bea's side every step of the way as she'd recovered from a serious spinal injury and the event had wound up bonding them as friends for life. Again, she cursed herself for being so petty and impulsive in bringing Liro down such a demanding trail and risking his safety this way.

'I'm fine.' He heaved himself up onto his elbows, his muscles straining against the dust-covered sleeves of his jacket. He grimaced as he tried to straighten further.

'You're hurt.' She flattened her hand against his chest to hold him still.

He looked up at her, stormy eyes glowing more green than grey today, obscenely ethereal in the sunlight. Eyes should not be such an unpredictable colour, she reasoned briefly, trying not to focus on the steady heat of his chest rising and falling under her explorative touch. She pressed his ribs slightly, watching his face for signs of pain.

'Surely the objective of taking me down this path was to allow me to fall to my death?' he asked, then immediately groaned as she increased the pressure of her touch.

'I want you gone, not dead.' She growled. 'Stop talking for a moment and catch your breath you…you little fool.' She cursed under her breath, holding his shoulder to force him still. He obeyed, his breaths coming shallow and hard as he lay flat on the ground. She took the opportunity to lift up his shirt to ensure there weren't any ribs poking out, causing his breathlessness. No protruding bones greeted her, only rock-hard abs.

'Little…fool?' he repeated.

She could hear the hint of a smirk in his voice and fought not to laugh, if only to break the terror of the past couple of minutes. 'I don't know...it just came out.'

'I thought that phrase was reserved for waifish heroines in period dramas. Do you think of me as a dainty damsel you've had to rescue?'

'I don't think of you at all.' She felt his eyes on her but refused to look at him as she stood up and smacked the dust roughly from her knees. 'Or at least I didn't, until you reappeared without any explanation, seemingly hell-bent on derailing my life at every turn.'

A heavy silence fell between them but she refused to apologise when she spoke the truth. Well, not about not thinking of him...of course that part was a bare-faced lie...but the rest of it. She had been on the verge of tears all morning then had been forced to put on her best performance during this ridiculous ride, only to have him bring up the past and question her choices.

She looked over to where his previously spooked mare was gazing peacefully near a tree, and felt a shiver course through her again at how close he'd come to injury. She should offer to help him up, she realised, but her body felt frozen in place. Everything about the past twenty-four hours was just too much.

If only Liro had just left again. If only he had never returned in the first place, like her father had done all those years ago. It was the one gift he'd given them, that clean break. It was far easier to forget someone when you could pretend they didn't exist. Having Liro here now made her feel as if all of her work in putting herself back together had been for nothing—as if just looking at him made her hurt all over again.

She had made her plans for this week and the months that would follow as she finally stepped into her role as Queen of Arqaleta. She refused to let the reappearance of one insufferable man throw everything off kilter.

His expression became gravely serious. 'Minerva... when I left...'

'I have no wish to discuss the past any more,' she said quickly, feeling a hint of panic creep into her voice. 'Once some time had passed, I realised that you breaking our betrothal was the best possible outcome for us both. I travelled the world and lived out my dream in a way I never could have if we had been forced into a marriage of convenience.'

'So you're done living your dreams, just like that?' he asked. 'Do you truly believe that any of these suitors will satisfy you?'

She froze at his cruel words, at how close they came to getting right under her skin. 'Is this the only reason you came back here? To question my choices?'

'Maybe I'm just here to try to make amends to someone I hurt. Someone I once considered a friend.'

She shook her head, hurt climbing her throat as she looked down at him where he still lay at her feet. 'Well, Liro, you're around fourteen years too late.'

The sound of hooves coming closer from a distance was a welcome distraction from how deep into unwelcome territory their conversation had got. By the time John's horse appeared from around the bend, Liro had sprung easily up to his feet.

'Everything all right?' the Irishman asked, his eyes darting shrewdly between them, as though he feared he'd made a gross miscalculation in trying to show off his horsemanship.

'The mare became spooked by the drop and threw her rider,' Minerva replied coolly. 'Thankfully Señor San Nicolau was not hurt.'

If Liro was surprised at her effort to spare him any embarrassment, he restrained himself from commenting. Instead, he focused on putting on the bravest face to belie the obvious bruising he'd endured from his fall. He walked over to his horse and swung up with only the tiniest groan under his breath, which he quickly disguised with a cough.

Minerva smiled behind the cover of her own stallion's flank as she pretended to tighten the saddle. For all he had insisted that the prince she'd known was dead and gone, this hint of vulnerability was something he couldn't help but show. She thought of the first few summers they'd been forced together, when she'd helped him get over his fear of horse riding, and he'd helped her with the remedial schoolwork she had been trying to catch up on for ever. They hadn't been close friends, but they'd never been enemies.

As they rode back towards the lake to meet up with the others, Minerva couldn't help but watch Liro closely for any other signs of pain. He remained silent, not speaking another word until he bid them goodbye at the stables and disappeared in the direction of the harbour. Stubborn man, she grumbled to herself as she was once again danced with attention by Jean-Claude and Prince Lorenz.

Prince Oliveiro might have adopted a new name and look, but when it came to hiding himself away without further explanation it seemed he hadn't changed so much.

* * *

Liro did not return for the informal dinner her mother hosted that evening, nor was he present at breakfast the next morning. Minerva resisted the urge to go down to the harbour to see if his ridiculously oversized yacht was still moored there, as a light fog had obstructed her view from her bedroom window the night before. Thankfully she had managed to fall into an exhausted sleep after the previous afternoon's horse-riding adventure had turned into an impromptu rowing lesson from Prince Lorenz on the lake. She had been surprised by his astute conversation and dry wit, and had vowed to give him an honest chance after his poor first impression.

But still Liro's voice was in her head far too often, asking her why now? Why the rush? He had got under her skin simply by reappearing in her life and then he had had the audacity to question her as well. His inquisition had only served to reaffirm her effort to get to know each of her three choices of potential husband. They truly were expert choices, showing her that her mother knew her better than she probably even knew herself.

The agenda for Wednesday began with an exhibition at their museum of cultural history in Albo's historical town square, one of her favourite places in all of Arqaleta. The curator had gathered and assembled an interactive exhibit of Arqaleta's rich history of weaponry, including their world-famous bow and arrow collections.

Minerva stood by her mother's side as the Queen gave a beautiful speech about the history of their beautiful island kingdom, a speech that Minerva knew came from the heart. Crowds had gathered, filling up their modest town square and spilling over into the surrounding streets. Street vendors sold sweet treats and their world-famous Arqaletan pastry, the honeybee, on every corner. The scent of warm honey and crisp, flaking pastry filled the air and made her mouth water.

She hadn't eaten much at breakfast, and would have loved nothing more than to cross the street and grab one for herself, but duty called. Still, her stomach rumbled as she gazed longingly in the direction of a young couple sharing a crisp, golden honeybee between them.

'Hungry?'

A low voice came from behind her shoulder. She turned sharply to find Liro, looking relaxed and pensive. How long had he been standing there? He was dressed in a fine navy suit today, his rich red waves smoothed back in a classic style that emphasised his strong nose and cheekbones. He had never been conventionally attractive as a teen, but every time she laid eyes on him now she found herself stricken anew by what a presence he made. He made no effort to hide his tattoos today, letting the curling black lines snake up from his open collar. She still couldn't make out what they were…a forest of some sort? An animal?

He noticed her staring and she turned away quickly away. Her mother's speech had ended, but the curator was talking through his inspiration for the exhibit now, and she had not been paying attention.

'You seem tense, *princesa*. Is selecting your favourite suitor from the bachelor buffet proving more difficult than you'd hoped?' He moved to stand by her side, using the handkerchief from his breast pocket to idly polish the sunglasses in his hands.

'You're still here.' She feigned complete boredom,

focusing her attention fully upon the display. 'When you disappeared again, I thought yesterday had finally convinced you to move on.'

'And miss finding out who your beloved new king consort will be?' He clucked his tongue. 'Not a chance.'

His handsome smirk sent a shiver along her skin and she resisted the urge to walk away, to leave him standing there alone. *Bachelor buffet…* Her mind whirled with discomfort at his words, the blunt reminder of the choice she had to make soon. They had an audience, she was a princess and princesses had rules. A princess did not cut people off, and she definitely did not stick her tongue out at them for good measure.

She settled upon turning her head politely to feign interest in the curator's speech, listening to the older man wax lyrical about primitive arrows and the very first cannon.

The heat was growing stronger by the minute and her stomach continued to growl softly as she put her best effort into appearing utterly engrossed. When the speech finally ended, she resisted the urge to sigh, knowing that now she would be forced to walk at a snail's pace around the exhibit when really all she wanted was to go straight to the bow and arrow section and see which pieces had been chosen.

The scent of melted sugar and butter teased her nostrils, seeming to have wafted across to her on a cruel breeze. But then by some miracle a pastry appeared in her vision, wrapped in a delicate white napkin in Liro's large, callused hand.

'A gift from an admirer, Your Highness,' he said,

placing the delicious pastry in her hands before she could say no.

He watched her, eyes sparkling with sin, urging her to cause a scene and refuse his gift. He had clearly been standing nearby for long enough to notice her gazing over at the food and he had gone and got one for her.

That realisation shouldn't have sent a glittering shimmer of warmth running through her, but food had always been her weakness. She was utterly ravenous, and the honeybee was her absolute favourite out of all the pastries he could have chosen. She bowed her head in the direction of the vendor, who smiled and gestured towards her excitedly. A queue had already begun to form around his stall now that the people could see the princess holding one of his perfectly baked confections.

'Consider it a peace offering,' Liro said. 'You could have left me in the dirt, or at the very least you could have told the embarrassing truth of what happened, rather than preserve the dignity of a *little fool*.'

His reminder of her phrase made a sudden snort of laughter escape her. She tried to hold it in, but it was too late, and a second bubble of mirth followed the first. Liro's eyes seemed to glitter with victory at the sound, making her wish he would put back on his sunglasses. He was…too much…and once again he was distracting her from her duty.

Sighing with defeat, she bit ceremoniously into a small corner of the pastry in the hope it would send him away. She was not prepared for the sheer perfection of flavour that met her taste buds. All royal teachings abandoned, she proceeded to finish the entire thing in less than three bites. She looked down at the napkin, filled with nothing but crumbs, and realised her lapse of propriety.

Liro leaned in, a smile on his lips. 'Don't worry, everyone is far too busy looking at your museum curator struggling to lift a bow to notice you inhaling a glorified croissant.'

'*He's* doing the demonstration?' She looked up, sure enough seeing the elderly curator lifting an ancient bow from its case. Her fingers itched with longing.

'Strange that they would choose an elderly academic when they have a world-famous Olympic archer sitting right here,' he mused. 'Or is this part of that new traditional image I've heard of?'

'I don't always have to take the spotlight.' She shrugged.

The look Liro gave her was one of complete disbelief. 'Your experience as an athlete on the global stage is a huge advantage. Teenagers had posters of you on their walls, for goodness' sake. Maybe they fear your power and influence.'

The crowd began to cheer around them as the elderly curator hit a weak arrow in the vague direction of the target. It was an utterly pathetic shot, but still she applauded. Heaven forbid anyone wound an old man's pride.

But still, as the display ended and the bell was called for the sit-down luncheon inside, Liro's words resounded in her mind. *Maybe they fear your power and influence.* Of course, she knew that her position as a female leader in a kingdom traditionally ruled by men was fraught with issues. Her own mother had hit many roadblocks in her reign, but she was confident that she knew which battles to fight and which to cede. Or at least, that was what she had been telling herself.

When they were seated, she watched from afar as Liro conversed easily among the guests at his table on the far side of the room. She felt his attention upon her at regular intervals and noticed his eyes narrow when the band started up and Prince Lorenz, John and Jean-Claude each appeared to ask her to dance. She indulged Jean-Claude first, laughing as she attempted to teach him a traditional Arqaletan slow dance. John stepped up for the next song, impressing her with his speed and agility as he led the dance. All the while, it took far too much of her focus not to let her eyes wander to the brooding red-haired hulk at the edge of the room.

It was on her third turn around the room, with Prince Lorenz this time, that she allowed herself to take a quick look—only to find his table empty. She craned her neck, looking around the hall, finally spying him standing in the far corner of the room with a familiar silver-haired politician, Robart. Minerva frowned as the two men shook hands, looking very chummy for brand-new acquaintances. Confirming her suspicions, Liro took out his phone and showed Robart something, earning a wink from the older man and a clap on the back.

When Liro looked up at her, she saw guilt cross his features and felt her stomach tighten. Her suspicions had been based only on a hunch, but one look in his eyes and she knew she had been right. He'd come here to conquer, to seize control in the shadows, just as his father had tried to do all those years ago.

The song stopped and she thanked her lucky stars. Prince Lorenz was a wonderful dancer, but he talked non-stop, and she just needed to breathe a moment alone. Something small and fragile ached in her chest, but she managed to maintain her composure as she walked past the tables filled with guests, up the grand staircase and out towards the rest rooms. Only at the very last moment did she realise she had changed her course and had slipped over the velvet ropes that led to the darkened display halls.

Automatic lights clicked on above her head as her heels clicked on the floors, the musty scent of wood polish reminding her of childhood visits here with her father. He had been an amateur archer himself, one of the only things they'd ever had in common. Her natural skill at the sport had never been enough to capture his attention, but still, she had him to thank for the introduction. It was woven into the very history of their country, in the talented bow-makers and fletchers for which Arqaleta had long been world renowned.

She came to a stop in front of a vast case filled with wooden longbows and bronze-tipped arrows, blinking at the faint reflection of herself in the glass. Another tiara adorned her head today, a small piece that had been designed to commemorate her Olympic gold medal. It was an accomplishment that many members of parliament had initially been against her seeking, deeming it unroyal and too time consuming. Robart had been one of the loudest voices against her suitability as future queen, so it stung to see Liro shaking the man's hand.

She didn't know how long she stood there in silence. When the sound of heavy footsteps approached slowly from the hallway, she didn't need to look up. Just as when they'd been young and she'd tried to avoid him, Liro always found her.

'Hiding from your duty, Min...?' He tutted, his hands

deep in his pockets as he came to a stop by her side. 'Your handsome bachelors will grow restless.'

'I'm surprised you noticed, with how cosy you seemed with Robart.' She laced her tone with saccharine sweetness, her words echoing off the high glass ceiling above them. 'Tell me…you're not trying to push your way into the harbour rezoning proposals by any chance, are you? The ones that my mother refused to sign? Would that be the reason you've refused to leave my kingdom for the past three days?'

Liro looked down at her, his stern expression breaking slightly. 'You already know about the harbour project?'

'People assume that, because I have stopped pushing the boundaries and chosen to step into my role fully, I have somehow stopped being the most focused person in the room.' She met his eyes, anger masking the strange sadness in her chest at the confirmation that she was right. That he had been toying with her these past couple of days, biding his time as he tried to close a deal.

Liro hadn't noticed Minerva leave the museum's function area at first, having been waylaid in conversation by that insufferable politician. Once he'd realised she'd gone, and noticed the distinct absence of the tall, dark and handsome Prince Lorenz, he'd made quick work of stalking down every exhibit hall until he found her.

Now here they were, arguing again. But this time about something he honestly had not intended to keep from her. They'd just been rather busy kissing, arguing and avoiding death by cliff-fall thus far. He took in the molten bronze ire in her gaze and shook off an inappropriate thrum of desire. Now was certainly not the time, not when he had myriad things to explain to her about his intentions with the development plans.

She raised a hand to stop him before he could say a single word. 'Save it. I knew about that project from the moment whispers began to circulate. I haven't raised my concerns because I don't have any.'

'You…don't intend to stop it?'

'My mother and I have very different views on what progress looks like. I believe that rigid control breeds secrecy and corruption, whereas compromise and fairness lead to more balanced results. I want Arqaleta to grow, and growth hurts sometimes, to lead to better things.'

He stared at her for a long moment, before he heard himself murmur. 'You're going to make an amazing queen.'

She turned from him, hiding her face. 'There is no need for you to continue attending events and stalking me for pretence, Liro. Finish your deal and go.'

He took in the rigid pose and the guarded look in her eyes and realised she believed he'd been using their past as a cover, to hide his dealings. If only that were the truth. He took a step towards her, irritation flaring as she took an equal step back. She wanted to keep herself at a distance while they had this conversation but…oh…that just wasn't going to work for him. He kept moving forward until she looked up at him with some of that glorious fury. He wanted her anger; he needed it, all of a sudden.

'That deal may be why I accepted the invitation, Minerva…but I think it's damned obvious to both of us that it is not why I stayed.' He stepped closer again, crowding her against the smooth glass of a display case.

'If you truly considered yourself a friend to me, Liro, you'd leave.'

'If I was your friend, I would tell you that you don't actually want to marry any of them. They won't make you happy.'

'That's rich, coming from you.' She stiffened, holding herself at a distance. 'I don't want a happy-ever-after, just a husband. The kingdom's tradition has always included a king consort and I won't be the one to break that.'

'Tell me what you need, Min,' he urged, moving close enough that their chests almost touched. 'When is the last time anyone bothered to ask?'

'Right now? I need to go back to the party.'

'Stay,' he said, softly enough for it to seem like a request. But the very idea of allowing her to run back to those preening fools, of continuing to watch from afar as they salivated and fought over her attentions like pups... His fists clenched involuntarily. She needed to be cared for in a way that no one else seemed able to see. She was so wound up, so tense and close to breaking point, he feared she might shatter. She put everyone else's expectations ahead of her own, living each day for her precious duty. Had she ever known a single day of true freedom?

'I should reveal your identity right here and now in front of everyone,' she whispered, her breath close enough to fan against his lips. 'I should have done it the moment I first recognised you.'

'You didn't, though. You were far too busy kissing me.' He tilted his head closer, caging her body in softly with his arms. Despite her threats, she hadn't made a single move to leave. A fact that made all of the blood in his body rush below his belt. 'I think you know what you need, Minerva. I think that's part of the reason why you're so determined to tear strips off me every time we get too close. We both have a lot of pent-up emotions that we didn't get the chance to work out.'

'Are you about to suggest that I hop into bed with you one more time for closure? Bang it out of our systems?' She scoffed, but he could see the way her honey-brown eyes tried to hide flickers of desire.

'I've wondered if one night of having you back in my bed would be enough. Wondered if it would make this burning need go away…or would it only stoke us back into a full-blown forest fire?'

He leaned forward, lifting her hand to press the ghost of a kiss against the inside of her wrist. She sighed and he felt it like a punch to the gut. He was so hard, he could barely think, but she needed to come to him the rest of the way. She needed to admit that what he was saying was the truth and that there was only one logical way for them to work this tension out and move on.

Because he knew that was all it could be—they both did.

'Tell me you haven't thought about it, Min,' he murmured softly, inching a second kiss upon her palm. 'Tell me that you haven't fantasised about me when your day is done and you're all alone in that big bed of yours. Tell me to leave you alone…and I'll go.'

His own needy words shocked him, an uncomfortable echo of his younger self that took him by surprise. He wasn't usually so unguarded with a woman. On the occasions he bothered to seek out company at port, he kept things brief. He treated his sex life much the same as his appearances in the board room—calm, rare and to the point.

But here...in this dimly lit, echoing museum hall as he waited for her to speak...he didn't feel calm at all. She reached up, placing a hand upon his chest, and for a moment he thought she might push him away. But she didn't. She left it there, a single maddening point of contact between them.

'I've thought about you,' she said quietly, closing her eyes tightly.

And there it was. He closed his eyes, taking in a single shuddering breath as his body strained hard against the seam of his fanciest dress trousers. When he opened his eyes again, she was watching him.

'Why am I telling you these things?' she whispered, sliding her hands up to his shoulders. Her fingers flexed upon his muscles and he flexed back shamelessly. Her slow smile was just a little shy and filled with the evidence of her desire.

'You don't want to be left alone, that's why.'

She bit on her lower lip. 'I don't know what I want. Not when it comes to you.'

He knew how easy it would be to lean forward and close the distance between them, to quiet her indecision with kisses. He wouldn't hold back; he'd instantly begin to show her exactly what he would do if she ever came back to his bed. One night with the woman who had haunted him.... One night to lay to rest all of the foolish memories he could never shake... He wanted it so badly his fingers shook and his throat ran dry. So why then did he find himself taking a step backwards?

What did he plan to do, undress her here on the cold

stone floor then disappear off to sea once again? Another final memory to keep, because that had worked so well last time, hadn't it?

Liro cleared his throat, looking back towards the exit. She was a crown princess with a museum full of people waiting for her to return; they could be found at any moment. She had so many people pushing her to comply with their needs, taking her kindness, using her.

She leaned towards him for a split second, a single glimpse of confusion in her eyes that she quickly covered up as she too seemed to come to her senses. Standing up straight, she pushed past him and walked away a few steps. She paused under an archway, flanked by two statues in gleaming golden armour.

'You said you'd go, if I told you one more time,' she said, her words echoing, cold and unyielding, in the cavernous hall.

Silence stretched between them. He knew what he had said and knew that it was the best course of action. But still, something within him growled in protest as she walked away.

CHAPTER FIVE

MINERVA RETURNED TO the function and threw herself into princess mode, speaking with everyone who sought out her attention and dancing until her feet ached. She didn't see Liro again. By the time the event wound down and she had returned to the palace, she was exhausted enough to fall into a dreamless sleep.

The next morning was a day filled with events, starting with a beautiful folk concert and poetry reading at the children's hospital. She resisted the urge to check if a certain giant black yacht had departed the kingdom yet, just as she resisted scanning the shoreline for it as her car drove past the marina. This week was about securing her path to the crown, not ruminating over the past like a moody teenager. She was good at compartmentalising her emotions. In a job where she was expected to be *on* at all times in public, she had to be.

Still, she couldn't stop herself from looking over her shoulder countless times throughout the long morning, and even longer afternoon, wondering if she might find a familiar pair of green-grey eyes watching her.

The sun was low in the sky when she and her mother were deposited at the bottom of the steps of the palace, but the idea of going inside and beginning her preparations for the evening's charity auction made her feel strangely empty. It would be a wonderful event, with all proceeds going towards so many causes close to her heart. But the idea of spending more time with John, Prince Lorenz and Jean-Claude made her feel utterly exhausted. She knew she had to begin to make her decision soon, before Mama's announcement. But all of her cool-headed determination from the past few weeks of preparation had begun to wane slightly, leaving her more than a little unsure of her decision to rush into a royal marriage of convenience.

She felt her mother's eyes on her as they walked along the corridor towards the family suites. Before she reached the privacy of her room, her mother pulled her away towards a quiet corner of the garden. 'Have any of the candidates I invited caught your eye yet?'

'I have it narrowed down to three.' She listed off the names of the men she'd chosen and saw a strange look cross her mother's features. 'What, you disagree?'

'Not at all, darling,' Mama said quickly. 'You asked me to send the invitations—the rest is entirely up to you. But…none of the others caught your attention?'

After a moment of hesitation, Minerva knew that her only choice was to lie and change the topic to the speech they'd been preparing for the announcement on Saturday. Her mother continued to look at her a little too closely, a fact that did nothing for the nervous energy that had plagued her since that moment in the museum hall yesterday afternoon.

When her mother finally excused herself to begin to get ready, Minerva knew she should follow along. She didn't have much time before the stylists and make-up artists arrived to do a quick change from her day look to evening formal.

The scent of citrus filled the air, floating over from the large glass conservatory hall where tonight's event would take place. She ambled towards her bedroom door, hesitating at the last moment. In the absence of her beloved sport, her thoughts had become increasingly tangled and harder to manage over the past few months. Time in the archery arena was time that she would usually have spent thinking about and working through the things that weighed upon her mind. But there was one place in the palace grounds that had always given her peace...

A hum of nervous energy seemed to zing through her at the idea, and before she knew it she had veered through an archway and was quietly cutting across the gardens in her polished ivory day dress. Her security team had remained in the upper hallway: the palace grounds were safe enough for her to wander a little. She would not be gone long; she just needed some time alone to breathe.

Minerva knew where she was heading instinctively, even before the tell-tale scent of moss hit her nostrils. She hadn't come down to their old lakeside haunt in many years. She had thought she had prepared well enough for the energy required to get through such a high intensity week of events, but nothing could have prepared her for him. He'd plied her with croissants, asked her for her secrets and cracked open all the tightly controlled longing she'd kept hidden away.

Three days ago, she had been fine. She had been more than fine: she had been *quite* content with the prospect of selecting a husband. Then he'd reappeared in her world with all the subtlety of an atomic bomb, making her question everything...planting seeds of rebellion, just as he had all those years ago.

Well, she was not the same girl he had used and discarded at nineteen, and it was high time he understood that. If he turned up at the auction tonight, she would give him a piece of her mind. She would tell him exactly how she felt, no punches pulled.

The stone archway was mostly covered in leaves and branches, and a wave of sadness came over her as she fought her way through the tree-covered pathway. The secret lake was still there, and blessedly not completely overgrown with foliage. The stone statues lay sleeping, as though they had been waiting for her return. She ran her fingers along the graceful neck of a marble swan, trying to adjust her eyes to the much softer light.

She didn't see the broad figure that lay in wait upon one of the stone benches, inhaling sharply when he stood and revealed himself.

'What are you doing here?'

'Probably the same thing that you are,' Liro answered, his expression more guarded than she had ever seen. 'I thought I would visit this place...before I leave.'

'And when will that be?' she asked, trying to hide how shaken she felt at the sight of seeing him here...in *their* place. They hadn't been here since that very last night when everything had fallen apart. The thought of being a royal bride had felt so exciting back then, while now she looked upon it as just another task she had to tick off in order to perform the job she had been raised to do.

'I'm leaving tonight,' he said. 'I had debated attending the charity auction, considering that I had already purchased my ticket, but I am sure the funds will still make it to the right places in my absence.'

Silence fell between them, along with a million unspoken words that Minerva wanted to say. Angry words, questions and above all longing. She wanted to tell him exactly how she had felt when he'd left, exactly how much his absence had shaped her as a person.

'I won't be backing down from my bid on the harbour expansion. But I have decided that I will not be personally overseeing the rest of the negotiations myself.'

He paused for a long moment before taking a step towards her. 'Everything I said yesterday was the truth, but I see now that it was unfair to return here. You've made it clear that my presence is unwelcome and...despite what you may think... I never set out to upset you, Minerva.'

She thought of the things he'd said in that darkened museum hall and felt heat blaze along her skin. *Tell me that you haven't fantasised about me*, he'd urged. *Tell me to leave you alone...* She hadn't been able to say either of those things with confidence.

The truth was she had fantasised about him more times than she could count. Just this morning she had awoken swollen and slick with longing, imagining his strong, capable hands doing truly delicious things to her. She'd only barely resisted calling out his name as she'd brought herself to climax, then had instantly felt raw and embarrassed afterwards as she got ready to go about her day.

'You said...' She inhaled a deep breath, nerves and indecision making it catch in her throat. 'You said that we both know why you stayed. I want you to tell me.'

'I stayed for you, Min,' he said easily. 'I stayed because, once I saw you again, I couldn't quite seem to leave.'

She took a step towards him. 'But you will leave. If I tell you to.'

'If that's what you want, then yes.'

Was that what she wanted? For days now she had told herself that she wanted Liro to disappear, along with all the complicated emotions that seemed to bubble up in his presence. She had been so consumed with holding herself together, with focusing on the celebrations and the matchmaking...

Tell me what you need, Min. When was the last time anyone asked?

She needed to kiss him. She needed it so badly, her hands trembled with the effort of remaining at a distance. Just once, she promised herself. One last kiss to get the closure she'd been denied fourteen years ago. She could see his fingers flexing by his sides. He wanted to touch her...and she wanted so badly to be touched. Before she could over-think, she closed the remaining distance between them. There were so many things she wanted to say, but words failed her as she reached for him, leaning into his warmth.

Her lips found his as though they had always known this was where she would end up. As though that very first kiss after she'd recognised him had simply been an appetiser, an initial spark of kindling upon the embers of their past. She had been smouldering for him for days now—she could deny it no longer. And, when his hands sank into her hair, she groaned against his mouth with relief.

'This…' she murmured as she paused for a breath. 'This is what I need from you.'

A growl came from somewhere low in his throat as he pulled her closer so that another inch of space was removed between them.

'If this is what you need from me, princess,' he urged, thrusting his hardness against her thigh. 'Then use me.'

His words felt wrong, somehow… But his tone was erotic and dominating so she let him take control for a moment, pushing her back against the tree trunk.

'You missed me.' His words were a statement rather than a question and she didn't have the energy to rebuke them as a shiver passed through her and reality began to encroach upon this tiny oasis of pleasure.

'I missed *this*,' she corrected, not able to give him any more than that. She'd gone so long without true connection to another and she was powerless to stop. They kissed until her back ached against the rough tree but, every time she told herself that it was time to leave, she didn't. In the end it was he who pulled back first, his eyes never leaving hers as he caught his breath.

'You make me feel like a teenager.' He growled, a subtle smirk on his lips as he traced the pad of his index finger down the side of her neck and along one collar bone.

His touch was feather-light and almost tender, confusing her even more. She didn't want softness from him. It was too much and yet entirely not enough. She pushed gently until she could slide away from the tree, needing to breathe.

'Your compliments are good for a girl's confidence.' She aimed for a light tone, failing miserably. 'Y-you've got better at kissing since then.'

Liro's voice was silky as sin as he replied, 'I've had a lot of time to think about it.'

This man… Minerva inhaled a deep breath, trying to cool off the instant heat that rushed through her body with his words. She knew that staying here and talking like this with him was dangerous. She knew it, and still she met his eyes with a direct challenge. 'I think sometimes time tends to embellish certain memories to make them seem better than they actually were.'

His eyes lowered to her lips. 'Well…there's only one way to know for sure.'

She didn't know who kissed whom first this time, not that it mattered anyway. The space between them was instantly gone and his lips were crushed against hers, his hands in her hair holding her just where he wanted her. Her body sang at his touch, a shiver of awareness spreading along the skin of her nape and down her spine like wildfire. The crackling heat of the flame finally being ignited between them was stifling. All rational thought of this being wrong was utterly consumed by a hunger so intense it took her breath away. She felt his hands tightening on her waist, pulling her closely against him so that she could feel the evidence of his arousal pressing against her lower abdomen.

God, how she had missed this feeling. She remembered once telling him that the intensity of her desire for him scared her. She had been younger then, a curious girl entering into her first passionate love affair. He had been inexperienced too, but had still always behaved like a gentleman. He'd held off on his own desires to make sure that she was ready before they took their relationship to the next level.

She was not a virgin now. Nor was he feeling particularly gentlemanly, judging by the way he pushed her back against the tree while his fingers frantically worked at the delicate pearl buttons at her throat. The front of her dress came open slowly, her simple cotton bra revealed to him inch by inch. His big hands splayed over the soft material, rubbing against her tautened nipples through the thin barrier. She sighed at the contact, fighting the urge to take over and remove both of their clothing quickly and efficiently.

She needed to feel his skin against hers, to enjoy it before either of them had time to rethink this madness. His lips teased her earlobe, kissing a hot path down the side of her neck. He flexed himself against her, clever hands peeling the fabric of her bra down so he could take one hard nipple into his mouth. Goose flesh spread down both of her arms and she braced herself against the rough surface of the tree trunk in an effort to remain standing; the pleasure was so intense.

He growled against her skin and she threaded her fingers through his hair, holding him in place as he worshipped her breasts. She hadn't realised how much she needed this. The tension of the past few days seemed to ebb away with every long, languorous lick of his perfect tongue. His hands followed the curve of her waist down to her skirt, pulling the fabric upwards. She felt cool air on her upper thighs as she impatiently reached back and pulled the zipper downwards so that the material could be pulled up around her waist.

He paused for a moment, something dark and unreadable in his narrowed gaze, before he took her hips in both hands and held her tight against the evidence of his arousal. His fingers hooked into the lace of her panties and pulled them to one side, giving him direct access to the hot centre of her. With each small circling of his fingertip, she tightened and moaned, grinding up against him. When he slowly slid one finger inside her, she thought she might expire completely. Her mind short-circuited, and for a brief moment of madness she wondered if her body might have forgotten what it was supposed to do.

But Liro clearly wasn't worried. He growled words of encouragement, asking if she needed more. She was vaguely aware of herself nodding, begging, until he added a second finger. Almost immediately, she felt as if she was seconds from shattering, emotionally and physically. She had resigned herself never to feel like this again, and now here she was, running headfirst back into the fire. Her barely contained moans only seemed to spur Liro on.

She bit down on her fist, fearing they might be heard if she completely lost control. He pulled her hand away from her mouth, his eyes dark pools of desire as he worked his magic.

'Come for me,' he urged under his breath. 'Let me hear you.'

She did as she was told, breaking apart in sensuous abandon and crying out without any regard for decency. She felt as though her body was unravelling with every slick movement of him inside her, the pleasure so intense she thought she might cry with relief. She was vaguely aware that he had begun stroking himself during their interlude and, before she even had the clarity to try to return the pleasure he'd given her, he growled low in his throat, his own release taking him over. It felt painfully intimate, watching him lose control so quickly, as though they had gone straight back in time to their trysts as young lovers.

For a split second, she worried that this was the moment the bubble would burst. But then Liro took one long look at her and cursed under his breath, leaning down to take her lips again roughly. Minerva melted into his kiss, her mind refusing to come back to earth after the intensity of her orgasm. She had forgotten what it was like to completely surrender herself to passion like this. To lose herself in it.

But, as he took a step back to clean away the evidence of his own pleasure, she felt the first cold breeze of reality threatening to creep back in. The silence spread between them as he helped her to put her dress to rights, his strong hands smoothing the ivory material back down over her hips. It was a strange thing, silence. Minerva imagined it like a wave of icy rain, snuffing out any embers of desire that might have remained. It created a distance between them, far more uncomfortable and insidious than words could ever achieve.

Minerva ducked her face away from his gaze, feeling

so vulnerable and over-exposed she could hardly bear it. She could feel his eyes on her the whole time and glanced up to see a deep frown marring his brow. He reached out, brushing some leaves from her hair, and her chest tightened at the tenderness of such a simple gesture. But still, he didn't speak.

She cleared her throat softly, forcing herself to stand tall and look at the man who stood silent and looming a short space away. 'The auction starts soon… I have to go back.'

'I'll walk you.'

'We both know it's best if you don't. I can't risk anyone finding us together…digging into your identity.' She shook her head, holding herself at a distance. 'This has to stop now, this *thing* between us. It needs to stop.'

'That would certainly be the most sensible course of action,' he drawled.

'It's the only course of action. Unless you fancy blowing up your fancy new life and inciting a royal scandal.'

'If anything, the revelation would cause Magnabest stocks to rise. I choose to live a life of privacy because it suits me. It brings me peace…' He looked down at her. 'You should try it out some time. I think life at sea would suit you…the sun kissing your skin while you recline on the deck…sea salt springing your hair into the wild curls they always make you tame down… Would you let me take you on an adventure, Min?'

'Perhaps. If things were different…' she whispered. He'd moved closer again and she swayed into him for a brief moment. His warm breath fanned the delicate skin below her neck. It was such a wonderful fantasy of relaxation; she could almost smell the sea breeze on the air. She swallowed hard against the knot of emotion that had formed in her throat, meeting his gaze. 'But we both know things are not different. I have to go… It's my—'

'Your duty, of course.' He nodded, one hand rubbing the back of his head in a movement that seemed so tense and at odds with the passion of moments before. 'I suppose this was the one area of things that we never had a problem with.'

Minerva bit the inside of her lip, feeling suddenly cold. For a brief window of time, his strong, muscular body had felt so warm against her, so right. For a moment she had seen the old Liro, the one she had longed for all those years ago. But now, with this cool distance between them, she knew that he was right—they had always had sexual chemistry. Even when she'd known she was about to be forced to marry him, she had wanted to cling onto the passion between them like a sticking plaster.

With one final touch of her hand against his cheek, she turned and walked away. It took every ounce of self-control she had not to break into a run. She held her arms tightly by her sides, a deep shiver coursing through her, even though the early summer night was warm and fragrant. She closed her eyes, refusing to give in to the sudden wave of sadness that had turned her legs leaden and cold.

She would not cry.

She'd done enough crying over Prince Oliveiro of Cisneros to last her a lifetime; she wouldn't do the same for his new alter ego, no matter how much more beautiful and confident he had become. She had spent years believing that she had got over the boy who had broken her heart, only to realise that the break was only held together with tape. Now it felt as if that tape had split, leaving her feeling just as raw and vulnerable as she had on the day she'd realised he'd abandoned her.

She'd chosen to kiss him and open all of these feelings back up again. She'd let him touch her, let him give her pleasure… The idea that this place, *their place,* was now the scene for yet another goodbye between them was an unbearably cruel twist of fate. But at least this time she knew that was what it was. At least, this time, she had been the one to walk away.

Liro had no idea how long he remained beside the lake, trying to calm down the riotous beating of his heart. When he finally emerged onto the open palace grounds, the long driveway was filled with cars. Elegant guests in tuxedos and evening gowns ambled around the gardens, bathed in the glow of the lamps. He walked alongside them, not caring that he looked dishevelled and unkempt in his sand-coloured chinos. He hadn't planned to attend the auction, not when Minerva had made it so clear that she wanted him gone. So why then did he find himself wandering through the glass orangery? The soothing sounds of string music enveloped him, the scent of exotic plants filling his lungs. A waiter passed by him with a tray full of drinks. Liro grabbed two.

It was the correct order of things, he reminded himself as the first glass of whatever kind of alcohol it was burned down his throat. Minerva was about to become queen, for goodness' sake. While he... Well, he had never fitted into royal life, even when he had been a prince. As if confirming his thoughts, an older woman passed by, glaring down at his informal attire, and Liro let out a harsh laugh.

This world placed so much emphasis on how one looked, how closely one kept to the narrow paths assigned to every member of 'polite' society at birth. There was nothing polite about how people stared at him as he stood in their midst, daring to have his sleeves rolled up and tattoos on display. He knew that he looked every inch the sailor he had been for the past decade. Minerva knew that too. He had always despised the confines of this world, chafed against it. So why, then, was he so resistant to leaving?

His father had blamed his youngest son's yearning for freedom on selfishness. They had never spoken again after the day he'd demanded Liro propose. Liro had believed himself selfish too, for a long time. He'd believed any number of terrible things about himself, a natural result of being raised in such a hostile environment. He knew now that he wasn't terrible, but that didn't mean he was good.

A good man would have felt remorse for what had just happened with Minerva at the lake. A good man would have left the first time she'd told him to. He knew that he wasn't good enough for her—that had never been up for debate. But Minerva had been so wound up and desperately in need of care. He knew how to care for her. He knew what she needed.

He took a slower sip from the second glass, staring

down at the ice cubes floating in the amber liquid. He had hoped to give them both some form of closure, a thought he had believed he could achieve. But, as he had watched her walls return in the wake of the orgasm he'd wrung from her body, the world had crashed back in upon her shoulders… and he had never felt further from closure with Minerva Argimon-Talil.

His mind balked at the idea of leaving without finishing what he'd started, without proving to her that their memories were not exaggerated. Maybe then he would feel free of whatever hold over him their connection had. He had come to Arqaleta to make a business deal, and that had not changed. But he refused to leave things the way they had been left fourteen years ago. It was his fault that she was being forced to choose from a ridiculous selection of thoroughly unsuitable potential husbands.

He could never have her himself; he knew that. He knew that he would never be the man that she chose. He knew that their lives were too different and utterly incompatible. But he was just selfish enough not to care right now. Not after he'd been moments away from burying himself deep inside the woman he'd chased from his dreams for years. Not when he'd seen how badly she still wanted him too.

A plan slowly formed in his mind, a perfect way for them both to have closure and for him to give her what she needed. He would have to ensure that he played his cards just right…and maybe this trip wouldn't have been completely in vain.

CHAPTER SIX

THE CHARITY AUCTION was little more than a glorified
gala dinner, and an excuse for the kingdom's wealthiest
and most famous individuals to dress up and be seen.
The palace's large greenhouse had been arranged into
an enchanted forest, with invitees taking part in an Arqaletan colour theme for their outfit choices. So far, Minerva had spotted at least seven gowns covered in bows
and arrows, as well as a handful of unfortunate banana-
yellow tuxedos that seemed to be aiming for the colours
of their national flag.

Everyone watched one another in the way that was
typical for these events, where the aim was simply to
be on display. There was the added bonus of being able
to flaunt one's wealth in the form of bids, but for most
part it was the kind of pageantry through which Minerva had to grit her teeth.

This was the first time she had been in charge of selecting the various organisations that would benefit, a
fact that made the opening speeches and endless greet-
ings slightly more tolerable. She had insisted that the
founders and beneficiaries of each charity be present
and offered the chance to speak if they so wished. Everything had been planned in the weeks beforehand;

perhaps that was why her complete lack of focus hadn't impeded the plans too much.

Her gown for the evening had been designed and hand-made here in the capital by one of their most famous up-and-coming couturiers. It was an off-the-shoulder confection of white silk and delicate blue beading that accentuated her waist and fell to the floor in extravagant waves. It was a gown made for movement, and it had taken most of her control not to twirl herself out on the dance floor as she had as a young girl. Her mother had beamed at her upon first glance, with a genuine look of surprise that there had been no complaints from her only daughter about the matching sapphire tiara and heavy necklace she was displaying as part of tonight's ensemble.

Truthfully, Minerva had hardly been aware of much of the past hour since returning to the palace. She'd nodded and smiled as her team had readied her, and discussed the details of the auction portion of the event, but mentally she'd replayed every salacious moment of the events by the lake.

Even her mother had commented on her distraction, and Minerva had tried to make an effort to pull her focus back to the present. She tried to remind herself how inappropriate today had been. How nothing good could ever come of it, of them together. But tell that to her rioting libido.

She had gone on a few dates in college, experimenting like most young people did. But, as a young royal, all her relationships had to remain secret, or else risk being on the front page of every tabloid. Secrecy, while temporarily exciting, had always ended up being a real mood-killer at some point for the people she had been attracted to. Pretty soon, she had stopped even trying to date, allowing her archery career to take up most of her time, and had returned to her duties in Arqaleta once she had graduated. No one had got under her skin the way he had.

Perhaps no one ever would.

She entered the grand ballroom, spied him standing on the opposite side of the room and the knot in her stomach only tightened further. She hesitated, knowing that ignoring him would be immature, but she truly didn't think she could be face to face with him in that moment without losing her composure completely.

He'd said he sought closure for them both but she hadn't had any need for it until he'd reappeared in her life like a ticking time-bomb. She had not thought of him; she had trained herself not even to think of him most of the time.

But as she crossed the room towards him, his eyes tracking her every movement with his usual leonine intensity, she felt something much more than discomfort building within her. She was excited. Seeing him here, meeting his eyes and knowing what they had almost done mere hours before… The dark thrill of it seemed to sizzle along her veins, filling her with the confidence to meet his gaze without any guile.

His eyes narrowed upon her, his nostrils flaring with awareness, and for a moment it was only them in the bustling crowd of well-dressed guests. Another moment in time called to her from the recesses of her mind, another evening of dancing and revelry in this very greenhouse that had first begun their short-lived affair. An affair that had ended with her in tears and him banished. She closed her eyes against the onslaught, opening them to find him moving towards her in the crowd, a look of intent upon his face.

Her anxiety piqued, panic climbing her throat as she tried not to see the parallels between that night and this one. She couldn't speak to him, not tonight. She was here to secure her future, not rehash a past she'd long buried and grown past. Did he believe her too proper to cause a public scene? Maybe she should show him exactly how much she had changed.

It turned out she didn't have that chance, because she was pulled away by the event team before Liro had even reached the middle of the dance floor. Her presence was needed on stage to prepare for her hosting duties while the announcements were made and the guests were seated in rows.

A string quartet began the evening's entertainment, and Minerva tried to enjoy the glowing music. But her eyes were constantly drawn to the man seated at the very edge of the front row, his attention firmly placed upon her.

The first items of the night were a selection of beautiful traditional Arqaletan paintings and statues. The bidding was healthy, but not a war by any means, and the items were sold off with relative ease. Minerva took turns with the chief auctioneer in announcing each lot, and even began to have genuine fun in slamming the gavel down, earning laughter each time.

Liro did not find any of this amusing, it seemed. His gaze remained serious and pensive as he surveyed the stage from his perch, his wide shoulders making him appear so much larger than the others.

When the final lot of the evening had been announced and sold off in quick succession, Minerva breathed a sigh of relief, hoping to make a quick exit to regroup before her inevitable showdown. She smiled and made to leave the stage, only to be stopped by the curator, who gestured to where her mother had stood from her seat, microphone in hand.

'There is one final surprise for this evening, a very special lot offered up personally by my daughter in honour of my birthday.'

Bea, seated in the front row alongside her elderly parents, met Minerva's gaze in confusion. Minerva shrugged, communicating with her eyes: *I have absolutely no idea.*

Queen Uberta continued, 'My daughter is excited, ladies and gentlemen, for tonight she will be auctioning off none other than a date with herself. For the highest bidder, you can have dinner and startling conversation with the Crown Princess Minerva of Arqaleta.'

Movement and chatter began immediately, the auctioneer smirking as he took control of the proceedings and guided Minerva to take a seat under a spotlight in the centre of the stage. Training and experience meant that her smile was relaxed and her posture didn't give away the extent of her unease. She looked down to find Liro's seat empty, her eyes darting to each side of the room in search of him, but he was nowhere to be found.

The bidding began and was instantly off to a quick start as John, Jean-Claude and Prince Lorenz calmly raised their paddles one after another without any sign of surprise that Minerva was the lot in question. Had they somehow known about this particular portion of the auction in advance? Was that why Liro had disappeared? The thought that he had chosen *now* to abandon her to her matchmaking duty, as she'd ordered him to, was suddenly utterly despairing.

Minerva looked to her mother, silently begging her to announce that this was a practical joke. Sadly, it was not, and soon the bidding began to intensify, Jean-Claude scowling as he bowed out, leaving only her other two suitors to compete. She wondered what on earth kind of dinner date she would be forced to endure.

Likely it would be Lorenz, with his much deeper pockets, but something about the prince still didn't feel quite right. None of them did, though she didn't wish to break her mother's heart by saying such a thing. She had made a promise to select one of these men as her future husband by the end of the week and she did not break her promises—most especially, not to her mother.

Prince Lorenz called out another bid, doubling his previous one and leaving the other men to stare at him in stern silence. A moment passed, then another, and Minerva gulped, resigning herself to the idea that she would be back to discussing performance techniques in college sports again some time very soon.

The auctioneer smiled, gavel already raised to pronounce the sale, when a smooth voice rang out across the chatter of the excited crowd.

'I'd like to double that.'

Minerva looked to find Liro had reappeared in the same spot he'd vacated, looking utterly bored and un-ruffled, as though he'd been there all along.

The auctioneer stuttered, calling out the final figure with a question. Liro nodded, his expression utterly neutral as he stared in the direction of the prince. Lorenz scowled, shock and disbelief warring on his finely chiselled features for a long moment before he sat down, placing his small white number firmly in his lap.

'Sold, to the handsome ginger fellow at the front,' crooned the auctioneer.

Minerva was furious.

As if it wasn't bad enough that Liro had paid an exorbitant amount of money for one dinner with her, but he'd done it in front of an audience, advertising his position as one of her suitors. Then, after he'd signed the contract for their date, he'd simply disappeared. No discussion, no opportunity for her to tell him exactly how inappropriate and inconvenient his little stunt was. Not to mention no chance for her to ask him why he'd done it, when they had already agreed that he needed to leave Arqaleta before his identity was discovered. He'd simply left without a word.

When a note appeared with her morning post, requesting her attendance on his yacht later that evening, she felt her irritation peak. No, he would not send for her at his convenience. Her schedule was empty that afternoon, in preparation for the grand ball tomorrow evening, and again that niggling voice of suspicion within her wondered if her mother had deliberately organised it that way.

Ignoring that thought, she showered and changed out of the chic linen suit she'd worn to that morning's poetry and arts event which she'd attended with a very forlorn Jean-Claude. The Frenchman had been predictably attentive and apologetic about having been unable to win her in the auction. As had the others, when they'd approached her for dances after Liro had disappeared. Prince Lorenz in particular had been bordering upon rage as he'd not so subtly questioned her about the red-haired shipping magnate who seemed so intent upon monopolising her time.

Blood pounded in her ears as she stalked across the lawns in the direction of the port, the wind lapping her unbound hair and the plain black smock-dress she'd grabbed in her hurry. If he expected a princess for dinner, he would be sorely disappointed. She fully intended to tell Liro exactly where he could shove his bought date for the evening. That was, until she arrived down at the dock, to find the man himself standing on the bow of his mega-yacht, dressed in a pair of ripped jeans and nothing else.

She had wondered what Liro might look like as a sailor. Judging by the way he easily hoisted a thick rope between his hand and elbow, twining it round and round, calling across to his crew and giving orders, she'd imagined he'd looked pretty much like this—like a handsome, ginger-bearded pirate, getting ready to set sail across the seas in search of adventure.

She had thought that her travels with the archery team

were thrilling—she had travelled all across the world, hadn't she? She had been given more freedom than her mother had ever dreamed of—a fact that the Queen reminded her of often enough.

But…she had never seen someone look quite as free as Liro did in that moment, the slightly cloudy sky shielding his fair skin from the harsh sun while the wind ruffled his thick red hair back from his forehead. The natural colour of his hair was even more mesmerising out here on the water. The richness of the bronze-red captivated her and made her fingers itch to run through it.

She gave herself a mental shake, clearing her throat, but the noise was drowned out by the sounds of the docks. Liro still had his back turned to her and was deeply engrossed in whatever he was doing with the heavy rope. He was working hard enough that sweat coated his brow and glistened on his bare shoulders as he heaved and pulled the rope around a large steel pole. The tattoo she had spied running up his forearm was in full view now, a winding design in black ink that formed an intricate sleeve across his right arm, shoulder and upper pectoral muscle. Minerva licked her suddenly dry lips, trying to ignore the mental image her treacherous mind produced in which she actually got to feel those muscles in greater detail…

Of course, he chose that exact moment to turn around, his green-grey eyes meeting hers with pure brazen confidence as he smiled broadly.

'You're a bit early for dinner.' His deep voice carried easily.

'I'm not here to eat,' she shouted back, crossing her arms over her chest as he moved down the ladder from the upper deck, coming to a stop at the open gangway directly across from her. He leaned against the railing, eyeing her up with the kind of slow precision that made her skin prickle.

'You look pretty hungry to me, *princesa*.' His lips quirked. 'Have you looked your fill already?'

'I wasn't *looking*, I was…staring.'

'Staring at me,' he clarified helpfully.

'You're practically naked up there, for goodness' sake!' she blurted. 'If I were to do the same, I'm sure I'd get some odd looks too.'

He laughed, closing his eyes for a moment as he gripped the railing hard.

Minerva growled under her breath. 'Liro, I came here to…'

He raised one hand to stop her. 'Hold on, I'm just trying to get a proper visual in order to make an informed rebuttal.'

'That is grossly inappropriate.' She fought not to laugh as he appeared to concentrate even harder, his eyes remaining firmly closed for a few more seconds.

'You're right. If you were up here topless, winding rope, it would be catastrophic for this whole crew.'

'Catastrophic?'

'I'd have to have them all fired, of course. Anyone who'd laid eyes on you would be severely punished.'

'Including you?' she asked, enjoying their back and forth far too much.

'Oh, I wouldn't need to look, of course,' he said

smoothly, the smile leaving his lips. 'I close my eyes and you're right there. Always.'

As she stood frozen in place, he raked his gaze over her slowly, from the top of her head all the way down to the strappy flat sandals she wore on feet. He met her eyes once more, showing her a brief glimpse of burning heat that took her breath away. It was the kind of look that she should have immediately turned tail and run from, if she'd had any sense. She was already too unsettled by this interaction, by *him*, to make the imperious speech she'd planned.

'You had no right, bidding on me last night. Why did you do it?'

'I don't like to lose,' he said, without a hint of remorse.

'You said yourself that you were never in the running.' she replied, fighting the urge to growl at the superior look on his impossibly handsome face. 'You say that as though you believe that this stunt has resulted in you winning.'

'You're here, aren't you?'

Minerva fought the urge to launch herself towards the ship to throttle him. 'I am not a commodity for you to bid upon or trade, or whatever it is that you are used to doing in your world.'

They were interrupted momentarily by the arrival of one of the yacht's staff, who needed Liro's signature upon something.

'If you have quite finished your speech, Your Highness, now that you're here, we might as well begin.' He turned to walk away towards the interior of the yacht.

'I have not finished.'

He paused but did not turn round, tension rippling through the ridiculously defined muscles of his gigantic shoulders. 'You wanted to discuss the past—this is the only way I will do that. I paid an exorbitant amount of money to have dinner with the Crown Princess, so get on the yacht.'

She hesitated, watching as he walked away from her and disappeared down a stairwell built into the polished wood. The question lay in the shape of the gangplank that separated them—five feet of wood and rope that separated her from the adventure he offered.

She remembered the wistful way he'd recounted his love of life at sea the night before. How he'd described it as healing, quieting something in him. This particular port wasn't quiet by any means, but the lulling sounds of the harbour had an oddly peaceful quality. For a moment she closed her eyes and simply listened to gulls cawing in the distance realising that, the longer she remained frozen in place, the further she was from getting actual closure on their past. Decision made, she boarded the giant yacht.

CHAPTER SEVEN

STAFF AWAITED HER to take her bag and offer refreshments while she waited for Liro to return from wherever he was freshening up. She hadn't taken any security with her and noticed that Liro didn't seem to have any here either. She was shown to the entertainment deck, where a large open-air terrace took up most of the space, overlooking the lower-deck pool and hot tub.

She wondered how many wild parties this vessel had seen, how many women he'd entertained in his entertainment deck. He was a handsome man, not to mention a self-made owner of his own shipping empire. He probably had a woman waiting for him in every major port in the world. She stabbed her toothpick into a cherry and almost didn't hear Liro slide into the seat across from her.

His hair was wet from the shower and he had changed into a black T-shirt and jeans combo that hugged his thick muscles while still managing to look effortlessly stylish. She forced herself not to stare down at how the denim framed his strong thighs; she didn't need to boost his massive ego any more than she already had.

'This counts as your first course,' she said quickly,

gesturing to the bowl of pretzels that had been placed on the table between them.

'Learning how to negotiate... I approve.'

His maddening smile irked her, even as she fought not to let her own lips curve. She wished that she didn't find him so entertaining, but it had always been this way. His dry humour was the perfect match for her, and he had always succeeded in pulling a laugh from her when most had failed.

But that was in the past. And if last night had showed her anything it was that their past would always be far too much to overcome. There were far too many things left unsaid, too much time had passed...and time was something she simply no longer had. Any other person at thirty-three would have had the luxury of time to consider what they truly wanted, where they wished to live and what career they wanted. But Minerva had simply been spinning her wheels for the past decade, never looking too far ahead. She had always known that one day the bell would ring and she would be obligated to fulfil the next step of her duty: a marriage of convenience, an alliance to strengthen her position, before she became queen.

There was only one person to blame for the fact that this cold reality now felt heavier than ever and he sat across from her at this very moment, looking as if he hadn't a care in the world as he stared out at the sea.

'Having me here on your yacht...is it supposed to have a specific effect?' she asked, idly twirling her glass. 'Am I supposed to see this lavish vessel that you've purchased for yourself and be jealous? Or did you hope I would be too distracted by you to remember that you had promised to tell me the truth?'

He was silent for a moment, his eyes scanning her face in a way that made him seem almost dangerous. He *was* dangerous...to her, anyway...to her plans, to her peace of mind. This man was a walking threat to everything she had fought so hard to contain within herself.

'This vessel is my home, Your Highness. I can give you the grand tour, if you like, once we're at sea.'

As he spoke, she became vaguely aware that the soft bobbing beneath her feet had turned into a rapid thrum. One look beyond the porthole behind her showed the harbour slowly slipping away from focus. She stood up, clenching her fists by her sides and looking down at him with full incrimination.

'Take me back to port!'

'I will, once we have completed our meal.'

'When I said I'd board your ridiculous yacht, I did not agree to leave the country.'

'You agreed to a five-course meal with me—the location is at my discretion.'

'You...you absolute *cheat*. Do you think that every tiny detail can just be manipulated and taken advantage of?'

'I do not cheat, Minerva. I pay attention to the details, in contracts and in people. How do you think that I went from deckhand to owner in less than a decade?' He met her gaze, taking the cocktail stick from her drink and popping the lush cherry into his mouth with a flourish.

Minerva walked to the railing and watched the edge of the palace grounds fade into the distance. She had no idea where he was taking her, no idea what he had planned. This date was turning into a living nightmare for a woman who lived her life on schedules and detailed itineraries. She had come here to take control and had wound up quite literally being swept away at Liro's will. She looked back to where he was watching her, his gaze completely unreadable, as usual.

Perhaps he was planning for some kind of poetic revenge. Perhaps Liro had hidden his cruel streak well and planned to steal her away, like the pirate she had accused him of being.

She shouldn't have felt a small thrill at that thought... and it had absolutely nothing to do with her capitulating and sitting back down on her seat.

Absolutely nothing at all.

Minerva remained mostly silent throughout their journey. It gave Liro more time to look at her, to think through exactly how he was going to talk about their past—something that he now knew he was going to have to do. As they disembarked onto a whitewashed marina and he guided her towards the street above, he had no need to slow down his pace, considering she almost matched him in height. She matched him in so many ways.

Minerva stood with her hands on her hips, eyeing up a small food truck surrounded by wooden picnic tables in the small seaside village where they'd docked. 'You sailed me across the sea to a mystery location...for food truck paella?'

'The *best* food truck paella you will ever taste.'

He waited a breath, fully intending to haul her back to the yacht and return her home if she ever actually said the words. But so far she had made a lot of eyes and grumbled but had not demanded to return. If anything, he felt she was relaxing into not being the one in control for once. As if she was almost enjoying their back-and-forth, just as she had when they'd been young.

Back then she had been the one who'd needed to be in charge, and he had simply gone along with it, happy only to be near her. So many things had changed, but the sudden smile that transformed her face was so youthful and reminiscent of that younger her that he remained frozen in place for a moment, almost forgetting that he was the one in charge of this date, until she nudged him.

'This is your second course and, yes, I *am* keeping track.' She looked around, her eyes landing on a large tourist sign proclaiming this quaint port town to be 'the Gates to the Cisnerosi Capital of Lodeta', which was a short drive away.

If she was surprised that he had brought her to his old home country, she didn't show it much. The only thing that had almost got a reaction out of her was when he'd presented her with a worn baseball cap and plain dark sunglasses.

'I've brought you here because, considering the history between Cisneros and Arqaleta, it's the last place anyone would think to find you. I wanted to give you something you haven't had a lot of: privacy.'

She looked around at the crowds of people passing them by and he could feel the tension rolling off her. He knew she had travelled to the Olympics, but always with a heavy guard. She had never been allowed to sleep in the team hotels or go out for spontaneous drinks in a crappy bar.

She'd lived her life on a leash.

He'd lived that life too and he'd despised every moment.

'Have you not been back?' she asked, looking around at the people eating at tables and looking out at the sea.

'I've been in the bay while overlooking my development plans here, but I never got off the yacht. I don't care if people recognise me. I don't need their forgiveness or adoration for all the work that I've done in fixing what my father ruined.'

His father had run their kingdom's economy into the ground through corruption, so it had been no surprise when people had mounted a coup. Liro hadn't known until it was too late, until the announcement of Minerva's and his betrothal was almost forced upon him by his father. And he'd rather Minerva suffer a broken heart from abandonment than have her name sullied by his father's sins and be bound in matrimony to Liro for ever. His father had died before he'd been brought to justice but his oldest brother, the crown prince, had spent some time in prison for the part he'd played. Liro hadn't spoken to either of his brothers since he'd left. Something a part of him regretted, despite their fraught childhood.

'I wish that I still had roots somewhere. Before my mother's death, things were different. He loved her and she calmed his worse impulses somewhat. I spent all of my childhood here, I grew up in this kingdom. But sometimes it feels like they erased my entire existence overnight.'

'When was the last time you actually set foot on Cisnerosi land?'

'I came back for the first time after being at sea for five years. I realised that I looked different and people didn't recognise me. And I liked it. So, I didn't tell them who I was, and I walked among them as a stranger in blissful solitude. And then, when the time came to set up the company, and as my success grew, I just kept burying my old self over and over until he no longer existed to me either. None of my family did.'

'Family is more than just blood. You can be close-knit without sharing an ounce of DNA, just as you can be hurt most by the people who gave you life in the beginning. I learned that with my dad—you can't choose who your parents are.' She exhaled slowly, folding and refolding the napkin in her hands. 'But you can choose how much of yourself you give them. The hardest thing I ever did was let go of my hope that one day I would have a relationship with him after what he did. Trust is a hard thing to rebuild once it's been broken by someone you love.'

Her words sat heavily in the air between them and Liro couldn't help but understand their meaning deeply.

'To our fathers.' Liro raised his glass.

After they'd finished eating, Liro took her to the funfair that had taken up residence in the town square for the summer. They walked through the fair and Minerva tried not to be nervous as people walked close by, jostling her shoulders. It was strange, walking with complete anonymity this way. Liro insisted that they try out the games set on stalls dotted throughout the fair, hooking ducks upon a stick in order to win tiny soft toys. He won quite a lot of them on his first try, and kindly donated the toys to a group of children that had been standing watching nearby.

'That was kind.' She watched the children scamper away, taking their laughter with them.

'Your turn now.' He gestured to the next stall of carnival games.

'Darts?' Minerva raised one brow.

'It's not a bow and arrow, but I believe the practice is the same. Try to hit the pointy stick into the red dot.'

'I am familiar with the concept of the game. Thank you.'

'How about we make it a little more interesting, then?' He raised one brow, mischief in his eyes. 'You get one question for every target you hit.'

Minerva eyed up the three boards; they were hardly a far distance away. 'You may as well just give me the answers I want to know, really.'

'Perhaps—but my date, my rules.'

'Get ready to lose, then.'

She stepped up to the metal stall's edge, grabbing three darts. They were much smaller than her arrows, but weighed much the same. She stared at the oversized target, black-and-red rings with scores in each circle. A small smile graced her lips as she instinctively took her archer's stance and sized up the distance.

'Not taking it too seriously, I see,' Liro murmured from her side.

She ignored him, eyes focused on her target, shoulders dropping, arm relaxing as she extended and readied. With one long movement she let her dart fly directly towards the target in a perfect smooth arc.

Only to find it hit directly to the left of where she had aimed for. She cursed aloud, cupping a hand over her mouth when she realised what she'd said.

'It's okay, you'll get the hang of it with a little practice.' Liro laughed.

She ignored his taunts; she'd had years of training through the distraction of crowds and commentary. This was a funfair darts stall, not an Olympic stadium... You could take the athlete out of the competition, but not the other way around. She turned back to the target, once again taking her stance, readying her dart and letting it fly with perfect precision. And once again at the very last moment it flew to the left.

'Impossible.' She turned to the young lady behind the stall. 'This game is rigged.'

'Excuse me?' A man appeared from behind the stall, placing one hand on the younger girl's shoulder. 'Are you accusing us of practising dishonestly?'

Minerva opened her mouth to begin reciting exactly how she knew that this entire game was rigged for customer failure, only to have Liro grab her elbow and lean across her, placing a handful of bills on the counter.

'Of course she's not,' he said calmly, smiling at the young girl. 'She's just a sore loser, that's all.'

'I am not—' Minerva made to protest once more, only to have Liro's arm pull her into his chest and deftly guide her away from the stall before she could speak another word.

They made it a few more stalls down before she swung round, pointing one finger directly in the centre of his chest. 'Oh my God, you knew that these stalls are all rigged, didn't you?'

'It's a funfair, princess, not a global tournament. They're just trying to make a profit.'

'Does everyone know that nobody follows the rules except for me?' she practically shouted. 'You had no intention of answering any of my questions, did you?'

'Rule number one—don't assume that everyone else is following the rules.' He held her wrist, stopping her from moving away from him. 'I planned on answering your questions no matter what. Once we get back to the yacht, you can have the answer to everything you can think of. But I didn't bring you here to rehash the past. I brought you here to show you why I left. I could never live this way when I was Prince Oliveiro. I could never do what I wanted.'

'So that's why you left? Because you wanted to be able to go to funfairs without the paparazzi following you?'

'You know that's not why...'

'I don't know, Liro. All I do know was that your father was forcing you to marry me and so you left. I thought we were happy, that we were preparing to celebrate our engagement. And then you disappeared and I had no idea if you were alive or dead. So forgive me if eating some paella and walking through a funfair doesn't feel quite as momentous...'

She walked away from him and was glad when he didn't immediately follow, giving her some space to browse through a small bric-à-brac tent filled with beaded necklaces and bracelets. She had no money with her with which to buy anything; she rarely made any purchases of her own at all. If she needed something, it was purchased for her, and for some reason she had never found that fact utterly ridiculous until this very moment. She was a grown adult and she had never browsed a store without a private appointment and security team in tow.

She realised then what he was actually doing in bringing her here. He was proving his point about freedom. Perhaps she should be annoyed at him for being so heavy-handed in trying to show her that the world was so much larger than the way she lived, but instead she felt a warmth in her chest. He had been more honest with her today in bringing her here and risking her wrath than anyone else in her life. He was showing her something real, something outside of her perfectly manicured sphere.

It was a gift.

She turned around to find he had purchased an aquamarine beaded bracelet, and he held it out to her. When she struggled with the clasp, he stepped closer, clicking it into place and sliding his thumb across the delicate beads. She looked up, meeting his eyes, and for a brief moment she wished that they were just a regular man and woman out on an exciting date at the funfair.

What would that actually have been like? What would they have been like if they had met under different circumstances? Would they have been so attracted to one another? Or had their love affair only happened because it had felt like a small rebellion of sorts?

And if she took him up on his offer of closure, if she went to his bed again, wouldn't that just be her doing the exact same thing all over again? She pulled away, walking slowly through the crowd, only to find his hand encircling her softly. This time, she didn't pull away. She relaxed into his hold and allowed him to guide her along, exploring together.

CHAPTER EIGHT

HE HAD ALWAYS passed this particular summer fair as a kid, but he had never been permitted to go, much to his tearful disappointment. His father had teased him relentlessly for being soft and he'd soon learned to hold his emotions in check. It was possibly the only skill his father had taught him, other than how to stretch the truth.

He pushed away the uncomfortable echoes of his past and focused on the woman he'd tasked himself with unravelling in the present. Minerva was seated upon the tallest white horse in the merry-go-round, waiting impatiently for the ride to begin.

'I thought for sure you would have chosen the boat, considering they are your whole life.' She laughed down at him, her eyes still hidden behind her sunglasses.

'What can I say? This hot-pink princess carriage called to me.' He grimaced as his knee became wedged between the tiny seats. Better to make jokes than reveal he'd chosen it simply because it had a perfect view of the white stallion she'd selected. 'I know this will sound strange but I don't actually care about boats.'

'Liro, you have literally lived and worked at sea for more than a decade.'

'The whole ship-hand thing just happened; I didn't

seek it out because of some unbridled love of the sea. I made a single promise to myself when I left, that I would go along with my instincts. And that's what I did.'

'I'm glad you trusted your instincts and you proved to yourself what you are capable of. I think you would have been quite bored by all of the sitting and smiling and waving—it is *not* for the faint of heart. Plus, you are huge now—we'd have had to have all the carriages adjusted.' She laughed, but he didn't miss the slight change in her tone.

'I never would have been bored with you, Min.'

'No?' She raised a brow.

'No. Not with you.'

Silence fell between them, only broken by the sudden tinny music that filled the air as the carousel began to move. Minerva smiled as her white stallion moved slowly up and down, leaning back to stick her tongue out at him and tell him to smile. Liro didn't smile—he was too busy watching. Back at the palace, the crown princess had been proud and regal. Beautiful, yes, but purposeful in every word and movement. Minerva unbound and free was…utterly breath-taking.

Her words played on his mind as they twirled round and round; her clear belief that he had left royal life out of boredom or disdain was wrong. In fact, he had fled to protect her from his father's crimes. Despite Liro being innocent of them himself, Minerva's court would never have seen it that way.

Once the ride stopped, he helped her down from her steed and tried not to laugh as she patted the painted horse's nose and thanked him for his service. Nearby, a large Ferris wheel spun in a slow circle to the sound of classical Cisnerosi folk music. Liro paid extra to have one small passenger car allocated just for the two of them. It was still early evening and no queues had formed. Parents and children began to fill up the rides around them, the noise of chatter rising and making it harder to hear, so he leaned across the space between them, reaching for one of her hands.

'You can be both, you know,' he told her, feeling the need to ensure that she didn't misunderstand him. 'You can smile and wave as their princess while also remaining true to who you are—the athlete, the woman.'

'You don't have to placate me, Liro, I'm quite aware of the pageantry of my position.'

'You were born to be the queen. That's the position you were trained to fill. It's a role that you had no choice in, but still, you were made for it. But Minerva the archer needs to be challenged, to feel in control and to feel like she is facing a new target, at all times.'

Golden-brown eyes met his, the lights of the funfair blinking around them.

'You can be both the queen and the archer, Minerva. You can be anything that you put your mind to. If anyone in this world can change a kingdom hundreds of years old to suit them, it's you. Push the boundaries, don't accept the cage for what it is.'

'Are you talking about my role as queen or what I must do before I ascend to the throne?'

'All of it,' he said honestly. 'You can call it whatever you want—it is someone else telling you who you are and who you can be. You are accepting it because there is a law involved, but you won't know for sure until you push.'

'What about the rules you set—can I push those too?' she asked sweetly.

'I wish you would.' He breathed, not bothering to temper his reaction to her words or to the images his mind created instantly at just how he wished those rules would be broken. No kissing, no touching… He had thought of little else every minute with her by his side and it was sweet torture to see her tongue dart out and lick at her lower lip. She bit down on the wet flesh, shaking her head softly, as though trying to clear similar images from her own mind. Did his princess have filthy thoughts too?

'Why would you make a rule that you have no intention of abiding by?' She breathed, her cheeks definitely flushed a little darker than they had been a moment ago.

'If I planned to break my own rules, I'd have done it the moment I had you alone on my yacht. That's not what today was about.'

'Then what was this about?' She frowned.

He leaned back, staring out as the fairground became smaller and smaller below them. 'I told myself that I just wanted to give you some time away from the pressure of the palace, away from your duty. Some time for us to get closure before I leave.'

'I want closure too,' she said softly. 'But I don't think I'm going to get that from a funfair.'

'What would you do, then?' he asked. 'What do you need?'

Her lips touched his, tentatively at first, as though she

was feeling her way onto uneven ground. He wasn't even sure when she had moved into the seat next to him but, once she had grown certain of him, she inched closer until her thigh practically splayed across his. She angled her face, her hand touching his beard and holding him in place, and he let her. He submitted to her kiss, knowing that was what she needed from him in that moment. She needed to trust in her own ability to break the rules he had set for them both, and thank god...because he had been one step away from kissing her senseless from the moment she had appeared at his yacht, eyeing up his naked chest.

When the wind picked up and their car began to rock side to side, he used the momentum to his advantage, lifting her to straddle his thighs fully, her centre pressed full against the evidence of his arousal. Far from being scandalised, his fearless princess simply ground her hips against him and carried on plundering his mouth, using him for her pleasure in the best way possible.

If this was all he could give to her, he'd do his duty over and over again. He wouldn't think of the consequences, of whatever came after, when she returned to reality and remembered why this was wrong for them both. It was only when loud laughter intruded upon their little bubble that they realised the Ferris wheel had moved around a couple more places and their bucket was now fully visible to the riders above them. A horrified elderly couple tutted loudly, while above them a group of young men wolf-whistled.

Minerva scrambled off his lap, making to move back to her seat, but Liro wound his arm around her waist to hold her close. She looked up at him, her eyes still a little kiss-drunk, and it took all his restraint not to haul her back onto him, audience be damned. Her hair had begun to escape her cap, curls rioting around her face as she threw her head back and laughed. And, without even thinking, he laughed with her. The wheel brought them back down to the ground but Liro handed the attendant another wad of cash to send them around again, this time buying up all the buckets around them too.

'Seems like a lot of effort to get me up here all alone,' she remarked, a slight hint of uncertainty in her gaze. 'Did you plan to finish what we almost started?'

'You'd like that?' he murmured against her neck, memorising the feeling of having her all to himself again. No interruptions, no audience to play for.

She sighed into his touch. 'It would be wild, reckless—so very out of character for a good girl like me.'

He growled low in his throat. 'You don't kiss like a good girl, Min.'

'How do I kiss?' She bit down on his ear. 'Well, I hope?'

'You are perfect.'

Their eyes met for a split second and he saw the glazed-over desire there, the heady wildness of a woman in over her head. But he couldn't help feeling that this was too much, too fast. That, if she had a moment to think it through, she'd realise that this wasn't actually what she wanted. He'd already pushed her onto his ship and taken her out of her comfort zone. If he followed through now with what she very obviously wanted to do, sure, it would be amazing…but for how long? Once reality returned, and they quite literally dropped back down to earth, would she hate him all over again?

He had entered into this ridiculous game of matchmaking for closure, for a way to draw the line under their past. But somewhere during the past few days he had begun to think less and less of the freedom he adored so much. His thoughts had become consumed with her. After more than a decade of control, he was fast becoming addicted to Minerva once more.

She sensed the change in him, pulling back on his lap. 'What's wrong?'

'Nothing is wrong. The sunset is beginning.' He gestured behind them, to where the sky had blurred from blue to pink and purple around the setting sun. He turned her in his lap, holding her steady...not quite able to not touch her.

'Why do you do that?' she asked softly, leaning back against his chest with a sigh. 'The minute I stop fighting you, you get cold feet and go off into your own world. It always maddened me when we were younger.'

Was that what he was doing? He frowned, holding onto her hand as she sighed and laid her head down upon his shoulder to watch the sky transform. He had always told himself he simply preferred his own company, that he just didn't need friendships or connection. He'd learned from a young age that his quietness wasn't accepted, that the things he enjoyed would be mocked.

But he wasn't a child any more—he was a grown man. The realisation that his retreat might not have been entirely to protect Minerva was uncomfortable and something he could not accept. He had loved her...

he had wanted to be with her…but he had known she deserved more than him. Deserved more than her reign as queen to be tarnished and criticised because of his tainted name.

As the glowing sunset erupted and the outside world blurred into a sea of colour, Liro couldn't shake the feeling that he carried more baggage from his childhood than he was willing to accept. Could such things really shape a person's actions for their entire lives? Surely not? He hadn't been beaten or neglected. He'd grown up a prince, for goodness' sake.

'I rather feel like I should have paid for this date, not the other way round.'

Minerva stared out, calm and still as she watched the crowds below them. This was a glimpse of the carefree princess he'd fallen for all those years ago before he'd ruined everything—this wild, free creature.

And she wanted him, she had made that much abundantly clear. She had to know that he would not deny her whatever she asked of him. He would not deny that getting her into his bed had been on his mind from the moment he'd walked back into her palace and laid eyes on her. But did that mean he should just take what he wanted, knowing that, afterwards, he would have to walk away and leave her to marry another?

He was so lost in his thoughts he hardly noticed the ride had stopped until he felt a hand gently pull at his elbow. They disembarked and wandered out into the rapidly increasing evening crowd of the fair.

A small stand was placed near the exit gate, selling tiny bags of sugar-coated nuts. He'd loved the smell of them as a kid. He watched as Minerva wandered closer, raising one brow in his direction.

'Looks like it's time for our final course.'

He didn't speak, paying for one bag and watching as she half-heartedly nibbled on the sugar coating. They strolled along the path to the marina in silence, her barely eaten bag of sweet almonds soon discarded in a waste bin once they had boarded the yacht.

'You didn't like them?' Liro asked.

Minerva hesitated, her gaze filled with a mixture of anticipation and a little uncertainty, an uncertainty that he knew he had put there. 'They weren't what I wanted.'

'You can't always get what you want.' He pushed her back against the door, turning the lock deftly in one slick movement before bracing one hand above her head.

'Are you about to burst into song?' She breathed, making a light attempt at laughter that quickly died once she felt the evidence of his erection against her. 'Oh, Liro...please don't stop again this time. I don't think I can bear it.'

'I won't be stopping, princess. If this is what you need... I won't stop until you're satisfied.'

'This...you...are what I need, Liro. Just you.'

He closed his eyes against the sensation her words unravelled in his chest, clenching his jaw against the foolish words he felt rise up his throat. Words that had no place there. His time with Minerva was destined to come to an end and once it did he needed to let her go, even if it tore him apart. Without thinking, Liro closed the gap between them and began to give Minerva exactly what she needed.

* * *

'I'd be lying if I said I didn't take you out today aiming for this to happen. From the moment I saw you again, this is all I've thought about—your sounds, your taste.'

Minerva watched as Liro dropped slowly to his knees before her. 'You have haunted me, Min, possessed me.'

His hands framed her naked centre, spreading her wide in a way that could have made her feel vulnerable and exposed. But instead she felt rather like a sculpture on display in a museum, scandalously adored and coveted. But he had no need to want her from afar, not now when they had so little time. She reached down and cupped the back of his head, pressing herself against his kiss without a hint of embarrassment or shame.

Those emotions could wait for the morning, along with everything else.

It had been so long since anyone had touched her. And this was so much more than the touching and kissing they'd already succumbed to; this was more and yet somehow it wasn't enough.

Will it ever be enough? that small voice whispered in the back of her mind.

Minerva tried not to let her body shake as she accepted the onslaught of Liro's attention. His mouth moved against her with devastating precision. She looked down to where his strong hands played along the skin of her stomach and thighs, snaking round to grip her behind and pull her closer to him.

He had never been this confident, this domineering, before. It seemed as if, without words, he knew exactly what she needed and where she needed it. But she had never been so eager to be dominated before either. Memories of their time together seemed to fuse with the present. They had been young back then, with no experience, nothing to compare to. They had simply been lost in their excitement and passion for one another's bodies. But now, with so many years between them, she felt doubts cloud her mind even as she tried to enjoy the ripples of pleasure working through her body.

'Stop thinking, Minerva,' he commanded, pulling back to look up at her. 'Stop thinking about whatever has you so tense and give in to me. Give in...and I swear I won't stop until you are completely satisfied.'

'It's not that easy.' She gasped, shocked when she felt his grip tightening on her upper thigh, holding her in place.

'You need me to switch off your thoughts another way?' He looked up at her, his mouth glistening with the evidence of her arousal. It was so torrid, so utterly wrong, and yet when he stood up and kissed her she revelled in that explicit action. It seemed to break through a barrier in her mind and she leaned into him, kissing him back with the wild abandon that she'd been holding in check. She'd been holding herself together for fear that, if she let loose, she would unravel completely, irreparably, never to be put back together again like some broken thing. Hadn't she been broken for so long already? Maybe this was exactly what she needed. Maybe, as he said, they needed closure in order to move past the place where they'd become stuck.

A snap decision made, she leaned into him, her fingernails digging into his shoulders as she raised her thigh to bracket his thickly muscled hip. She moaned and ground the evidence of his arousal against her, separated only by a thin layer of her lace underwear. He was so hard, so large and, gods help her, she wanted nothing more than to climb him like a tree. She wanted to stop being angry and take what she was owed.

She would take this one night…one night without thinking like a princess. One night to feel just like a woman—his woman.

It was as if he sensed her change of thoughts, how her resolve had solidified her decision in the way her body had changed towards him.

'There you are.' He growled, tracing kisses down along her neck.

'This night.' She gasped. 'This one night is ours.'

The loose sundress that she wore was bunched around her hips and she could feel the cool breeze of the night air on her legs. He lifted her as though she weighed nearly nothing and carried her over to a canopied daybed. It provided slightly more privacy than the open top deck, but not enough that she didn't feel the thrill of possibly being caught.

'No one will disturb us.' He growled, setting her down slowly as though she were made of glass. He looked uncertain as he stared down at her, and for one prolonged, awful moment she thought he had reconsidered this madness they had both willingly agreed upon. If he'd been thinking, he quickly came to a decision, smiling as he pulled her panties away from her body in one smooth movement. The sound of lace tearing was unbearably erotic, as was the glimmer in his eyes as he took a moment to obviously savour the bare flesh he had uncovered.

His eyes were dark and thoroughly locked upon Minerva as he moved over her, bracketing her in with strong arms and tracing one long kiss up her centre. This time, he would not stop until she was thoroughly satisfied—wasn't that what he had said? She didn't look away; she watched him as he pleasured her and sighed loudly as her release began to build. He added two fingers, curling them just where she needed them, and the pleasure built even further.

Liro's low, rasping compliments moved around her, echoing under their cocoon along with her increasingly harsh breaths. She was coming apart, losing herself. When he felt her begin to tighten, he commanded her to *just let go* and, to her surprise, she did. She let go of it all, shattering over and over again until her lungs ached from crying out and her mind was completely blank. When she became aware of herself once more, she only wanted one thing: him.

'Make love to me, Liro. Now,' she said, stretching her arms above her head and offering herself to him fully to do with as he pleased. She didn't care if he was gentle or rough, only that it was him, and they were together.

CHAPTER NINE

LIRO RAISED HIMSELF up over Minerva's thoroughly pleasured body, his biceps bulging with the effort of not plunging into her immediately. He was too worked up after seeing her fall apart like that for him, too close to losing control, and he hadn't even thought to bring a condom. But then she'd asked him to make love to her, so very sweetly...and he'd been a lost cause.

'*Si, princesa,*' he murmured against her lips as he fought not to notch his hard length against her. 'We need to get protection, then you can use me as much as you need.'

She shuddered against him but then stilled, her golden eyes spearing him in place. 'I'm not using you, Liro,' she whispered, breathing hard as she punctuated her words with soft kisses along his chest and jaw. Her hands traced his pecs and his tattoos, coming to rest right above his heart. He closed his eyes against the vulnerability he saw there, the softness...

He'd been prepared for the frantic wildness of their initial joining, knowing that, so long as it was just sex, he could give her what she needed. He could be the man who made her orgasm over and over and still walk away at the end. But this... Having her look at him like this was almost more than he could bear. So he took the coward's way out and gathered her into his arms, carrying her into the darkness of his bedroom. He didn't turn on the lights, knowing exactly where to find the small square box of protection in his nightstand. He'd never brought anyone here, not even for a date. This had been purchased with Minerva in mind.

'I can't see you.' She laughed huskily, reaching for him.

'Use your other senses,' he commanded, moving behind her and sneaking a quick kiss on the back of her shoulder before grabbing her wrists and holding her in place.

'How can you see a thing?' She asked, out of breath from their play. Liro could just about make out the curve of her lips as he laid her down on her side, sliding himself behind her and entering her in one hard thrust. She inhaled a sharp breath that turned into a groan as he filled her fully.

'Tell me what you need, Min,' he murmured against her ear, using one hand to hold her thighs apart but firmly in place, stopping her from rocking against him.

'I need you...to move.' She gasped, craning her neck to seek out his kiss.

'Like this?' he asked softly, moving the barest few inches before stopping again. She moaned in protest so he moved again, the scantest couple of inches, before stopping.

'Liro, please,' she half-laughed, half-begged.

'You want more?' he said silkily, withdrawing completely and lying back on the bed. 'Don't ask me, don't beg. Take it from me, *princesa*. Take what you need.'

'I… I can't see you.' Her voice was a husky murmur as she turned over, hands outstretched.

'You'll find me.' He watched, jaw clenched, as her hands found his skin and she guided herself into his lap. He didn't know why he was playing games, only that he needed this. He needed to know that it wasn't just him going out of his mind with need here in the darkness of the night. He wanted her to be fully in control—maybe then the ache in his chest would ease. Maybe then he could stop counting down the hours until this night would be over and he returned her to where she belonged. To the royal life in which she had been born to flourish, the kind of world to where he could never follow.

He wasn't the right man for her in the daylight but here, under the cover of darkness, he knew that he could give her everything she had always been afraid to demand. He could show her the power she had over him, the power she had always wielded with effortless grace. If only she knew…

He waited patiently as she guided herself over him, resisting the urge to enter her as hard and fast as he had before. Teeth gritted, he hissed as she slid tentatively down onto his length with a sigh. He couldn't see her face but only imagine the satisfied smile he might find there.

Suddenly he regretted the decision to move them into the dark—he wanted to watch her as she took him. Reaching over to the bedside table, he flicked on a lamp to its lowest setting, bathing the bedroom in soft amber light. Sure enough, the sight that met his eyes was more beautiful than he could ever have imagined.

Minerva's eyes were heavy with pleasure as she found

her own rhythm, her hands braced on his abdomen and her breasts… *Dios*, her breasts…

This was a queen seated atop her throne, conquering him with every slow circle of her toned hips. She used her thighs to grip him tighter, urging him to move faster and deeper and, after the slightest moment of resistance, he complied, smiling as she took exactly what she needed over and over again until he was the one falling apart under her control. She leaned down to kiss him as her own release sent her body into spasms and she finally went limp against his chest.

Liro felt as if he'd been hit by lightning, unable to do anything for a long time other than run his fingers along her dark curls and hold in the words that threatened to spill from his lips. When he felt Minerva's breathing deepen, he arranged her onto the pillows alongside him and waited for the silence of the wide, open sea to soothe him to sleep as it always did.

But there was no soothing the ravaged beast that he had awakened within himself tonight. He'd been a fool to think that having Minerva in his bed one more time would be enough. He knew that he could not have her, but he had meant it when he'd said she shouldn't have to marry at all.

His mind moved over the various possibilities that they might both get what they wanted but came up short. It seemed that, no matter which path they chose, one of them was destined to lose something important. And he knew that, if he had to choose, he would take that loss himself.

Every time.

* * *

Minerva awoke in the circle of Liro's arms, her face pressed tight against the centre of his chest. His eyes were closed, his face peaceful, and she took a long time just simply to look at him. Never once had they fallen asleep all of the times they had been together as young lovers. Their meetings had always been rushed and secret, overshadowed by the worry of being caught. Last night Liro had come through on his promise not to stop until she was satisfied. They had made love twice more after that first time.

With no clock or watch to go by, she could only guess that they had slept for a few hours: the sky outside the portholes was still pitch-black, but with a tinge of violet to signify that dawn was not far off. Dawn meant that her day of freedom was officially over…and, with it, her time with Liro. She moved slowly out of the circle of his arms, sliding her bare feet down onto the plush sand-coloured carpet. Her body felt heavy, warm and satisfied in a way she didn't think it had ever felt, not even after her most gruelling Olympic training sessions.

She stared around properly at the lavishly decorated space for the first time, taking in the inner sanctum of the powerful shipping mogul he'd become. Despite the obvious wealth and quality of everything aboard his yacht, Liro's bedroom was quite warm and minimalist in its appearance. A tall shelf of books filled one wall, coupled with a comfortable-looking arm chair that faced out towards the tall windows. There were no family photos or mementos, but it felt lived in. Liro had said he'd chosen this vessel as his only home and she could feel that was what it was.

His bathroom was almost the same size as the main room, with a large double tub and a shower stall that took up the entire wall towards the end. A surprising ache formed in her chest as she spied his toothbrush sitting in a cup by the sink along with the mint-flavour paste. She stared at the mundane items that filled the open vanity cabinet, studying them, needing to know who he was. How he had lived for all these years when they had been apart.

She stepped into the shower stall, closed the door behind her and stared up at the confusing high-tech display. Her eyes unfocused as her mind continued to race. Had Liro brought other lovers here? Had they shared his bed and used this luxury shower the way she was doing now? Frowning, she tapped a few buttons, gasping when cold water instantly streamed down over her body. She frantically tapped the display again until it turned off, leaving her shivering but kind of thankful for the jolt away from her uncomfortable thoughts.

Everything about his world made her feel out of her depth: the fancy appliances, the lack of rules and routines. She knew nothing about this version of Liro, only that he wanted closure from their past just as she did. He said he had thought of her, sure, but had he missed her the way she'd longed for him? If he had cared half as much, surely he wouldn't have been able to leave? She leaned her head forward, seeking the cool, glossy wall tiles to calm her racing thoughts, only to see a shimmer of moonlight on waves.

This was not a wall at all, she realised with a start, but a window. She gasped aloud, covering herself with two hands.

'It's one-way glass,' a voice murmured from behind her. Minerva instantly moved to cover her bare breasts and relaxed once she saw Liro sliding open the shower door and stepping inside. His red hair was ruffled from sleep, his face slightly flushed. He looked infinitely younger...almost like the young man she'd once known.

She might not be able to name what he meant to her but she knew it wasn't just freedom, a warm body to use or any of the things he had accused her of. It was more that he had always meant more to her than he was supposed to.

'I didn't know how to work it.' She gestured to the shower and stepped back as he moved around her, fiddling with the display. Hot water fell from the wide waterfall-style attachment above and the scent of lavender essential oils filled the air.

'You don't look as blissfully relaxed as I hoped you would after last night's efforts.' He frowned, one large hand cupping her cheek. 'Talk to me, Min.'

'I'm okay,' she said quickly, avoiding his eyes and how much they always seen. He moved closer, caging her in against the glass as the steam whirled around them.

'You're lying,' he said. 'Want to know how I know?'

'How?' she whispered.

'Because I'm not okay either,' he murmured. 'I woke up alone in my bed...and I thought you'd gone back. And I wasn't okay, Min. I wasn't okay at all.'

He leaned in, every inch of his warm, wet skin pressing against hers. It wasn't a sexual embrace, it was comfort. She closed her eyes, feeling the emotions within her peak. How could a night feel so perfect and so terrible all at once? How could one person be everything you needed and everything you could never have?

She felt the final wall she'd built to keep him out fall and crumble. This day…all the emotions he'd made her feel, all the pleasure…had torn away all the defences she'd spent so long creating to keep herself safe. Now she was raw and fourteen years' worth of emotions had risen to the surface.

'Why did you have to leave?' she heard herself whisper. For a moment, she thought the noise of the water might have drowned out her needy words, but she felt his body tense, his head dropping down to her shoulder.

'I already told you—it was the best thing I could think to do. I didn't know what my father had done but, even so, marrying me would have ruined you.'

'I understand why you walked away from the betrothal. But why did you leave *me*?' she said, not bothering to hide the tremor in her voice. 'You never even thought to talk to me first. Never thought to say goodbye.'

Minerva watched him rub a hand along the back of his neck, his jaw tight as he stood up straight under the hot spray. He looked tortured, his throat working as he tried to speak, then he gave up, shaking his head. 'I should have. I wish I had.'

'Did you know that I always hoped to see you?' she whispered. 'Every city I travelled to, I looked into the crowds and wondered if I would see you. I always hoped...'

'And if you'd found me?' he asked softly, his voice cocooning her in the steamy air.

She turned away. Of course she understood his meaning, even if it hurt. What *would* she have done? Would she have abandoned her duty and run away with him? Would they have lived out their days in the bowels of a shipping freighter? Or would he have stowed her away in some port city, returning every six months?

'I left the way I did because I didn't trust myself to say goodbye,' he said, his hands sliding down to sit heavy on her waist. 'You were just having a fling, determined to perform your duty by marrying me. But Min... I was in love with you.'

His words snapped like a whip in the silence, stealing the breath from her lungs as she let them sink in. She couldn't move, couldn't do anything but stare out at the thin line of the approaching sunrise beginning to peek out from the inky-black horizon. She closed her eyes, feeling his deep sigh against her back.

'Why didn't you...?' She bit down hard on her lip. 'You never said.'

'You remember how shy I was. I barely spoke for the first few summers. But I watched you from afar.' He laid a gentle kiss on the top of her head, turning them so that the water warmed their rapidly cooling skin.

'I think I fell in love with your confidence first—I was captivated by how determined and capable you were in everything you did. How kind you were to everyone, even the awkward, scowling prince who followed

you around the palace grounds. I was always drowning
in my own thoughts, my own insecurities, but when I
was with you... I could breathe. So, yes, I fell in love
with you long before my father revealed our betrothal. I
thought that maybe your feelings for me would develop
and we might make things work. But then that day...'

He didn't need to clarify what day he meant; she
knew. Every failed relationship has one—the day that
changed everything. The day that sealed their fate. She
had seen misery in his eyes but had thought it was his
own regret at being forced to marry her.

'I asked you why you wanted to marry me,' Liro continued. 'And, with your reply, I saw myself through your
eyes. I saw how things would be, with you calmly taking me on as a husband of convenience while I pined for
you. I was young and impulsive and angry—so angry.
The idea of having you but never truly having you... In
my mind, there was no other option but for me to leave.'

The light in the bathroom revealed more details hidden within the curling tattoo designs that she had in-
spected before. The dark ink covered his shoulders fully
but in the middle of the swirls she spied a familiar shape:
their lake. And on the banks stood the dark silhouette
of a woman gazing up at the moon.

'If you think I walked away and never thought of
you, you're wrong. I carried you with me, Minerva.
Right here.'

She placed her hand over his heart, drawing in the
warmth from his skin. From the words she'd never
known she needed to hear so badly—that she'd been
wanted, loved even, even if it was all in the past. He

had loved her once, back then. He hadn't just used her for her crown or played a part that he'd been forced to by his father.

She closed her eyes, wondering how different things might have been if she'd not been such a coward and kept him at arm's length. In her mind's eye she remembered his face, younger and so earnest as he'd asked her why she was going ahead with the wedding. As he'd gone cold at her abrupt answer. She'd believed herself to be the only one with a broken heart that night... Of course he'd run from her—she'd driven him away.

Now, here in the present moment, the idea of admitting that she had been in love with him too seemed utterly absurd. Would he believe her? Or would he see it as a pathetic attempt for her to rid herself of some of the guilt crawling up her skin, making her shiver? She closed her eyes against the force of her own regret and the desperate longing that came with it. She couldn't look at him, not when she knew she was so close to losing control and admitting everything.

Her love for him then...and now.

Because she suddenly knew without a doubt that nothing could possibly hurt this much and not be love. And it was absolutely terrifying. Shivers covered her skin, breaking open that small, vulnerable part of her that she'd kept hidden away. The part that told her that every man who claimed to care for her would leave, that no one was truly reliable or trustworthy. It was a hard, cynical way to feel and she despised it. Had she been so affected by her parents' relationship that she'd used it as a blueprint for all others?

She had never even attempted to bond with someone new after Liro, had never gone beyond the odd casual date if she felt like some fun. A small part of her had welcomed the royal marriage requirement as a way to appease the constant questions about when she'd find the one. She knew that, for her, true love and happy marriage would not exist, so giving herself a week to select a stranger to marry hadn't been a big deal at all.

Now, the idea of returning to Arqaleta and choosing another man as her husband made her feel wild with the wrongness of it. But they had both known that was the way it must be; they had made their deal knowing that this was only a temporary reprieve from reality.

'You're breaking your own rules again, princess.'

His voice stirred her from her thoughts. She looked up at him and thought she saw a brief mirror of her own pain before he stepped closer and pressed his naked body flush with hers. 'This time is not for talking and thinking about the past. Not when this is all we have.'

He claimed her lips in a scorching kiss that chased away all the overwhelming emotions that threatened to swallow her whole. In their place, it was only him—only Liro. He kissed her for what felt like hours, his hands in her hair. He kissed her like the drowning man he'd described, as if he was drawing in every breath of her.

CHAPTER TEN

LIRO AWOKE TO the to the glorious sight of Minerva, fully nude, arranging a modest breakfast upon the table near his bed. He didn't move immediately to speak or alert her that he had awoken; instead, he simply watched her, taking in the graceful focus she put into arranging toast upon one plate and heaping some eggs alongside it.

She had cooked for him… He had let the crew take the night off once they had returned to the ship the evening before. The captain and a small skeleton crew would stay on the opposite end of the ship, where the engine room was, to ensure that all remained well on the vessel, but the cleaning crew and hospitality staff were gone.

'I can feel you staring.' She turned to face him, her eyes sparkling with mischief. 'I wore a robe when I went into the kitchen. This is pretty much the only dish I can make, so…'

'Does this count as course number five?' he asked, 'Or am I breaking your rules again?'

'I think we broke more than one rule last night.' She smiled shyly, hiding her face behind her dark curls as she laid their food out on a tray and put it in the centre of his bed.

He reached over, unable to stop himself from cupping her face with his hand and claiming her lips in a soft kiss. The kiss deepened and his simple need to touch her and taste her became more, his hands pulling her closer.

'The food will go cold,' she chided, sliding out of his grasp with a happy sigh.

The ate in a companionable silence. She poured his coffee, he buttered her toast. But all along he felt an undercurrent of tension building in his gut. He glanced at the clock that showed that it was almost eight, and he knew that her first event of the day began in less than an hour. Once they had finished eating and clearing away their plates, Minerva flopped down onto the bed, looking at him with hooded eyes and wiggling her finger in a 'come hither' motion.

Liro inhaled a calming breath, knowing that his body would doubtless hate him for what he was about to ask, but...

'I would love nothing more than to spend the entire morning in bed with you—you must know that.' He watched as the playfulness left her eyes, replaced with a guarded expression. 'You have duties to return to.'

'I took the day off.' She bit her bottom lip. 'I called my team and organised for my mother to run the event solo this morning.'

Liro froze. 'Why would you do that?'

'I thought that you would be pleased.' She frowned, reaching down to pull the sheets over her bare breasts, guarding herself from him. 'I was taking your advice and doing what serves me. But now I feel kind of foolish that I didn't ask you first. You probably made plans to sail off somewhere today. I can call them back, get someone to come pick me up.'

He stopped her before she could begin grabbing her things, hating the look of uncertainty on her beautiful face. 'Minerva, trust me, I would love nothing more than to disregard the shadow of your duty hanging over both of us. I would love to keep you here on my ship—'

'Then keep me,' she interrupted, reaching out to pull him towards her. 'Let's ignore the real world for a while longer. Let's pretend it's just me and you for one more day.'

He closed his eyes as her lips traced the skin below his navel, moving down. Her hands moved around to his buttocks, gripping him, holding him just where she wanted him. He let her take control, tilting his head back as his mind continued to work against his body. Common sense told him to force the issue, to prevent her from neglecting her duties and blaming him for it in the future. But another more selfish part of him asked... what future? This was it. This was all that he would get of her, this small window of stolen time that he himself had pretty much forced her to give him.

He had told her the truth last night—that he had broken the betrothal because he'd been in love with her. He'd spoken about it as though those feelings were firmly in the past to protect his own pride. But he knew his feelings were still there, raw and burgeoning against the surface of his control.

She'd seemed shocked at the revelation, but she hadn't said she felt the same. They'd made love again twice and now she wanted to stay...but did she want to stay for him or what he made her feel? That selfish voice within told him to shut up, to live in this moment and not invite reality back into their bubble.

In the end it was Minerva's lips that took control of the situation, pushing away all rational thought as she gave one long, languorous lick down the length of his erection.

'Still thinking about my duty?' she asked, her voice a husky rasp as her eyes met his and her lips worked his length, taking all of him in, worshipping him.

He couldn't speak, couldn't think, as her brown eyes held him in thrall, making him feel a depth of emotion he had thought he would never feel again. His hands wove through her hair, holding her with gentle deference as she brought him to climax with a swiftness and intensity that he had never experienced.

Her sweet smile as she looked up spoke of pride and victory. She had conquered him truly. He knew then at that moment that he would do anything for this woman. He finally admitted to himself that he had come back here for her, that he had received that invitation and immediately set sail for this island as though he'd been shown the way to a treasure he'd thought he would never see again. She was his treasure—she had been from the moment he had first laid eyes on her. He hadn't known how important she was to him then…not until he'd lost her. But now, taking her into his arms and holding her close, he knew that he would never allow anything to hurt her ever again.

But what if the biggest danger to her perfect future as queen…was him?

* * *

Minerva knew that she was playing a foolish game, pro-
longing their time together this way. But, as she watched
Liro dive off the bow of the yacht, then smiling from
the crystal-clear water below, she couldn't quite muster
the energy to feel regret.

She could feel a shift in the air since his mention of
her duty earlier. Perhaps that was why she had been so
insistent on bringing him to climax that way for the
first time. The power and the erotic pleasure of it had
astounded her; she had already been halfway to an orgasm of her own simply from having him fully under
her control and feeling him come apart.

Of course, a more sensible woman would have awoken the morning after a passionate one-night stand with
her ex and immediately left to return to reality. Especially when that reality involved a very imminent and
public elevation to queen of an entire kingdom.

But, when she had opened her eyes in the early-morn-
ing light and felt Liro's arms around her, she'd felt free.
The idea of getting dressed and walking off his ship,
going back to reality, had set a riot of angry hornets
flying around in her mind. Her fingers had shaken as
she'd typed out the email to rearrange her schedule. Just
one more day, she'd told herself. Then she'd feel ready
to walk away.

Liro crooked his finger up at her, mischief in his eyes
as he trod water, waiting. She stood poised on the out-
ermost ledge, taking a moment to feel the breeze in her
unbound hair.

'What are you waiting for?' He laughed, splashing cool

sea water up against her legs. Strong hands slid around her calves as he moved up against the side of the ladder.

'I'm not waiting for anything, that's the point.' She smiled, sighing as he gently kneaded the tension from her body.

'I'm surprised there's any tension left after the amount of times you've made me come in the past twenty-four hours.'

'You were always this way.' He dropped a kiss on her knee. 'Strung tighter than one of your bows.'

She let a noncommittal sound escape her lips, her thoughts feeling more and more clouded by the minute.

'Do you miss competing?' he asked, pulling himself up to sit alongside her.

'Sometimes,' she said, leaning against his cool skin. 'I loved seeing the world and meeting new people. But some of the other archers saw me as a hobbyist rather than a serious competitor. There were many unfair terms thrown my way—some of it from jealousy or dislike, but some were deserved. I can be overly confident, maybe even a bit tunnel-visioned, when I want to do well at something. I was always conscious that I had a very privileged upbringing with some of the world's best trainers. Even if I lost everything, I returned home to a palace, which wasn't the case for my competitors.'

'You deserved your success, Minerva.'

'I worked hard but, once my mother told me of her wish to step down, it wasn't a difficult decision to leave it all behind, you know?

'What about you?' She tried to appear casual. 'Do you ever miss royal life?'

'I miss the version of royal life that existed before my mother's death. Being in Cisneros brought back some old memories that I'd forgotten. But that life doesn't exist any more.'

Minerva nodded, wishing she had the courage to ask the question she really wanted to: *would you ever return to royal life...for me?*

She closed her eyes against that foolish thought, tilting her head up to the sun as though the burning heat might chase away all the shadows that had begun to encroach on her little oasis of freedom. But an oasis was all that this could ever be—a temporary illusion of peace and tranquillity—no matter how much she wished things were different.

'You have shadows in your eyes again, Minerva.' Liro tucked his fingers under her chin, turning her to face him. 'Is this whole shipwrecked fantasy doing nothing for you?'

She laughed, loving how easily he made her smile. Loving *him*. 'You might have the luxury of being a runaway pirate prince, Señor San Nicolau, but I have to go back eventually.'

Liro's firm grip tightened ever so slightly around her wrists. 'If I were a true pirate, I wouldn't return you. I'd keep you right here.'

'Would you hold me to ransom?' She laughed. 'Make me walk the plank?'

'I'd tie you to the mast and have my wicked way with you for a while.' He nuzzled her neck, nipping his teeth against the soft skin there. 'Yes... I think I'd find endless ways to enjoy my stolen booty.'

'An endless booty call. Is that what we're calling this now?' She laughed. 'I don't know... I think you'd tire of me eventually.'

'A good pirate knows when they've found a treasure so rare they could never part with it.' Liro's eyes met hers and Minerva stopped breathing for a moment, fearing she might burst into tears if she spoke.

She fought to find the right words, wanting to lay out every messy emotion within her heart for him to see. He cared about her, that much was undeniable. *But he can never be yours*, that tiny voice within reminded her softly. Even if his identity wouldn't be a scandalous risk to public opinion about her;...even if he didn't run his own shipping empire with the world at his feet...deep down, she knew he was still the boy who had longed for freedom from royal life.

The royal role that she adored and worked so hard to keep was part of a life he despised. To ask him to consider being with her, when he knew that she needed to marry immediately, would be selfish. He had already been used as a pawn by his father years ago; she would never do the same thing to him. Not when he had told her how happy and peaceful his new life made him. He already had everything he had ever wanted...

Liro cleared his throat, ducking his head from her view. 'Of course, I'm not an actual pirate. Let's make that very clear for any Arqaletan coast guards who might be within hearing distance.' He raised both hands up for theatrical effect before he dove back into the water.

'Thanks for making that clear.' She chuckled to herself, pushing away her morose thoughts as she slid down into the crystal-clear water. It was warm and she welcomed the silence as she let herself sink down under the waves.

Liro's arms were around her in an instant, their bodies twining around one another and their lips meeting as they floated back up to the surface together.

Minerva woke to the sound of beeping. It was coming from her phone by the side of the bed. Eyes half-closed, she grasped for the device, jabbing her fingers at the screen until the noise stopped.

She lay back down on her pillow with a sigh. The room was quiet but for the sound of Liro's soft breathing. She turned towards him, taking the opportunity just to look for a while. It was late in the morning, and Minerva could stall no longer. Tonight was the grand ball and with it her mother's announcement. It was time for her to return to Arqaleta and do what she'd set out to do.

Unease crept up her spine, making her turn from Liro's handsome face as she pondered what must come next. She'd lain awake for a while last night, after she and Liro had spent a full day doing nothing but eating, laughing and making love. She'd forced herself to think of the practicalities, to prepare herself for her return home and the decision she would have to make.

Of all the suitors she'd entertained, Jean-Claude struck her as the most suited to the role of king consort. He was a descendant of European aristocracy, was handsome, confident and had excellent public speaking skills. She would set a meeting with him this afternoon, formally propose marriage and it would be done. Another item ticked off her list.

'Good morning.' Liro's strong arm curved slowly around her waist, his lips tracing kisses along her bare shoulder as he pulled her back against his gloriously nude body.

'Good morning to you too,' she murmured, melting into his embrace. He was hard and she was weak and one last time of having him inside her seemed like the perfect way to say goodbye really.

She laughed as he moved up over her, covering her with his full weight and spreading her legs wide. But, just as he made to enter her, another sound filled the room, this time a more serious tone coming from the intercom upon the wall.

'Ignore it,' she pleaded as Liro apologetically stood up and walked over to press the button on the intercom. She understood that aboard a vessel there might be emergencies... Well, at least she understood that on a logical level. It would take quite a lot of fire and brimstone for her to be happy about not making love with Liro again.

She watched as he spoke in a low voice. She could tell something was wrong as his eyes instantly darkened, his brows knitting together. He thanked whomever was on the other end of the line for telling him, his tone serious enough to have her sitting up straight in the bed.

'Who was it?'

Liro's eyes met hers, his expression starker than she'd ever seen it. 'My publicity team. My identity has been discovered and made public.'

CHAPTER ELEVEN

MINERVA'S HEARTBEAT THRUMMED in her ears as she opened her phone screen to see a newspaper article published one hour ago. It had been sent by Liro's PR team, accompanied by no less than twenty-three missed calls in the past forty minutes since she had put her phone on silent mode. The article was headed: *Mysterious Shipping Magnate is Long-Lost Banished Prince!*

'Oh, God…' she whispered. 'How did they find out?'

'Someone was bound to eventually.' Liro stared blankly at the photograph filling her screen with an image of his younger self. 'I never intended to hide my past for ever. But I didn't plan for it to happen like this, when your kingdom is at such a pivotal moment.'

Minerva thought of her mother, of her vow to do whatever it took to repair Minerva's standing in public favour. She had been so close to fixing everything, so close to being ready to make her mother proud. To making her people proud.

Having this reminder of the past splashed all over every newspaper on the day her mother planned to announce her abdication wasn't just inconvenient…it was a disaster.

She turned, looking around the bedroom floor for

items of clothing that had been discarded the night before. The bed sheets lay in complete disarray, towels strewn on the floor after they'd finished making love in the hot tub after a lazy dinner.

Everywhere she looked, she was met with reminders of their time here together. Not that she needed them. The memory of Liro's love-making wasn't something she would ever forget. Nor did she want to. She didn't regret it. She had planned to tell him that, before she left his yacht, but now everything was in chaos and she had no idea what to say.

She picked up her dress, throwing it over her body. There was no time to search for her bra, not when at this very moment her mother was likely hunting her down.

'Min, calm down. You can't just rush back to the palace like this.'

She shook off his grip, moving to step around him to find the rest of her things. 'I need to go and help with the damage control.'

He blocked her path. 'By damage control, do you mean rushing to announce your engagement to one of your mother's more appropriate suitors?'

Minerva sucked in a breath, feeling her chest ache. 'That's what I should have been doing all week, instead of running away. It's my fault that this is happening. I should have gone back yesterday.'

'Who is going to be the lucky man?' he asked harshly. 'The prince?'

Minerva shrank under his cold demand. 'Actually, Jean-Claude makes the most sense.'

Liro's grey eyes darkened to obsidian. 'All of this

pageantry has been to bolster you in public opinion, to make the public view you as a suitable queen. What will people think now, Minerva, seeing their perfect princess walking off *my* yacht?'

He walked over to the balcony doors, opening them up to reveal the sound of shouting and commotion. Sure enough, a small crowd had formed further down the marina, held back by a makeshift barricade of Liro's security guards.

'If you rush out of here dressed like this, there is not a single person with eyes who wouldn't know what we have been doing all night.' He moved closer, staring down at her with that same intensity. 'Are you so eager to run off and select your new fiancé so quickly after leaving my bed?'

'This is how it needs to be.' She shook her head, 'It's my duty to my mother to fix this as soon as possible but I can't calm the press with you here. An announcement of a royal engagement to Jean-Claude will distract them for a time.'

'No.' Liro growled, wrapping one arm around her waist and hauling her up against him. 'I don't want you near him. I wouldn't let you off of this ship if I could manage it.'

'You've done your deal; you've had your closure… There's nothing else keeping you here.' Her breath heaved with the effort not to sink into him, to run back into the physical pleasure she craved. But this was so much bigger than them now: this was fast on its way to becoming a royal scandal.

'Your public image was already in question. You need

to control this news to avoid disaster, Minerva. You need *me* here to control it.'

'You've admitted you had no public image at all for the past decade, not even with Magnabest. What good could you do?'

'We have been through this once before. Surely you know the answer?'

'No.' She shook her head against his words, shaking off the painful mirroring of their past and present. She wouldn't entertain history repeating itself this way— she *couldn't*.

'You need another announcement, one that would overshadow this one.' Liro met her eyes, cold and unemotional. 'We will announce our engagement immediately.'

Liro would have been lying if he'd said that this wasn't what some deep, dark part of him had wanted from the moment he'd set his course to return to this kingdom. He wanted her with every fibre of his being and the thought of having her by his side…in his bed, in his arms for ever…made some hungry part of him want to grab at this opportunity with both hands and make sure that neither of them could ever turn back.

He wanted Minerva for himself…but not like this.

'It would only make everything worse.' She shook her head, staring at him with the exact horrified expression she'd worn the first time they'd had this conversation. This time, at least, he had been the one to propose.

'Make the announcement, Minerva,' he said roughly. 'Your team know how to spin it as a grand love affair.

The public will be appeased. Your mother can go ahead with her plans to abdicate. Two scandals solved for the price of one.'

'It would be that easy for you?' she asked, tucking her arms tightly around herself. 'You would marry me, walk back into this world?'

He fought off the instinctive discomfort that her words evoked—the memories of his younger self, of always feeling unsuitable and unwanted. Was that how she would see him now? She had been so ready to choose another as her king consort, to send him away. Perhaps a better man would have obeyed. But he was not a better man. He might not be her ideal choice for a royal husband but he was more trustworthy than any of the other men she'd been prepared to choose between.

'I was never guilty of the crimes my father committed. So, it's the best solution,' he said, avoiding her eyes lest she see right through this poor show of bravado. 'You would only have to remain married to me for a short time, long enough to get settled as queen. After a year or so, we could divorce. It's not as if that has not happened—'

She winced and he realised, far too late, the gravity of his words. Minerva did not speak of her father often, or the public divorce that had shadowed her early teenage years. He closed his eyes, pressing thumb and forefinger against the bridge of his nose. 'I didn't mean to speak ill of your parents.'

'No, it's the truth. The public have already recovered from one broken royal marriage. Seeing as history is already repeating itself, we may as well lean into the charade, right?'

'Minerva.' He moved towards her, freezing as she raised her arms up to hold him off, warning him not to come closer, not to touch her. How was this happening? Less than an hour ago, they had been blissed out from a second night of pleasure and now she could barely look at him.

'I need to return to the palace, Liro.' Her brown eyes were cold and flat, as though every ember of happiness had been extinguished within her. The idea that facing marriage to him had affected her this deeply hurt now, more than it ever had the first time. Back then they had been young and naïve and his love had been a fragile thing.

Now, it was deep enough that this rejection hurt like a knife sliding between his ribs. Like an arrow, aimed at him with every furtive look of disapproval she threw his way as she finished dressing and putting her hair to rights in the bathroom mirror.

But at least now he would not be foolish enough to hope that a marriage between them could be anything more than a temporary solution. He would not be so naïve as to believe she would come to do something as ridiculous as love him. But she would not marry the Frenchman or any of the others. She would marry *him*.

He had walked away from Minerva once, leaving her alone to pick up the pieces, and he would not do that again. The next time he walked away from Arqaleta, it would be once she was seated firmly upon her throne and needed no one else to keep it.

He watched silently as she slipped her feet into her shoes one at a time, her voice a low monotone. 'I need to speak to my mother alone. Discuss our options.'

'Discuss me, you mean.' He remained still. 'Because, if marriage is on your agenda, I am the only eligible bachelor you will be selecting.'

Minerva closed her eyes. 'You are...impossible.'

'You can keep fighting me, but we're not so different in this regard. Once I make up my mind on what I want, I get it.'

She shook her head, fists balled tightly at her sides. 'You don't want this. You don't—'

'What will you tell her about where you've been?' He cut across her anger. 'How will you explain how you of all people didn't know my identity?'

'You were gone a long time. I'll tell her I wasn't sure.'

'You recognised me the moment you truly looked at me, Minerva. You knew me.'

He waited for her to respond, not knowing what he wanted her to say, only that they couldn't leave things like this. He couldn't be about to become engaged to the woman who had haunted his dreams for so long only to have her look at him as if he was the villain of her fairy-tale. As if she despised him. Or, worse, as if she was completely immune to him.

Another brief window of happiness before the world came crashing in... His mind mocked him as he watched Minerva get escorted by his security team to a waiting car, cameras flashing from the crowd of photographers up the street.

Their time on his yacht would now haunt him more than any of his other memories of her. He had walked away once before; he had forged a new path for himself knowing that he was giving her the freedom she deserved. He would not do that now. He would marry her if she still wished for it. He would enter a royal marriage of convenience. He would do it...even if it tore him apart.

But he would not submit to it without ensuring she had every other option available first. She was only in this situation because of the rules of the world she had been born into. And, as he had told her many times, he did not often like to play by the rules.

Decision made, he tapped his phone to call for an urgent meeting with his team at Magnabest. Likely they were all still celebrating their win and planning for the huge development project that lay ahead for them. They would not be pleased with what he was about to ask them to do. But, as he looked from his office windows in the direction of the palace, he knew this was what he needed to do.

Once back at the palace, Minerva threw herself into damage-control mode. Her mother was absolutely furious in a way that Minerva had not seen in a long time. Public scandal was always a difficult subject for her to navigate, and seeing her usually calm, controlled mama so stressed brought a heavy sense of shame upon her.

The news of Liro's identity had swept through the kingdom with surprising swiftness, along with paparazzi photographs taken of them at the fair in Cisneros. The entire public relations team was already working overtime to try to ensure they had some control over the story.

'Minerva, honestly, I thought that you had more sense

than to be photographed in this way! When were these photographs taken?'

'Two days ago…when I said that I was taking the evening to rest. Liro took me to a fair.'

'You were…not resting.'

'No, Mother.' She waited for the inevitable ranting to begin about her deception and her lack of care about her duty. She deserved it; she knew that her behaviour had been inappropriate and reckless… But still, she waited and nothing came. In fact, when she looked up into her mother's face, the other woman was smiling.

'I think your amusement is possibly more disturbing than the scolding that I expected.'

'Darling, you are a thirty-three-year-old woman who is readying to take over an entire kingdom. I am not about to scold you.'

'You're not?' Minerva frowned. 'I thought for sure that you would be furious. You invited him here believing him to be a shipping magnate, a catch…and it has led to scandal because of my inability to face the truth.'

Her mother shook her head, her eyes drifting away towards her secretary for a split second. A look passed between the women, a widening of the eyes that drew Minerva's attention instantly. 'Neither of you are surprised…and you both admitted to putting extensive research into your matchmaking solutions.'

Her mother grimaced.

'Please tell me that you did not know who he was… That you didn't seek him out on purpose?'

'That depends, Minnie, my love…did it work?'

'You lied to me. You had me sneaking around, trying

to stop you from finding out, and the whole time you knew what were you doing? Placing bets on how big of a scandal this would bring down upon us all?' Minerva choked out the words.

'I chose your happiness over the threat of scandal, my love. You told me to choose you a selection of the best possible partners. I could not do that in good faith without inviting back the man that I knew you had loved, the young man that I wrongly banished through my own anger at his father.'

'What happened before was not your fault. I told you that.'

'It was not within my power to stop you from having your heart broken before, but I would not be able to allow you to enter into a loveless marriage of my own doing…if I hadn't at least tried to give you back the one that you deserved.'

Minerva felt hot emotion threaten to choke her as she processed what her mother had done. Of course her mother had known… Maybe she simply hadn't wanted to see that herself.

The love that she deserved… She thought of Liro's offer of marriage and felt her jaw tighten painfully. 'I'm pretty sure that all of your meddling has been for nothing. We are right back where we were fourteen years ago—staring down the barrel of a forced royal marriage of convenience.'

'I don't see how. It's as clear as day to everyone that man is head over heels in love with you.'

'Any love he may have would be stifled by having to remain here. He hated royal life in Cisneros. He would rather have disappeared than remain here and clear his name.'

'This isn't Cisneros. And you are not nineteen any more. He knows what he wants.'

'You don't know that.'

'Don't I?' Her mother stood up, 'I have it on good authority that half of parliament met with the heads of Magnabest today. There was only one item on the agenda.'

Minerva stared down at the royal memo her mother placed before her, sent over from their prime minister to inform Her Majesty that their investor had placed a freeze on its plans until the Crown Princess signed off on it...as Queen.

'He can't do that, can he?' Her fingers trembled as she read the short memo again, hardly believing the ramifications of one simple act. In the time since she'd left him, it appeared that Liro had been in a plethora of meetings with her mother's parliament. He'd purchased the land and he owned it outright now. Freezing his plans would lose him valuable time in developing it—there was no logical reason for him to wait. Emotion tightened her throat painfully so that, when she finally spoke, it was with a hoarse croak.

'He's holding our government to ransom to ensure my succession.'

Her mother nodded. 'Tell me that is not the action of a fool in love.'

Minerva swallowed the pain of that statement, re-alising that there was a very real possibility that her mother was right. Liro had told her he'd been in love with her before everything had torn them apart. But the fact remained that she would become queen. She would remain here in this palace for much of the year, serving her people and carrying out the plans she'd spent years forming to make their lives better. This was her life's work, her vocation. There would be little time for spontaneous trips or adventures; everything would be planned and ordered. That was everything that Liro had told her he despised.

'I thought this would make you happy.' Her mother frowned.

'It does make me happy. *He* makes me happy, even when he's not terrorising the entire Arqaletan parliament in my honour.' Minerva felt bittersweet tears threaten, wiping them away quickly with the pads of her fingers. 'But the fact remains, I can't expect him to walk away from the life he chose to come and stand by my side. I can't force him back into the royal world that he despises, all in the name of love. Eventually, he will resent me. And we both know where that leads.'

Her mother's eyes widened with understanding and Minerva felt ashamed. She knew it was irrational still to be so affected by her father's abandonment, but there it was. When she thought of marriage, she thought of her parents and the circus that had been their very public divorce. Going through that with a man she barely knew had been a risk she'd been willing to take, but not with a man she adored.

'Minnie...your father never resented royal life, he left because he fell in love. Yes, it was selfish, and I wish he had taken more care with you. But our marriage was arranged and we were so different. The only thing we ever agreed upon was how wonderful you are. It was a relief when he asked for a divorce, even despite the scandal.'

'I just don't know if I can bear it.'

'You don't have to be the only one in this. Go to him. Let him make that choice for himself. Figure it out together.'

Liro stood at his office window and watched the kingdom of Arqaleta disappear behind him. He hadn't intended to leave today but, with a large storm set to come in tonight, his crew needed to pay a visit to the mainland. Truthfully, after a long day of arguing in a boardroom alongside Magnabest's corporate team, he needed space.

Since his identity had become known, he had felt more of an outsider than ever. His CEO had even attempted to bow to him when they had first met in the hallway. He had known the man for years, but it seemed hiding one's true identity under a persona made people upset. A fact he supposed he understood, even if he knew he had his reasons.

Still, he had done his part in ensuring that Minerva's future was made up of choices rather than just duty. He had seen the faces of the men and women who ran the parliament and had seen how they'd known instantly that their plans had been felled. And he had never been more glad he had trusted his own instincts.

She was free now, safe in the knowledge that she did not have to appease anyone by marrying in order to secure her crown. It was hers without question.

Maybe that was why he had chosen to remain aboard when his staff had informed him of their need to return to the mainland for the afternoon. The grand ball was to take place in a matter of hours, and he would wait and watch while the Queen announced her imminent abdication to the world. Minerva would become Queen immediately, but in essence she already was at this very moment. He had watched as the Prime Minister had signed it into existence.

And with it he had felt something within him tighten. Some deep-seated knowledge or old pain that, once she knew she didn't have to marry him, she would be relieved. He knew that she had not been false in her emotions during their night together. He was confident in her physical attraction to him, and their chemistry together. But as for her heart… She had never mentioned love to him, not once. She had never alluded to the fact that their relationship was anything more than just sexual, passion and freedom.

When she became queen, she would have no need for his adventures and freedom. She would be required to have almost every moment of her day accounted for and planned. She had prepared for this moment for her entire life and, while he was brimming with excitement for her and full of confidence that she would do amazing things, a small, selfish part of him still rallied against what he had done. He had almost had everything he wanted, and he had quite literally signed it all away when he had made the deal on behalf of his shipping company, ensuring Minerva had a choice in her life.

He was so lost in his own thoughts that he hardly

noticed when the movement and the noise of the waves slowed, almost as though had they had begun to stop. He looked out and sure enough there was something amiss. A loud siren blared from outside as he opened up a porthole and stuck his head out to investigate. What he saw shocked him to his core.

Four Coastguard ships had surrounded them, the grand Arqaletan coat of arms emblazoned on their sides. Sirens blared along with a voice commanding them to come to an immediate stop and prepare to accept boarding. Liro pressed his intercom directly to the captain's cabin.

'What is the meaning of this?' he demanded.

'They are ordering us to return to shore,' the captain shouted over the noise of sirens.

Furious, Liro bounded out onto the deck in the direction of the part of the vessel nearest to their unwelcome visitors. He'd had quite enough of the government of Arqaleta trying to have its say in his business. He had absolutely no patience for this happening now. Rain had begun to fall hard and fast but he ignored it, climbing the emergency ladder to get to the captain's board fast.

It was only once he was high up on the top level that he looked down and saw a sight that sent his blood running cold.

'Minerva.' He breathed.

She was standing out in the rain, her blue sundress billowing in the gusts of wind as a team tried and failed to aim a rope-bridge device towards his yacht. She shouted something he couldn't hear, putting her hands out to take the device herself even as the men shook their heads.

'Don't you dare,' he hissed under his breath, frozen in place as he watched her take stance and aim. The rope bridge unfolded and she looked up, meeting his eyes with triumph.

'No, Minerva, stay there.' He launched himself down the ladder, determined to reach her before she began the dangerous journey across. It was a short distance, but still the slippery rope and plastic were treacherous and all it would take was one wrong foot…

Terror striking his heart, he bellowed again for her to remain on her side, but she had already begun to make her crossing.

Minerva could just barely hear Liro shouting over the noise of the wind, the waves and her own frantic heart-beat as she tried to be graceful in navigating her way across the rope bridge they'd secured between the two ships.

'Stay where you are, damn it!' Liro roared, his voice reaching her on a gust of wind. She looked up to see him climbing down from the top deck like a madman as a handful of his staff watched.

Minerva looked back towards the Coastguard ship to find it was much further away than she'd thought. She was pretty much halfway now. Her knees buck-led as her hands slid across the wet ropes, holding on tight with all the strength she had. She gritted her teeth, looking down at her sandalled feet moving one step at a time, until a wooden ledge appeared under her feet and she realised she had finally reached the other side. She barely had a moment to stand up before strong arms grabbed her, pulling her head up against a warm, hard chest. She didn't need to look up to know who it was—she knew Liro San Nicolau's heartbeat better than she knew her own.

'I told you to stay.' He growled, his hands in her hair as he tilted her head up to face him. 'You could have fallen to your death! You should have waited for me.'

'I'm the one who sent the full Arqaletan Coastguard to stop you from leaving me—the least I could do was let them stay dry.'

'You thought I was leaving you?'

'Well yes, considering arrived down at the dock to find your huge, hulking yacht disappearing into the horizon.'

'So you armed your own armada to stop me?' His eyes were wild. 'My crew needed supplies from the mainland before the storm hit—we were only planning to be gone for a couple of hours.'

'Oh.' Minerva grimaced. 'I suppose I overreacted slightly?'

Liro stared down at her for a long moment, then he laughed, deep, barrelling laughter that eventually made her laugh too. The wind whipped her hair across her face and Liro pulled it away, studying the long curls that swirled loose around her shoulders with a sudden thoughtfulness. For a moment, she wondered if he planned to kiss her, but then his hands dropped from her face and he took a step back. 'Tonight is a big night for you, for your mother… I know we argued, but I wouldn't have missed it.'

'She told me what you did today. What you're risking.'

She watched as his eyes darkened and felt a sliver of fear in her chest. A hint of doubt that maybe she had been foolish to assume he'd done all this for her out of love.

'Why did you do it?' she asked. 'Why not just go ahead with marrying me?'

'I wanted to offer us both another way.'

'I told you that I would not force you down the aisle.'

'There is no version of this life in which I would ever need to be *forced* to marry you, Min. Not then, not ever. I walked away from you once in an effort to save you, and in doing so I wasted fourteen years that I could have spent with you in my bed, in my arms, in my heart... I am selfish enough to grab this opportunity to make you my bride...but I loved you too much to have it happen this way.'

'Loved...as in past tense?' she asked. 'Because I know you loved me once and I came here to ask you if you could give me another chance. If you could love me again, the way I love you now.'

'Love...as in, every place, every time. Always.'

She threw away all her plans to be romantic and poised in her own declaration, throwing her arms around his hulking shoulders and pulling him down halfway to meet her lips. She kissed him with all the love she felt, all the fear and all the joy. She kissed him until the wind almost pushed them both overboard and the captain called out across an intercom for them to get inside to safety.

'Mad woman,' Liro drawled under his breath as he gripped her behind through her wet gown. 'I don't know anyone else who could have made that shot with a rope bridge in a thundering storm. You're terrifying when you're furious, you know that?'

She gasped as he climbed over her, tearing away her wet dress as if it was tissue, grumbling about her catching a chill. It was laughable to think her body would have the chance to get cold with him nearby. He had them both naked in minutes, his hot skin evaporating any rain water that dared to remain upon her.

'Ask me to marry you again.' She breathed as his hands began to travel down her stomach to where she craved him. 'Ask me to be your wife, Liro.'

She waited for his answer, her breath coming faster as his fingers found the centre of her and dipped in, drawing slow circles upon her right where she burned for him. Her practical mind argued that they should be fully clothed and serious as they discussed something as pivotal to their future. But, then again, so little about their relationship had ever followed the rules.

'God knows I have wanted nothing more in this life than to hear you beg me so prettily, *princesa*. But there is something that would make me happier.' He paused, a smile transforming his lips. 'I want to watch you become Queen in your own right, just as you have always dreamed of. When I propose to you…when I finally claim you in front of the world as my bride, my wife, my queen…it will be because that is what you want.'

'What if I want it right now?' she challenged.

'I'd obey, without a question, Your Highness.' He smirked, placing a kiss upon her breast with reverence. 'When are you going to realise it, Min? If you decided that you want to get married right here, right now, I would do it. I would wear the giant crown. I'd be paraded through the entire capital in the open carriage, no questions asked.'

She laughed, feeling joy burst through her fears as he kissed her again, deeper and softer than before. A kiss that was filled with promises.

'I like your plan better,' she whispered. 'It feels almost like a normal courtship.'

'I plan on sneaking you out for as many dates as I can manage, Your Highness.'

They had soaked the sofa through with their clothes, and the storm outside was only picking up with every moment, but in his arms she felt warm and secure. He leaned down, pressing his forehead against hers.

'I vow to you right here and now that, whatever our life needs to look like on the outside, you will have it. Because you have me. As long as we both shall live.'

EPILOGUE

QUEEN MINERVA OF ARQALETA was crowned in late November, after six months of already acting as Queen of the realm. Her mother, a monarch globally known for her stoic manner, sobbed throughout most of the ceremony and sought regular comfort from the handsome ginger-bearded man by her side. Once the rumours of the banished and formerly disgraced prince had surfaced, it seemed that the public had been more interested in their relationship than in his family's unhappy past— a fact that they had decided to use to their advantage, giving tactical teases about their passionate love affair while simultaneously insisting upon privacy.

Their numerous romantic getaways had dominated the headlines of most of the world's press, bringing an unprecedented amount of attention to their tiny kingdom during the transitional period after her mother's abdication. The fact that the new Queen was still as yet unmarried had not been an issue. In fact, her public approval ratings were now the highest of any new monarch in the kingdom's long history. It seemed that the people of Arqaleta had been hungry for change, and Minerva intended to give it to them. Her mother had not fully disappeared from palace life, of course, and still took part in monthly summits discussing the future of their beloved kingdom.

A weekend of festivities followed the coronation, with not one but two public holidays declared to celebrate the coronation.

'I didn't fidget with the crown once.' Minerva smiled at Liro as they finally returned to their private apartment in the palace, shutting the door on work for the day. Here, they were just Min and Liro, and that was the favourite rule they'd made up once they had formally moved in together last month. He was upon her in an instant, his hands deftly pulling the pins from her hair and massaging her scalp as he pressed his nose to her neck and inhaled deeply.

'I know these big events with all of the public adoration are a part of the job, but damn if it doesn't get any easier sharing you.' He growled, pulling her closer to claim her lips with his. They had not had a single private moment all day and Minerva groaned into the kiss, relaxing into his quiet strength. This was her favourite time of every day. Their passion for one another had not waned much in the wake of their tumultuous reunion—they'd already made love twice that morning before they'd had to begin to get ready for the ceremony. But that did not stop Liro from lifting her bodily into his strong arms and bounding through the apartment in the direction of their bedroom.

'I don't know if the carrying is approved in the handbook.' Minerva smirked, tracing the perfectly trimmed edge of Liro's beard with reverence. He smelled like sea air, adventure and home. Even now when they were living full-time at the palace he still managed to make every single day feel exciting and rich with possibility. Truly, every reigning monarch needed a brooding ginger pirate by her side.

He laid her down upon the bed, removing both her shoes and throwing them away without any care for propriety. Her stockings were removed next, and then the skirt of her gown rolled up around her hips.

'I can take off the dress.' She laughed as he growled with impatience, burrowing his head impatiently under the material.

'And ruin my fantasy?' he chided, disappearing fully beneath her gown.

'Wh-what is your fantasy?' she asked, shuddering as she felt his lips tracing a slow, determined path above her kneecap.

'My fantasy, Your Majesty…' he murmured, emphasising each word with another kiss, 'Is that one day, in the distant future, we see this coronation gown in the royal museum…and I get to lean down and remind my queen of the time that I brought her to the best orgasm of her life while she wore it.'

His words scandalised her in the best way and she opened more for him, watching as he laid claim to her body in the most primal way possible. Her intimate folds were spread wide and his eyes met hers, silently demanding that she watch him as he tasted her in slow, teasing strokes. His mouth conquered her slowly and completely, sending her into a haze of incoherent babbling within moments as she begged, 'Yes...' and, 'There...' and, 'Please, Liro, please...'

He knew just how to hold her right there, making her beg for just the right amount of time before granting her mercy. His name was wrung from her lips on a shocked cry as she fell apart, blissful waves crashing outwards through her body and leaving her boneless in a cloud of silk and tulle.

Happy Coronation Day, Queen Minerva, she thought with a giggle as she let her head drop back onto the bed.

Only then did he unzip her dress slowly and free her from the restrictive fabric. He had a strange look on his face as he undid each tiny button and hook on her complicated corset, his fingers stroking along her skin where it was marked from the pressure. Tears pricked her eyes as she realised he was always there to kiss her better in the aftermath of whatever her day had involved. He had become her own personal island kingdom in the sea of obligations and duty—her home.

Consumed with the need to reciprocate and show him just how treasured he was, she took advantage of his apparent distraction and flipped him onto his back, stranding him before he could protest.

'This was not part of my plan just yet...' He began to speak, stopping when she slowly angled herself to notch his impressive erection and rolled her hips in a tease. His eyes narrowed upon her, his breath leaving him on a low hiss as his head fell back onto the pillow in apparent surrender.

Minerva's victory was short-lived as their sensual haze was immediately interrupted by the sound of scrambling paws in the distance. Moments later, a small ball of honey-coloured fur bounded through the doorway in a chorus of high-pitched barks. Liro quickly covered them both with the coverlet just before the mischievous pup jumped up onto the bed to join them.

'Flecha, down!' Minerva made an attempt at a stern voice, trying not to laugh.

'I told you, now that you've let her sleep here once...' Liro chided, rubbing the ear of the excited pup while she made quick work of trying to chew Minerva's antique pearl earring from her ear.

'She missed us, didn't you, *mi amor*?' Minerva crooned, laughing as Flecha attacked Liro's foot under the covers.

An impromptu sailing break that she and Liro had taken along the northern coast of Cisneros the month before had ended with them finding a new-born pup abandoned on the beach. After taking the pup to a local shelter for medical attention, and confirming there was no owner missing their pet, Minerva had been surprisingly bereft at the idea of leaving her there.

Liro had been the one to suggest they adopt her and he had also suggested the winning name—Spanish for 'arrow'. Together they had worked their schedules so that one of them was always close to their newly renovated palace suite. But, for times when they were away, she had employed a royal dog-sitter just for the occasion. She watched as Liro beckoned the pup to come back to his side of the bed and tried not to laugh as he again tried to teach Flecha the 'sit' command.

'You know, *darling*, I am queen now...independently,

as planned,' she mused aloud, wondering how to broach the next subject without seeming completely overbearing. Which she knew she kind of was, but hadn't he said he loved her taking control?

Liro paused for a split second in his dog wrangling. 'Yes, I was there.'

'It's just… I was thinking… Well, actually, it was my mother who made the observation earlier that, while the people have been quite accepting of our unconventional union for the moment…'

Liro sat back, a strange smile on his lips. 'Are you okay?'

'I'm fine. I'm better than fine! I'm so happy, I truly am… I just kind of thought you'd have gone caveman by now and challenged me on the "no ring before the crown" agreement.' She lost her nerve, standing up to pace the room. 'It's unbearably selfish and ungrateful, because now I have the home and the crown, and even a puppy for goodness' sake, and I just—'

'Minerva!'

She snapped up her head, noticing the odd way that Liro was holding their squirming pup in place upon his lap. She looked closer and saw that a square pink box had been tied to Flecha's little pink collar.

'Oh, it's a… *Oh.*'

Liro tried not to burst into laughter as he realised he had succeeded in rendering the Queen of Arqaleta absolutely speechless. She took a step back, eyes wide above the perfectly manicured hands she'd clapped over most of her face to hide her shock. It was happy shock…he hoped, unless he'd read all the signs wrong. With only mildly shaking fingers, he removed the box from the pup's collar, throwing a treat on the floor to distract her for a moment. To his absolute delight, Minerva was still visibly reeling.

'You were trying to teach her to sit all week…for this?' she whispered.

'Sadly, it was a fruitless effort. Our dog has no sense of discipline.'

'How long have you been planning this?'

'If it had been up to me, I'd have had you wearing my ring from the moment you finally told me that you loved me. I still sometimes don't know how I've restrained myself. But I vowed to wait…to watch you become the queen you were born to be…before I asked you this one very important question.'

'Yes—the answer is yes.' She moved to reach for the ring then stopped, realising she'd interrupted him mid-speech. 'Oh, sorry… Continue.'

Liro laughed, expecting nothing less. Without breaking eye contact he sank down to one knee beside the bed, looking up at where she gloried above him in the lamplight. She had never looked more beautiful than she did at this moment, her cheeks still warmed by the afterglow of his ministrations. He had agonised over this proposal for weeks, wanting to make right all the wrongs of the first time. Wanting to give her the perfect moment she deserved…a moment worthy of a queen.

But, in the end, he'd realised that this was all that they needed—a moment that reflected who they were and who they might become as husband and wife. So long as she said yes, of course…

He took a deep breath, feeling the sheer weight of getting this moment right hit him square in his chest. 'Min, the past six months have made me happier than I had ever dreamed possible. You gave me a second chance; you gave us a second chance when most people would've simply given up. We haven't had the easiest path…but I wouldn't change it for the world.'

He opened up the box, revealing the ring that he'd had hand-designed by a jeweller in the old town. The design was a stunning gold band with a pear-shaped diamond, held in place by a swan-like symbol on one side and a graceful archer's bow on the other. The glitter in Minerva's eyes became full-on tears from the moment she saw the ring, so much so that he barely heard her gasping, 'Yes,' between wracking sobs.

'Yes?' he asked, holding her as she sank down onto her knees on their bedroom floor beside him.

'Yes!' she practically squealed, holding her hand out for him to slowly slide on the ring. Once he realised that it was a perfect fit, the bands of anxiety in his chest relaxed somewhat enough for him to claim her lips in a frantic kiss. She had worried that he would feel restricted by the return to royal life, when in reality he had never felt more at home anywhere in his life than he did in this palace.

As he looked down at his fiancée…his queen…he thanked destiny for sending them on this wayward path. He wouldn't have had it any other way.

* * * * *

THE BILLIONAIRE'S ACCIDENTAL LEGACY

MILLIE ADAMS

MILLS & BOON

CHAPTER ONE

JESSIE HARGREAVE HAD been taught to believe that there were two kinds of people. The *frightened* and the *frightening.*

Raised by a narcissistic, sociopathic millionaire crime lord, she and her sister Maren had been taught to hold the wants and needs of others in low esteem. All that mattered—all that could ever matter—was what *you* wanted. And what you could manipulate others into giving you.

Their soft, flighty mother had never been able to stand up to their father, and eventually she'd gone away. Off to greener pastures with easier rich men who didn't demand quite so much in return for a life of luxury.

That left Jessie and her sister behind.

"I am frightened now. And we aren't frightening," she could remember Maren whispering tearfully after she sneaked into Jessie's room the night their mother had left.

Poor Maren, who had the same peculiar mind as Jessie but with the focus skewed less toward facts and numbers and more toward human frailty and emotion. It overwhelmed poor Maren at times. Jessie felt like protecting her sweeter, softer sister was her greatest mission.

Eighteen months younger than she was, Maren was her baby sister, and Jessie would die for her if need be.

She just felt having minds like theirs meant no one should

have to do anything half so dramatic as dying. They'd been given the gift of great thought. So they ought to be able to use it to solve their own problems.

"There must be a secret third option."

She'd said that so pragmatically she'd believed herself instantly.

"What is it, Jessie?"

"I don't know. I'll figure it out."

And so she had. They had.

They were neither frightened nor frightening. They had learned to thrive in the shadowy space between extremes.

They had become gray opportunists who used the frailties of those who fancied themselves as *frightening* against them.

Jessie hardly saw herself as Robin Hood, though she did *only* rob the rich. It was just she wasn't handing out alms to the poor. Unless she considered *herself* a member of the poor. And hey, for a long time, she had been.

But she wasn't now. Neither was her sister, thanks to all their work.

They'd spent the past three years playing in casinos and private high-stakes poker tournaments, amassing wealth, gambling it and turning it into yet more wealth.

This game was the last game.

She hadn't learned much from her father, other than what a person ought not to do.

She and Maren had decided at twelve and thirteen that they wouldn't be part of their father's games, but they'd also decided they'd have to have a clear path to escape before they tried to make a move.

Their father was like them. He didn't miss anything. They'd have one shot; it would have to be perfect. They'd had to get IDs—their father had never provided them with any—birth certificates, falsified naturally—and figure out where they would stay.

They squirreled their contraband beneath the floorboards of their bedroom in their father's compound, and then finally, they'd made a real plan of escape.

Their father used them to exploit banking systems—that was his world. He had an obscene amount of money and made more loaning it to people he could exploit for favors.

He used Maren and Jessie to help with those things.

Jessie could remember when her father had asked her to get all the info she could from talking to a certain man at a train station, and she had. She'd pretended to be lost and he'd talked to her to calm her down.

"His name is Marcus," she'd told her father. *"He has a granddaughter he loves very much. Her name is Eloise. She and her parents live in London."*

If only she'd known then how her father would use that information.

The images still haunted her. Every image did.

So she'd done what she always did. She used her brain to solve her problems.

She'd centered herself, and she'd gone into a big room in her mind and imagined a ribbon, made of pretty blue silk. She'd imagined it was tied to her feelings, connecting her thoughts to them. She'd taken out a pair of gleaming scissors and cut that ribbon. Severing it entirely.

She didn't need feelings anyway.

She and Maren had escaped five years ago, finally, at seventeen and eighteen. She had purpose. She didn't need feelings.

They would *not* be frightened.

They would *not* be poor. They would never be vulnerable or endangered, *ever.*

They would use every asset they had to make themselves safe and secure, to play their way to the kind of lives they really wanted.

They had also decided that there would have to be an endgame.

Because once you were willing to dip your toe into the murky waters of theft and con artistry, it was easy to lose yourself. Easy to drown. That was where crime lords came from. It was how your morals began to strip themselves away entirely.

She could not ever allow herself to be quite so lost.

So this was it. The last show.

Their long con had been shockingly easy. Because they were new, they were young and they were women. Beautiful women, at that.

It wasn't vanity for her to think so. Beauty was nothing but a well-fitted dress and some brightly colored makeup. In these circles, beauty could be put on and taken off like a costume, with relative ease.

No one was looking deeply at the features of her face. They were looking at her bold red lip and her cleavage. End of story.

The cleavage went a long way in ensuring she was underestimated. By all those men who were so sure they were smarter, better.

Men who believed that they could read any room. And above all else, men who believed they would always triumph.

She didn't feel guilty about it.

If you gambled, you might lose. And when you underestimated an opponent on sight, you were a fool.

That was one saying she did believe to be true: a fool and his money were soon parted.

And if she was the instrument of that grand divorce, all the better.

Especially when it ended up in her pocket.

But they had decided there would be a limit.

This exclusive poker game had been an absolute mission to gain an invite to. Partly because she and her sister were not notorious.

That was important.

They had done their very best to move beneath the radar. They didn't want to draw the attention of their father, and in general Jessie found the concept of painting a target on your back foolish.

Young women getting big prizes at poker games might have been headline grabbing, were they not haunting private games, games played by royalty, by criminals. People who did not wish to have attention shown upon their habits.

They weren't masters of disguise; they didn't have to be.

A change in gown color, hair color and makeup meant that they were rarely remarked upon. They also hadn't played the same crowd twice.

Tonight would be different. Tonight would be high profile. And that was why tonight was the end.

But if they won, it would be by far their biggest score, and they would be able to be done with all of this.

To truly begin again.

Or rather, for the first time. A life that was theirs. Truly theirs.

It was Maren who had caught wind of tonight's game. A secret poker game being played at an old English estate house out in the countryside.

Invitation only.

Maren's special skill was her softness. She was lush and pretty and had wide, round eyes that always looked just a little bit wounded. Men loved a wounded bird. She would sigh and listen to them and express sympathy, and they would give her the world.

She'd been working at a gentlemen's club when she'd heard about the game.

She'd taken the job for information, of course. It could never be said that she or Maren had ever done an *honest* day's work in their lives.

Honest work didn't pay well enough.

Maren had the ability to get info out of anyone, using her soft voice and very large eyes. She was so good at seeming stupid. But then, was it their fault people often perceived the hallmarks of femininity as less? Maren used that, and she used it well.

She wasn't a siren; she was the sweet, childlike one who needed to be shepherded along. And if she could be shepherded to lucrative poker tournaments...then all the better.

They weren't pickpockets. That was base.

And far too small.

With feigned interest, and a couple of well-placed giggles, Maren had found out about *this* game.

And about the invitation. And with her photographic memory, had committed the layout of the invitation to memory. As well as the particulars of how the invitations were disseminated and whether or not they would be able to make a counterfeit.

In the end, Jessie had taken the information and contacted the assistant of the organizer of the event, and managed to convince her to send out an invitation to her and her sister's aliases, on the pretense that their uncle had told them about the game. Of course, they had all of their fake uncle's details as well. Including the serial number on the ticket.

She smoothed her silver dress, and it shimmered over her curves like liquid metal.

Maren was in gold tonight, all the better to set off her red hair—fake, of course.

They were not there to look like sisters. Jessie had naturally dark brown hair, which for the night had been dyed black.

Maren's hair was a lighter shade of brown that skewed cinnamon nicely.

They would be playing in different halls tonight, at different tables. There was no point competing against each other.

Jessie knew just who she wanted to play today.

Ewan Kincaid. The Duke of Kilmorack.

A *duke*. It was so archaic and hilarious. He had spent the past few years whoring his riches out to any old table, disgracing his title and his father's name. He won vast sums, and was considered by many to be the best card player in high-stakes games. He was a wretched playboy. A debauched, dissolute gambler.

And absolutely the most beautiful man Jessie had ever seen.

She did her best not to think of him, but God help her, she did. Ever since she'd seen him for the first time in person.

She'd seen photos of him before, of course—he was infamous. Which was why that day on the casino floor fourteen months ago, she'd known instantly who he was.

But she hadn't been prepared for the impact of him.

Hadn't been able to forget.

He had been on the casino floor, not in a closed back room but in public for all to see. He liked a show. She did not. She'd been haunting the edges of that particular casino, hoping to sneak into a high-roller room, and there he was.

Head and shoulders above everyone around him, dressed in a close-cut black suit that showed off broad shoulders and a lean waist. He was devastating to her sanity. To her desire to be something other than what she had long feared she might be.

Wicked.

Across the room, their eyes collided. There was no other word for it. And in that moment a reel of fantasies she'd never had before played through her mind like a symphony. Building, building, exploding.

Images of his hands on her body. His broad shoulders without a suit jacket on...

He had consumed her from that moment.

She'd seen him again from afar in Monaco the next month. She'd made sure to keep her distance from him. She'd stared, from the upper floor in the casino down to where he was, until he turned and she'd run away.

Her breathing had been labored, her heart beating fast. Not from physical exertion.

From him.

And then there was Capri.

She'd been in a high-roller room at a table of whales, and she'd been winning. And he'd come and taken his position at another table. He'd seen her.

And later when she'd gone to collect her winnings, he'd followed her out.

"I know you."

It had been a singular moment. She'd been seen. And it was like that neatly trimmed blue ribbon had fashioned itself together in that moment, her heart taking flight along with her imagination.

Her breath had caught. *"You don't. I'm no one."*

"You were in Las Vegas. A few months back."

"I've never been to Vegas."

A lie. She'd been born in Reno. She'd been to Vegas more times than she could count. Even before all this.

And she'd been mesmerized by his eyes.

Blue. But on one side a fleck of green. On the other, gold.

"Liar."

"You have me confused with someone else."

"I am never confused."

He'd touched her then. The edge of his finger skimming her bare arm.

"I have to go. I have a prize to collect," she said.

"I wouldn't be opposed to adding myself to the prize packet."

Her heart had started pounding so hard she'd been dizzy.

"Not tonight."

And again, she'd run.

She'd acted like the *frightened.*

And she'd never wanted to be frightened.

It was one reason tonight she felt like she needed to conquer him. He'd scared her. He was under her skin.

She wanted him.

And she wanted to run from him.

Here she was, hoping to best him.

She had not, of course, said anything to her sister about his beauty.

Or her opinion on it.

They had rules about men.

Very strict rules. And she was...pushing things. She knew it.

She knew that she would have to start at an early round table, and that the likelihood of being placed with him immediately was low.

In fact, she wasn't entirely certain she would be put in his tier. But she had no problem putting herself there.

Her body went languid just thinking of being near him again.

She swept through the grand manor and took a glass of champagne off the tray. She was allowed three sips of champagne, and the rest of the night she simply mimicked the act of drinking.

One thing she had learned was that your behavior had to blend. Melt seamlessly in with the people around you.

They were narcissists. Every last one of them. All humans were. To one extent or another. And they were always much more concerned with their own behavior than with yours. But it was important that they didn't feel you challenge their behavior. To make declarations about not drinking made others uncomfortable. Who were constantly then attempting to justify their actions and paint them as being inside normality.

And so Jessie pretended to drink. In fact, she found it was a boon because the more she drank, the more those around her often felt comfortable drinking. And she was always happy to have her opponents' wits slightly addled.

Not that she needed it.

She could win even if everyone was playing their best. But what she didn't want them to note was why she won. And how she did so with ease.

She always lost a couple of times. Enough to throw off suspicion.

She sidled up to the waiter. Not one of the waitresses, and not one of the straight men. She knew exactly who to speak to. She needed someone who wouldn't feel threatened by her beauty, but also wouldn't want it for himself.

"I know that we are not supposed to do this, but do you know which table Ewan Kincaid is playing at?"

The man looked at her, and his eyebrows lifted. "If you know you're not supposed to do it, why are you doing it?"

"I'm sorry." She tried to look both ditzy and overcome. "I have a bit of a crush on him. And I just want to make sure that I can sit at his table for a moment. I'm not very good. Honestly, I'm only here to…you know."

His smile went naughty. "You want to get lucky."

"I do," she said, smiling.

Definitely not in the way he meant. But yes. She was here to get lucky.

"He's been placed in the West Wing game. It's really high stakes. But he is…"

"So hot, right? I'm not worried. I can buy my way into any of these rooms. I was invited, after all."

"And you're just here to throw it away on a night in his bed?"

"I hear he's worth it."

"He definitely looks like he is, but you know he gives it away for free."

"No one gives anything *good* away for free."

"I suppose that's true."

She put her hand on his forearm. "Thanks. So much."

She wiggled away from him, unable to take large steps in the very tight dress.

Hopefully, he wouldn't get in any trouble. But the exchange had been brief enough. She had not been placed in the West Wing. But she managed to talk her way past the door, and get a seat set up, all by giggling and claiming it was because of her little crush.

Her fingers tingled. She felt alive right now. She was so good at this.

She was…

She was done.

After this she was done. They'd agreed.

If she won tonight, she'd won the whole game. She had to remember that.

At the end of this she would have a whole new life. So much money. And she would never gamble any of it again.

This was the game they'd been planning for two years now. Win, invest. Win, invest. In clothes, and access to the right rooms. In the ability to have enough money to buy their way into the games in the first place.

But this was the thing with gambling. So Maren reminded her. Eventually, you had to call it good. Had to call it a day. And you had to walk away.

Especially when you gambled the way they did.

Her father was brilliant. He could've used his brain for anything. But the problem was, he was more than a narcissist. He was a sociopath, and he enjoyed testing people. He needed to do it. He was smarter than everyone else and he was desperate to prove it.

They weren't the same.

She was nearly certain.

Sure, she got satisfaction out of winning, but she didn't need to do it. She wanted to be happy. She wanted to be comfortable.

She wanted to be *free*.

And if she felt a tug of sadness over losing this...

The thrill of a mark. The thrill of the chase...

Well, she wouldn't dwell on it.

This wasn't a charity game, and no one here was playing for any reason other than that they could. They treated their wealth lightly, and they treated the lives of others as if they were nothing.

Ewan Kincaid was a fantastic example of that. His family name was old, respected, and he dragged it through the mud.

His industry was debauchery.

Bars and party yachts and exclusive clubs where the very rich could act out their wildest fantasies.

Everything about him was a scourge on respectability.

If she had come from a family like his, she would've treated it with some care. He respected nothing, including his fortune. Which he now slung hither and yon with as much care as his penis.

None whatsoever.

He was not discerning.

She reminded herself of that when his face presented itself clearly in her mind's eye. He was a rake.

It shouldn't excite her.

Just like gambling shouldn't excite her.

But both did.

She sat down at her assigned table, and smiled at the men around her.

Ewan was not among them; he must be at one of the other tables in the room, but that didn't matter. It was perfect. She was opening at a table of all gray-haired men who would assume she was even younger than she was, and likely twice as dumb.

She played it up, giggling and making her movements seem nearly childish.

Men loved that.

A woman who acted like a girl but had big boobs. She and Maren had gotten their minds from their father. And their figures from their mother. And she supposed in the absence of any moral character, she should be thankful for those two gifts they had received from their parents.

Because those assets certainly made cons easier.

She lost the first hand deliberately. And then won all over the next two games, advancing to the next table.

Where she cut a swath through the tournament like a shark.

There was so much money. So very much money.

And finally, the room was down to one table. And when she sat down, she felt as if the entire world had been tilted on its axis.

Because there he was.

And no amount of press coverage, of illicitly taken viral videos of him caressing women on dance floors of his clubs, or photographs of him in the media could prepare for the impact of him in person.

Her memory was perfect.

And even her memory hadn't captured this.

The man was an absolute thirst trap. Which was public knowledge.

But that was all looks. A still photo could never capture this.

The magnetism.

His dark brown hair was pushed off his forehead, and she could see strands of gray, just there at his temples, adding an air of sophistication to the man sitting before her. His blue eyes held anything but sophistication. They were wicked. And filled with promises that made her feel overheated.

The lines around his eyes spoke of secret smiles shared with countless lovers. And she trembled. He didn't move, and she tried, tried her very best, to remain still, and yet could not. She had a will of iron. She always had. Her brain was always a flurry of activity. It was like that when you could remember everything. Unavoidable.

And yet, because of her memory, it was very difficult to surprise her. She'd seen him before, after all.

Her observational skills were unparalleled. And the speed at which she synthesized all the images in her brain made it so she was always one step ahead.

But right now she was breathless. Right now there was no thought beyond him.

And she could not recall a time when she held just one single thought, not ever, not once in her whole life.

"Hello there," he said, that rough Scottish accent making her feel as warm as it had the first time she'd heard it.

He knew her.

She could see that.

She pretended.

"Hello," she said, allowing herself to blush. It was the easiest thing.

The easiest thing ever, as she searched his face. She'd memorized every detail the first time she'd seen him. It was what she did.

Every line, every minute piece of him.

And yet, now she did it again. As if she was committing him to memory for the first time.

The green fleck in his left eye, the gold in his right.

The slight impression of a scar on the right side of his upper lip. Not a razor blade. Nothing surgical. A fight. She knew exactly what a scar that came from a fist hitting flesh looked like.

She knew what her memory, what her words, could bring about.

She knew what it sounded like when a girl was being tortured for the sins of her grandfather.

You saved her.

At least there's that.

But she'd been caused pain, and that couldn't be erased.

Her eyes dropped down to his hands, the way he touched the deck of cards.

Ewan touched her once...

No, that wasn't what she should be thinking of.

He wasn't the dealer. You did not deal your own cards in a game this high stakes. And yet, he was touching the deck of cards and no one had tried to stop him.

"Can I get your name?" He was looking at her as if she was the only other person at the table. There were others.

With her peripheral vision she had taken in every detail of their appearance. They did not signify. They did not register.

It was him and only him.

And she saw something just then. A light in those eyes. A brighter glint to the cold. Something sharper in the green.

He moved around like he was a feckless playboy, like he chanced into his winnings, but he didn't.

She could see it.

He was a predator, this man.

And he made her shiver.

She watched his hands closely, seeing if anything came out of his sleeves. If there were any extra cards.

"Cat got your tongue, my beauty?"

"No," she said, forcing herself to meet his gaze. "I confess I'm a bit overwrought. You are quite famous."

Her words were breathy, and incredibly false, and she had to wonder if he could sense that.

Maybe he didn't recognize her.

Her hair had been red when they'd last met.

"Overwrought?" His mouth quirked upward. "You don't seem the type."

"Surely that's something you're used to. Women losing their powers of speech when in your presence."

"Yes. But there isn't usually a card table between us then. In fact, there's usually nothing between us by the time their speech fails them."

She couldn't control her response to him. And she controlled everything.

She was not inexperienced with men by accident.

On the contrary, she knew everything there was to know about men in an academic sense.

But she and her sister had rules. An agreement.

The problem with a mind like theirs was that they did hang on to every detail.

Trauma, they had decided, would be a particular beast when one couldn't forget. They'd already had their share.

They were far too clear on everything that had ever happened in their childhoods. They did not need to go tempting memories of an infatuation. Of heartbreak.

Sexual encounters that would burn each minute detail into their brains.

That would always live there. In that vast catalog of drawers in the back of her head.

Her sister had a *mind palace*.

Jessie thought it was a stupid name. And she thought it was a waste of imagination. Her sister kept all of her memories in a great library in a castle out in the middle of the sea. It was all bright and airy and *pink*.

Maren was a romantic. Maren was *good*.

Jessie was more pragmatic. Sometimes she worried if her sister was good, she might be wicked. So she leaned into the organizational aspects of her personality rather than the wickedness. She liked a file cabinet. And alphabetizing.

Not a color-coded organization system that made absolutely no sense.

He was red, she decided just then, and she was annoyed.

She didn't want to assign a color to him.

Red was intrusive. Strong. It was passion. Anger.

And she knew right then he would be filed under red forever, and she was deeply, deeply irritated about it.

Maren would think it was hilarious.

This was why they had rules about men.

An agreement. Until they had succeeded in getting themselves secure, they stayed well away from them.

The risk was too high. For them especially.

They could not afford to be compromised before they had finished.

Before they were safe. Before they were secure.

"I have to confess," she said, hoping that this would throw him off. And make him complacent about her skills. "I might have worked my way into this room just to sit with you. I'm a fan."

"Well, then, I'll be sure to sign something for you later."

His eyes caught hers, and held.

Everything in her went still.

Her throat dry and scratchy.

"Aren't you going to take the cards from him?" she asked the dealer.

She'd betrayed more of herself then than she would have liked.

"Of course," said the dealer, removing the cards from the center of the table. Was everyone under his spell? No one seemed concerned.

He lifted a brow in question. And she tried to simper.

"Just wanted to make sure you don't have anything up your sleeve," she said, trying to keep her tone sweet.

"I never have anything secreted away except for an extra bottle of whiskey. You have no need to worry."

No. She decided then that he wouldn't cheat. Not like that. It would be clumsy and inelegant.

But there were other ways. And she knew them all.

Gameplay began. The cards were dealt. And bidding began.

He was relaxed. And he didn't have a tell. But she was keeping track of where the cards were.

And everyone else had easy tells.

By process of elimination, she had figured out several hands.

When the dealer dealt the cards, all she had to do was keep watch on the edges.

It was easy for her to approximate where they then folded and who they went to. What was still in the deck and what might still be at hand.

It required concentration, but if she lost it at any point, she could simply call back the image in her mind.

Right now Ewan had a particularly good hand.

There were a couple of cards she could not account for,

of course, but she had a fair idea of everything that was happening.

And so, when the bidding became intense, she folded.

She would have one more round to take all.

And this was where things became complicated.

Knowing when to trade. When to hold. When to fold.

He won, quickly and decisively. And he took the pot to himself.

Good. Let him think it would go his way.

Her adrenaline spiked.

Several left the table. Done for the evening.

Two were eliminated.

And there she remained. Her heart beating faster, her blood singing. She was doing it. Like she always did. It felt so good.

Winning.

The next hand went out.

She nearly breathed a sigh of relief. She almost had a full house. One card short. And if she traded... It was still there. It was in the deck.

"I'll take one," she said.

She slid the card forward.

And the one that came back to her was exactly what she had hoped for.

She kept her face impassive, and then allowed her forehead to pucker. Let him wonder.

Bidding began in earnest with many more people making trades.

Another round, three folded.

The pot was growing, bigger and bigger.

She was getting to the top of her budget.

And suddenly, it was just her and him. Seated across from each other with chips in between them. Her whole future riding on this moment and yet...

Right now the moment felt bigger than her future. It was just her and him. This man she'd set out to conquer. This man who haunted her.

You'll either lose everything or you're finished.

She was finished either way. She'd vowed to be finished.

She didn't have any more money to gamble with. Any more and she would be reaching into Maren's pot, and she had no way of knowing how steep of a game her sister was involved in.

They were the only two left.

She prayed he would call.

"I raise you," he said.

The amount of money he raised exceeded what she had. By so much it was impossible.

She could win this. She wouldn't fold.

She wouldn't lose.

And that meant… That meant it was time to take a risk.

"I… I see you," she said, her eyes locking with his. "And I raise you…my body."

CHAPTER TWO

IT WAS HER. He knew the moment he saw her. The woman from the casinos, all those months ago. Months in between, and he had not forgotten her. He couldn't. She'd changed her appearance. Her makeup, her hair, the style of dress. She'd altered her appearance all three times he'd seen her and still he'd known.

You could not cover the electricity that arced between them with a change of hair color. He'd seen her that first time on the casino floor and it had been like a match strike against the hardest part of him.

But it was more than sex.

He could have sex anytime he wanted. But this… This was something more.

She intrigued him.

And it took a lot to intrigue him.

She was a bold thing. And there was something else to her, and had been from the moment they'd met.

She saw him.

Ewan had been an emotional child. He'd been filled with sadness, laughter, anger and above all else, hope.

His mother had died and he'd wept until he couldn't breathe, and then his father had beaten him until his tears had mixed with blood.

He'd stopped showing how much he cared that day.

And he'd begun plotting revenge.

The facade of the playboy was a perfect one. People underestimated him. It was how he'd made his own private fortune in investments. In the beginning people were always willing to sell to him for a bargain-basement price and think they were fleecing him.

Ewan had come out on top, every time.

He laughed easily, he smiled, he made merry with every woman he encountered, but it was a surface kind of pleasure.

When he'd touched *her*, it had gone down to his bones.

She had ignited an intensity in him he'd thought long banished.

For her part, she'd seemed nervous, and he could see that she had also tried to make him feel certain she was ditzy.

She'd had different energy the other times he'd seen her, and he knew she was nothing that she appeared to be on the surface.

The woman was like a lure, twisting beneath the surface of a loch. Sun catching her sparkles and making her shine.

There was a hook buried in there, though, he knew.

She was not dithery and she wasn't inexperienced at cards. She was brilliant. Sharp. She had taken every man at the tables to get here, and she would take him, too.

He would ensure it.

Ewan Kincaid was an expert at reading people. And all of their desires.

He was certain of two things when it came to this woman.

She was a liar. And she wanted him.

She had from the very first.

And she was not at all what she seemed to be.

"You are offering…?"

"One night. My body. Whatever you wish." She looked at

him from beneath her lashes and he could see glitter there. Not just attraction. Something else.

She knew she was going to win so her offer wasn't sincere.

And yet, it was.

She would have him, if they were alone. She wanted him, desperately, and that was the only honest thing on her face.

"Unorthodox. Imagine if Sir William was still in the game."

"He is not," she said. "You are. It is a specific bet. For you to win…or lose."

She said it with no clear hint of provocation and that, in and of itself, was a red flag to a bull. She was so cool. A mystery. An intrigue.

All so hard to come by for his jaded palate.

"I see. So you have no more money."

"I confess, I find myself unable to raise you." She didn't sound worried. She seemed cool. Collected. At ease.

She wasn't afraid to lose, which meant she knew she wouldn't.

Or she wanted him that badly. But with the amount of money at stake, he doubted it.

He did not have a reputation for coming at a high cost.

"You may have to forfeit the game, then. Because I could simply offer more money. But then, that would require I determine the set value of your body."

"This is unorthodox," said the dealer.

Men like him were not paid to deal in the unorthodox. Thank God Ewan's life was more interesting than that.

"You do not have to facilitate," Ewan said, looking at the man. "The lady and I will work out our own terms."

Everyone around the table was staring at them, hushed. Watching this woman prostitute herself.

But then, she had said that she'd attempted to get to his

table. Was it for this purpose? Was this all an attempt to seduce him? Because this was quite a lot more work than most women put in to get into his bed.

He was notoriously easy.

He was a man who liked to party. A man who liked the pleasures of the flesh in all ways.

He liked women. He liked sex.

In vanilla and every other flavor that might be on offer.

All she would've had to do was walk in and ask for sex; he'd have given it to her.

He was hungry. Always. For every experience that might be out there. So it could only be that.

Plus, she was far too good at playing cards.

Far too good.

She was a card counter. That made sense.

The way that she looked at him, and everything else, was sharp and astute. He'd have likely lost to her even if he had *not* intended to lose tonight. His next offer had always been one he'd intended to make. Losing the estate was his goal, and doing so in a way that would make headlines.

It was a shame he had no intention of taking victory here. Because he wouldn't mind winning her body.

"You're right. It is impossible to volley with something of equal monetary value. And so my return offer is this. Upon my father's death, my title and my estate."

Her response to that was imperceptible. As he knew it had to be.

If she appeared surprised, or too eager, then it would be easy for the casual observer to see that she was certain she had a win on her hands. She was very good, this woman.

If she lost, she would be his for the night.

But he did not think she would.

He had, by design, lost a good deal of money over the past few months. It mattered little to him. Money was easily had. The entire point was to make it look as if he was on the verge of a breakdown. That he was careening right off the edge of a cliff, and that he would take his dying father's title and empire with him. The old man only had a couple of weeks left. Long enough to see him lose the estate. Long enough to know that it would be leaving the family. They had an archaic inherited title that meant nothing.

But he had already vowed to his old man that he would never have a child, never pass the estate on. The bloodline would end with him.

Of that he would make sure.

"I call," she said.

"Then put your cards on the table."

And when she did, a gasp went through the room.

She had done it.

She was dizzy. She could hardly breathe. She had won and the triumph of it was intoxicating beyond reason.

She had won.

She had won the game.

She had won his estate. His title. She wasn't even sure such a thing was possible. She was a woman.

And this was not the eighteen hundreds.

But it didn't matter.

And he was not... He was not disappointed.

She could see it.

Yes, he was affecting a laissez-faire sort of attitude. The posture of the kind of man who didn't care whether he won or lost anything.

But he didn't care. He had lost by design. And he had lost this very particular prize by design.

Against her will, she found herself intrigued by him.

Even as she was trying to grapple with the fact that she had just won millions of dollars. And an estate.

She had a home.

After all these years, Jessie Hargreave had a home.

And they really could be finished. Even if Maren didn't win her game.

"Congratulations, Miss…"

"Lockwood," she said. "Jessica Lockwood."

She found it best to keep the first name as close as possible to her actual name.

Anyway, the world was littered with Jessicas.

But her last name was one of her many aliases.

"Thank you," she said to the dealer.

"Your winnings will be wired to the bank account information that you provided earlier. As to the rest of the… unconventional bet. That will be up to you and the duke."

He grinned at her, slow and lazy.

She needed to find her sister.

"Have the other games concluded?"

The man checked his watch. "No. There is a particularly fierce game going on in the East Wing. It does not look as if it will conclude anytime soon."

"Thank you."

She didn't necessarily wish to go and connect herself to Maren. So they would have to convene when they could.

And she was grateful in some ways that this moment was hers and hers alone.

She loved her sister. Her sister was never tempted to bask in these sorts of moments. She was never tempted to glory in the wrong things. Jessie couldn't say the same for herself.

And when she looked at Ewan Kincaid, she felt like indulging in the wicked even more than usual.

Her heart was thundering hard. She had bet herself. Her body. She had known she wouldn't lose. With almost complete certainty.

There was that possibility. That small possibility. That she might've lost. And she would've honored the bet.

The very idea sent a jolt of something sensual through her. She had never been touched intimately by a man before. Had never kissed one.

She wanted to.

She and Maren had worked so hard, all this time, and Maren had been very clear they needed to draw lines, and Jessie agreed. She did.

But she was tempted. And this was the last night, the last hurrah. The last window.

She should be overjoyed to walk away, and while on some level she was, while she was buzzing with the absolute triumph of all that she had just achieved, she felt sorrow as well. For this was where she shone.

It was where she was the best. She wasn't afraid here. She wasn't small. Not the insignificant unwanted daughter of a crime lord who had wanted a son, but had seen value in herself and her sister because of their minds.

No, she was using her mind on her own terms, and using it to benefit her.

It made her feel good. She could admit that now, without her sister close by her.

It thrilled her. Hell, a win like this turned her on.

And sitting across from the man who had ignited her imagination from the moment she had first seen him…

This was it. She would never run into him again. She would have no reason to. But tonight she would have reason to convene with him privately regarding her win. They would be alone…

"Shall we adjourn?" she said.

"Anxious?" he asked.

His manner was smooth. Unruffled. He didn't seem to care that he had just lost…everything.

"Yes. I would hate for you to back out. You seem awfully resigned for a man who has just lost his title and his estate."

The corner of his mouth lifted upward. "You assume that I care about those things."

"I suppose when you have so much it's easy to disavow the care of something others would find essential."

He ignored that.

"I have a suite of rooms upstairs. You will join me there. Perhaps for a drink as well as a discussion."

"Yes. I would like that."

He stood, and her mouth went dry. She had forgotten how tall he was. How broad.

He was nothing like the other men here. Who were either overstuffed with their imports and rich foods or self-consciously lean in a testament to their dedication at finding some sort of meaning of life in fitness. Accomplished from cycling in too-fitted Lycra and days spent playing pickleball.

But not so, Ewan Kincaid.

Who looked as if he spent his days out in fields lifting boulders. Moving them about the Highlands.

The Highlands.

Scotland.

That would be where his home was. His ancestral dwelling.

She had never been to Scotland.

It was, she thought, such a fascinating thing to have inherited. And it was the kind of decisive victory she could not have ever dreamed of. Not only had she more money than she'd ever seen in her life, but she also had a home.

He moved to her, putting his hand on her lower back, and everything in her went molten.

It was as if someone had reached inside her and taken everything she knew and squeezed it down tightly in their hand, so that it became small.

And she became reckless.

She would never be here again. Never have this moment again. Where she was the winner. She had claimed victory over him. And why could he not be her prize as well?

She had been prepared to surrender her body to him on the very off chance that she had lost the match.

In fact, part of her had been excited by it.

It was that sort of wickedness that she had always been afraid lurked in her veins.

And it did. In this moment it did. It was burning to the surface. Why not indulge it?

Because this was why they had decided they had to end the charades. It became too much a part of who you were.

If this was her last moment to be wicked, then why not dive in? Put her head under water. Drown in it.

They wove their way through the crowd, and into an elevator.

Everyone had been looking at them, but pretending they were not.

"What is your real name?" he asked, when the doors closed on them.

"I told you my name."

"It is not your name. I've seen you before." The breath left her body. "This is what you do. And your name is not Jessica Lockwood."

"Does it matter what my name is?"

"You want legal ownership of the estate? This is not money wired into your fake account. You want your name on the deed."

She froze. "I cannot have my name easily found. I'm certain you will understand."

"I'm happy to wrap it up in a business of some kind. But your legal name ought to be buried somewhere in there, don't you think?"

"I'm nobody. Nobody to you. But I am somebody who might be harmed if I'm found by the wrong person."

"A con artist."

"Nothing about what I did was a con. I beat you."

"But how?"

She lifted her chin. "By having better cards than you."

"Yes, that would be the assumed way. But you also won the game at the casino in Vegas. In Capri. And then again in Monte Carlo."

"You saw me."

"I always see you." It was like the world stopped, right then. And she would be just fine if it never started again. His voice lowered, his eyes meeting hers. "Redhead, brunette." He reached out and touched her hair. "Raven's wing. It doesn't matter. You are not an easy woman to forget."

She was a woman who couldn't forget. She had often wondered what it would be like to have the sort of brain that protected you from trauma. From pain. That shielded you from what you'd seen or heard.

She would never know.

She had a clear accounting of all of it, filed away forever. A constant cluttering of details in her mind, no matter what.

But she would be happy to remember this.

To remember him telling her that she was hard to forget.

"If I give you my name, you must swear you will not let it get out. You must protect me."

"Darling, this will be in the news."

She knew that what he said was true, and that there was no way around it.

"And that's fine. My father... My father will not pay attention to a news story about the duke losing his family home, but if my name appears..."

"Jessica Lockwood will be your name as far as the public is concerned. But I want to know your real name."

Just then the doors opened. They walked out into an empty hall, and he paused in front of the door, pressing a key card to it, and she heard the lock give.

They walked into a modern-looking penthouse, so different than the rest of the estate home.

But clearly, the upstairs had been remodeled as a place for guests to stay.

"You have my word," he said, turning to face her. "I have no wish to harm you."

"Why would I believe that? Why would I believe it given that you just lost a game today, and you accused me of being a con artist?"

He treated her to another wicked grin. "Because one con artist recognizes another."

She scoffed. "You're not that good."

"I'm only not that good if I intended to win. Tonight... Tonight I intended to lose. My entire life is a con, lass. Make no mistake."

The way he said that, the way his Scottish accent rolled over the syllables, sent a shiver through her body.

This was all so dangerous, and the danger of it made her heart beat faster, but not with fear.

She wanted to remember tonight.

She wanted this last night to be bold and bright forever.

"Keep me safe," she whispered, "and you can have what you failed to win."

He lifted a brow, and then walked over to a bar in the corner. He picked up a decanter of whiskey, poured a measure of it and took a drink. "Are you offering me your body?"

She lifted her chin. "Yes."

"What sort of man do you take me for that you think you might need to trade sex for safety?"

"A man."

He took a step toward her, his eyes never leaving hers

even as he took another drink of whiskey. "No. Darling, you're welcome to give me your body because you wish to give it. Because you cannot say no to the desire that has taken you over. But you will not trade me for your safety. I am the most debauched man on the continent. I can have whoever I wish. Whenever I wish. I do not need a body offered to me as a sacrifice. I give you your safety. Freely. I do not want my estate. I lost it, and in the most scandalous way possible in order to destroy my father."

"I won," she said, aware that she sounded like a petulant child. Unable to do anything else.

"You did."

"You couldn't have beat me if you tried."

"I have no trouble believing that. I chose to stay in the game when I knew that I would lose. But losing was the only thing on my cards tonight."

She was shocked to discover the revelation didn't diminish the thrill of her victory. She had beaten everyone in there tonight to get over to his table. He had his own game. But then, so did everyone.

It was the way of it.

If anything, this made it all the more exciting.

"Before anything," he said. "Your name."

She trembled. On a knife's edge. Did she tell him? Or did she not?

The trouble was, she trusted him.

Even if she didn't know why.

"Jessie," she said. "Jessie Hargreave. *Jessica*, actually. So you had half the truth as it was."

"You're smart. Don't deviate too far from the truth if you wish to create a convincing lie."

"A very basic truth."

"Your father wishes to hurt you?" he asked.

"He's a dangerous man. Though I would say it's more

he doesn't like to lose. And he lost me. He will want me back, I'm afraid."

"He would be Mark Hargreave, I assume."

She should have been prepared for that, and yet she wasn't. "Yes. I'm not surprised that you've heard of him. And you can understand why I don't let my name lead."

"I do. And now you have my word, he will not find you. You will be protected."

"Thank you."

"Here's the paperwork."

He turned to a locked cabinet, produced a key from his pocket and proceeded to release it.

He opened the doors and brought a stack of papers out before her. "You will sign it. With your legal name. And you will be assured that it is yours."

"All to get back at your father?"

He chuckled, and the sound made her body liquid. "I don't think I'm the only one here with daddy issues."

The word shimmered through her body.

The way that he looked at her, those enticing, unforgettable eyes looking into her.

She let out a breath and took hold of the papers, looking them over.

"Can you really give your title to me?"

"I've no idea. But you can claim it."

"And what is the purpose of this?"

"Revenge. Quite simply. My father is on his deathbed. This paperwork, by the way, ensures that it all passes to you upon his death. An agreement between yourself and me. We will have final papers sent to you once he draws his last breath. But I will ensure that he is aware that the line is ending with me, before he slips into hell. That's all I ask."

"That seems fair to me." She didn't need to question why

the man hated his father. People were entitled to hate their fathers. God knew she hated her own.

She looked over the paperwork quickly, and signed.

The air between them became thick.

"I'm leaving gambling behind me," she said, stepping away from him, arousal making her warm.

This had been the most exciting night of her life. And he was an unexpected and thrilling opponent.

They had both won a victory tonight. And why should they not bask in it?

"Are you?"

She shrugged. "You have to stop eventually."

"Do you? I don't intend to stop until I drive my Ferrari into a brick wall. And then maybe I'll slow down."

"When you're dead?"

He shrugged. "Perhaps."

"That doesn't seem a recipe for a happy life."

"I don't want a happy life. I want *everything*. When I want it. All the time. I want excess. However long that lasts, I don't care. But a man like me isn't exactly made to sit in a rocking chair in his twilight years. A man like me isn't made for twilight years."

"That seems grim."

"Perhaps I'm grim. Maybe that's my secret. But in between the moments of grimness, I'm told I can be a good time."

"Show me." Her pulse was pounding.

"Why don't you show me?"

With his whiskey firmly in hand, he turned away from her, went and sat on a large armchair in front of windows that overlooked the back courtyard.

"I am told," he said, "these windows overlook the valley below. And we are on a cliff's edge. So no one can see. That's what I'm told. I suppose we can't be certain."

He took a sip of whiskey, those eyes burning into her. "Show me the prize I failed to win."

He was asking her to strip.

She didn't know how to strip. She had played the co-quette, she had played the seductress, but none of the games that she and her sister played ever demanded that they follow through.

Tonight wasn't a game. Tonight was a claiming. She was cashing out. Why not cash out her virginity as well?

She reached behind her back, and before she could allow nerves to overtake her, she began to unzip the dress. She let it go loose, let it fall to her waist, her breasts bared for his perusal.

"Gorgeous," he said, his jaw going tense.

She knew the rumors about him, and he did as much as confirm them just now.

He was a man who did what he wanted, when he wanted to do it. He'd had more sex than he could likely catalog in an evening's time.

And he was aroused by the sight of her naked body.

He shifted, and she could see the evidence of his arousal, just there at the apex of his thighs.

She trembled.

"More," he demanded.

She pushed the gown down over her hips, so that she was wearing nothing more than the small white thong she put on earlier, and her sky-high heels.

She hadn't intended for anyone to see this. It made her feel sexy. Helped her play the part.

But now it felt as if it was for him. As if perhaps it always had been.

He lifted his hand, and crooked his finger. "Come here."

Jessie was not, as a general rule, obedient. But his voice

was liquid velvet, and it poured over her like a soft, sensual promise, and she could not deny him.

She took a step toward him, and then another.

Until she was standing just before him, wearing nothing but those very brief underwear.

"It's a good thing I didn't intend to win, Ms. Hargreave. Because I would've found it nearly impossible to concentrate with you sitting across from me. And seeing you uncovered... You're even more exquisite than I could've imagined."

"Why do you remember me?"

She remembered everything. Everybody.

But she remembered him different. She remembered him red.

He didn't go in a file cabinet. He never could. He couldn't be classified, alphabetized, organized.

He was heat and light and burning passion, whether she wanted him to be or not.

And she knew that not everybody remembered the way that she did. But he remembered her. Surely it meant something.

She needed it to mean something.

"Because I want you," he said.

"You want me?"

"From the first moment I saw you. At that casino in Las Vegas. I was in the high-roller room, and I had won a ridiculous sum of money in the sort of game that makes my father livid.

"And I saw you there. You looked so young. So innocent. But you aren't. You are an enigma. And you have been to me from that first moment.

"You wore a wig then. You don't wear one now."

She shook her head. "It's dyed darker now."

"Your hair looked short. Just to your chin then."

She nodded. "That was a wig."

"It was very pretty. Though I prefer this."

She shook her head, made her inky dark hair shimmer over her breasts like an oil spill. He growled, his hips bucking upward.

She had never felt so beautiful. And more to the point, she had never cared whether or not she felt beautiful. It had been a tool. Always. This body. This face.

It had never been anything she cared about.

"And then when I saw you again. In Monte Carlo. You were up on the second floor."

"When did you see me? I didn't..."

She hadn't realized.

She'd made mistakes with him. She had never made mistakes with anyone else before.

And she was standing naked before him now, and that should serve as a warning. A warning that he wasn't safe. That she needed to guard herself. She didn't make mistakes, and yet she did with him.

She didn't make mistakes, and yet she was standing before him naked.

Almost naked.

Her pulse was throbbing between her legs, and she wanted nothing more than to move forward and straddle his lap. Rub herself against him and satisfy the ache within her.

She was familiar with the desires of her body.

In her imagination it was vivid.

But this... This transcended imagination.

It was big and bright and real. It was red.

Suddenly, he reached out, his large hands gripping her hips and pulling her forward. And then he pressed his mouth to her stomach. Just beneath her belly button.

She shivered.

He had yet to kiss her lips, and yet his mouth, hot and impertinent, had touched her stomach.

"You are delicious," he said roughly. He looked up at her, moved his hands up her waist, just beneath the swells of her breasts. Her nipples went tight.

"Get down on your knees."

"I…"

"You have to earn it. Your right to be here. With me. Show me how much you want me. Show me you could be a good girl."

Her knees were trembling as she sank down before him, and he looked down at her, then reached out to cup her chin. Tilted her face upward. And closed the distance between them as he bent down to press his mouth to hers.

It was firm. Hot. And then he angled his head, and it became fury.

He parted her mouth roughly, pushing his tongue deep. A raw cry escaped her throat, and she kissed him back. Allowing him access. Surrendering to him.

She had thought to seduce him tonight, but this was different. She had thought to claim a prize, but he was nothing of the kind.

He was living and breathing and powerful. The furthest thing from cold, soulless money as one could be.

And he was not biddable. Pliable. She could not manipulate him.

That thrilled her deeper than anything else ever could have.

It had been exciting, knowing she had beaten him.

It was intoxicating to know she couldn't.

That he was a man with his own game running. A man with his own set of rules.

That he was perhaps her equal.

You're kneeling before him.

Yes. But because she chose to.

He began to undo the buckle on his pants, as he took his mouth away from hers.

He undid the button, the zipper, and revealed his hard, thick length.

She knew exactly what he wanted. And she wanted to give it to him.

She was about to lean forward, when he reached behind her head and pushed his fingers deep into her hair, drawing her head toward him, bringing her mouth down to him.

She parted her lips, and took the head of him in, that salty, musky flavor sending a sharp burst of desire through her. "Go ahead, pretty girl. Give me what I want."

With trembling hands, she wrapped her fingers around his thick shaft and began to work him as she sucked him into her mouth. She knew what a blow job was. She knew how they worked. She didn't have to have had personal experience giving one to know that.

She took him in as deep as she possibly could, and then… Then she lost herself.

It was like the light in that back room of her brain had been turned off. She couldn't see the file cabinets. She couldn't access the vast bank of memories that drove her, that assaulted her at all times. There was nothing but this. The taste of him. The feel of him. She had never done this before, and it was wholly new. Wholly terrifying. Wholly wonderful.

She was lost in the taste of him. The hardness.

The heat.

The deep growl that he made in the back of his throat when she did something he liked.

She was, perhaps for the first time in her life, fully in the moment. Not in the past, not in the ever present, entirely too detailed memories that made her who she was.

Suddenly, she was lifted away from him, brought up onto

his lap, and they were kissing. Fiercely. He was untethered. A man without a rudder, she realized.

It should maybe be terrifying, but it was the most exhilarating thing she'd ever experienced.

She was having sex with a stranger.

Well, she was *about* to.

She'd just had the most intimate part of him in her mouth.

And now he was consuming her. Claiming her for his own. And she had never wanted anything more.

Wicked. Wicked. Wicked.

And tonight it would be only a good thing.

Tonight she would let it carry her into her darkest fantasy.

Tonight she didn't care about rules.

Because this was it, so what was there to behave for?

He saw her.

He knew she was a con artist.

He didn't care. He wanted her anyway.

He put his hands on her hips again, lifted her so that her knees were on his thighs. Then he grabbed the edge of her underwear, and pulled them to the side, exposing the heart of her to his inspection. He moved his hands around to cup her ass, and brought her up against his mouth.

A short scream escaped her as he began to lick deep within her.

Each stroke of his tongue created a white-hot streak of pleasure that rioted through her.

He moved one hand down between her thighs, and stroked where she was wet and needy for him, pushing a finger deep inside her from behind as he continued to lick her. Suck her. Taste her.

She lost control of herself. Completely. And that was another new experience. Because she controlled everything. The way she breathed, the way she looked, every step she took.

She ground her hips against his mouth, sought more, and

then he pushed a second finger within her and she let a raw cry escape her lips.

"Yes," she said. "Yes."

"You are a very bad girl, aren't you?"

He had seen her. Seen the fear that lived in her. Was she wicked? He thought so. And he loved it. Reveled in it.

Made her like it, too.

It was so good. So good, it nearly hurt.

He growled that against her sensitized flesh, and she could only tremble in response.

He continued to lick her, and suddenly, it was like the whole world fell away.

And she along with it. She unraveled, as pleasure rolled through her like a wave.

Her internal muscles tightened around his fingers, and she had to grip his shoulders to keep from collapsing.

Dimly, she registered that he was still mostly dressed, while she was undone and naked before him.

She was about to say something, but he stood, bringing her over his shoulder like a caveman, one hand gripping her ass firmly, the other around her knees as he carried her through the penthouse and into the bedroom.

He threw her down onto the bed, and stood away from her as he began to undress.

And she just lay there, legs splayed, still wearing high heels, watching as he revealed his glorious body to her.

He undid his tie, the buttons on his shirt, his cuffs. And her mouth dried as he exposed the hard, heavy ridges of muscle that made up his chest, his abdomen.

His body was covered in course-looking golden hair, and she had to bite her lip to keep back her cry of desire as he took off his jacket, shirt, pants. As he revealed every bit of his body to her. His muscular thighs, and that thick, glorious member.

She'd already come once, but she was ready for more already.

He moved over to her, and grabbed the front of her underwear, pulling them down her legs, and off completely.

Then he returned to her, kissing her ankle, the inner part of her knee, running his tongue along her inner thigh before moving back to the heart of her, and pushing his tongue deep inside her.

Her hips bowed up off the bed, and she nearly screamed his name.

He moved up, to her breasts, taking one nipple deep inside his mouth and sucking hard.

If this was debauchery, then perhaps she had always been made for it.

But there were worse things, she supposed. Worse things than being debauched. Worse things than being wicked.

Worse things than knowing that every detail of tonight would linger in her mind forever and ever and ever.

She would go have a quiet life after this. But not tonight. Tonight she would be loud.

He opened up the drawer of his dresser and took out a condom packet, tore it open and quickly rolled the latex over his arousal.

And then he moved back between her legs, hooking her leg up over his head before he thrust hard inside her.

She had not been prepared for that.

She gasped, pain tearing through her.

"What the hell?" he asked, frowning fiercely.

"I'm all right," she said, putting her hands on his lean hips and urging him to stay there. "I'm fine."

"You're a virgin."

"Not now."

He gripped her chin and held her face. "What game are you playing?"

"I'm not playing a game. We played that game already. And I won. But I *saw* you. The same as you did me. I haven't been able to forget. I just wanted tonight. That's all. I just wanted you to be the first one."

Maybe the only one.

She just wanted him. That cost her nothing to admit it because she would never see him again. All she would have was tonight. This beautiful, raw memory of tonight.

"I cannot give any more than this," he said.

"I don't want any more than this. I couldn't take any more than this. My father is a crime lord. I've spent the last few years running from him. Trying to make a new life for myself. Trying to make myself safe." She refused to bring Maren into this. It wasn't her sister's fault that she had decided to do this. "I won tonight. I made myself safe. I'm going to go off and have my life. But I just wanted this first."

"But I will make it a night you don't forget."

If only he knew.

If only he knew she would never forget, no matter what. Not one breath. Not one heartbeat. Not one moment.

But she was grateful that he would make it wonderful. He withdrew from her, and then pushed back inside, and the delicious friction made her wild.

She wrapped her legs around his lean waist as the pain began to recede, as need replaced it.

His thrusts became hard, less measured.

And she felt her arousal tightening within her.

Felt herself climbing toward that peak again. But this wasn't an unraveling.

This time, when she came apart, she shattered. It was violent, intense, her body gripping his hardness, drawing him deeper within her, and he responded with an animal need. His thrusts wild and hard. And when he lost control, she felt like she was staring into the center of the sun.

Because it wasn't only she who shattered. But he as well. And in the aftermath of it all, they lay there together.

She wondered if she would have to leave. If it was time for her to go and find Maren.

"Stay there," he said, getting up and going into the bathroom.

He returned a moment later with a towel. "I will get you cleaned. And rest with you for a moment. But if tonight is all you have..."

"Yes," she said, relief rolling through her. It wouldn't be just once. "Show me *everything*."

CHAPTER THREE

His father was dead. He wasn't sorry about that.

He had, however, expected to feel triumph.

He'd won, after all. His father had died alone in a care home and he had survived him. Instead, he had felt smothered by a blanket of heavy black darkness. It hadn't been grief. He knew grief. It had been something worse.

Futility.

He had outlived his father. He had made sure the old man knew that the line would end with him, that the estate was no longer part of the family.

But on the other side of that had been...nothing. Nothing but a strange finality he had not anticipated.

It was like he could no longer find the man beneath the mask. He'd always imagined he'd be there, somewhere. Healed when his father died and yet...the closest he'd felt had been with her.

He had been utterly unlike himself, as had the desire he'd carried for her every day since. She had aroused something deeper in him. Something dark and intense. He'd never been like that with a woman before.

Then he'd gone back to himself. To the Ewan he put on every day along with his suit and tie. And now his father was dead.

Everything was still broken.

Or perhaps that was Jessie.

He hadn't felt anything like triumph since that night he had spent with Jessie.

Five months and he hadn't gotten the woman out of his mind. Not just because they were connected by her winning the estate.

Jessie…

He had lost the taste for everything since that night. For anyone else.

That she had been a virgin was a shock. A gentleman would have taken her just the once. Allowed her to recover.

He was not a gentleman. But even beyond that…his behavior hadn't been about playing into the idea that he was a debaucher. He'd been lost to it. To her.

With her, he'd found something gritty and dark within himself. He'd made demands of her, and she'd met them. It had felt like meeting an old friend, or perhaps just a part of himself long buried.

He'd been a child when he'd smoothed that charm over the top of his intensity, and so he'd never had the chance to connect it to sex and need and desire.

But they had.

He had taken her every which way. He'd bent her over the couch in the living room. He'd had her in the shower.

He'd tied her hands and pleasured her until she had begged for release. And he had refused her until she was sobbing.

It had been the single most intense night of his life. And it should've faded into that hazy pool of memory where he kept all sexual encounters.

But it had not faded. It had stayed there. Bright and determined.

Perhaps that spoke volumes about how jaded he had become. It had taken a virgin to show him something exciting. And now he could find no interest in anything else.

Or perhaps it had been that night.

That finality he'd felt having surrendered his title, the estate, severed his ties with that house and his father forever.

She had been a conquest. A victory. And he'd been hers.

The mutual desperation had been unlike anything he'd ever experienced before.

She had been like liquid fire in his hands. And she'd begged for everything. And he had given it. Over and over again.

He had left no part of her without his brand. She might have been a virgin when she came to his bed, but she had left with no more firsts to be given. They all belonged to him.

Even now, sitting there thinking of it he grew hard.

Even now, she was the only thing that made him feel.

And that was a strange thing, given he had not managed to find excitement for a woman standing right in front of him in the months since.

This was, without a doubt, the longest stretch of celibacy he'd ever endured.

And he had certainly never imagined that he would endure it simply because of his own lack of interest.

But maybe that was to do with the death of his father.

The way it hadn't fixed the cracks inside him. The way he wasn't restored, and everything from the past was still past.

Nothing was changed.

He sat there in his office, a billionaire in his own right, free of the man who'd poisoned him, and asked himself what the hell he had expected.

That he was fixable? Now, after all this time?

He knew better than that.

Or perhaps he hadn't.

Perhaps somewhere inside him a scared little boy had thought he was slaying a dragon, when in reality a bastard of a human being had died and his death didn't erase the scars he'd left with his existence.

Idly, he found himself looking up the articles on when she had won the estate.

It had been quite the headline. Tabloid fodder, to be sure, but that was exactly what he'd wanted it to be.

Jessica Lockwood. Kincaid estate.

But what he saw was not what he had expected. As he sat there in his gleaming office, he felt fire ignite in his chest.

There was a brand-new article. Just from yesterday.

And there she was. His beauty. Jessie. Round with a pregnancy.

He curled his fingers into fists. It had to be his baby. It had to be.

They'd made love countless times that night, and he knew that there had been a point when desire had taken over everything, and condoms had become an afterthought.

Because she had ruined him.

Changed him.

She had made him into a man who didn't care about consequences or anything that happened beyond that night.

Was he more than the playboy that night—a man given over to hedonism without a care for how it impacted anyone?

Or less? A man who felt it down deep, who wanted it, needed it. Who wasn't easily succumbing to temptation for the hell of it, but who had been beyond himself in the moment. Beyond anything but the need he felt for it.

And it had felt incredible.

But there was the consequence of incredible. Right there in front of him. A magazine article that could not be denied.

His child.

He had sworn that he would not carry on his bloodline. His family name.

He died thinking you wouldn't. He died thinking that you had surrendered the estate.

His blood was at the estate whether or not he acknowledged it.

Of all the tricks that could possibly have been played.

His child would be the heir whether he staked a claim or not.

His child.

His child.

A baby.

He pushed the intercom button on his phone. "Natalie," he said, barking his assistant's name. "Have the private jet ready to leave. I need to go to Scotland."

"Yes, sir."

His tone brooked no argument. He made sure of that.

Other than that, he could not think straight.

Jessie Hargreave was pregnant with his baby.

He had to see her.

As quickly as possible.

Even though doing that meant a trip into hell.

"I don't know how anybody got in here with a camera without us knowing."

Jessie looked up at Maren, who was pacing the length of the dining room.

"It's fine," said Jessie, not feeling fine in the least.

"You won't think so if our father finds us." Maren's eyes were round with fear and whenever Maren was afraid, Jessie wanted to protect her.

Maren needed to be handled gently, and Jessie had always known that. She was soft. A little pink marshmallow of a human who had to be gently coddled.

"He didn't find us when the first news stories were printed," Jessie pointed out.

And she had a security detail, reporting her father's moves and making sure they were safe.

Maren frowned. "Yes, but more is just tempting fate."

It wasn't their father that worried her.

"You know me, Maren," said Jessie. "You know I'm not going to let him get us. He thinks he's smarter than us because he made us and that will always, always be his downfall. I've always been better at a math equation than him. Always better at angles. And you? You…"

"Will feel an intense emotion at him?" she asked, blinking slowly, her face placid. She was being dry, but with Maren it was hard to tell. It was part of her *innocent creature* persona.

"What are Dad's weaknesses?"

"His ego. His dependence on wealth, and his aversion to hard work."

"Issues we don't share."

"You can come with me," said Maren. "In just a couple of months I get to take occupancy at the castle that I won. I'm going to be a princess. I'll keep you safe."

"On your country that literally spans only the width of the rock the castle is on?"

"Yes. I will."

"I'm a duchess," Jessie said, even knowing that her claim to the title was specious. She needed it in this moment so she was taking it. "I'm perfectly capable of protecting myself. And my baby."

Finding out she was pregnant had been… It had been terrifying. And she had kept it a secret from Maren for as long as possible. She felt guilty about that.

The night of the poker game, her sister had also won an amazing prize.

The castle, and all the money that went with the place. It was a whole kingdom, really, even though nobody lived there full-time.

It was only that she had to wait several months to take up occupancy. And in the end, that had been good.

But at the time it had felt…suffocating.

Maren had suspected something the night of the game.

Because Jessie hadn't come back until morning, and by the time she did sneak back into their hotel room, in the same dress as the night before, the sun had begun to rise.

"We have a rule, Jessie. For a reason."

Maren looked tired, angry and wounded.

"I know."

"I won my game."

"That's great."

"You weren't there," Maren said, accusing.

"I had my own business to see to. I won an estate."

"I know that. Everyone was buzzing about it before I won my game, but you were nowhere to be found. You went off with him."

"It was our last night, Maren. It's done. It's over and finished, and there's no reason that we need to be worried. There's no reason to keep being so careful…"

"You're wrong, Jessie. There's always a reason to be careful. When you become careless, you become like Father."

"Well, maybe I am like our father."

Maren had looked immediately regretful.

"You aren't."

"I might be. Just a bit more wicked than you."

"It isn't wicked to desire a handsome man. But I just worry… I worry."

"I know you do. But all is well."

"You aren't hurt?"

"I just had about thirty orgasms. I'm fine."

All of that came back to haunt her when she missed her period. And then another. When she was forced to take that first pregnancy test, and when she opted to keep it a secret.

The first day she threw up in the morning was the day that she knew. The day that she knew she couldn't keep it a secret anymore.

"I'm pregnant."

Maren had simply nodded.

"I know."

Maren would have made the better mother. They both knew it. But Maren wouldn't be this careless.

"How?"

"Nearly imperceptible differences with your appearance. But noticeable all the same. Plus, you seem sad. What are you going to do?"

"I don't know."

She had kept right on not knowing until she had felt it was too late to make any sort of drastic decision.

Maybe she'd done that on purpose. For she was not an indecisive person by nature.

In general, she was extremely confident. Always knew what she wanted the minute choices were presented to her.

She had known that she wanted Ewan from the moment she'd seen him.

So she'd had him.

But she couldn't imagine a baby. And maybe that was the most difficult part. What a baby made by her and him might look like.

She couldn't fathom it.

And maybe in the end that was why she hadn't decided

to end the pregnancy. Because it was a mystery. Because it was something she hadn't anticipated.

Because in many ways she had finally caught herself.

And anyway, what were they doing out here? They were starting a new life.

She had intended to go to school. To find something she wanted to study, a job she wanted to do. She was interested in so many things…

But she had all the money she could possibly need, and now she was going to…be a mother.

She wasn't entirely certain she was maternal. She and Maren had barely known their mother, and she had been deeply uninterested in them.

Their father was evil. She knew what *not* to be.

And again, perhaps that was why she thought maybe… Just maybe it would be worth having this child.

Except now it was in the paper, and she wondered if *he* would see it.

He may not do anything.

He didn't appear to want children. He had given up the estate in the interest of disavowing his bloodline, after all. He hated his father.

As for her…

He was too much for her. On top of all of this, the reality of knowing she was going to be a mother, she couldn't take him on with it.

He did things to her. He made her feel things.

He made her feel beyond herself.

She was going to have to find a way to…feel. Just for the child. Just open herself up just enough to be what her baby would need. She couldn't have him anywhere in the vicinity when she was…open.

He saw too much already. She couldn't take the risk.

She had to be the best mother she could be—and she had no earthly idea how good that actually was.

She had deliberately avoided looking at any photos of him in the months since they parted. She didn't think she could stand to see him with another woman, and worse, if she did, she would never be able to get that out of her head. And at night she replayed the hours they'd spent together. He was so beautiful.

Her memories of him were so vivid it was like she could reach out and touch him.

As if she could feel it all over again.

He was red.

And so was wanting him.

It painted every day.

It was why he needed to stay away.

"We can go away to my castle," Maren said stoutly.

She was adorable when she tried to be the protector.

"No. This is my home. Mine. And if I have to hire a security detail to keep me safe, then I will do it. But I won this place. It belongs to me. Just like your castle belongs to you. We set out to make new lives for ourselves, and I'm doing it. I'm…" She decided it was time to say it out loud. "I'm going to be a mother."

"Oh, Jessie," said Maren, her eyes filling with tears. "Do you want that?"

"I don't know. But it's happening. At least it was because of something I did. Think of all the terrible things that we went through in our childhood because of what our parents decided for us. I went to bed with him of my own free will. I wanted him. I wasn't careful. I knew better. I realized that the time when… I knew he didn't get a condom. The last few times. I didn't care. I didn't care about anything but having him. It's my consequence for my mistake. From the beginning I made mistakes with him. He's the only one who has ever affected me like that..."

"I don't ever want that," said Maren, looking away. "It sounds terrifying."

"It is," she said. "But it was wonderful."

"*One night*, and you're going to have a baby that you have to take care of for the rest of your life."

"In fairness, it isn't going to stay a baby forever," Jessie said, putting her hand on her stomach. "I really do need to see a doctor, probably."

"Yes. You definitely do. But thankfully, you have enough money to have private visits at your estate."

"Very thankfully."

It was the roar of an engine that broke the conversation. Not a car engine. The plane. They both startled.

And she ran as best she could to the back window of the sitting room, to look out at the vast field behind them. Just in time to see a sleek white plane disappear behind the rise of one of the hills. There was a landing strip back there; she knew that. One of her favorite parts of the estate was the horses.

And even though she had to be a bit careful riding, she had gone on very mild rides in the past few months, all over the grounds. And she had explored what was obviously a place for planes and helicopters to land, plus a few other spaces that spoke to the wealthy excess of the previous owners. She knew. Immediately.

"He's here," she said.

"Father?"

"No, Maren. It's the duke. Ewan Kincaid."

CHAPTER FOUR

As THE PLANE touched down, adrenaline fueled Ewan's veins.

It was as if he was descending into hell, not down to the shocking green of the Highlands.

But this place was hell to him, and had been all his childhood, since everything had been washed in crimson and stained forever.

Destroyed forever.

He tried to push the images back. He didn't have time to dwell in the past. He didn't have the mental energy to devote to it. The past was the past.

Death was final.

As soon as the plane stopped, he stood. "Be quick about it," he said to the flight attendant, who began to open the doors.

This was not him, he knew. He could see it in the faces of his staff members. Had seen it from the moment he had asked for the plane to be procured.

Normally, he was affable. Easy. He was a playboy, after all. His business was pleasure clubs. And he knew that you caught more flies with honey than vinegar. And he preferred to apply his honey liberally.

But it had all left his body when he'd seen Jessie round with his child.

He'd only had one thought. To get to her. To get here.

Only then would he be able to make sense of it.

Only then would he be able to find a way forward.

He was not a man who sat still.

His father was entrenched in tradition. Frozen at an archaic point in time.

Medieval. And cruel.

The sort of man who would beat a little boy for daring to be frail enough to cry for his mother. A man who had a near wild-eyed commitment to the name, to the legacy. Who cared more for his dead ancestors than he ever would for his own living child.

Ewan had never wanted to be thus.

And he never had been.

But now he was close to it. Touching the edge of it as if he was putting his finger to a flame.

It pained him to know that he could understand his old man. But in this moment, he very nearly did.

Because what did he care for the comfort of those around him when he felt as if he was being dismantled from the inside out.

He walked down the plane's stairs, to the staircase, and continued straight into the green.

He walked up over the rise, and could see the estate down below.

He was wearing custom-made Italian shoes. Not practical for moving across the soft ground here in the Highlands.

His suit jacket wasn't practical, either.

And they were suffocating him.

This place. God in heaven, this place. He hated it. It was as if there were hellhounds here. Lurking on the edges of the wood. His heart pounded hard, and then it was like he couldn't breathe.

With speed and efficiency, he took his jacket off. He

cast it down to the ground, then bent down and untied his shoes. Both of them.

He left himself barefoot. It was practical because the ground was soft. It was not desperate.

Then he ran.

Toward the estate. Toward her.

Until she was in his sight, they would be nothing but this. This confusion. This jumble of sound inside his soul.

This fractured feeling.

Was it his child? It might not be. He had been her first. He had been the man to introduce her to pleasure, and so maybe he had awakened a hunger in her.

She had been an eager lover.

It was possible the baby belonged to someone else.

Does it matter?

What manner of father could he be?

All he knew was pain in that relationship. A father and son.

He had spent his life avoiding attachment.

He had none.

He changed assistants at least once a year. The staff on his private jet never remained the same. His clubs were constantly in a state of flux, as clubs often were. The ambiance, the employees, all shifted continually.

And he didn't stay long enough to truly get to know anyone.

He had tried to the best of his ability to escape this place. This place. As his feet met with the damp ground, it felt as if it was mocking him. Bringing up pieces of his childhood. Of the pain there.

He had been left outside in the cold before. Unable to warm his feet as they sank into the soft grass.

Huddled in a corner of the property trying to find some shelter.

He had been beaten. Shut away.

Starved. His father had always been cruel. His grief had driven him mad.

Turned him into a sadist who hid behind a raft of rules and a need to control, control, control the son he'd borne. To make him the perfect heir as he would be the only one, the only hope.

He did not seem to realize that the way he'd treated his heir could have killed him.

As if bleeding his own pain out onto his son might heal him in some way. Like draining the poison to Ewan would fix something.

So Ewan had decided to deny him in every way. He'd cut off the estate. He'd disgraced their name. He'd decided there would be no children.

It was what his father had deserved. And so how was there a child now? How was he *here*?

How was he here?

That thought propelled him to the back door of the estate.

And he was ready to kick the door down when it opened. And there she was.

She was wearing a red flowing gown that poured over her curves. The neckline was plunging, showing her overflowing breasts. And the rest of the gown was loose, flowing easily over that baby bump.

"I knew it was only a matter of time," she said, shaking her head.

Her hair was lighter now. A chocolate brown rather than the raven's wing from five months ago. She was no less beautiful. If anything, even more so, with her curves rounded by her pregnancy.

She was clearly unwilling to appear even the least bit surprised. That cool calculation of hers he'd seen at the poker tables was visible here.

That, at least, was the same.

Though when her eyes dropped down to his feet, she could not hide her shock.

"Have you had an accident?" she asked.

"Other than the one I'm staring at just now? No."

She ignored that. "Where are your shoes?"

"I left them to the fields."

With his coat. He realized then that might have been sort of a mad thing to do, but he wouldn't show her that he doubted his own sanity.

"All right, then. You might as well come in."

He could see her. Doing mental calculations. Trying to figure out just how she was going to manage this. How she would come out on top.

He could think of nothing. Could strategize nothing. Because his brain had ceased to function. He was there. Standing before her. And she was pregnant.

"The child is mine," he said.

He'd meant it as a question. It had come out a statement of fact.

"Oh, no," she said. "I mean, it *could* be. But it's actually nearly impossible to say. I have just had endless sex since last we met. So many lovers I can't even begin to—"

He'd thought that. Had the suspicion himself.

But when she did...

When she did it was clear to him it was a lie.

"I knew you would say that," he said. "It's not even a good con as cons go."

"But you can take it as the answer, if you want to," she said, looking at him. "I don't know who the father of my baby is. I've had far too many lovers to keep track of. It could be anyone's."

She was lying. She didn't have a tell. And that was the biggest tell of all. For if she had told the truth, he had a feeling she would look much more vulnerable. As it was, she was defiant.

But she was offering him a chance to walk away.

But he had no honor, no connection to family or blood. That was what she didn't understand.

He wasn't here for *honor*.

He'd had to see. Like some beast had possessed him. Because she was here.

Here and pregnant.

And it had driven him here even though he now had no idea what purpose he served.

"You and I both know that's a lie," he said.

She shrugged, as if she didn't care. "Suit yourself."

He'd walked into the estate, and felt an oppressive sense of cold fold itself around him. And right then he hated that he had decided to take his shoes off, because being in here with his feet touching the floor felt far too much like being at home.

And this was not his home.

She tossed her hair. "I don't know if you realize this, but I'm a millionaire."

He laughed. Because at least that jarred him out of the moment he had found himself sinking into. The thoughts of the past that were threatening to reach up and strangle him.

"I am aware, as you achieved that status in part by taking a substantial amount of money from me."

"That's incorrect. You *lost* a substantial amount of money to me. And this estate. I am quite well, and taken care of."

"I'm not here for *you*," he said. "I'm here for the child."

But his head was beginning to pound and the ghosts of this place hung thick around him, pressing in hard, harder.

"What could you possibly want with a child?" she asked.

"What do *you* want with a child?" And suddenly, everything crystallized for him. She was a con artist. Beautiful.

The sexiest woman he'd ever been with, but a con artist all the same.

She was not fit to be a mother. Any more than he was fit to be a father.

One thing he knew, as he stood there in this oppressive place, was that he could not consign a child to a life of misery.

But they'd made one.

The poison had done its job. It had spread.

He was looking at the devastation.

Not only was she having a child neither of them were fit to raise, she also seemed to not understand the danger such a thing could represent.

But he knew.

He knew all too well.

"I'm having the child," she said. "It's kind of out of my hands now."

"That isn't true, and we both know that."

"I've decided to have the baby. So. That's what I want with the baby. I'm having it. And I want to see where it goes."

This girl had no idea. She was treating this like it was nothing. Like it couldn't be the death of her.

"It isn't a poker game, Jessie. Pregnancy is dangerous. And that is only the shortest bit of this. You cannot simply have the child and see if it goes your way, and fold if it doesn't."

Color mounted in her cheeks. "How *dare* you? I've spent the past four months coming to terms with this. Deciding what I was going to do. Do you think it was easy? And now you've come and you questioned me and you're acting as if you've put more thought into this than I when we both know you could not have known about the child for more than a few hours."

"It's clear to me. I don't need months to think about it. The baby is mine."

"Again..."

"Liar," he said, his voice fierce. He took a step toward her, and he pressed his thumb against her lips. "This mouth is mine. That lying tongue is mine. You did not spend all those years of your life untouched because you lacked opportunity. What we had was different. And you would not have gone off into someone else's bed after. You know that."

"Do I?"

"Yes," he growled.

Why did it matter? Why did it matter to him that she'd been with no one else? If she had, he could walk away.

She let out a hard breath. "Why are you here? Because we both know that you don't want a baby."

"And you do?"

She shrugged. "No. And yet, like you it seems as if I'm having one. What is there to be done? What is there to be said?"

"You know that two dysfunctional humans can't combine to become a single functional parent. We will only make this worse if we are together."

"I'm not suggesting we be together. But perhaps we need to figure out how we might both..."

"What whole thing will two broken shards make?" he asked.

"I don't want to. I want a life that's mine. You don't want a baby. So why can't you leave?"

She was offering him freedom. He wanted her.

But the idea of a child...

He could think of nothing worse.

Because all he could imagine was that night. The moment that changed everything. Destroyed it all.

A pale, still woman, and a baby that never cried.

Why was he here?

He could not endure it.

She would be better off without him. Because he was entirely tangled up in the monstrous legacy of this place, and the loss that happened here. The pain after.

And fathers with demons were nothing but devils.

He knew well enough that he could be Satan himself if the wind turned wrong. How could he deny it?

It was in his blood. Perhaps that was the best reason of all for his mask. For cutting off all that he'd been as a child.

Maybe his father had hated him so much because it had been like looking in a mirror.

Blood he'd been intent on cutting off. Blood that he…

But she was here and he wanted her. He knew nothing beyond that. It was desire that had brought them here and desire was the one thing he could understand.

Why was he here?

For this.

And he found himself closing the distance between them.

Then he lowered his head, and pressed his mouth to hers.

CHAPTER FIVE

JESSIE FELT LIKE she was on fire. She wanted to cry, and she wanted to keep kissing him and never stop.

This was unconscionable. She couldn't allow herself to be…seduced by the father of her baby. While he was standing there in a fury.

Why not? The damage was done.

In so many ways, the damage was done.

Why couldn't she have him? Maren was here. In the other room. But if they went upstairs now, she wouldn't see them. And even so, she would just have to apologize for her continued weakness later.

She was weak for him.

But she had a feeling that he would leave after this, because she had given him means of escape, and he would take it. She couldn't blame him.

It would be the best thing. The best thing for both of them.

But she'd never felt what she did when she was with him. Not before. And she never would after.

More than that, she couldn't afford to. She had to let it go. She had to.

But she needed him again. She needed to feel like that just one more time.

She'd lived so many years cut off from her feelings. Until him.

It was bright and terrifying and something she should run from. But not now. Not now.

"Have me," she whispered against his mouth. "Please. One more time."

"Yes," he growled.

She didn't know this man. She still didn't know this man. Pregnant with his child, at the mercy of his kiss yet again, and she didn't know him.

She didn't understand why he was here barefoot, or why he had given the place away to begin with. Why he had come at all, and why he would leave since he'd come all this way.

She'd known from the moment she'd met him that he was more than he seemed.

But there was even more than she'd seen.

He was broken somehow.

Tortured.

Hurt.

She hurt for him. For herself.

Why was he here?

But she wondered if he didn't know the answers to that question, either. Any more than she could answer why she'd decided to carry this child.

And so she simply let herself get caught up in his kiss. Consumed by it. By him.

He lifted her up with ease, her dress trailing behind them as he carried her up the stairs. Because of course he knew this place.

Of course he knew the way to the master bedroom that she called her own, and he found it with ease, kicking open the door and sparing it no examination as he closed it again and walked her to the bed.

The gown she was wearing fluttered around her as he placed her gently at the center of the mattress.

"I did not think I would find such a thing so arousing. But seeing you, round with my child… Knowing that I've made you this way…"

He had no idea. No idea the depth of it. He had made her this way. She'd gone twenty-two years without ever much thinking of sex. Just a bit, when she was alone in her bed.

But he had taken her and made her a creature of need.

He had changed her in so many ways, and she could only stare at him, at those eyes, and wonder if she had changed him, too.

This felt out of control.

It seemed like perhaps she had.

She truly wanted to believe it.

She truly did.

And so, as he began to undress himself with shaking hands, she knew that he was as undone as she was.

She watched as he bared that gorgeous, perfect body for her, and she knew a moment of shame, because he was still perfect. Rippling muscles and utter glory, while she was round and…

When he uncovered that most masculine part of him, all of her insecurity vanished.

He was hard for her. And the need in his eyes was like an inferno.

He reached down, gripped the top of her gown and pulled it down, exposing her breasts, and then he divested her of the rest of the garment, leaving her only in a pair of lace underwear, her belly round and *obvious*.

She had decided to get dressed up like a femme fatale because there was no way to avoid him, and anyway it was how she fortified herself when she ran a con. She had decided to meet him where he stood because she knew that there was no other real option.

She hadn't anticipated *this*. Or maybe she had. Maybe

somewhere, deep down, this was what she had always wanted it to become.

Maybe it was what she needed.

They could come together again, and it would never be enough. She knew that. Because there was some kind of sickness in them.

Something that made them need each other like this.

It wasn't just sex for him; she could see that.

Because he was not happy to be here. He didn't want to want this, and somehow, that made her feel even more aroused. Because it made her feel even more special.

This thing between them had always been real. Specific.

It had never been simple sexual desire. It had always been something deeper.

They were powerless in the face of it even now. Even as they attempted to cope with this new reality. The pregnancy.

Even as he was angry. She didn't know at what. Not her. But at something. Some darkness that seemed to be pushing at him.

"Beautiful," he said, his voice a growl. "You are stunningly beautiful. And mine."

She wasn't his.

He was leaving.

And it hurt her more than she wanted to admit.

She'd told him the baby wasn't his so he would leave. So she could have her independence. She was fine.

She was fine.

She was fine.

She didn't need him.

But now she *needed* him.

He bent down and pressed his mouth to her stomach. She shivered.

And then he looked up at her, and she saw something so raw, so painful, in his eyes that she had to look away.

He cursed, low and harsh, and then lifted her, putting her on her knees, with a pillow beneath her to help brace her stomach. Then he put his large, rough palm against her ass and squeezed her, before moving her underwear to the side.

And he was inside her before she could take her next breath.

And she wanted to weep with it. Because it felt right. It felt like home.

It was all the memories of what had come before, but something new. Because the desperation between them was real.

Because this was a goodbye she didn't think they would ever say.

But each stroke brought them closer to the end.

She'd already thought they'd found the end. But no. They were having to do it again.

She would have his baby. A piece of him, always.

As if the memories weren't enough.

As if he wouldn't always be red. And everything she saw. Everywhere she looked.

"Mine," he growled.

And it was that, that edge that pushed her right over.

"Ewan." She cried out his name as her orgasm broke over her, and he gripped her hips tight and followed behind, pouring himself inside her as he growled his pleasure.

Her cheeks were wet with tears, and her body was trembling.

"Go," she whispered.

"Jessie…"

"You're right. Neither of us knows anything about having a baby. And what are we going to find out together?"

"Nothing."

"Just go, and know that everything will be fine."

She was breaking. She needed him to leave.

If he would leave someday, he had to leave now.

He had to.

"If you can't handle things…"

"I'll get help. I promise. I can't have you here." Her voice broke. "I can't."

"I would stay," he said. "If I didn't think I would cause more harm."

"It's okay."

And he dressed, and left her there. And she thought that she was going to shatter. Into a million pieces.

A million ugly pieces. And she would never get that image out of her head, either. Of herself breaking apart without him.

She had never really loved anybody except for Maren before.

But there was something with him. No matter how much she wished there weren't.

"Go," she said again. Because she had to save as many pieces of herself for her child that she could.

Because she couldn't keep breaking for him.

CHAPTER SIX

THE FOUR DAYS following his departure from Scotland were like hell.

He didn't compare it to hell lightly. He had lived in hell before. At that very estate. He had lived it that day his mother had died. The day that he had seen his younger brother. Cold and still.

Dead before he even drew breath.

Everything good he'd known had died that day.

He knew all about hell. Most assuredly that it was a place on earth. He did not doubt that for a moment. But being without Jessie... Having made the decision to step away from her and the child...

In this decision he'd discovered a new level of hell.

And when he'd descended into those depths previously it had been beyond his control. This was not.

He could change it. He had the power.

He was no longer a child held hostage in the Highlands. He had ascended on his own, taken his status and little else out into the world and built an empire not apart from his father—better—an empire to spite him.

He could go back.

But for what?

For her?

He'd had to walk away.

It was the only way to spare them both.

Because what lay on the other side of this...

He had gone to her because he had to see. Or perhaps because he'd simply needed to see *her*. It had been foolish.

But he had gone.

It was hell. But he'd been with her. He'd known he wouldn't stay.

She didn't need him.

She'd wanted him gone. She'd made that clear when she'd declared the child wasn't his.

Or perhaps she was just giving you a choice?

It didn't matter.

He had done what he'd had to. He had done what was best.

If he had thought for a moment that his presence in the life of his child would...

If he had thought for one moment that he could be of good. That he could do something good as a father. But the problem was he didn't believe in the benevolence of fathers in general.

You left her.

He had.

Unbidden, images of their last time together flooded his mind and infused his veins with fire. He'd made love to her again because he'd been unable to stop himself. Because when it had been clear she wanted him as he wanted her, he'd been powerless against it.

That weakness was why. It was why hc had to turn away from her. It was too much like his father, and if there was even a chance this flame could take all he'd made himself and forge him into that monster, he had to deny it.

But he worried. About the baby.

He didn't know the woman. And what he did know was a concern.

The daughter of an infamous criminal.

A con artist.

And she would be raising his child. His blood. But what did blood mean?

He had seen his mother's blood. Staining the white sheets after she bled out. His blood, too.

But worse, he had seen his father's blood, and how it had turned following the death of his beloved.

His father had never been a particularly warm father. He had loved his wife, and that was it. She was much younger than he was, beautiful.

She'd had him, and for years after they had tried to have more children. She had been driven by her need for more children, and his father had never seemed to care one way or another whether Ewan was there or not. He was an heir. A convenience as far as passing down the family line, but that was all.

He meant nothing more.

But his mother... His mother had loved him. Being a mother had been her proudest achievement. She had put it above being a wife, and Ewan hadn't been able to escape the truth that his father had resented him slightly for that always.

But he had also loved his wife, and lived to give her what she wished. So they had tried for more children. Baby after baby.

Lost.

Most in the very early stages.

But finally, when Ewan was eleven, she had managed to carry one to term.

They'd had the very best doctors brought in. His father hadn't trusted that she would be safe in a hospital. He wanted total control over the environment. There had been high-tech medical equipment, and entire teams of people.

But everything had gone horribly wrong, and to this day, he didn't fully understand what or how. It had been like a scene from the past. They hadn't been able to stop her bleeding. Not with anything, and at the same time, the baby had been in grave distress.

And she had been begging. Begging that the child be saved. And when it was clear the baby would never breathe, he was convinced that she had just chosen to slip away.

It was the moment when she had stopped fighting.

The very moment.

And then she had been gone.

And he had watched it all unfold. A frightened boy crying in the corner.

His father had railed against the medical team, and then had clung to his wife's body, wailing.

The baby was an afterthought. Lying there still and blue.

He had filled Ewan's vision. This boy who would have been his brother. Who had taken his mother from him. The fury and despair that had filled him with equal measure was a shattered, sharp memory. One that robbed his lungs of air even now.

He would never forget it.

He would never not be marked by that. Or all that had come after. The truth was that the poison had always been in his father's veins.

The loss of his wife had let it flow unchecked.

All the rage his father had ever carried over Ewan taking his mother's focus away had poured itself out on him. And the need to correct what he saw as softness in him.

And everything to do with babies and pregnancy... Ewan couldn't fathom ever facing such a thing. Above all else, he had yet to see why a child might need a father. He had needed a mother.

But she had died.

His child would have his mother. And no other poison.

You don't know that. You don't know what manner of parent she'll be. You don't know her. She is a woman whose arms you spent a pleasurable few hours in.

He couldn't imagine Jessie being cruel.

Why? Because she gave you her virginity? Because you think that makes her pure in some fashion?

No. That wasn't why.

She hadn't tried to bleed him for more money. She hadn't tried to exploit the fact that she was carrying his baby.

Yet.

And perhaps the issue was there was a bigger fish. A mark that she had in mind. She'd said she'd had other lovers. He didn't believe her. But maybe he should.

He growled, sweeping his papers off his desk.

He should go to one of his clubs. Find a woman interested in performing a scene and have her there in front of everyone.

He wasn't opposed to such things. No act was off-limits for him. Provided everyone involved was willing.

But he just…

He couldn't. Not as long as the memory of her skin beneath his hands haunted him in this way.

He stood up, realization pouring through him.

He would have to go back.

That decision was made and he was moving before he had a chance to fully process all of it.

He *couldn't* stay away from her.

He couldn't stay away from the child.

To what end?

At what cost?

He would hold her at a distance. Just because he was with her didn't mean he had to touch her. Perhaps there was a middle ground?

It nearly made him laugh.

He was not a man who knew a middle ground.

He burned bridges to ash and laughed at the destruction.

It was important to him to be confident in what he did, always. When he had broken away from his father, from his family name, he had been determined that he would make something new. And even if it was partly just to spite his old man, it had been his and his alone.

And now there was her. She had brought him back to the estate, a place he swore he would never go again, and he had gone back.

And here he was, poised to go back again.

The intercom in his office came on. "Mr. Kincaid, there is a woman here to see you."

Jessie filled his mind. Only Jessie.

"Send her in."

A few moments later the door to his office opened. The metallic disappointment he felt when he saw it was a redhead, and not Jessie, was disorienting.

"Mr. Kincaid," she said, bobbing into a quick, ridiculous curtsy. "Your Grace."

He lifted his chin. "I don't answer to that title anymore."

He'd given it away, even if it had only been a public showing of frivolity and nothing of weight.

The pretty redhead advanced on him, her brows low, her lips making a snarl. She was like a very mad kitten. "You abandoned my sister. And she needs you. *We* need you."

"Ms. Hargreave, I don't have the time…"

She leaped forward, and she pushed him with the edges of her fingers. It actually hurt a bit. "Don't act like I should care about your time! Our father found us. Please, Mr. Kincaid, she's too proud to tell you, but we need your help. You need to protect her. You need to protect your child."

Jessie had been looking into the cost of a personal security detail ever since she'd gotten that phone call out of the blue from their father.

"Aren't you going to congratulate me on becoming a grandfather?"

The ice that had dripped down her spine…

She was terrified. And Maren was even more terrified. She had begged Jessie to call Ewan back, but she couldn't do that. Her sister didn't understand. She was a virgin. She didn't know what it cost her to even think about Ewan. That in the days since he had left her she…

She had been altered, forever, by the passion between them, and she simply couldn't cope with having him near, not again. Only to have him leave.

Yes, she had promised that she would let him know if she needed him, but she wasn't entirely confident that she did.

It was unsettling that her father knew where she was.

But she had no real evidence that he wanted to hurt her.

It was far more likely that he would wish to manipulate them into working for him again. Using his connections and their past misdeeds to make enemies for them.

Their minds were incredibly valuable, and while he possessed the same sort of mind, three were better than one.

Maren had vanished yesterday, with a cryptic comment about getting help herself.

Fine. Maybe her sister's new palace and title would get her what they needed.

Maren was going to be a princess.

That had to hold some weight.

She stood up and went to the window, looking out over the vast green.

And then she felt a flutter in her stomach.

She put her hand there. "Baby? Is that you?"

Could she really feel her child moving?

She was stunned by that.

And then gripped with a vicious feeling of protectiveness.

"If that bastard comes after us, I'll kill him. And I will relish the memory of it. The one that will never go away. Because it won't."

But her baby being like her? It made her want to weep. For the first time, she thought of the baby as a person. Not a circumstance that had been imposed upon her, but what would be a human being, independent of her. Walking around in the world.

"I don't want to hurt you," she said. "But I'm afraid. I don't know how to be a mother. I don't know how to be anything but a con artist. I was never taught anything different or better. Your aunt Maren and I were taught nothing about how to love. About how to be a family. We were only ever taught how to use people. But I want you to learn better. She and I have learned how to care for each other. To put each other first. We'll do the same with you. She'll help me. And anyway, she's a princess. Which is pretty cool."

And just then, she saw a white plane descending.

There was no doubt what that meant.

"No," she said.

He was here.

She couldn't bear it. She couldn't bear to be confronted by him, not at this moment. Except…

Maren.

This was Maren's doing.

"I take back everything that I just said. Your aunt Maren is a turncoat. She's… She's not to be trusted."

She grabbed her phone and called her sister. *"Maren,* what have you *done?"*

"I'm making you safe," said Maren.

She could hear commotion through the phone. Likely the opening of the plane door.

"I told you not to involve him. He doesn't want anything to do with me or the baby."

"That isn't what he told me."

"Hey."

"Jessie," and she would know that voice anywhere. "You have no choice. This is exactly the kind of thing that you said you would tell me about."

"I have assessed the risk and determined that it does not require you or your intervention."

"It requires me."

"It doesn't."

She heard a car door close. "I will not watch you bleed out and die, do you understand me? I will not lose you or this child. I will brook no argument on the topic."

"You have no authority over me," she said.

"I am the Duke of Kilmorack. And I will exercise the authority in my blood."

Fury filled her. "*Technically*, you gave the title to me."

"*Technically*, you can't do that." And then he hung up.

She growled in frustration and flung her phone down onto the couch.

She knew they would be here in only a couple of minutes.

Now she was afraid, and angry and she didn't know which was worse.

She paced back and forth, the length of the room. And didn't stop moving until she saw a black town car pull up in front of the estate. She could see her sister and his Royal Dukeness sitting in the back.

They got out of the car, and she was struck by the way Ewan towered over Maren. He was such a tall man. And he looked good walking next to her sister.

She fought back a wave of jealousy. What a ridiculous thing.

She had no claim on him. She didn't want one anyway.

And Maren certainly didn't want him.

It was just that they were both very beautiful.

And together, even more so.

She swallowed down that surge of ridiculous anger and walked downstairs to the vast entryway of the estate.

Her home, which was supposed to be a place of tranquility. Instead, it had been nothing but drama.

It's not the house's fault that you decided you needed to jump Ewan after winning it from him.

No. She supposed not. And in the end, the pregnancy was why all this was happening.

Her own lack of self-control.

It wasn't fair. She had been controlled all of her life.

She had never made a mistake.

Except this very tall, very handsome, mistake that was spidering out of control into lots more mistakes.

When the front door opened, she was standing there with her arms crossed tightly over her chest.

"And what exactly do you think you're going to accomplish by being here?"

But then his stormy eyes were on her, and he was moving toward her with purpose.

With single-minded intent.

He reached out and grabbed hold of her, pulled her against his body. "There is no question about what happens now, Jessica. Your father knows where you are. You owning this estate isn't going to insulate you from that fact. You need something stronger. You need my name."

"I need... What?"

"My name. You will be the Duchess of Kilmorack, Jessie Hargreave. You will be my wife."

CHAPTER SEVEN

HE HAD KNOWN this was the only real option from the moment Maren had told him what was happening.

Hell, he had been on his way to that conclusion anyway.

He had been ready to board the plane back to Scotland even before he'd found out there was a real threat of danger.

And he did not doubt that he would've decided *this* before it landed.

Maren had simply crystallized it all.

He could sense her vibrating with barely contained anxiety behind him.

"I'm sorry, Jessie…"

"Don't tell me you're sorry. You did this on purpose." Jessie in a fury was a sight to see. He'd seen her passionate, and he'd seen her contained, playing a role. He had not seen this. This uncontained, incandescent rage. "Why couldn't you just listen to me? Why couldn't you let me handle it? You're always so cautious, Maren. If it wasn't for me, we wouldn't have any of this. I'm the one that led us through. You had all your *stupid rules* all the time. And maybe if you hadn't been such a prude, maybe if you hadn't insisted that we not touch any man, I wouldn't have lost my mind over this one." She jabbed her thumb toward him but didn't look his way.

He looked between the sisters. "Is that true? Did you have rules?"

Maren looked up at him in a beseeching way. "Well, yes. We have… Has she not explained this to you?"

He looked down at Jessie, his *lover*. The woman who was carrying his child. The woman he knew almost nothing about. "I know that your father is a career criminal. A dangerous man. I know that you are both con artists."

Maren sniffed. "We are not. We *were* women experiencing con artistry."

"Is that a thing?"

"Seems more fair. I don't think *con artist* is what we want to be defined by."

He turned narrowed eyes to Jessie. "And you?"

"I can own it." Her own eyes glittered, all the rage simmering there multifaceted, like a particularly sharp jewel. "Con artist fits. Why not use it?" She turned away from him, clearly wanting to put distance between the two of them.

"Other than that," he said, looking back at Maren. "I know very little about her."

"She's a genius, you know. We—"

"You're card counters. I know that. I actually saw you both months before the last poker game. While I was building up to losing my family estate and titles."

"You're kind of a con artist yourself," said Maren.

Jessie whirled around. "He is *absolutely* a con artist. And a coward. You had every opportunity to claim me the last time you were here and you walked away. So now what? Now that you get to play the part of Batman you're happy to storm in? Now that you get to be the night, and vengeance and whatever else, owning up to the fact you knocked me up is cool enough for you? You didn't want to marry me then."

If she was remotely close to the truth it might have made him angry. But she wasn't.

"I can't say that I want to marry you *now*," he said. "But it has become a necessity. The truth is, Jessie, if I thought for one moment that my presence would have added something to the life of you or the child, I would never have left. But listen to me now. I am not the hero of your story. Not then, and not now. However, now... Now I know that you need me. Now I know that you need me to keep you safe. The scales have balanced. My absence is now more harmful than my presence. And that's why I'm here."

"I have done a damned good job of protecting myself. Protecting us for all this time. I don't need you."

"I'm afraid that we do," said Maren. "And if you're willing to take the chance with us, that's fine, Jessie. We've always taken chances by ourselves. But the baby..."

"Don't talk to me about the baby," said Jessie. "The baby is mine. Mine. You," she said, turning to face him again, "were ready to leave us."

"I was on my way back before Maren came."

"I'm going to leave you two to talk," said Maren.

"Coward," said Jessie, her eyes narrowed.

"Maybe," said Maren. "But mostly, this isn't my fight."

"You *made* it your fight," said Jessie.

"No. I just brought in the person that you should have been discussing this with all along."

Once Maren was gone, Jessie rounded on him.

"I'm not going to marry you."

"Don't be a fool, Jessie. What is the point of having this estate? What is the point of having this life if it's under threat?"

"You don't want this."

He wanted her. That much was clear.

But… He did not possess the capacity to be a husband. He did not see what benefit he could be as a father.

"My name will protect you. And while we work to ensure that your father is put behind bars, you need that name."

"My father, behind bars? Do you really think you can accomplish that? Many have tried and failed."

"I have never failed at a single thing that I've ever put my mind to. I don't intend to start now."

"So confident. For a man who ran from here only a few days ago."

"Every decision that I've made so far has been about what I thought would be better for the child. Believe me when I tell you, there are worse things than having no father."

She looked at him, that luminous green boring into his soul. "You think I don't know that? My father is the person creating all these problems now. Of course I know that. But you…"

"What? You think because we have incendiary sex we can make something more of it?"

"Not anymore. Because I already know who you are. You walked away from me. For five months, you were away from me. You knew where I was. And then you came back, and you saw that I was having your child, and you left again."

"You told me to leave," he said.

She jerked backward as if he'd struck her. "A gentleman wouldn't remind me."

"I am not a gentleman." He moved toward her. "We are strangers, Jessie. Nothing more than two people who found pleasure in each other's bodies. That does not make us fated. But if you need some things explained to you, then I will do so. I never wanted to return here. This was a house of suffering. Why do you think I hate my father? Do you think it was because he would not increase my allowance when I asked? Do you think that I'm a poor little rich boy? Is that what you suppose? My father was a monster. He starved me. Beat me. Neglected me. Under the guise of making me stronger. Because the weak perish. And I would either become strong or die. He would see his line carried on by an honorable man, one like him who never turned a public scandal." He grinned. "So I became public scandal."

The color drained from her face. "But you… You were his son…"

"Yes. But he was mad. And you cannot reason with a madman. Or an evil one. So believe me when I tell you, I have no interest in attempting to do so with your father."

Her throat worked. The evidence that she was affected by what he'd said written in the paleness of her skin.

"It will be a marriage in name only, and I will be here until I'm certain you're safe. I cannot ever be a real father to the child. Do you understand that? I can never be a real husband."

She glared at him. "I don't want you to be."

"You seem angry about me leaving."

"It's complicated, Ewan. I don't like feeling abandoned, and I don't like feeling manipulated and all of it's happening all at once. I have to be a mother, and I don't have the energy for you, but I hated that you left even though I asked you to. I am pregnant, my father is a narcissistic sociopath and I refuse to be reasonable because I feel I deserve an outburst!"

He reached down and gripped her chin, and regretted that the moment his thumb and forefinger made contact with her soft skin.

"I'm sorry," he said. "That things are this way. That I am this way."

She looked away. "So tell me, how many times a year do you have to deal with something like this?"

"Never. I'm always careful."

"You weren't careful with me."

He shook his head. "No. I wasn't."

"You admit it."

"How can I deny it?"

She shook her head. "I don't want you here. I don't want to marry you. I don't want you to be high-handed and…"

"It has to be a big wedding, and it has to happen soon. It must be visible. You must, for all the world, be the wife of Ewan Kincaid. Do you know why?"

"Yes. Because coming for me will be visibility my father won't want. But as long as I'm nothing and nobody squirreled away in the Highlands…"

"Exactly." He looked at her. "You're not a foolish woman, Jessie. You did not get where you are by denying reality. You and I both know that."

She tilted her head to the side, as though she'd just had a realization. "It's a con."

"If that makes you feel better."

"It makes *sense*. My father is nothing more than a con artist willing to shed blood. He fancies himself some kind of a mastermind. But it isn't anything quite so exciting. He's a petty con man who started killing people. That's it."

"Why does he want control of you?"

"We are strangers. You don't need to know that."

And with that she turned and walked away, leaving him standing there in the entryway of this house that haunted him in so many ways.

CHAPTER EIGHT

JESSIE HAD THE door locked firmly, as she sat in her tepid bath, angry that it couldn't be hot for the safety of the baby, and angry at her sister, and Ewan.

The firm knock on the door jolted her.

"I'm sorry," said Maren.

"No, you aren't."

"I'm sorry that you're mad at me. I'm not sorry about what I did."

She craned her neck to hold her chin above the water. "Then your apology means nothing."

She felt bruised. What he'd said about this place, about his father. Mostly because it made what he'd done somewhat understandable and she didn't especially like that.

She didn't want to humanize him. He was right. They didn't know each other. And she felt strongly that perhaps they shouldn't.

"I didn't know what else to do."

"Well, Maren," said Jessie. "What you could've done is at least talk to me. At least…"

She sighed heavily and got out of the bath, wrapping herself in a towel.

She stepped over to the mirror and looked at herself. She looked exhausted.

She had been sad and miserable ever since Ewan had left here four days ago, and all of this was only making it worse.

She went over and unlocked the bathroom door, then turned back to the mirror again. There was a firm knock again.

"Well, come in," she said.

Except when the door opened, it was Ewan.

She gasped and took two steps away from him.

"You said to come in."

"I didn't know it was you. I'm naked and soaking wet."

He lifted a brow. "You've been naked and soaking wet beneath me on multiple occasions."

Heat consumed her and that just made her angry. "You know what I mean. That was beneath you."

"You have been..."

"Stop."

"You are the one who needs to stop."

His tone was grave, his eyes on her body far too keen. And she felt as if he could see straight through the towel. He might as well be able to. He had seen her, after all. She had no shame with him, no self-control. If she could take back any one thing—other than giving herself to him that first night—it would be the way that she had surrendered to him when he had come just days ago. When he had left her.

You pushed him away. You didn't want him. And he was happy for the excuse.

It was true.

They had both been searching for ways not to deal with each other. And they had both been happy to take the reasons they had found.

And now things had changed. And she was loath to admit it.

She wanted to solve the problem. Because she always solved the problem.

Maren was the dreamer. Maren saw things in ways that Jessie often couldn't.

But Jessie made the plan.

If Maren dreamed it, then Jessie articulated it.

Mind palaces and file folders. That was how they were different.

And she had to admit, even if privately now, that if Maren couldn't see a way out of their current situation, even with her dreams, even with her more naturally optimistic personality, then there was no way out.

It would be great to get their father arrested, but complicated. They knew there were a few of his men inside law enforcement and they'd agreed it was a bit too risky. They could find themselves back at the compound or in a cell.

No way in hell.

She hated that. Hated that truth with a passion, because the man standing before her was likely her salvation.

"Speak now, then," she said, trying to sound imperious.

"What did your sister mean?"

"By what?" she said with an exasperated breath. "My sister has said a lot of nonsense today."

"About you. Your mind."

She looked at him from the side of her eye. "We're card counters. You know that."

"It isn't that simple, though, is it?"

She decided then that not answering would just make him more interested. And she'd rather have him cheerfully skip off to Narnia.

So the truth it was.

"It's an eidetic memory. Not the most extensive ever recorded, but it's a lot. I can often remember what happened on a precise date. I can recall with perfect detail situations that I was in. Maren and I spent a lot of time training ourselves. So that we were not bombarded constantly with un-fettered memories. You have to keep them in files, you see."

"Really?"

He looked at her like he was interested. Not like she was a specimen, and she found that was different and notable compared to the way many people looked at her, especially men.

But even more surprising, it made her want to talk to him.

"Yes. That's how my father has grown his crime empire. He has the same kind of mind. And he has designs on ours. We were tools to him. That's why we ran away. We decided we wanted a different life. And that is also why we decided there was an endpoint on the con. We were made to be grifters from birth. We didn't choose that. But using those skills, we decided to find a way out of that life."

"He doesn't want you out."

"No. At least, that's the concern. And I don't want anything hanging over my head. Or Maren's. Or the baby's. The baby most of all. Maren and I didn't ask for this predicament. But... The choices I made are why I'm pregnant."

"The choices I made, too. So let me help you."

She felt her expression get petulant along with her tone. She couldn't help it. "You left."

"And you're upset about it now."

"I'm upset... I'm upset at myself. I'm upset about everything. I lied. Okay? I'm a good liar. I lie easier than I do other things. I lied to protect myself. I lied to myself. I told myself it would be easier if you weren't there, but it hurt me that you rejected the baby. It hurt me that you wanted to take the excuse."

He stared at her for a long moment, and she felt exposed. "Jessie, what do you suppose this is? What do you suppose can be made of this?"

She knew she was inconsistent. But she'd never been pregnant before. She'd never had a lover before. It was confusing. All of it.

She wanted him here, but she did need some boundaries. Badly.

"It isn't about me. It's about the baby. I don't want you to reject your child." She suddenly felt tired, and soggier than she would like. "Can we step out of the bathroom, please? I don't need to have maidenly modesty in your presence, but I do want to get dressed. I'm starting to get chilly."

Unfortunately, she did feel a measure of maidenly modesty; she just didn't want to demonstrate it to him. So as soon as she exited the bathroom, she let the towel fall to the floor and walked with as much cool as she could muster to the closet, where she disappeared inside before selecting an outfit.

She'd ordered a great many loose and flowing things.

And leggings that stretched infinitely. She emerged again a moment later with a very large sweatshirt and some of those very leggings.

"Sorry. It isn't exactly the clothing of a seductress." She did a small shimmy for effect.

But he was staring at her, and she could see the heat in his eyes.

He should have laughed at the shimmy.

He hadn't.

"No. If I agreed to marry you for the sake of the baby, for protection, we have to have very clear ground rules. You and I do not play well together."

"The problem with you and I is that we play rather too well."

She sighed. "But we can't just have sex constantly."

"Agreed, but I'm curious. Why do you feel that way?"

"Because it cost me too much. Because I remember everything. Don't you understand that? Everything. Every detail. That's why we had rules. That's why we could never take lovers. Because of this. Because when I think about that night it's a film that plays in high definition in my mind over and over again, and I can't stand it. I can add to it. I can't... I'm not in love with you. I don't want to be. I don't think I could be. I don't want to be obsessed with you, either. It isn't fair. It isn't right. I want more for myself than that. I want to have this new life. I want to have it on my terms. Being forced to do anything because of my father is unconscionable to me. But I acknowledge that this is out of my hands. Out of my control. But I won't... I can't. Not again."

"You will have to marry me. And at as public a venue as possible. It will have to be a story. About that poker game. About that passionate night. It will need to seem as if we are madly in love. Because your father has to believe that there is a wall around you so protective, he cannot cross it."

"He won't care..."

"He will. And if it doesn't work, then he'll be entrapped. Because I will have men set around you. I will keep you safe, Jessie. I promise you. I will keep the baby safe."

He lowered his head. "I don't have a high opinion of fathers."

"Neither do I. For obvious reasons."

"I do not know what I can offer this child. I don't know what I can give. But what I know is that there is a graver sin and that's not offering protection now when I could."

"I think that I would be fine if..."

"No. We have to make it impossible for your father to come at you. We have to make you safe. It is paramount that we do so. It is essential. And if I were to stand by and allow him access to you and something were to happen to you, I would never be able to forgive..." He shook his head.

"I do not need forgiveness or redemption. But I need you safe. And the baby."

"Why?"

She was truly baffled by it. He had been willing to walk away from her, to accept that she was able to take care of herself on her own before her father had been introduced into the equation. He had felt no particular loyalty to her then, and no draw to the child. So why now? Why had this made a difference? She truly didn't get it. She wasn't someone with an innate moral compass. She could acknowledge that.

She was all right stealing from people as long as they were the right sort of people to steal from. She had been totally fine having sex with him when he was a stranger. She hadn't been a virgin out of any sense of moral obligation to purity or treating sex like it was special. Her morality was fixed by being raised by a criminal. And otherwise, it was based on largely not wanting to cause harm. But in a blanket sense. She didn't have the impression that he was much more keyed into honor or morality than she was. So what the hell?

"I cannot and will not allow you to be harmed," he said. "That's all you need to know. Because in my mind, there is a very thin line between a man that actively harms those in his care and a man who allows harm to occur because he does not act. This place is hell to me. I will not allow it to become hell for you. Do you understand me?"

It made her feel small and somewhat wounded. And she had no idea why. She did not expect anyone but her sister to truly care about her. She didn't expect Ewan to care.

But it was far too easy for her to think back on the night they'd spent together, and the time here in the estate. His hands on her skin. His lips on hers.

To feel like that must have been caring.

It wasn't.

It never would be.

"So you feel...obligated?" she asked.

"Yes, I feel obligated. I might as well jump out of the highest window of this house if I cannot bother to put myself to use keeping you safe. Can you understand that? My life would be forfeit, and I would be nothing. No amount of money can erase such a sin. No amount of power. There is nothing worthwhile on this planet that a man could claim if he fails those around him. When they are most vulnerable."

She blinked, uncertain when tears began to fill her eyes, only certain that they had. He had so much conviction in that statement, and sometimes she was afraid she lacked conviction. She liked to win. She didn't know much else about herself.

"You said you don't know me."

"I can get to know you."

"Can you? When you do, will you let me know who I am? Because I don't know. I'm still trying to figure it out. I'm still trying to decide. When I was born, I was nothing but clay for my father to mold, and the problem with a memory like mine is you don't forget anything. So I remember all of his lessons whether I want to or not. Everything that he ever taught me about how I have to look out for myself. And now I have to figure out how to be a mother. Isn't that essentially caring for someone else more than you do yourself? I was never taught that."

"We'll begin by letting me care for you."

She stood there for a long moment. And she realized that if there was even a chance that her father might hurt her, and she had turned down his protection... If she had the opportunity for him to intervene and she hadn't taken it, and the baby was used against her... She would never forgive herself. And that was an introduction to a new thing about herself.

"I'll marry you," she said. "Until the threat of my father is neutralized."

"Well then, you best get prepared. Because this isn't just going to be a wedding. This is going to be a whole Cinderella story."

"I've never wanted to be Cinderella."

"Who did you want to be?"

"The fairy godmother. She's an independent woman who can turn a pumpkin into a carriage. All Cinderella could do was get the attention of a prince when she was wearing enchanted clothing. I want to be the one who does the magic tricks."

"That's an interesting way to look at it."

"You heard a little bit about my childhood. *Interesting* is the only way I can look at anything."

"We will put a marriage announcement in the paper today. I will alert the media. We will marry in two weeks' time."

"Two weeks?"

"You object?"

"That's hardly time to plan anything."

"Suddenly you care?"

How strange. She sort of did.

"Not really. I never thought that I would get married. I'm not especially attached to the idea, but you know if I'm going to have a wedding, maybe it should be kind of pretty."

She had not realized that she possessed even the slightest bit of a romantic bone in her body. She thought that was entirely Maren's territory. And here she was, saying things like that about a wedding.

"You know what," she said. "I only care because there are going to be pictures of me everywhere."

"I don't believe you."

"Well, what about you? Did you ever think you would get married?"

"No. I very much intended not to. But my father didn't live to see the day, so I suppose every cloud has a silver lining."

"Indeed. How nice to be a cloud."

"A sexy cloud."

"A cloud that you aren't going to touch."

She didn't know why his compliments affected her. Men had always called her beautiful. Sexy. It didn't mean anything to her because they didn't.

And that right there was a troubling revelation. Ewan was a playboy. He was used to complimenting women. He was accustomed to flattering them. It meant nothing. It meant *nothing*.

And she meant just as little. He wanted to protect the baby.

But still… No one had ever been protective of her other than her sister. And they were more protective of one another.

But the sensation of wanting someone to protect her, even if it was because she was a vessel for the actual main attraction… It did something to her. She didn't want to admit it, but it did.

This was just so damned difficult. And complex.

But she was smart. She hadn't gotten this far being emotional, and she wasn't going to start now.

You're going to have to be something for the baby.

Well, yes. But she had months to figure that out. So… She would take months.

But she only had two weeks to think about the wedding. And the fact that she was going to be a bride. She only hoped that she had the wits necessary to withstand him. She could make her brain work in her favor. She forgot nothing. And while she couldn't convince herself anymore that he was simply a vacuous playboy—there was more to him than that—it was the part he chose to play.

If there was one thing she understood it was that the commitment to a role could be stronger than the truth about someone's whole personality.

She knew because she lived it.

She knew because it was her.

And when the wedding came around, she would be smart. And when they got married, she would remember that it was only until she and the baby were safe.

Because they had created this accidental child together. And they would protect her together. She looked at him, and suddenly she felt resolved. Like the two of them might have something deeply in common.

Neither one of them had been protected by the people who should've protected them most.

And together, they would not allow the same fate to befall their child.

On that, they could agree. No matter what.

"Two weeks," she said finally.

"And it's going to be a hell of a party."

"Great," she said. "I love a spectacle." Though usually, she liked a spectacle because it was distracting from the con. And this was indeed a con, but she wasn't entirely sure it was a con designed in her favor.

But the thought of a con at least made her heart beat a little bit faster. It was a relief to have her heart doing that over something other than Ewan.

CHAPTER NINE

THE ANNOUNCEMENT HAD created a splash in world headlines, just as he had predicted that it would. Just as he had
known it had to. But there was one more thing he felt he
needed to see to before he would feel good about the direction they were taking things. Yes, he had private investigators working to find what evidence was required to take her
father down. But the thing about Ewan was he was a man
who did not intimidate easily. Or at all. When you were
raised by the very devil, what could frighten you?

He shut the image out of a limp blue baby.

There was nothing to be scared of in the past. They were
only memories. And he was doing his very best to make
sure that those memories were not his future.

Or the future of the child who had not asked to be con-
ceived. Let alone by two such broken people.

Broken though they might be, he was nothing if not bold.

And that was what brought him to her father's front. It
was an office building, like any other. One could be for-
given for believing that it was actually a legitimate business.
But of course, he knew it wasn't. He knew the authorities
were well aware it wasn't, either, but so far the man remained untouchable. Whether because there was a laby-
rinth of crooked police officers or other more complicated
reasons, he did not know. But he intended to find out.

He also intended to walk into the other man's office today and throw down a gauntlet of his own.

Because he knew that the other man would've seen the headlines.

And he knew that he would have been making plans.

Ewan intended to upend those plans.

He moved through the reception area, barely glancing at the secretary.

She wasn't there to check people in, after all.

There was a metal detector, of course. He was searched for weaponry when he got off the elevator. He was not so foolish as to bring a weapon into the building.

There may be a day when it came to that. But he would choose his venue. And it would never be on Mark Hargreave's home court.

"You have an appointment with Mr. Hargreave," the man waving the magnetic wand over his body said.

"No," he said. "However, he will know that we have a connection. Ewan Kincaid. Duke of Kilmorack."

"Indeed you do," said the man, proving that he was more than just a goon. He was someone who was privy to the conversation in his boss's office.

"Yes. And it is about the business that you would expect."

"Then he will look forward to an appointment with you."

"He doesn't even have to anticipate it. I'm here."

"You know he has many people hoping for an audience with him."

"But only one of them is the father of his first grandchild."

The man chuckled. "We'll see if he'll see you."

He disappeared behind the door and opened it a moment later. "He's feeling generous today."

"Just my luck," said Ewan.

His playboy charm was turned up to eleven, and he knew

that it was likely to irritate the other man, so he made sure that his smile was brilliant.

He walked in as if he didn't have a care in the world. Much less a plan.

"Mr. Kincaid," said Hargreave from behind his desk.

He could see nothing of his daughters in the man.

Perhaps they weren't his. But then, if what Jessie said was true, they had his mind. But the girls were beautiful and petite, and this man had the look of a blunt instrument.

You could put a wild jackal in a suit, but that was what he remained. And Ewan should know. His father was of noble blood, for all that it meant, and he had still been a jackal.

A scavenging hyena that just wanted to pick the bones around him clean.

"I thought that we ought to become acquainted with one another. Since we are about to become family," said Ewan.

"You have something that belongs to me."

"By that, I suppose you mean your daughter? A bit old-fashioned, don't you think?"

He spread his hands over his desk. Shiny, glossy and wide. He was wearing a sharply cut suit. His American vowels were broad, out of place almost, and Ewan had a feeling Hargreave traded on that. "I'm a traditional man."

Ewan nodded. "And so am I. It's why the two of us are getting married before we welcome the child. I don't care, of course, and my love for her transcends such ridiculous notions as marriage. But I do want to do the right thing by her. Or the right thing by you."

"What do you want?"

"I want nothing. Except for you to stay away from my wife."

"She's not your wife yet. And she was my daughter first."

"She left. She doesn't want to be with you. I have to warn

you that I take it very seriously and very personally if anyone makes what's mine feel threatened."

"It's funny. I was going to say that I take it very seriously and personally when somebody takes what's mine," said Hargreave.

"Again. Your daughter removed herself from your possession. She doesn't want to be in your life. And you will respect that."

"Do you think I couldn't have you all eliminated? You, the baby. My daughter is of some use to me, but the rest of you..."

Ewan fought back blinding, violent rage. He had to stay cool. Make it clear he was in control here. He could not let emotion lead him.

It was the strength of the emotion that shocked him. "Do you think I can't have the same done to you? And now if something happens it will be easily traced back to you. Isn't that the only thing keeping you here, in this office building? That plausible deniability. But now you've made threats, and I've heard them. And I will make sure that it's known far and wide unless you steer clear of us. I know that you're a powerful man, but you have no idea who I am. Not really. The whole world doesn't know who I am. But I'm happy to introduce them."

"A compelling speech. You are nothing and no one to me. A playboy billionaire."

"A member of one of Scotland's oldest and most important families. Descendent of the clans in the Highlands. Back then, I simply would've taken a broadsword and separated your head from your shoulders. We were given this land and title by the British. But I'm from Clan McKenzie. And it is rooted deep in our history and our blood to keep our women safe. Our children safe. And it suits me to have the world think of me as a playboy. Have you never thought of that? In much the same way it suits you to have the world believe that you're some sort of altruistic businessman. Someone who is always adjacent to dangerous things, but it can never fully be attributed to you. That benefits you for obvious reasons. But you've never stopped to ask if it might benefit someone else? Are you too much of a narcissist?"

"You're on dangerous ground."

"Unlikely. Since I own much of the ground. I could buy this out from under you tomorrow. You might have a criminal empire. Worth millions. I'm worth billions. Your fortune could be mine in mere seconds. At the snap of my finger. The only thing that could give you an edge on me is if I was not as ruthless as you. But I am. Stay away from her. And if you don't, expect that retribution will be swift."

"I could have you killed now." But he could see that he'd struck a chord with Hargreave.

"You know it's strange. I've already called the police. They're outside. If something were to happen to me... Well, that would be inconvenient. They know that I'm here."

"Such a powerful man you have to call the cops?"

"Such a powerful man I have contacts everywhere. And I'll use them. Don't forget it."

He turned and walked out of the office, and he didn't look back over his shoulder, for no matter that the other man was issuing threats, he refused to let him put him on the back foot. He refused.

Then he walked out into the sun and smiled. This was back in hand.

Nothing was ever going to change his past.

But today he'd been a different man. Today he hadn't been the playboy. He had done the right thing, and it was a novel enough concept to make him feel.

And now. He had a wedding to plan.

CHAPTER TEN

"SHOPPING FOR wedding dresses is supposed to bc fun," said Jessie, pacing the length of the room in the estate.

"It will be," said Maren.

"It will not be. I'm round as an egg. And it's going to be impossible to figure out exactly what size to get. Even though the wedding is in just two weeks."

Two weeks. Already, the headlines had exploded. Already, they were under so much scrutiny, and it had been one day. So technically, she had thirteen days until the wedding.

And he'd said that they would shop for wedding dresses. She wondered if there were any down in the village near here. She could hardly imagine it.

He was intent on making a spectacle, and she wasn't entirely sure what that meant yet.

And that was the thing about him. He came and went as he pleased.

He had been in London on business, so he said.

And when she saw the sleek jet landing just over the rise, she thought about the butterflies in her stomach.

She had no reason to be filled with butterflies.

Not at all.

They were doing this to protect their baby.

When he appeared in the estate moments later, she did

her best to look bored. She experienced a mountain of messy, horrible feelings whenever she thought of him and it was killing her slowly. By inches.

She couldn't find that neat visual marker she'd counted on for so long.

She tried to imagine a ribbon with his name on it, tied to her feelings, so she could cut it ruthlessly in her mind.

But it was red.

And it just made her angry.

"So are we going down to the village or what?"

"We aren't going to the village." He looked borderline scandalized. "We're going to Paris."

"Paris?"

"Where else?"

That was how she found herself ensconced in the private jet. She hadn't ridden in it yet. She'd never been in a private plane.

It was... It was a stark reminder of just how far apart their positions were.

She had an estate that she owned free and clear and that was a big boon.

She had a couple of million dollars in the bank.

Another boon.

But this man was a billionaire. And he controlled more wealth than she would ever be able to fully comprehend. Well, this much wealth.

Butter-soft leather couches on a private jet wealth.

Bedroom on a plane wealth.

Lobster on a plane.

"This is almost outrageously fancy," she said.

He leaned back, his hands behind his head. "When did you miss the memo that I am outrageously fancy?"

She stared at him. Then leaned in and stared harder. He leaned back slightly and that satisfied her.

He was just so ridiculous. As if she hadn't seen him intense.

As if she hadn't seen him as he really was.

Good girl.

The memory of that kept her up at night. It made her sweaty.

Which was not sexy but it was true.

And whatever with that. She saw him. That was the truth of it.

It was, perhaps, the most real reason he'd run.

And that he'd seen her was the biggest reason she'd sent him away.

"I get that that's your facade. Or whatever. It doesn't exactly match up with what I've seen of you, though. You like to play the fool. But I knew the minute I sat down across from you at that poker game that you weren't a fool. I knew the first time I saw you in the casino. Your eyes are too intelligent."

"I'm amazed to hear that you think anyone is intelligent. Given what I know about your gifts."

She shrugged. "It's not a gift. It's a tool. And it isn't intelligence. Just the way my brain is wired. I don't take any particular pride in it, though I have used it, and will continue to use it. I'll be able to remember every stage of our child's development with perfect ease. You know, I wonder about… I have heard so much about the way nostalgia turns memories hazy. I wonder sometimes what that would be like. To let things grow soft so that you can gain a different perspective on them. I never can. I only ever have the perspective I had at the moment. Because I remember everything I saw at that moment. Everything I felt. It robs you of something, I think. Though there are many things that you gain on top of it. I'm not complaining. But I do think that it wouldn't... It's not beneficial for me to be too full of myself about all that. It just isn't."

"That's an interesting perspective. I never thought of it. But I will tell you the memories of my childhood have never grown gauzy. I have never been infused with nostalgia. What was confusing to me as a child is confusing as an adult. And even if I've tried to sort out what it all means now, I find that I'm unable to."

"Well. That's disappointing. I sort of liked imagining that there were people out there who had it together."

"I have certain things together, that's for certain. And there is something blessed in allowing anonymous evenings to turn into a blur. But our night together never has."

"I suppose I shouldn't be pleased about that," she said.

"You can be pleased about it if you want."

"Then I will be pleased about it. And I will remember that you told me I could be pleased about it for the rest of my life." She didn't bother to hold back the small smile that tugged at the corner of her mouth. "But don't feel too excited about that. After all, I can't forget anything."

"Yes, of course. I promise not to let it go to my head."

"Why Paris?"

A flutter of excitement began to take off in her stomach and it made her feel more than she would like. She had never been to Paris. There had never been a reason to go.

She had spent most of her childhood in the United States until her father moved them to London. Likely running from the law.

But they had never gotten out to see the world. She had traveled since then. She and her sister, running their cons, but it had been to specific places where gambling was a feature. And for the most part, that wasn't major metropolitan areas. Not mainstream ones anyway.

She'd been to Las Vegas more times than she could count. But never Paris.

And she ached with the knowledge that she would go now. With him.

She shut that off. She enjoyed the meal that was served on the plane, and then she went and reclined on the bed for a while, just because she could. When they landed at the airport, they were swept immediately into a luxury car that drove them through the beautiful streets. The architecture was glorious. All stone scrollwork and famous glories. The Eiffel Tower. The Arc de Triomphe. She committed everything to memory. Every detail. She wanted to remember this. Forever. She loved it. She realized that she had her face and palms pressed to the glass on the window. And she felt mildly embarrassed. But not enough to stop. Because these would be her memories. Her chosen memories of this moment.

Paris and all its glory.

"Is it everything you hoped?"

She shot him a shady side eye. "How do you know I've never been here before?"

"You look far too eager for someone who remembers everything. And anyway, you look as if you're trying to save this forever."

"Maybe I am."

"You don't need to be prickly about it."

"Why do you care? What I like, what I'm interested in…"

"It seems like I should know something about the woman who is having my baby."

"Based on what? What do you or I know about functional families?"

"No. On something. Though I can't say what. Movies I've seen or maybe Jiminy Cricket. Isn't that what your conscience is supposed to be shaped like?"

She couldn't help herself. She laughed. "All right. As long as a cricket told you to ask about me, then I allow it."

"Good. Tell me about your mother."

That brought a cascade of images. Her mother laughing, tossing her silky hair over her shoulder. She could remember every time she'd seen her mother do that. Down to the very last time. The time she had left then never come back.

"She was beautiful. Is beautiful, I suppose." As if she had never looked up her mother's picture. She was a socialite who very much enjoyed her visibility.

Jessie was always amazed that her father had let his wife go like that. But she supposed it had to do with starting over in England. Making his new life there. Why bring an American socialite who would offer him nothing in terms of social cachet? Never mind that she was the mother of his children.

But she'd walked out before that anyway. "She was not very interested in being a mother. She was very good at styling hair and letting us try on her gowns. I will give her credit for that. She wasn't protective of them. She treated designer pieces like they might as well be our dress-up clothes. She enjoyed that part of having daughters, I think. She let us use her makeup. She let us play dress-up exhaustively in her bedroom. But then she had her own life to see to. And I can't blame her. Except she left. And I kind of do blame her for that. Which isn't fair because I also left."

"But she left you," he said.

"My father would never have allowed her to take Maren and me. We were too important to him. Too valuable. When we were fourteen and fifteen, he was already using us to crack codes for him and remember things. To run cons. We were better than a computer, he said.

"No. He would never let her walk away with us. She was beautiful. But that was all. She wasn't a real asset to him.

It would've put her in danger to bring us, and she never would've been able to start over. Though I think it might be easier for me to forgive her if I truly believed that she missed me."

She felt a slight crack in her heart. It had been there for years. It was just that now she'd become aware of it.

She did her best not to let it show on her face.

"He taught us to be very analytical. Because our brains do hold so much information. And to access it rather than be bombarded by it you have to learn to use it a very specific way."

"You mentioned files."

"Yes. I keep my important thoughts in files. I can walk through the room that's filled with file cabinets and I can go through them alphabetically. That allows me to put them away so that I'm not assaulted by them when I don't want them, and it allows me to come up with a system to help me go through the vast amount of knowledge I have. The other thing he taught us to do was read body language. And manipulate people based on who we assess that they are."

"There's a term for that, isn't there?"

"Yes. A mentalist. I suppose that's what I am. I'm sure there must be some very good things that could be done with the skill set, but I was never shown them. It has helped me, though. To insulate me. Protect me from being swallowed up by my emotions. I learned early on what was important."

"Protecting yourself."

"Yes."

"That's how life is when the adults around you don't protect you," he said, his tone far too knowing.

"Yes."

"But we are protecting our baby. He or she will never have to wonder. And he will not have to build up those defenses."

"But she might need them," said Jessie. "Imagine if she has a brain like mine. I hope she doesn't. I hope she's desperately normal. And I'll think she's exceptional all the same. All mothers do, don't they?" She laughed. "How quickly I forgot my own story. My mother didn't think I was exceptional."

"And you were. Objectively. And so I think the conclusion to be drawn here is that when a mother does not find her child exceptional it is not a commentary on whether or not the child is. It is simply a commentary on the mother."

"Maybe. What about your mother?"

He cleared his throat. "She thought I was exceptional. She loved me. More than anything. She told me all the time she never understood what her life was about, who she was or what the day-to-day meant until she had me. When she was alive, I was happy. But I didn't realize just how much she held everything together. I didn't realize just how much she was protecting me. Because once she was gone, I was no longer under the illusion that my father felt similarly."

"I'm sorry... What happened?"

"We don't need to speak of it."

And she realized that he couldn't speak of it.

"Okay."

For the first time in her recent memory, she was comfortable letting something go. She wasn't certain why; it was just she knew she didn't want to hurt him. She cared about him.

It was such a dangerous thing because when he had left her days ago, she had felt so bereft. Even though she had asked for it. She wasn't reliable when it came to him. Not in any way.

She had made one mistake after another with him. And she was used to being unerring. Analytical. She had never been analytical with him, not for one moment of their association. And she continued not to be. Her own mind made no sense around him.

Her mind was playing tricks on her, and that was part of why she had grown up so analytical. To make it so the mind as strong as hers could never do that.

She turned to face him, looked at his strong profile. Those beautiful eyes...

And it was all feeling when she looked at him. Nothing to do with analysis or equations. She couldn't even tell what he was thinking.

She realized that with alacrity. When she had first met him she felt like she could read him, and now the more she got entangled with him the less she felt like she could.

It just felt like...

Feeling. It was all she could think to call it.

"Are we nearly to our shopping destination?"

"Yes. There will be people there, waiting to take a picture. I called ahead. The best paparazzi photos are staged."

"Really?"

"Of course. If you ever see a photograph with favorable lighting that immediately tells you what brands the woman in the picture is wearing, you can be certain that she called the photographers out to the scene herself."

"That is brilliant."

"You're a con artist. That never occurred to you?"

"Shocking though you may find it, I have not often spent my time ruminating on celebrity. I had bigger fish to fry."

"Well, fry your little fish out of the car," he said as they pulled up to the curb. "And smile."

CHAPTER ELEVEN

HE WATCHED AS Jessie got out of the car and posed like an absolute champion for the photographer that was waiting.

She caught on quickly, and she understood the need for all of this.

He got out of the car and followed behind, doing his own best to look irritated by the proceedings. He put a protective hand on her, another hand on her stomach. Each moment that he spent touching her was like pressing his palm against a naked flame.

This woman. Would he ever get used to the proximity of her? She was asking all kinds of questions he didn't easily have answers to. Well, he could have easily answered how his mother had died, except the words often got stuck in his throat, and he didn't want to speak of his dead brother. More than anything he did not wish to speak of that.

But also, she was asking how he knew what a child needed. And perhaps the answer was in the deficits. He leaned in and whispered in her ear as they walked into the door of the boutique where he had made a private appointment for them. "I think I know what our child needs because I know what we didn't get."

She turned to look up at him, eyes wide, her lips parted slightly. And he knew that would make a fantastic photo.

As soon as they were inside, they had privacy.

"It's more believable if we keep this entirely private."

"Right."

But he stopped talking about believability because the designer and a seamstress came into the foyer of the store and greeted them.

"Miss Lockwood," the woman said—they had agreed to use Jessie's alias while they traveled, because why court trouble? "Very good to have you here. We have pulled aside some of our most popular and accommodating designs."

Jessie laughed. "I assume you mean to accommodate my stomach."

"The baby," the woman said, smiling, tapping Jessie's bump, which caused Jessie to look up at him in irritation.

He shrugged.

He followed Jessie and the two women back into the dressing room. Where she was summarily divested of her clothing, without even being ushered behind the curtain.

"Isn't that…" He couldn't help but lean forward in interest when Jessie's bra was removed. "Dressing room?"

"No need," he said. "Nothing I haven't seen."

She opened her mouth like a fish, opened and closed, opened and closed. But then said nothing.

He had a feeling he would get an earful about that later. But he didn't mind getting an earful from her.

As he sat there watching as she was wrapped in gown after gown, he realized something very strange.

He had lived a very lonely life. He couldn't recall having a relationship that was long or strong enough with someone else to be able to anticipate what they would do in response to something. But with Jessie, he could already imagine it.

She would lecture him, on her modesty. And maybe then afterward she would tease him. Like she had done coming out of her bath the other day. She had dropped that towel and showed him the whole of her beautiful backside before dressing herself. She wasn't shy, and even if she were, it was clear that her desire to one-up him outweighed any kind of modesty she might possess.

She knew that he responded too eagerly to her body to ever remain completely cool and collected when she was nude, and she was happy to dress up, in that red dress as she had done that day that he had come to find out about the pregnancy, and again that day when she had dropped her towel.

He had a feeling it wouldn't take her long to figure out how to use this to her advantage.

He was excited then, not because he was getting a good view of her body, though that, too, but mostly because he knew that about her.

He *knew* her.

At least in some capacity. And it was a strange and unique feeling that he didn't want to let go of.

She tried on many flowing gowns, with the last one being more fitted, showing off the swell of her stomach, and there was an elemental need that fired through his veins that he had no control over. He stood. "That one."

"The lady gets to choose her own gown," the designer said, sniffing.

"I am paying for the lady's gown, and I like her in this one. I want to see her body. I want to see her curves."

"Just for that, I think I might agitate for one of the others," she said, but he could see by the way she looked at herself in the mirror that she liked this one best, too. It annoyed her she agreed with him. He was amused by that realization.

"She'll take this one."

She bought shoes and a veil, and by the time they swept back out onto the Paris streets, their packages safely ensconced in their town car, she was glaring at him.

"We're walking just down this way to go and get some dinner. I've made us a reservation."

He sensed her soften beside him. The mention of food might be enough to tame her.

"Oh."

"I thought you might enjoy a nice meal."

"No. You thought there might be some nice pictures from the nice meal."

"I can think both."

"You are just as much of a con artist as I am. You said that. But I don't think I fully realized it until now. You're always operating on multiple frequencies. That's what you have to do."

He nodded. "That is what you have to do. At least, it's what I've had to do all of my life."

She fell into step beside him. "You're not a playboy, are you?"

"Oh, I am."

"I didn't mean it in the way that… I mean, I'm certain you're a slut."

He barked a laugh. "What?"

"Yes. You have a reputation for sleeping with anything that moves."

"Not anything."

"Okay," she relented. "Not anything. But the overriding opinion is that you are free and easy with your favors."

"I am. And you aren't."

"Out of necessity."

"Understood."

"But I mean you aren't shallow. Or an idiot. That's a game that you like to play because it lets you be in control. People underestimate you. I get that. That's what I do with my looks. I go out of my way to get written off as a bimbo. It's funny. You know my sister seduced so many men without ever letting them touch her. She flattered them. Appealed to them. And she could get them to give her so many things without actually giving them anything. It is amazing what people do when they think you are stupid and they can show you something. It's amazing what you can get from them." She frowned. "I hate that. I hate that I know that. I hate that I think that way. I think maybe I'm not a con artist, and yet I have been forced to live as one. I like gambling. I like winning, and it has taken me until this moment to really…" She trailed off, suddenly looking worried.

"What?"

"Do you ever worry that you're wicked?"

He thought of his father. Who had been difficult always, but had gone into some sort of darkness that terrified Ewan mostly because…he recognized it. "Yes. I do."

"Me, too. All the time. How can you not worry when you're so like…? When you're so like him?"

She was talking about herself, and he knew that. Yet, he shared that feeling. It resonated throughout his entire body.

Because yes. He knew that. He knew it well. "That's when you dedicate your life to revenge," he said, his tone dry.

She laughed. "Oh, I don't have the energy for that. I want to have a life. That's what I was trying to do."

They arrived at the restaurant, and he could see more people taking their pictures, just as he'd anticipated. He overrode the doorman and opened the door for Jessie himself, ushering her inside with a protective arm. They were then led to a table in an alcove. It was a small restaurant with only ten tables, but they were right by the window so that they could be photographed.

"And what exactly have you decided to dedicate your life to?" he asked when they were seated and assured the waiter that they would be taking the prix fixe menu.

With no alcohol for the lady.

"To being happy. At least, that was my plan."

"Win enough money to be settled."

"Yes. When I won the estate, I was…overwhelmed. Overcome. I couldn't believe I'd done it. I'd set myself up for life. And given myself a home. There was never a moment when my father's house felt like a home, no matter where it was. I was always so aware that it was simply his domain. The place where he and other criminals hatched schemes and took advantage of people. It never felt safe. Even being part of his circle. Or maybe being part of it most of all."

"You were part of it. You're not so different from me. Your father made decisions for you. About how comfortable you would be. About how you would spend your time. You are nothing more than a thing to him." He twirled his wineglass on the table. "I spoke to your father."

Her eyes went round. "You what?"

"I decided to go and introduce myself to him. Since I am going to be his son-in-law, after all."

"He's a dangerous man. I thought the entire point of this was to avoid him."

"No, the entire point of this is to get rid of him once and for all. I'm not a man who lets other people determine how I behave. Your father needed to understand the power balance."

"He's dangerous."

"So he told me. Repeatedly. Men who are so dangerous don't need to tell you. Anyone who has any substance whatsoever will simply show you. He's violent, that's clear. But he is not half as clever as he thinks he is, and that is going to be the end of him."

She looked away. "He doesn't forget, though."

He reached out and cupped her chin, forced her to meet his gaze. "Perhaps not. He remembers everything, just like you, but I think that because of that he often does not see. Often does not understand. That some are smart in other ways, and who might have stronger motivation than he realizes." He let that sit with her for a moment. "He's a sociopath, isn't he?"

Her eyes widened a fraction. "Yes. I suppose that's a fair characterization."

"And you aren't."

"How do you know that?" She suddenly looked worried. "I mean really, how do you know that? Because I worry sometimes. I was just saying to you I don't like conning people, and I think that's true. But sometimes... When I won that poker game against you, I felt like I was high. I might as well have taken an illegal substance. I was so thrilled with myself. And I knew at that moment that it was a little bit sad that I was finished with my games because my games made me feel alive."

"You're not a sociopath, because you worry that you might be. Do you think your father has ever given one moment's thought to whether or not he was hurting the people around him? Do you think he just does what is expedient for him?"

"You're right."

"My father wasn't a sociopath. In many ways, that's worse. He was often in a cycle of shame and regret but then his rages were unparalleled. His lows were more than the entire sea."

"I'm sorry," she said. "It sounds horrible. But your mother..."

"We can be done with this."

Dinner was served after, and it was delicious, but he could not keep his mind on the meal before him when he was consumed with Jessie.

"Dinner was delicious," she said when they finished. They walked back out onto the street. He couldn't escape the feeling that he should be touching her. And yet, he couldn't bring himself to close the distance between them.

"The hotel we're staying in is just down there."

"Okay," she said.

"Do you wish to know about my mother?"

He kept that space of air between them, made sure that he wasn't touching her at all.

"It seems like the thing you want to tell me least."

"That isn't an answer."

She stopped and looked at him. "I don't want to hurt for you. But I do. I already do. You make me act so out of character. You make me... From the moment that I met you, and I mean, saw you, not met you, I have thought of nothing else. I was obsessed with you. And that has never happened to me before. I'm focused. I've had to be. But you have disrupted everything. You wrecked everything. Look at this. Look at me," she said, gesturing to her stomach. "You have changed me forever more, and there has never and will never be anything the way that it was. I can never have that uncomplicated and free life, because of you. *Because of you.* I'm not even sure that I want it. Because it feels good to change. But I'm afraid. I'm afraid of hurting even more for you. Feeling even more for you. I'm already carrying your baby. I don't want to crack myself open. Not again. But also, I have a feeling that this is the one thing that you need to tell me. Really."

"Is that a yes?"

"Yes."

He nodded and turned away, continuing to walk down the street. "When I was eleven years old, she died giving birth."

It was a surprisingly easy thing to say. Such a surprisingly simple thing. No real explanation was required, and he was shocked when that story fell out of his mouth. So complete, with so few words.

"Oh," she said. Not a simple sound, but one as if she had been punched in the stomach.

"I saw it. Her. And the baby."

"I'm sorry…"

"There's no need to be sorry."

Her eyes filled with tears. "I'm sorry." She said it as if she was full of wonder. The strangest tone.

"I just… It's terribly sad."

"Yes, it is. But there's nothing you can do about those sorts of tragedies. They just are. If you're lucky they don't turn you into a monster. My father wasn't so lucky."

"Did it happen at…the estate?"

He nodded.

"That's why you don't like being there. You don't. I can feel it."

"No. I don't like being there. But it's less about that and more about what happened right after, and years that followed. He beat me after she died, to stop me from crying."

"Ewan…" She breathed the word, a note of shocked horror.

"He would have his heir be perfect. And then there was all the time after. All the time that I spent being abused and locked away by my father. All the rage that I felt, all of it swamps me when I go back there."

"That's terrible. It's an amazing thing that there are so many different kinds of terrible in the world. I've only lived one of them. My life has been so sheltered and small that I've only ever really put thought into my sort of terrible. Maybe that's why I worried I was a sociopath. Well, that and my father. You do worry that that sort of thing is hereditary."

"You love your sister."

She nodded. "I do. And Maren… She's soft. And all I ever wanted was to protect her softness because it's so beautiful and lovely in this ugly, ugly world."

"But what about you?" he asked. "Who protected you?"

"Maren tries. You've seen it."

"But you saw things, didn't you?" he asked, his voice heavy.

She nodded. "When Maren and I were girls we were sometimes used as decoys. Once I pretended to be lost in a train station, specifically to catch the attention of an elderly man. He comforted me, and he told me about his granddaughter. I told my father his granddaughter was his weakness."

"How old were you?"

He could see remorse rising in her like a tide; he could see it in her eyes. "Nine. But it didn't matter. My father kidnapped the man's granddaughter. They hurt her. I could hear her screaming. The man told my father he'd give him anything he wanted...anything at all."

"And then what?"

"That night I helped them both escape. I knew exactly how to get them out of the compound. I knew every code. But I will never get the sound of screams out of my head. I will never be able to make that moment any less clear."

"Did your father find out you did it?"

She smiled. "Of course he did. I made sure he knew Maren had nothing to do with it. I accepted his beating and I considered it a trade. He would have killed that girl. But I realized that I couldn't walk through life feeling so much. I couldn't have emotion attached to every image, or I'd never have a sleep that wasn't made of nightmares. So I cut them off. I worried maybe I would never be able to get my feelings back. But..." A tear slid down her cheek. "I met you and felt something. We made love and I felt something. You told me that story and I feel something. This story is very sad indeed."

He looked at her and he felt...indescribably desolate for having caused her tears. This was perhaps the best reason of all to continue to be the playboy. That man felt so little he could never have such hollowed-out feelings over his mother and dead brother.

He could never feel like killing Jessie's father with his bare hands.

Or offering comfort to Jessie, like he wanted to do now.

Even though he wasn't certain how to do it.

"You went to see my father?"

"Yes. I'm not afraid of him. I don't feel fear for myself. I was broken of that when I was a boy. Because there were a few times when I was certain I was going to die. I knew what dying looked like. When you go through those things as a child, I think you become dead to them later on. I don't worry for my own life."

They continued walking until they reached the hotel, which was glorious naturally, but mostly, he just saw her.

"Our room awaits," he said.

They went through the lobby—all sleek black marble and highly polished gold. He realized then that he could have her if he wished. Because she looked soft and sympathetic to him. And their bodies already knew what to do when they were alone. They already gave in to such things. They had already built a pattern of falling into each other's arms because it felt right. Because it felt necessary. Because it would erase the pain that he felt over having bared his soul to her in regard to his mother.

And he needed to avoid it. He needed to tell himself no. Because he had to prove that he had control here. He had given in to her because it was easy. Because he had let himself believe for a moment that he was the playboy that he pretended to be.

He'd been so dead inside when his father had died that he'd told himself there was nothing left in himself that felt.

And then, when he had come to her the day he learned about the baby, when he had run...

He had run away.

Like the frightened boy he'd been. A boy who hadn't been able to run. Who hadn't been able to escape the estate. And it was as if he had fled on behalf of that child.

But he would not fall into a lack of control now. He would not give himself over to this thing between them. Because he had agreed to come back. He had known he needed to care for her.

To marry her. To make his child legitimate, whether he felt that mattered or not. He would give his child everything.

And then, in the end, he and Jessie would live their own lives. Separately.

Because she needed him now. The child needed him now. But they would not always.

Tonight he would not touch her.

Tonight he would be...different. Not the playboy, but not himself, either. Something better.

When the elevator reached the penthouse, he let her get off first. It was a mirror of that night they had spent together. And he would not allow it to end the same way.

"Go and get your rest. You must be tired."

She looked at him, somewhat shocked. "Yes. Of course. That's... It's a good idea. I will get some rest."

"We can do some sightseeing tomorrow if you like. And then we will go back to Scotland."

"Sightseeing and everything. For a whole day. You know how to show a girl a good time."

"We could go straight back."

She fixed him with a pout that was far more charming than it had the right to be. "Don't be mean. You promised to show me Paris."

"I suppose I have."

CHAPTER TWELVE

JESSIE FELT ODDLY DEFLATED having been sent to bed by herself, but she knew that it was a good thing.

She knew that it was better for her to learn to spend some time with him without...

Well, too bad for her in the way her brain worked; all she did was think about him naked, and picture him in excruciating detail whenever he came to mind.

So maybe that was the thing. She needed to build some new images around Ewan.

It was so difficult. Because she liked the naked ones.

But he had promised to take her out and about in the city today. So she supposed she needed to act happy. And grateful.

She paused, putting her outfit on for the day. Just a black stretchy dress that covered her baby bump, and a pair of boots that were also black. She looked a bit witchy, and she liked it.

She was using him. She was using him the way that she had always used people.

The way her father had taught her to.

And now that she felt things—more and more things—it made her ache.

She hadn't meant to. She'd wanted so badly to get away from it. To get away from using.

She wanted her own life that she could have on her own terms. She didn't want to use anybody. She really didn't.

But she didn't know another way to be either.

That made her feel indescribably sad.

Did that make her a better person because she felt sad at the thought?

How did you ever know if you were or weren't using someone? She had used him that first night to lose her virginity. To experience pleasure. She had used him that second time for the same reason, but also to try and stop her heart from bleeding out, to do something to make her feel like she could hang on to a memory of him. And now she was using him to keep her safe. Using his money, using his power and influence.

Did people only ever use each other? Were they all like her father, just on different sides of the law? Did they use people with varying degrees of selfishness?

She had no idea how she was supposed to know.

This was why she didn't feel. Or why she hadn't historically. Because with feeling came worry. Trauma. Guilt.

She loved her sister. But the truth was, Maren was very easy to love. And Jessie had known her all of her life.

Maybe if she hadn't, she would simply use Maren, too.

Or maybe she did. Because she needed Maren to tell her whether or not she was being a good person, and to set boundaries and parameters for her. Maybe she used Maren as her external conscience. Her cricket.

She did love her, though. She was certain of that. She really was certain of that.

She put some red lipstick on and decided that she looked like a very Parisian witch, so there was that.

Then she met him out in the living area. She had not been prepared for him. She never could be. He was wearing a white shirt, the sleeves rolled up to his elbows, showing his spectacular forearms.

He had the most beautiful hands she'd ever seen. And she could remember every pair of hands she'd ever seen if she tried hard enough.

"Good morning," she said.

"Good morning," he said.

He gestured to the table. "I had an array of baked goods brought for you. I thought we might want to eat before we go get to the sightseeing."

"So," she said. "Is this primarily to make more splash in the press, to make my father feel like he can't make any moves toward me?"

"Yes," he said.

"And here I thought you just liked me."

He looked at her, his gaze cool and assessing. "You know you have a gold fleck in your right eye?" she asked.

"What kind of question is that?"

"It's an observation and a question. But I noticed that your eyes were different the first time we met. And I wondered if you had ever noticed."

"I don't spend that much time staring at my own face."

"You should. It's a decent face," she said.

His expression was cool, but she could see amusement in his eyes. "Thank you for that."

She inclined her head. "Of course."

"And don't take it personally, Jessie. I don't like anyone."

She frowned. "Do you think you'll like the baby?" It would be difficult if he didn't. But then, would she like the baby? She had no experience with babies. It was a concern.

"Do most people like their own children?"

"I don't know. There are certainly TV shows that suggest some people like their children. And in fact, choose to spend time with their families. I guess I choose to spend quite a lot of time with my sister. But we never really had a choice. And soon she's going to be a princess and move into a castle."

"I don't really understand that."

"She won a castle. She just can't move in until Christmas."

"Well, all right, then. But what exactly is your point?"

"I'm not sure if I would've chosen to spend that much time with her if I didn't have to. So I guess I'm saying I don't have empirical evidence that people like their families."

"Did you want to go sightseeing or not?"

She nodded vigorously. "I very much do."

"Then let's go."

"It's okay that you're using this to get to my father," she said once they were in the car headed somewhere she didn't know.

"Thank you. I'm glad to have your approval."

"I was just thinking that we all always use each other. It can't be helped. You're only with people when you need things from them."

"I can't say that I ever thought about it."

"I think about it a lot. My whole childhood was so isolated. It isn't like we went to school."

"Never?"

"You did?"

"Yes. A boarding school. But still. I was with other children my age." He looked away from her. "I had friends."

"How nice. That you did get a reprieve from being around your father." She meant it. She wished she'd had a reprieve from hers, but she didn't resent him.

"Yes. School was my only real escape. This persona was very effective there. People like the one who's always quick with a laugh or a sarcastic comment. I found that it could obscure the reality of things. I made myself who I am because of that school."

"I think I never had the chance to develop a *persona*." What she'd done with her feelings wasn't about showing a particular thing to others; it was about protecting herself. "I've been many different people. It all just feels more like a mask that I take on and off at the end of the day. It would be nice to have a persona. It feels a little bit more stable."

"So you were kept at home. How did you get an education?"

She laughed. She couldn't help herself. "I remember everything. Everything. So if I read a mathematical formula, I remember how to implement it. Also, that kind of thing just makes sense in my head."

"Right. You're a genius."

"I suppose. Though I think it's more of a very helpful party trick. Regardless, the education part wasn't the issue."

"You didn't have friends."

She shook her head. "Only my sister. Who at least understood me, but the problem with that is… When someone understands you so well you don't have to learn to be understood. You don't have to learn to connect. We just think the same. I don't know how to make another person understand me."

"I think most people don't know that. And it's what causes a lot of the great strife in the world."

"Humans are needlessly complicated," she said.

"On that, we can agree."

They ended up walking along the river and stopping at various market stalls.

He bought her lunch at a café, and then they continued to walk until they got to the Musée d'Orsay.

"I could take you to the Louvre, but I confess that I prefer this one."

"Why is that?"

"It's more than expected."

"I just think you're a hipster," she said.

And much to her surprise, he laughed. "That's a new one. I've never been accused of that before."

"Have you ever known anyone well enough to have them accuse you of anything?"

He looked at her for a long moment. "No."

Her delight in everything was infectious.

She was odd. And he hadn't noticed how much that was true when she had been playing the part of the seductress the night she had won the poker game. When she was angry, her quirks were also not as apparent.

But he was peeling back the layers on her, and he could see that it was true. She didn't have experience getting to know someone. Not outside of a con.

It was something they had in common. Because he wasn't certain when he'd last gotten to know someone, either.

She had appreciated everything, but when they walked into the museum, everything was different. She looked around; her jaw dropped as they walked through the first wing, filled with statuary. Then they made their way through various art exhibits, and she took everything in, and he wondered what it would be like to remember every detail. Of such beauty.

There was a van Gogh display in a black room where your senses were cut off from everything but the gloriously detailed artwork.

And when Jessie stood in front of *Starry Night*, her hands clasped tightly and pressed against her chest, he watched as tears formed at the corners of her eyes and slid down her cheeks.

"Are you all right?"

"Yes," she said. "It's just… I've seen this painting. It isn't the same. It isn't the same as seeing it in person. And I will remember every detail of this forever. And what a gift. To be given such a beautiful memory."

Memories.

The most valuable gift that can ever be given to her, because they were indelible.

His chest felt like it had been split with a large ax. Because he had never given to anyone before.

Revenge was a selfish pursuit. He had been consumed in his own need to harm his father for so many years that he… He had not made connections.

He had lost touch with those friends from school as he had made himself into a crasser version of himself as the years went on and he'd perfected his facade.

But this was real. The joy on her face. The way that she looked at him.

There was no artifice here. No revenge, no con.

Just connection.

And it did something to him. Shifted something inside him. Changed him. Utterly. Absolutely.

He didn't know if he was intrigued or if he wanted to turn away. He'd wanted to find something other than the facade he'd cultivated. He wanted something other than the ash that was left in his mouth after his father died. The bitterness of revenge gone satisfied, and cold.

She'd shown him he could feel something.

He could not deny this moment. The look of pure ecstasy on her face as she took in every brushstroke of the artwork in front of her.

He vowed then to give her more memories. There were so many gifts that could be given away. Thrown away. Forgotten about.

The memory would stay with Jessie forever, and he realized that made his every interaction with her so much more perilous. So much more precious.

She was a rare thing. And she had been abused all of her life.

He felt the sudden urge to shield her entirely. From anything unpleasant in the world.

She stayed at the museum for hours. Until it was dark outside.

And he had never fancied himself a great lover of museums, but watching her was something that he might never tire of.

What a strange thing. To care for someone like that.

The thought brought him up short.

Caring for her.

And she was at risk.

He thought of her father again.

He would kill that man himself before he ever...

And there it was. His father's violence making itself known, crowding into this moment when he had felt human.

He hated that. Hated his old man with a burning passion.

It had become everything he was, and yet...

He had not changed a thing.

He was having a child. He had not ended the bloodline.

His father was dead, and his mother was still gone.

Nothing was fixed.

When they finally finished and went back to the penthouse, he left her again, without touching her. Because he needed to distance himself from these feelings.

He couldn't afford to have them.

He couldn't afford to have any.

CHAPTER THIRTEEN

JESSIE WAS STILL lost in the beauty of their trip to Paris when the day of the wedding came.

Maren was fussing about, and arranging her skirt, fiddling with her flowers.

"This really should be you," said Jessie, looking at her sister.

"Why?" Maren asked.

"Because you're a romantic. And I never have been."

Maren laughed. "I think you probably are a secret romantic."

"Why do you think that?"

"The dress that you chose is the definition of a princess wedding gown."

"It is the definition of a dress that wasn't going to get too tight for me in a couple of weeks between when I bought it and today."

"Sure."

The annoying thing was her sister was right. It was difficult not to feel romantic.

They were getting married in a beautiful chapel down in the village, and she happened to know for a fact that the entire thing had been decorated with white lights and manzanita bows that made the entire thing look like something out of *A Midsummer Night's Dream*.

She would've said that she did not believe in the romance of weddings, or fairies, but being in Scotland with Ewan made her feel slightly different.

He hadn't touched her, though.

In the two weeks since he had returned, he had not touched her.

He had taken her to Paris, they had bought a dress. He had taken her to the Musée d'Orsay and he had shown her something so beautiful she did not think that she would ever recover from it. And he had not touched her.

She didn't understand why. He didn't want her anymore. She was getting fairly round with the baby, and it was entirely possible he wasn't attracted to the shape of a pregnant body.

That made her feel sad, but she supposed it was understandable. People had the taste that they had, after all.

As if she hadn't made all kinds of proclamations when she had said she would marry him. About not wanting things to be physical. She had to. But it felt like things were shifting between them.

Why do you think that?

She stood there and stared at her reflection in the mirror. The woman there was unrecognizable. She had her natural hair color. Something she saw so rarely that it just didn't feel like hers.

She was wearing a wedding gown. She was pregnant. She had makeup on that was designed to highlight her features, not shift them into something else.

She was Jessie. She supposed.

And she had never really been all that familiar with Jessie.

By cutting her emotions off, she'd cut herself off with it. She'd done it to be safe. He'd challenged that, and at first, she'd been afraid of it. At first, she'd gone back and forth, wanting it but fearing it all the same.

But then she'd seen him. And he'd seen her.

And somehow it was helping her see herself anew.

She walked up to the mirror without thinking and touched it, her finger pressed against the reflection of her own hand.

"Are you okay?" Maren asked.

She jumped and took a step backward. "Yes. I'm fine. We should probably head to the church."

"Probably," Maren agreed.

It was going to be a huge and highly publicized event because in the time since they had announced their engagement, the headlines all over the world had exploded. There was going to be a made-for-TV movie about their romance. Well, not their romance, but one just like it. About a man who loses his estate in a poker game, and then falls madly in love with the woman who won it.

A great story, she thought. But not…theirs.

But it was having the effect that he'd wanted it to. If anyone made a move toward her, it would be so highly publicized, so apparent, that nobody would ever be able to walk away from it without a life of imprisonment.

She was no longer an asset to her father that outweighed the liability of acquiring her.

And that was the gift.

It really was.

So she supposed it didn't matter if he touched her or not. Her feelings didn't matter.

She didn't even know what her feelings were. But she had them now.

Did he?

She had been drawn to him from the first moment she

had seen him. She knew it was the same for him, but would he ever let himself feel it?

They were both broken; he was right about that. But they'd seen each other. Didn't that matter?

It had changed her.

Would it ever change him?

She'd seen hints of it. She knew he wasn't the man he'd pretended to be for so many years. He was caring, and intense. He was strong and he was...

Ewan. The same way she was just Jessie.

"You look sad," said Maren.

"I guess I'm a little sad. I never dreamed about getting married. I sort of wish I had. So that I could enjoy a part of this."

"Is that really what's bothering you?"

She didn't know what was bothering her. She was trying to figure it out. Her brain was a fantastic and useful computer and it couldn't seem to put the data set together to figure out what exactly was the issue now.

So what good was it to her?

"Come on," said Maren. "You have to get married."

Maren was irrepressibly excited and Jessie had a feeling it was down to her bridesmaid dress being princess-like and frothy.

She allowed herself to feel a small measure of happiness that Maren had gotten through all this with her... Maren-ness intact.

That was, perhaps, the greatest testament to what she'd done in the years they lived with her father. She'd protected Maren. She was still able to be soft and excited.

And you?

Well, she'd committed graver sins.

You saved that girl; how long will you punish yourself for being a pawn?

She wasn't punishing herself; she was protecting herself. But not now.

No, not now. She couldn't, not with him, and she'd known that from the beginning.

It was why she'd pushed him away, then been angry about it. Because she wanted it, but she'd been afraid of it.

So much of her life was grounded in fear.

The fear of what her father might have made her.

The fear of her own complicity in the things he'd done.

She was tired of being afraid.

Ewan had given her new feelings. Bright feelings. Glorious feelings. She wanted to feel them, and with that there was the possibility she could feel bad things.

But she was Jessie. Wholly. And that made it seem worth it.

The drive to the church seemed to go on forever, and when they got there, she was shocked by the sheer number of people milling about. She was ushered through a side door where she would be concealed from everyone, including Ewan.

She was his pregnant bride. She was surprised how unbothered by that people seemed to be.

They had been given a brief overview of the way the ceremony would work, and after they had been there in a side room for a few moments, Maren was ushered out the door to walk down the aisle.

She was walking by herself, the only member of the bridal party, but she was obviously the maid of honor.

The most important person in attendance.

And then the music changed and it was time for her.

Of course, her father wasn't giving her away. She was giving herself away.

Because she owned herself. She owned her life.

And she was using…

She stepped to the edge of the sanctuary, all the thoughts dissolved in her head.

Because there he was. Standing at the head of the altar in a black suit jacket and a kilt. The dark green-and-blue tartan was perfect, masculine and went with his eyes, and she wondered if it was a family pattern.

It was hard to say with him because he did resent his father, but also against his will seemed to have some thoughts about bloodlines and succession. He was here, after all.

And he was handsome.

His hair curled around the collar of his suit jacket, just perfectly, pushed back off his forehead, and his eyes were stunning.

She just kept her focus on those eyes as she made her way down the aisle.

Her heart felt sore.

And as she got closer, it only felt like it was getting even more sore, as if it was growing, even.

She took his hand in hers when she reached the front of the room; all eyes were on her, she suddenly realized. It was as if this missing piece had locked into place, and everything suddenly became clear.

She could make sense of what she was thinking because she wasn't thinking.

She was feeling.

And she'd kept wanting to make it all clean and neat.

She'd kept wanting to make it all a con. She wanted to think about who was using whom, and why. She wanted to try and figure out the plan, the aim, the end goal.

And yes, she was using him in some regard to keep her and the baby safe. But mostly, she liked being with him.

Mostly, he was important to her.

Standing in front of him was like standing in front of *Starry Night*.

Every detail on his face, every line, every beautiful element that made him who he was, filled her, consumed her. Made her want to weep.

She couldn't put names to all of this because they were feelings.

She had never been taught to prioritize feelings. She'd been taught to push them down. Put them away.

She had been given the mind that she had because it mattered more than her heart.

And she realized now that wasn't true. Right at that moment, her heart mattered very much, and it was the thing driving all of this.

Her heart was now pounding so hard that she felt dizzy.

She felt for him.

She could feel.

She'd always been able to care. She had just been afraid to. Because much like desire, it would be something she would never be able to forget the finer details of.

And it would be horrible. And wonderful. All at the same time.

And if she lost him, if she lost this, then what would she have?

And she would lose him. Because this was never about forever.

The vows they spoke were traditional, and they made her tremble. Because she'd never had traditional in all of her life, and here she was in a white wedding dress holding hands with the most beautiful man she'd ever seen, saying sacred words in front of a priest.

She was pregnant, so there was that. That bit of the nontraditional, which at least made her feel like herself.

And when it was time to kiss, her heart leaped up to her throat, and he reached out and caressed her face, his fingertips moving slowly down her cheek. She searched his eyes for a sign that he wanted to kiss her. For a sign that this was real. For a sign that he felt anything at all, the way that she did.

Because she felt too much. Everything.

And then he leaned in, and it was like the whole world slowed down.

This was different. Different than the first time, which had been driven by uncontrollable lust. And different than the last time, which had been all lust and anger and desperation.

This was different. Because she knew that it was more than sex. Because she knew that it was more than a decision she'd made by thinking.

This was nothing less than her whole heart.

Then he leaned in, his mouth touching hers, and she ignited.

There in a church in front of everybody.

She wrapped her arms around his neck and clung to him, every beat of her heart trying to teach her a new language.

This language of feeling.

It was new and it was terrifying. Wonderful and debilitating.

She felt like she was being set free and shackled all at once, and maybe that was how everyone felt in these sorts of situations, but how would she know? Because she had never known anyone who could tell her.

His kiss was everything she remembered and more. Warm and wonderful and perfect.

And she breathed him in and clung to him, the memory of the vows they had just spoken a promise that echoed through her soul.

And when they parted, everyone in the church clapped for them as the priest announced them as man and wife.

She didn't know any of these people. All these people out

in the crowd wishing them well. And she knew that it wasn't real. That it was all based on their feelings for him and his proximity to power. But she couldn't deny that it made her feel something. This moment when it seemed as if she was part of a community of people. Rather than on the outside.

It was also…strange. Now that she had opened herself up to the possibility of feeling, it all seemed muddled. Intense beyond the rational.

But she supposed that was the issue. She had moved beyond rational. She had gone to another place entirely.

She had opened up her heart. And that was the thing she had always been the most afraid of. Because her heart wasn't full of files.

She had all this knowledge in her head, and yet it wasn't any use to her when it came to this. To feelings.

She didn't know what to do with all of this.

She didn't know what to do with herself.

But she was there with him, and they were married. But it was nothing. For nothing except the protection of the baby.

Suddenly, she felt like she couldn't breathe.

But he was there. He looked at her and squeezed her hand, and it was easy for her to believe it was because he felt something, too.

It was easy for her to believe that it was because he was swept up in the same tide of emotion. In the vows they had just spoken as strangers clapped for them.

He wasn't, though; she could see it. In his eyes.

Because she had clear memories of those eyes. And she knew what it was like when they were filled with passion. She knew what it was when they were filled with emotion. Vulnerability, as they had been when he had told her about his mother.

It made her ache. Tremble. She felt as if she was having an episode.

Because it was like a wall had come down within her and suddenly, she was just so aware.

She had been pleased that she was hurt for him that night in Paris, as it had been evidence to her that she wasn't a sociopath.

But it was beyond that now. She wasn't pleased that she had feelings. She simply had them.

It was like all of her self-protection was gone.

All of it.

And all she could do was cling to him, the object of this pain, and let him walk her back down the aisle.

She smiled, because she was very good at playing a part, above all things, even when everything inside her was eroding.

They got into the car that was waiting for them, and she began to breathe a little bit better. They would go back to the estate; they would...

She realized they were driving away from the estate.

"Where are we going?"

"To the airport."

"What?"

"We are going on a honeymoon."

"I don't understand. Even if we were doing that we could fly out of the estate."

"Too private. I am ostentatiously taking you on a honeymoon."

Of course he was. Because this was all about the show, and she had to remember that. Before she let her tender heart begin to beat in response to the idea of him taking her on a romantic trip, she reminded herself that this was about showing her father that he cared for her, so that her father would believe that the hammer would fall upon him were he to make a move toward her.

"Oh. But Maren..."

"She knows. And don't worry. She's been secreted off to her very own luxury private chalet where she will be well insulated and protected from harm."

A good thing, so Jessie could be annoyed at her. "She's a traitor."

"I think she likes me," said Ewan.

"Well, don't feel too pleased about that. Maren likes everybody. She has quite literally never disliked someone until they proved that she ought to. And even then, she has a difficult time with it."

"But not you."

She looked at him out of the corner of her eye and denied the new tenderness surging through her.

Perhaps it was hormones.

That would be more comforting. More comforting at least than believing that proximity to him had done something permanent to her.

"I don't like anyone. As a matter of course."

"That's sage, Jessie. As people are in general useless."

"Where are we going?"

"Don't you want to be surprised?"

"I had thought that we had gotten to know each other at least a little bit."

"Be surprised, Jessie."

She felt stirred up as they boarded the beautiful private plane, which she still wasn't used to, and allowed herself to be served nonalcoholic drinks and cheeses.

She didn't know that she wanted to be surprised; it was yet another thing she couldn't envision. Couldn't label her trust.

She already thought she was wandering in a dark room, and she just wasn't accustomed to that feeling. She was used to having a reference door that she could open up in her mind to try and understand it. Even though sex with him had been *knowing*, she had a cursory understanding of the act and what it was.

She had been able to figure out exactly what should pass between them.

And even though the sensations of it had been something different, she had a guidebook, essentially.

And the guidebook felt important.

But there was no guidebook to this. She was afraid of what it might be, but even then, she had no way to look at it. No way to understand it. No way to examine it.

It was all just too much. A swelling feeling at the center of her chest, the tightening of her stomach, a restless sensation in her limbs.

This feeling that whatever was happening to her was too big for her body to sustain.

She was already carrying a baby so that just seemed unfair.

She was living life for another human. It seemed over-the-top.

But then, so had Ewan, from the first moment she had seen him.

She had never been the kind of person who could bring herself to believe in destiny. If destiny was real, then why had she been born to her father?

Divine Providence was difficult to latch on to when everything was just…hard. When you were left to the devices of a sociopathic madman; when your own brain was an enemy because it could be used as a weapon, either against her or… She had used it as such against other people. Even though she thought they deserved it.

But right now she wondered. Because when she went back to that moment she had first seen him…

It was so hard to say because there was no room for magical thinking in her world. Her brain trapped every detail, so remembering him had not seemed significant.

But it wasn't the remembering; it was that he had been there. In her path all the time, but she had difficulty sorting that out. Was it fate, or was she a mastermind? She had finagled her way into the game, but only through Maren's speaking to the right man.

Maybe this was the problem. She gave herself entirely too much credit. Because she gave herself so much credit, it was easy for her to dismiss anything slightly miraculous in the world.

She always figured it was because of her own machinations.

But maybe it wasn't.

She stuffed a slice of cheddar cheese into her mouth. Because at least that grounded her to the moment.

"Are you all right?" he asked, lounging back in the comfortable seat.

"Not especially. I would like to know where we're going."

"But don't you think it will be exciting to be caught unawares?"

"No. Because I'm a woman. Who has had to navigate the rather unfriendly streets of the world, and I can tell you, nothing good happens when you are caught unawares."

"This will be good."

"Do you intend to seduce me again?"

She tried to sound cool. But she rather hoped that he would.

"No. I intend to be true to my word. You wanted this to be a marriage in name only, and you will have your way."

What if, she said only to herself, *I have changed my mind?*

She didn't want to say it to him because she felt tender. Wounded.

She would have; only a week ago, she would have.

But since she'd had a chance to turn over everything that had passed between them in Paris, she didn't want to.

Because he was the *Starry Night*.

And she realized suddenly that when they'd made love when they'd been strangers, it had been like looking at a printed copy of that painting.

But this, knowing him, knowing the ways he had been hurt, knowing the ways his father had devastated him...

Confiding in him, being near him, sitting with the reality that she was carrying his baby. That they had made a child together...

These were the details of an original work of art. A masterpiece.

And she was overawed with them, and it made it impossible for her to keep her normally flippant facade up.

"Be surprised," he reiterated.

She napped, and when they landed hours later, the jewel-bright water was rushing up to greet them.

"Where are we?" she asked.

"An island in the Caribbean. Private, naturally. Easy to have supplies brought in daily, but we will be isolated. Not a soul in sight the entire time."

"That seems excessive."

"I thought we'd been through this already. I am excessive. In all things."

Except as she looked at him, she could see how much of that was a facade.

He had cultivated a persona of excess, but it was not who he was.

He was not the libertine that he pretended to be. Not that he hadn't engaged in the business pursuits, but she did not think he did so because he lacked self-control, or because hedonism was a siren's call he couldn't stay clear of. No, she had the feeling that it was all to do with his vengeance. And it irritated her that he was playing a part even with her, and yet... She shouldn't be surprised. She didn't think he had planned to let her guard down when he had told her about his mother. It had been circumstantial.

She intended to think about that more, but as soon as the plane door opened, a rush of fragrant floral air greeted her, and she could only step outside, her mouth dropped in awe.

"This will be our home for the month," he said.

"The month... And Maren will be safe the entire time?"

"Yes. Believe me. She has been moved somewhere equally luxurious, and just as private. Plus, she has an entire security detail surrounding her."

"Okay," she said cautiously.

Well, at least she would be able to rest. Yes, there were some difficulties emotionally. But she would be safe here from her father, and it was glorious.

A car whisked them along winding oceanside roads, and she couldn't tear her gaze away from the water.

Crystal clear and an extraordinary shade of aqua all at once.

The white sands were so bright that she had to put on sunglasses to keep her eyes from burning.

They began a winding road that went away from the water, and up the mountain at the center of the island. And at first, she didn't see where they would be staying, but then suddenly, she saw it. Buried in the trees, a part of the landscape itself.

The house was on multiple levels, with bridges connecting different quadrants. It was made of honey-colored wood, with large windows that were highly reflective, and made it appear as if it was just more greenery, rather than a massive home.

"It's like a treehouse," she whispered.

She sounded more like Maren right then. Like she'd found something fresh and sweet inside herself.

She looked at him. He made her feel that way. It had scared her at first.

She liked it now.

She liked him.

"It is quite something," he said.

"Whose is it?"

"It's mine. One of the many properties I own."

"That's right. You have clubs. Sex clubs."

Her lips tingled when she said the words.

"I don't know that I would go so far as to call them that. But they are designed for people pursuing decadent pleasure, that is certain. The sex usually happens away from the club, though."

"Usually?"

"There are private rooms. And sometimes gatherings in there get…intimate."

"I see. And do you participate in such things?"

He shook his head. "No. To be honest with you, group sex has never appealed."

"That surprises me. You're an exhibitionist."

"No. I'm not an exhibitionist. I was making a show of certain things to build a facade. But I am not at my core someone who likes to expose every part of himself."

"I see."

It was all she could think to say. Because it made her think of that night in Paris, and what he'd said to her about his mother. And it made her realize that he was a man who kept many things tightly locked away.

It was true that she had a treasure trove of different personalities that she put off and on like the wigs that she had often worn during her gambling days.

But the Ewan that the world knew was a fully constructed personality that didn't exist.

She felt that she had seen under the persona even that first night she'd been with him, but she wondered if he would ever admit that.

If he would ever acknowledge that she had truly met the man he was beneath it all.

She had her doubts.

He parked the car at the front of the house, and they got out. She looked around at the gardens, the paths that wound around the different quarters and quadrants of the building.

There were bridges above that stretched across rocky chasms and connected to different suites of rooms, and a staircase that went down below them, to a platform that seemed to extend well beyond the face of the mountain, likely offering glorious views.

"This place…"

"It is where I come to be alone."

And he had brought her.

"Well, it's beautiful."

When they walked up the path, the inside was glorious. Natural rock and slate tile, cement walls with cracks that had tropical vines growing through them, bright pink blooms adding color to the room.

Everything inside was both luxurious and natural all at once. And it was another thing she knew she would never forget. But for a moment she had forgotten that she was different. For a moment she had just been there, taking it all in. Enjoying. As she had done that day in the art gallery. This was like art. This place.

"You will find that everything you need is already in your room."

"Thank you."

"It's up the stairs, and across the first bridge."

He didn't follow her, and she made her way up wood stairs that seemed to float and then down a long corridor that led to an enclosed glass walkway that stretched over the canopy of trees, and connected to another mountain ledge with a glorious suite that was all glass, offering an unobstructed view to the nature around it. The bed was white with white curtains surrounding it, and there was a giant deep tub. It was also beautiful. The most glorious honeymoon suite anyone could've ever thought of.

She smiled. And then she stretched across the bed and began to weep.

CHAPTER FOURTEEN

HE THOUGHT THAT he may have made a mistake leaving Jessie alone, and yet he found he needed the separation.

She was so devastatingly beautiful. And as his bride, she had been beautiful beyond belief.

He wanted her. He had never imagined taking a wife. Just as he had never imagined having a child.

But the sight of her in her white dress, her baby bump not concealed at all by the flowing fabric, had done something to him. And he could not afford to be in such a state.

He was doing this for the safety of her and the child.

By the time they returned from the island he anticipated that her father would be in prison.

He would be sure of it.

His investigators were working round the clock to find exactly what was needed to put the other man in prison for the rest of his life.

He would keep his family safe. He would...

They are not your family.

The only family you ever had died.

You are nothing but tragedy and poisoned blood.

And so he would leave Jessie to her isolation.

No matter how hurt she looked.

Because he was protecting her.

Whether she understood that or not.

* * *

She crept out into the main part of the house late that night.

She was starving.

It was true; her room contained everything she could possibly want.

There was a computer, and there were books. There were soft, silken pajamas, and she had put them on, then climbed into bed and read for several hours.

It was strange, to be so well taken care of. She had been grappling with that feeling ever since she had won the estate. Ever since she'd had enough. And hadn't had to work to keep herself comfortable.

But this was different still. A level of luxury she had yet to enjoy.

But now she was starving.

She walked back across the bridge, down the stairs, into the main part of the house.

The kitchen was a couple of levels higher than the living area, and she went inside and admired the beauty of it. More plants everywhere, and concrete countertops gave it a natural cave-like feeling.

But mostly, she was headed right for the overlarge fridge. She opened it up and saw platters of prepared foods, and took one out eagerly, uncovering it and taking some fruit off of the board while she continued to look inside.

"I see that you found what you require."

She turned around and saw him standing there. He was wearing a pair of sweatpants, low on his hips, and no shirt. There was sweat beaded there on his muscles and she thought he might've been working out.

Hunger was what kept her up. And missing him. She wondered what kept him up.

"I skipped dinner. And I don't skip meals. Not right now. Not ever."

"When you were with your father did he make sure you had plenty to eat?"

She shrugged. "I suppose so."

Her gaze kept going back to his chest as if it was a magnet. And she tried to cast her mind back to living at her father's compound. That was not a sexy thought. Not in the least.

"You don't sound definitive."

"It wasn't about us. It was, at best, about my father and his wants and needs. He had a private chef that provided him with whatever he wanted. His favorites."

She rooted around the fridge, looking for something specific; she just wasn't sure what. She only knew she would know when she saw it. "I remember when Maren and I escaped and we had our first win. We went and bought a whole bunch of things from the grocery store, and tasted them all. And we went out to a restaurant and we ordered everything. Trying to figure out what our favorite foods are."

"And what did you decide?"

"I love breakfast sandwiches. Eggs and bacon and cheese. On a croissant. Maren prefers cereal. I love pasta of all kinds. Though specifically ravioli. I think it's delicious. I love Caesar salad."

"I think you might find one of those in there. And some pasta."

She did and managed to make herself a large bowl of salad, and then reheated some pasta with lemon and vinegar and sat down at the concrete countertop, eating quickly, and under his far too careful gaze.

"What about you?" she asked around a mouthful of lettuce. "What are your favorite foods?"

"I don't know."

"What?"

"I don't know. I have been fed a steady diet of the best and richest foods that the world's top chefs have to offer. I've never really thought about what was better or worse."

Because he was never him. He was the playboy. And it wasn't actually about pleasing himself, but about crafting a personality aimed at his father.

She'd been grappling with similar. She'd cut her feelings off so she could avoid pain, and sorrow and disturbing memories, but he replaced all that with enough good she didn't need it.

Not anymore.

She looked at him, at his beautiful face, and she put her hand on her rounded stomach.

It was a revelation.

The bad was still there. All her memories. Especially the one that haunted her, of the way her father had hurt that child, had used her to gain access to that child.

For the first time she was able to feel...like it was finished. The child had gotten away; Jessie had helped her. Her memory had kept the bad part of it alive, so vivid it was like she'd never really gotten out.

But she had. And somehow standing there with her future in front of her, with the possibility of good things feeling bigger than what had gone on before it, she could find the good that much easier.

And there was so much good.

"Well, we can't have that. You need to figure out what your favorite food is."

"Why?"

"Because everyone should know that. Food is one of the most glorious indulgences that we have been given as humans. Taste is purely for pleasure."

"That is actually not true. Taste also tells us if something is poison."

She sniffed. "I like my version of that better."

"It doesn't make it true."

His logic was both sound and infuriating.

"Well, be that as it may. Taste buds are one of the few frivolous parts of our bodies."

"Not the *only*, though. I believe there is one part of a woman's body that exists only for pleasure."

His eyes met hers and she felt a fizz of desire skate down her spine. Her internal muscles clenched tight, and she wanted to cross the distance between them and slap him on the shoulder.

Because it was mean to bring that up. Especially when he was refusing to seduce her.

You're seduced. Utterly, entirely and permanently. You could just seduce him.

She could. But she was enjoying the conversation. And the problem with them was she already knew the sex was good. But they hadn't had conversations like this.

"That is true. But that part of your body does not tell you if something is poison. Something very bad can feel very good."

"I suppose that is also true."

"But in the interest of pleasurable pursuits, I do think that we need to figure out what your favorite food is."

"Shall I place an order to the mainland?"

"Yes. And we shall have a tasting. That's what I want to do. For our honeymoon. But it can't all be good foods. You have to get packaged foods. Processed foods. From America. Because they are the best ones."

"You say that with a great deal of authority."

"I *know* so. We did another grocery trip our first time back to America. We grew up there, you see, but of course, then moved to England."

"Yes. I did realize that."

"So we shall place an order."

"I'll leave that to you, Jessie, since you're the one with so many opinions."

"You're about to get a few more of your own."

CHAPTER FIFTEEN

HE DIDN'T KNOW quite why he had allowed his wife to take the wheel on this. Perhaps because it didn't matter. Perhaps because it made her happy, and that made him want to... He wasn't exactly sure. Make her smile, perhaps, because she had been quite unhappy with him right after the wedding.

And this had seemingly made her happy, and that made him... It was something.

When he came downstairs after spending a few hours going over his accounts, two days after they had first arrived at the house, he found Jessie sitting with a pile of food packages around her, and a wide grin on her face. "I'm setting up a tasting."

"Jessie, this is maniacal." He looked around and saw boxes of unnaturally colored toaster pastries, and brightly colored cereals and that was just the breakfast section.

"They were able to fly in hamburgers from a couple of restaurant chains. They're in these little thermal containers to keep them warm. Is it not delightful?"

"It's insane."

"Come be insane with me, then. We are going to figure out what your actual favorite food is."

He'd never thought about it because he didn't care. He was powered by the desire for revenge. The need to destroy his father. The need to play the part that he was required to in order to accomplish what he wanted to.

Build his own empire. Disgrace that family name. Then he had done so. Along the way, there had been pleasures, but none of it had been specific. The food had been good. The sex was satisfying.

Being with Jessie was specific. And now she was asking him to find that with food.

It was a strange thing, and yet he found he couldn't deny her.

"All right," he said, sitting down on the low sofa across from all the food. "Bring me something to eat."

She picked up a box of toaster pastries and laughed happily while she opened it. "These are my favorite. They're wild berry."

"Is a wild berry neon blue and purple?"

"These magical mystical wild berries that are fashioned in a lab are. And they're delicious. All we have to do is put them in the toaster." She took the little silver package and shook it in front of him. "Come on."

"This is very strange, and so are you," he said.

"You say that like it's something that should bother me. But you know that it doesn't. I'm perfectly happy being strange. I never had a hope of being normal."

Neither of them had, he supposed. The toaster pastry heated quickly, and he could honestly say he wasn't a fan. She took it from him and finished what he didn't. "Too sweet, you say?" she asked.

"Definitively."

"We can probably skip the sugary cereal, then. But I find that highly suspicious."

"What do you find suspicious?"

"That anything could be too sweet."

From there they went on to hamburgers and French fries;

he did have a definitive favorite there. What had to be the cheapest one, that had an association with arches, he believed.

"I don't know why it's good," he said, taking another bite.

"It shouldn't be," she said. "Objectively speaking. And yet, it is. Absolutely delicious."

He couldn't disagree. He'd had some of the best gourmet food in the world, and yet, he could see this being something he wanted again and again.

Jessie demanded that he rank and score everything, and by the time they were finished, it was dark outside, and he felt vaguely ill.

But Jessie looked cheerful, and she was still snacking on chips.

"So we have your favorites. A favorite fast food, and you have decided that your favorite overall food is…"

"Steak."

"That is incredibly masculine of you."

She had scooted closer to him during their tastings, and he found that looking at her too closely was like staring at a sunrise full on.

And then she drew closer to him, and he knew what she intended to do. And he found himself unable to turn away from her.

She pressed her mouth to his, and it was like the world had stopped.

"You're the only man I've ever kissed," she whispered against his lips.

"Perhaps we should bring an array of men to the island."

Even as a joke, he didn't care for it. Even as something that would never actually come to pass, he hated it.

"It's funny," she said. "I know that I don't need to. Because when I was a girl, and I saw other foods on TV shows, foods that were not my father's favorites, I wanted them.

And as soon as I had the opportunity I went out and I made sure I got them. Because you know how I am. I never forget. And because I never forget I remembered each and every food that I wished I could try that I'd been denied. I hold on to things. And that gives me a certain certainty about my cravings, I suppose. But I could've had any man I wished. And yes, Maren and I had rules. But you know me. I'm happy to violate Maren's rules if it suits me."

"Yes," he said, his voice rough.

"I don't need to kiss a whole line of men to know that kissing you is my favorite thing."

"This should not go further," he said, his voice rough. But he didn't know where that came from. The need to make her keep her distance.

"It doesn't have to. I am content to simply kiss you. Because we didn't do that the first time. We raced right ahead." She pressed her mouth to his again, and it was so soft and sweet. He had never kissed simply for the pleasure of it, but with her, he found himself settling right into it. He put his hand on her cheek and parted his lips, letting her tangle her tongue with his. Letting himself get caught up in the moment. He found himself cupping her face, smoothing his thumbs along her jaw as he kissed her deeper and deeper.

She moaned, and it took all the self-control he had not to push her flat on her back, amongst all the food wrappers, and have her then and there.

But she had said they would only kiss. And it was foolish to do anything else.

Because his control had been severely compromised the last time he had been with her.

What control? Already she's pregnant with your baby.

He pulled away from her, and the soft smile on her face nearly undid him. Yes. He had indulged himself all these years. With rich food and with more lovers than he could count. And yet, none of it had ever really mattered. And it was because of how big the moment felt that he pulled back now.

"I have a new favorite thing to add to my list."

His voice was so rough it was barely recognizable even to himself. And he waited, waited to see if she would move back and kiss him again, because if she did, then he would be overtaken. If she did, he would not be able to resist her.

But instead, she sat back, with a sweet smile on her face.

"So do I."

CHAPTER SIXTEEN

THEY DIDN'T MAKE LOVE. For two weeks they were on the island, and they didn't make love.

They talked. About food now, since he knew what his favorites were, and about his friends at school.

It was difficult to dig deep enough to get to a personal part of Ewan. Because it was clear to Jessie that he had done everything he could to minimize that part of himself.

It was all related to the fact he hadn't even known his own favorite foods. The degree to which he had given himself over to his desire to hurt his father had shaped everything he was.

It was frightening, sometimes.

He seemed like a warm, carefree playboy, and he was anything but.

It scared her sometimes, wondering how deep that core of destruction went within him. And if there was anything of a man left.

But that night when he had kissed her, just kissed her, she had found something helpful to hold on to.

You're just as broken as he is.

Sometimes the voice whispered to her. Like now, when she was walking through the outdoor bridge system up inside the trees, enjoying the weather and the view through the fronds of the ocean below.

Sometimes that voice whispered to her that she wasn't different. That this time away hadn't transformed her.

She remembered what Maren had said.

That they were nothing more than women experiencing con artistry.

She had never needed that sort of buffer between herself and the decision she'd made.

She had seen herself as a con artist.

But what was she now? She was a woman about to have a baby.

She was…

She was falling in love with him.

They'd gone about everything all backward. Inside out. Except perhaps they hadn't. Because the moment that she'd met him something had taken hold of her that she had not been able to get rid of since.

The moment she had first laid eyes on him.

He had made her feel things she'd never felt before, and she'd been driven by them.

If they'd struck up a conversation first, they both would have run in the other direction.

They had both constructed their entire lives in such a way that it had made them unable to get to know people. He had been surrounded by revelers, by parties for all these years, and yet he didn't even know himself. And Jessie knew only Maren and protected her actual identity above all else.

It was almost necessary, then, that they'd made love first. Which had bonded them together by way of the baby.

She had been thinking more and more about the baby, too. As not just a baby, but a baby that would grow into a child.

A child who would need a mother.

She had never known what a real mother was supposed to do, what a real mother was supposed to be. She had images, saved in her files of TV and book moms, and the flashes of brilliance that her own had brought to her life before she had left forever.

But she didn't want to be a mother constructed simply of images.

Of knowledge.

She was learning that she needed to begin to build things from her heart.

And there was no certainty there.

She was so used to certainty.

To the absolutes of her mind, and life was more than absolutes. It was these messy uncertain spaces, where she had to do battle with her own doubts. Where she had to try to find a picture of something that she had never seen before and figure out how to walk toward that.

An image of herself holding her baby. An image of herself hugging a small child before that child went to school.

Of loving that child when they were messy, crying and inconvenient.

Of giving that child all the things she had never had.

Love, she realized, filled the blank spaces. It was love that allowed you to feel what you could never know.

Love was the most important thing, and it wasn't as simple as something you kept in a file in your mind.

She felt changed out here. With so many fewer things to see you, and know and learn.

Left behind with only her feelings.

With the silence of the trees and the sounds of the waves.

With the beat of her heart, and the need in her soul to find more than what she had been given up until this point.

She didn't know what she was doing. But she would use love to fill in the spaces.

She was very afraid that she was beginning to love him.

Very, very afraid.

Because she wasn't sure what more he had inside. Because she wasn't sure if there was more to him. She wanted there to be. There were moments when she was almost certain.

You know what you have to do.

She did. But it was frightening.

But they had done all this backward. Sex first, a baby and now they had gotten to know each other.

But there was still more in him. She was certain of it. There was still a part of himself that he held back.

And she realized that they were at the point now. The point where she ought to seduce him.

Because it meant something different now.

Because they had changed.

She had cut her feelings off to protect herself from the horror of their lives. From the pain she'd caused due to her father's machinations. So much so that she had, for a time, forgotten what feeling was. So much so that she had denied it to the point that she was afraid she didn't have it.

She had stopped protecting herself in some ways, but she was still clinging on to pieces of that protection.

She had to stop. Because that was the key to change. To her actually becoming new. To her actually being the mother she needed to be. The sister she wanted to be.

The woman she had always wished she could be.

And that meant taking a chance.

The risk. But this was different from gambling. When you gambled, the prize wasn't specific. Not generally. It was just a pot of whatever the fools decided to gamble. And this was only her heart.

That was all. And it had to be him, or it would be nothing and no one.

That isn't true.

Even if he can't do this, you'll have your child. Even if he can't do this, you'll have Maren.

All the ways that you've changed.

It was true. She would.

It fortified her. It made her feel strong.

She grasped the railing on the bridge and looked out at the view, then tilted her head back. And took in a deep breath.

She didn't connect the moment to memory; she didn't go in and open up her files. She simply was. She simply felt.

And she smiled.

Because she could do that now. And somehow she knew that it would be okay. That it had to be.

A sliver of fear wound its way through her. Because perhaps, for a while, it would feel like it wasn't okay.

Perhaps for a while, she would be broken.

And she would have to figure out how to put herself together again.

But she was strong.

She knew that she was.

She was Jessie Hargreave. And she wasn't the con woman her father had made her.

She was the woman she had decided to make herself.

Looking at Jessie had become almost a physical pain. Ewan had never experienced such a thing before. He had never desired a woman and denied himself that woman. He had never desired anything and denied it. Because he had never allowed anything to become bigger than his pursuit of revenge.

And yet, it was gone. That revenge. The thing that had made him who he was. And he had experienced that moment of emptiness. Then he transferred it. To Jessie's father. He was fine when he was being driven by a desire to destroy.

Hands that wanted nothing more than destruction could never touch Jessie.

And so he didn't.

Apart from that kiss they had shared two weeks ago.

But it was killing him. Killing him to deny himself.

Because denial was associated with being controlled.

And somewhere in the middle of all this it had ceased to be about his control over himself and had begun to feel like the torture he had experienced as a child.

This need to make himself into something acceptable. Something different.

He walked across the bridge from the room he was using as his office, and into his bedroom, and stopped. Because Jessie was standing there in the middle of the room. Naked.

Her brown hair was loose around her shoulders, long enough just to brush the tops of her breasts, not long enough to conceal the tightened, dusky buds there.

Her belly was rounded from her pregnancy, and it aroused him deeply. Filled him with a sense of triumph to see her changed by him.

Her hips were generous and lovely; the dark triangle at the apex of her thighs made his mouth water.

And there was no thought to be given to control. Not now. Not in this moment.

"I like talking," she said. "Don't get me wrong. But I did think that perhaps we were missing something that this honeymoon needed badly."

She took a step toward him, and that was all he needed.

He released his hold on everything. On his control, on everything that was tethering them to the earth, and moved to her, wrapping his arm around her waist and drawing her flush against his body.

"I want you," he said, the words guttural.

"I want you," she said. "But I want all of you. All the things that you are. All the things that you hide. I made my-self my mind. Only my mind, and it was only when I made love with you that I was able to turn it off for the first time in my life. That night we were together, all I did was feel. I was not crowded with thoughts. And ever since then, even if it has taken work, I have been able to find my way back to that place, because now I know what it is. You gave me a gift. You allowed me to unlock a door inside myself and walk into a room that I did not know was there.

"It is all me. But it is me that I kept hidden. The part of myself that I kept most protected. And I learned something. That it is not protection. It is prison. I kept that part of myself imprisoned. What do you keep locked away?"

She was searching him, her gaze far too keen, far too sharp. And he wanted to turn away from her. He wanted to tell her there was nothing. Nothing.

Because he had not locked a part of himself away; he had hollowed himself out. Bled himself dry the way that his mother had done.

Because there had been no choice for him that day. No other way for him to survive.

And as he looked at her, suddenly that glory he'd felt a moment before over seeing her round with his baby was overshadowed by fear.

Fear.

That was what he kept locked away.

Because as long as he was vengeance, then he was out there taking control of the world and making things right. Balancing the scales.

But the truth that it hid, the thing that he denied the most, was that he would never be able to stop injustice.

He would only be able to fight it afterward, again and again.

But there were some things in this world that you could not stop. Some things that you could not ever have dominion over, and that was the thing that frightened him most.

It was the thing that made him feel like a small boy who walked out in the cold, starving and freezing.

And the worst thing was it was his father who held the

key to all of that; it was…some power that simply laughed at the misfortune and destruction of humanity.

For he was angry at his father for a great many things; his father had been forever the demon in his life, but his father had not killed his mother, and he had not killed his brother.

It had been a force that he could not seek vengeance on. A force that he could not control.

And he would never be able to protect Jessie, either. He would never be able to protect the child.

He pushed those thoughts away, and growled, kissing her with all that he was.

He would not speak anymore.

He knew how to deny all of this. He knew how to keep it hidden.

How to keep it secret.

He knew.

So he opened up the part of himself that embraced nothing but feeling, sensation, and he consumed her.

He moved his hands over her smooth, soft curves, kissed her neck and down to the plump swells of her breasts.

He took one nipple deep in his mouth and sucked hard until she cried out.

"You're more sensitive now," he growled, his mouth against her flesh.

"Ewan."

The way she said his name, broken and pleading, ignited a fire inside him.

And he decided to let it burn him.

Because at least that was all-consuming enough to block out everything else.

He kissed his way down her body, that rounded swell of her stomach, and he refused to let himself think.

He buried his head between her thighs, licking that sweet center of her.

He had missed her. He had missed this.

"My very favorite delicacy," he growled.

The broken cry that was elicited from her lovely mouth told him everything he needed to know.

She was as lost to this as he was.

They didn't need to bring their conversations to this.

They didn't need to bring the changes that had happened between them these past weeks. This could be sex. Simply.

As it had been the first time.

It was never just sex. It was never simple.

He remembered. The first time he'd seen her.

In the way he'd known was awake even then.

That moment in the casino, and had never gone away from him. Not one detail lessened by time.

As if it was one of Jessie's memories, and she had planted it in his own mind.

He pushed back against that, licked her deeper until she was screaming, until she was trembling.

Until he tasted her climax over and over.

He tried to picture other women. Tried to make this familiar, but all he could see was her.

All the times he had seen her.

As if the path to this moment was inevitable. As if it was fate.

He refused to believe in something so cruel as fate.

He refused.

How could it take his mother from him, and give him his father? How could it give him Jessie when he was too twisted and destroyed to care for her in the way that she deserved?

No. He could not believe it was fate.

He could not.

He stood up, lifting her off the floor and wrapping her legs around his waist as he carried her to the bed. He consumed her. Took her mouth with his and claimed her utterly and thoroughly. Did everything he could to block out the thoughts that crowded his mind.

But nothing could block out the feelings that bled into his chest.

He felt like he was dying. Like something inside him was shattering.

When he brought her up over his body and thrust deep inside her, looked up at the view of her, over him, his hardness buried deep within her, he felt undone.

As if he would never be able to separate from her again. As if he would never be whole again if he could not be inside her like this for all time.

The picture that she made was so erotic he could barely breathe.

Her rounded stomach, her glorious breasts. The expression of pure ecstasy on her face.

She was glorious, and at that moment, she was perhaps everything.

And so he lost himself, in the rhythm that she created as she began to flex her hips. As her internal muscles rippled around him, she began to climb closer and closer to another climax, and he found himself perilously close to the edge of the same.

He had made a mistake. Because this wasn't the same. He had thought that if he was in her again, it would all be familiar. Because not only had he been with countless women, he had her before as well.

He had thought it would bring them back to familiar territory, but this wasn't.

It was new. It was something bright and wholly different than anything he'd ever had before.

He'd had sex.

This was making love.

This was what happened when your soul saw someone, and they saw you, and then your bodies became one.

This was something he had never believed in. More than that, it was something he had never wanted.

Because this...

This was the precipice of a man's sanity.

This was him, unmasked.

This was him, without any of the artifice, any of the control.

This was where a loss would make him jump off to the jagged rocks below, and damn the consequences.

This could make a man destroy everything around him, and he was powerless to fight against it.

Powerless to do anything but surrender.

To her, to this.

To the need that pounded through him.

It was the one thing he had vowed never to do. The one thing he had never done. At the hands of his father, under the fist of his grief, he had never surrendered.

And yet, in her arms, buried in her body, he could do nothing but.

He shouted his release as she gave a hoarse cry and found her own, and he was lost. Spiraling into the darkness. But there was light there. And he did not want it. There was light there, but it frightened him more than anything else ever had.

And then she whispered. Into that light.

"I love you."

And just after that, his phone rang.

CHAPTER SEVENTEEN

SHE WAS STILL SPENT in the aftermath of what had passed between them, her body vibrating with the pleasure that she'd found in his arms, and he was moving to the nightstand, grabbing his phone. "Yes?"

She listened intently, worry for her sister filling her chest.

"I see. Thank you." He hung up the phone. "Your father is dead."

She did not know what she had expected to feel under the weight of such an announcement.

But the burst of joy that went through her was not expected. Still, she supposed it was fair.

He had threatened her baby, and he was gone.

He was gone. All the power that he'd had all this time over her life, over her choices, over her safety, and he was gone.

"What happened?"

"He decided to have a gunfight with the police rather than going quietly. It is better this way, Jessie. Even from prison, he could have..."

"I know," she said. "I do. I... I know that it's for the best. I'm not sad."

"Good," he said. "It's a good thing, too, that I am confident now that I'm not without feeling because I might've thought so now. It's cold-blooded to be happy that your father is dead, I suppose.

"But it's for our baby. I am happy for our child that he won't be there to cast a shadow over their life."

"No. He is gone."

And she realized then they didn't need to stay married. Because she was safe. Maren was safe.

There were choices now.

Choices she'd never had before.

This was real freedom.

"I'm free," she said.

"You are," he agreed.

And she looked at Ewan, and she knew that his father's death had not brought that same freedom.

She wished that she could fix it. That she could break open the thing inside him that still held them in chains, but she didn't know what it was, and she didn't know how.

She felt helpless then. Helpless to do anything but hold on to him. "I love you," she said. "I want to say it now, now that I have all the choices in the world. All the freedom in the world. Nothing is hanging over me, and nothing holding me back. I love you."

"Jessie…"

"Why don't you feel the same? Why did your father dying not make you feel this? Because I no longer live underneath his shadow, and neither do you."

"It isn't that simple."

"Why not? Why does he get to decide who you are, what you are? He was cruel, unimaginably so. He left a little boy to wallow in his grief, and he caused him more pain."

"I thought that when my father died, I thought that when I got my revenge on him, everything would be right. But it wasn't. I was left with nothing more than emptiness, and do you know why?"

"Why?"

"Because my mother is still dead. He did not kill her.

My brother is still dead, and he did not kill him. It was...
the hand of fate. I don't know. But they are dead, and there
is nothing in this whole world that I could do to fix it. Revenge did not fix it. Nothing can. The world is the same as
it ever was for me."

She shook her head. "No. It isn't. Don't say that. Yes,
tragic things happen. They do, and we can't control those
things, but they don't get to decide..."

"They do. Jessie, I could not bear watching you bleed
out. I could not lose you. I cannot..."

"Isn't that love?"

"If it is then I want nothing to do with it."

"You can't stop it from happening if it's going to happen," she said. "You can't will it away. You cannot be venge-
ful enough to blot out what will be, or to take away your
own feelings, and why should you? I did that. For so many
years. I ignored my own feelings. I denied them."

"I don't want you away from me. I could not stand it.
Not now. But I'd... I cannot be what you are asking. I can
never soften myself. I can never..."

"Then I won't stay with you."

It cut her open to say it. It made her want to die. Then
and there. Just lie down on the floor and stop breathing al-
together because it seemed easier than bearing such a loss.

"I love you, Ewan. I have never let myself love. Not anyone other than my sister. I never let myself be wanted. I
never let myself feel. But I do now. I do now. And I just want
more than anything in the world for you to love me back. I
want us to win. I don't want the dark things to win. I don't
want the terrible things to win. And believe me, I know,
because I remember. There are endless stories where the
darkness wins and the hero dies. But there are also stories
where they live. We have to choose it. We have to choose
to live. All the way. With everything we are. We have to

choose to do it with the fullness of ourselves because no one will choose it for us. The world is tragic. But I am choosing to trust in what I cannot see. And what I know in my heart to be true. There is no file in my brain that tells me that everything will be fine. That it will be fine. But I believe it in my soul."

"I cannot."

"Let me believe it for the both of us. If I can do that, if I can have just a small bit of hope that someday... That someday you can, then I don't need to walk away from you."

"I can't," he said.

And something inside her broke away. Something she knew that she would never get back. "You know where I am."

"Jessie..."

"I just can't, Ewan. Not after everything. I want to be loved. The way that I love. Because you are my favorite thing. And I don't need to taste an array of pleasures in this world to know that. To know that you are what I want. To know that you are what I need, too. You helped me find all these things out about myself. And I tried to do the same for you. I can't be less to you than you are to me."

He said nothing. He simply stood there, naked and ragged, his body so beautiful it made her want to weep, his eyes so full of pain that she did.

"I'm going to call the private plane. I'm going to go home."

She turned and walked away from him, walked across the bridge, and made her way down to the main part of the house before her knees gave out. Before she began to weep. Even as she took out her phone and put in the order for the private jet.

She had to do this. Because she had to trust.

In the evidence of things she could not see. In the gaps that her mind could not know.

In love.

Because it was the newest and greatest thing she had learned. And hope, because it was what it was saying to her soul even now.

Because she had been a woman without those things. She had been hard and isolated and lonely.

She didn't know everything, it turned out. But she knew this.

But in the end, love was worth taking a stand for.

And she had to hope that it was bigger than vengeance could ever be.

She was gone. And he felt gutted. Hollowed out.

It was not the first time he'd felt this way. It was a grief that transcended breath.

He should let her walk away. He should let her go and find happiness. With someone else, somewhere else.

What could he possibly give to her? What could he possibly give to a child?

Nothing.

As long as your hands are bound by fear.

It was the truth, and he knew it; he simply didn't know where it came from.

What untried part of his soul had this level of wisdom?

He had made himself nothing.

And when his father died that had become apparent, because he had lost his purpose and his meaning.

Now that her father was dead, he felt the same. Except... She was still here.

She was still here, and the promise of his child yet existed.

When his father died, his mother had still been gone. His brother had still been dead.

And he had felt helpless in the face of that reality. Of that grief.

Jessie was still here. And that meant that at this moment he was choosing fear over her. Over his child.

And that made him rage.

At himself. At everything he was.

He had rejected her.

And he was nothing now, nothing more than that boy who'd walked away.

Dammit all, his father still held the keys.

He had never escaped. The vengeance had never been his.

He had spent all these years drinking poison and waiting for it to kill his father. His father had died of old age. His father had died after a long, bitter life.

Ewan had been allowing his father to kill him. All these years.

What he could be; what he could have.

Any hopes, any dreams, any love.

Jessie. He wanted Jessie.

He wanted to feel no fear so that he could have her.

You won't. You always have the memory of your mother. You will always have the memory of your brother.

He sat there in that certainty. It was true.

He would always remember their deaths. He would always remember that tragedy. And the abuse that had followed.

He had to accept it. Something that happened. Something that was part of him.

And he had to find it in himself to choose to have more.

To be more than pain and suffering. To be more than his father had allowed him to be.

He had to stop letting that old man destroy him.

He had to stop letting tragedy define who he was.

Otherwise, his child would be marked by these things as well. Forever and ever.

He had to stop it.

He had fought to break the chain by stopping his bloodline. But he realized something now.

He had to break it even with his bloodline carrying on. And it was not something fate would handle for him.

He had to do it himself. He had to break those chains with his own hands.

And by God, he would.

Because Jessie loved him.

Despite all that she'd been through, she loved him.

Despite everything she knew and all the things she remembered, she loved him.

He did not remember everything. But he knew that when he drew his last breath he would remember seeing her for the first time. Remember watching her look at that painting. Remember her standing naked in his room ready to seduce him. He knew that those memories could become bigger than the ones that held all of his pain.

But only if you let them.

Only if you let this love be bigger than fear.

He stood up and turned the knob on his bedroom door. It was not locked.

Because he was not a prisoner. Not anymore. It was simply a matter of choosing to walk out of the cell.

And so he did.

For her.

For love.

CHAPTER EIGHTEEN

MAREN HAD PROVIDED food and fuzzy blankets upon Jessie's arrival. She had shouted invectives and made physical threats of violence while Jessie cried.

"I will kill him!" Maren announced. "With...pillows. I'll smother him."

It almost made Jessie laugh.

"No, Maren, you don't need to engage in soft murder on my behalf."

It was clear that she was unnerved by the fact that it was not Jessie who was being bloodthirsty.

But she simply didn't have it in her.

Not right now.

Mostly because she wasn't angry at him, as much as she would like to be.

She was just sad.

"Love really does sound terrible," said Maren.

"It is," said Jessie. "But wonderful all at once. I wouldn't trade it. I wouldn't go back. Because I'm finally who I want to be because of all of this."

"I don't think I understand that."

Jessie laughed. "I don't think I do, either."

Maren had gone to a meeting about the acquisition of her new property, and Jessie was still lying on a chaise longue next to a window in the estate when she saw the sleek white plane begin its descent.

Her heart leaped.

"No," she whispered. "Don't do that. Don't hope."

No. Hope. Because you can. She stood up, and she found herself walking out the door, and then running.

Running up over the grassy hills that led to the landing strip.

And then she saw him. Just on the other side. Barefoot. And running toward her.

"At him," she whispered.

And as much as she could, she ran toward him.

And when she reached him, he pulled her into his embrace, and simply held her.

"I love you," he said, his whisper fierce and hard.

"I love you, too."

She couldn't wait to hear his explanation. All the things that had shifted and changed inside him. But she didn't need them to know that she loved him.

She didn't need them for this moment.

"I'm sorry that I was afraid."

"Life gave you a lot of reasons to be afraid."

"I could never believe in fate. I thought it seemed cruel. But right now it doesn't. I thought that I needed to destroy myself to destroy my father. But there are more ways to break a cycle than I believed. We can break it now. By being different. By choosing love. By choosing that over power. Over all else."

"Yes," she whispered.

"I love you, Jessie. More than I'm afraid of losing you. More than I'm afraid of pain. I love you more than all the pain and suffering and glory on this earth. And I always will."

"I love you, too."

Jessie Hargreave had been raised to believe that there were two kinds of people. The frightened and the frightening. She had believed the only way to beat that system was to be a con artist. Someone who wove her way through the margins of fear. But now she realized that none of that was true at all.

Because there was love.

And it changed people. It changed them from frightened creatures, it changed them from con artists, into something wholly beautiful, wholly wonderful. And entirely worthy.

And from their love they would grow enough good, big, beautiful memories to make the darkness seem small.

She knew without a doubt, that what she would teach her child was that in the end, the greatest thing of all was love.

EPILOGUE

EWAN DIDN'T BREATHE the entire time Jessie was in labor. He had chosen love, but it didn't mean that his bad memories didn't still exist inside him.

Part of embracing the truth of himself had been grieving. His father had cut his grieving short, and then after that he'd cut off his own grief so he could embrace his chosen persona.

So now he felt sad sometimes when he thought of his mother. Anger when he thought of his father. A peculiar sense of missing something when he thought of the baby brother he'd never had a chance to know.

Above all else, when he looked at Jessie, he felt love.

So even though his emotions weren't all pleasant all the time, the love was always there.

But his daughter was born screaming and healthy. And Jessie was laughing and beaming within moments of their daughter being placed on her chest.

And that was when he realized that things could be okay.

That he could have something glorious and beautiful.

That he was truly able to be more.

Now he had a family. His wife, their little girl. Even Maren had become as a sister to him, and that had healed that broken part of himself that had lost a sibling.

His life was full now.

And he was himself. As he'd always been meant to be. No masks. No games.

He leaned in and kissed his wife on the temple, and brushed his finger along his daughter's downy cheek. "I love you." He let out a long sigh. "I was willing to endure pain to love you. But I realize now even more... I want to be happy. Loving you. I'm ready for joy."

She looked up at him and smiled, and he knew right there was all the joy he would ever need. "So am I."

* * * * *

COMING SOON!

We really hope you enjoyed reading this book. If you're looking for more romance be sure to head to the shops when new books are available on

Thursday 31st August

To see which titles are coming soon, please visit

millsandboon.co.uk/nextmonth

MILLS & BOON

MILLS & BOON®

Coming next month

INNOCENT'S WEDDING DAY WITH THE ITALIAN
Michelle Smart

"Do you, Enzo Alessandro Beresi, take Rebecca Emily Foley to be your wife?"

He looked her in the eye adoringly and without any hesitation said, "I do."

And now it was her turn.

"Do you, Rebecca Emily Foley, take Enzo Alessandro Beresi..."

She breathed in, looked Enzo straight in the eye and, in the strongest voice she could muster, loud enough for the entire congregation to clearly hear, said, "No. I. Do. Not."

Enzo's head jerked back as if she'd slapped him. A half smile froze on his tanned face, which was now drained of colour. His mouth opened but nothing came out.

The only thing that had kept Rebecca together since she'd opened the package that morning was imagining this moment and inflicting an iota of the pain and humiliation racking her on him. There was none of the satisfaction she'd longed for. The speech she'd prepared in her head died in her choked throat.

Unable to look at him a second longer, she wrenched her hands from his and walked back down the aisle, leaving a stunned silence in her wake.

Continue reading
INNOCENT'S WEDDING DAY WITH THE ITALIAN
Michelle Smart

Available next month
www.millsandboon.co.uk

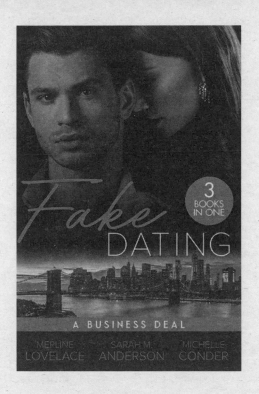

LET'S TALK
Romance

For exclusive extracts, competitions
and special offers, find us online:

f MillsandBoon

🐦 @MillsandBoon

📷 @MillsandBoonUK

♪ @MillsandBoonUK

Get in touch on 01413 063 232

MILLS & BOON

THE HEART OF ROMANCE

A ROMANCE FOR EVERY READER

MODERN

Prepare to be swept off your feet by sophisticated, sexy and seductive heroes, in some of the world's most glamourous and romantic locations, where power and passion collide.

HISTORICAL

Escape with historical heroes from time gone by. Whether your passion is for wicked Regency Rakes, muscled Vikings or rugged Highlanders, awaken the romance of the past.

MEDICAL

Set your pulse racing with dedicated, delectable doctors in the high-pressure world of medicine, where emotions run high and passion, comfort and love are the best medicine.

True Love

Celebrate true love with tender stories of heartfelt romance, from the rush of falling in love to the joy a new baby can bring, and a focus on the emotional heart of a relationship.

Desire

Indulge in secrets and scandal, intense drama and sizzling hot action with heroes who have it all: wealth, status, good looks…everything but the right woman.

HEROES

The excitement of a gripping thriller, with intense romance at its heart. Resourceful, true-to-life women and strong, fearless men face danger and desire - a killer combination!
